DEATH
PARTS US

Alex Walters

Print ISBN 978-1-1912175-61-1

Also by Alex Walters

DI McKay Series

Candle & Roses

PRAISE FOR CANDLES AND ROSES

'Alex Walters' crime debut is a great read, it is exciting and intriguing and I simply loved this detective novel.'
Caroline Vincent - Bits About Books

'I felt like one of Alex Walters victims as before I knew what was happening he had taken my breath away.'
Susan Hampson - Books from Dusk till Dawn

'As police procedurals go, this ranks way up very close to the top of the pile. I found it to be authentically and sympathetically portrayed with superb characterisation of the two lead characters, DI McKay and DS Horton.'
Anita Waller - International Best Selling Author

'Candles and Roses is a gripping crime thriller that certainly kept me on my toes. With a likeable protagonist, you can't help but get drawn into his life and work and can't wait to read more about McKay and his team.'
Sarah Hardy - By the Letter Book Reviews

'Candles and roses for me was a spellbinder I absolutely loved it from start to finish. Alex Walters ...a brilliant book.'
Livia Sbarbaro - Amazon Reviewer

To Helen. And to the (increasingly) occasional sons—James, Adam and Jonny

CHAPTER ONE

She fumbled with the key, as she always seemed to these days. Her eyesight was fading, her fingers less steady.

Eventually, she unlocked the front door and dropped her small bag of shopping onto the hallway carpet. As she straightened, she already had a sense that something was wrong. She couldn't have said what – a slight unaccustomed chill in the air, an unfamiliar scent or sound. Something she couldn't pin down.

Suddenly anxious, she hurried to the door of the living room. The television was burbling away, as always, some mid-morning talk show, the volume too low for her to make out the words.

Jackie's chair was empty.

She took another step into the room, peering past the armchair as if Jackie might somehow have concealed himself behind it.

Panicking now, she returned to the hallway and checked the bedroom, the bathroom, the room they still called Kirsty's, even though it was decades since she'd last lived there. Finally, she turned back to the kitchen.

Where had he gone? These days, she could barely persuade him to leave that chair, even when he needed the lavatory, or when she was faced with the nightly task of getting him to bed. When she was out of the house, he just sat there, his eyes fixed uncomprehendingly on the television screen.

As she entered the kitchen, she realised why the house felt colder than usual. The back-door to the rear garden was standing wide open. She blinked, baffled by what she was seeing.

In the days when Jackie had still been prone to aimless wandering, she'd had two deadbolts fitted to the door to prevent him slipping out without her realising. The keys were left hanging from the hooks near the sink, but she knew Jackie lacked the wit or initiative to find them.

Except that, somehow, he had.

She hurried over to the open door and gazed out into the garden. It was a decent spring day, the pale sun trying to break through a layer of thin cloud. The garden – little more than a square lawn surrounded by a narrow border of bushes – was empty. She stepped outside, looking uneasily around. 'Jackie?'

There was no sound except the faint brush of the sea breeze through the leaves, the cawing of the gulls from the bay. She was genuinely confused now. How had Jackie managed this impossible disappearing act?

She stepped out on to the lawn.

It was only then she saw it. The familiar low straight line of the fence at the rear of the garden was broken, the panelling cracked outward as if some heavy object had been thrust against it.

She remembered Jackie erecting the fence when they'd first moved into the bungalow, all those years ago. They'd wanted something to provide shelter from the winds and weather off the sea, but not so high that it blocked the view. The fence stood a little lower than chest height, and if you stood by it, you could see the panorama of the bay spread out before you.

In their early days here, she and Jackie enjoyed watching the view together. In the summer, on the rare bright days, the narrow beach would be crowded with families, in from the surrounding villages or up from Inverness. Sometimes, they glimpsed the dolphins out in the firth, playing tantalisingly close to the shore. Outside the short season, the view was more desolate but often just as striking, an endlessly changing pattern of sun and cloud, grey seas washing against the shingle, waves breaking against the seawalls at high tide.

It was a long time since she'd bothered with any of that. The last few years had offered little but grind. She'd kept her head down and got on with it, knowing there was no alternative, not allowing herself to think how life might have turned out differently.

Distracted by these unbidden thoughts, it took her another moment to register the significance of the broken fence. Even then, she could barely bring herself to believe it.

She walked forward across the soft grass. The bushes were sparse at that point, and she had little difficulty pushing her way through them.

The bungalow, just off the high street, was set on the steep hillside above a row of houses fronting onto the sea. The house immediately below was a small cottage, now occupied only as a holiday let, its banked rear garden some twenty feet beneath her.

Scared now, she peered cautiously over the broken panelling down into the neighbouring garden.

And she began to scream.

CHAPTER TWO

*B*leak, McKay thought, looking around the cramped sitting
room. *Nothing but bleak.*

The young man from the agency was still enumerating
the bungalow's many virtues. Closeness to the sea. A decent local
pub. Good restaurant in the season. Convenience store. McKay
already knew all that and didn't care much about any of it.

In his head, he was trying to decide just how bleak the place
was. As bleak as Caley's chances of winning the SPL. As bleak
as a Labour politician's odds of becoming First Minister. As
bleak as –

'So, what do you think?' the young man interjected. He'd
finally recognised that McKay wasn't listening.

'Ach, it's fine. I'll take it,' McKay said.

Bleak was what he wanted right now. This anonymous
bungalow, furnished with shabby, charity shop cast-offs, fitted the
bill perfectly. He just wanted out of what had been their home.
Give Chrissie the chance to move back in. Let them both have the
opportunity to get their heads straight. Then, maybe, there'd be
the possibility of giving it another shot.

Aye, in your dreams, he added silently to himself.

The young man was still blethering on. There were patches
on his face untroubled by acne, but they were relatively few.
McKay wondered whether he'd ever been young like that, full
of clumsy, well-meaning enthusiasm. No doubt he had, but
it was a long time ago. These days, all he had left was the
clumsiness.

'I've said I'll take it,' he said. 'I'll come into the office this
afternoon to sort out the details.'

'Right.' The young man looked nonplussed, as if he'd been hoping for some different outcome. 'Well, that's grand. I'll see you later, then.'

'You do that, son. New to the job, are you?'

For a moment, the young man looked affronted. Then, he shrugged. 'Aye, just a few weeks. Is it that obvious?'

'Only to a trained detective, son. You did great.'

The young man laughed. 'That what you are, then? A trained detective?'

McKay remained blank faced. 'Detective Inspector, son. Twenty odd years on the force.' McKay paused, as if thinking. 'Bloody odd years, most of them.'

The young man looked around, clearly wondering why the hell a presumably well-paid DI would want to live in a place like this. 'Must be interesting.'

'Aye, son. I suppose it must. And now, I ought to be getting back to it. I'll see you later, then.' McKay turned and made his way out of the bungalow, pausing briefly to glance again into the bedroom and bathroom, reassuring himself that this place really was as pokey and unprepossessing as he'd thought.

Outside, he blinked in the unaccustomed sunshine. He was a short, wiry man with slicked back, greying hair. He was old enough to believe that a suit was still the appropriate garb for work, but Chrissie had finally managed to persuade him not to bother with a tie. That had been in the days when she cared about what he wore. These days, most of his younger colleagues looked as if they'd just come in from a night clubbing. Some of them probably had.

He'd left his car down by the seafront, so he stomped back towards the centre, enjoying the sight of the blue firth spread out before him. The young man had reckoned the bungalow offered a sea view. Aye, maybe, if you stood on your tippy-toes in the kitchen and peered between the rooftops.

He was halfway down the hill when he spotted the pulse of blue lights. As he reached the beach-side road, he saw that a marked patrol car and an ambulance were parked a few hundred metres along, effectively blocking the carriageway. There were a couple of uniformed officers and a small crowd of onlookers milling about.

McKay was nothing if not nosey. It was, he told himself, one of the qualities that made him a good detective. He strolled along the street and placed himself in front of one of the uniformed police.

'I'm afraid we've had to close this road for the moment, sir,' the officer said. 'You can walk along the beach or back up along the high street.'

'What's going on?' McKay asked.

'If I could just ask you to move along, please, sir —'

'Aye, son. You can always ask.'

The officer opened his mouth to respond, but McKay was already brandishing his warrant card under the man's nose. The officer leaned forward, clearly registering not just the rank but also the name. McKay's reputation tended to precede him.

'I'm sorry, sir. I didn't realise —'

'No bother, son. You were just doing your job. What's going on?'

'Accident, sir. An elderly gentleman has fallen from the garden up there. Looks like he cracked his skull, unfortunately.'

'Dead?' McKay had already read this in the young officer's eyes.

'Looked like it. The medics are with him at the moment. But I think he was already dead when he was found.'

McKay peered past the young man. 'How the hell did he manage to fall from the garden?'

'Not sure exactly, sir. The fencing up there was broken. His wife reckons he suffered from Alzheimer's.'

McKay was staring up at the rear fence of the bungalow above them. Something was stirring in his mind. 'Have the Examiners been called?'

The officer blinked. 'Well, no, sir. Not yet. We thought, as it's an accident —'

'How do you know it was an accident?'

'Well –'

'How do you know his wife didn't just get tired of looking after the old bastard and took her chance to push him over the edge?'

'With respect, sir –'

'Aye, son. Always treat me with respect. You'll find it pays. Look, most likely you're right, and it was just an unfortunate accident. But don't make assumptions. I'm not joking about the wife. These things happen.'

The officer nodded. 'Sorry, sir. Wasn't thinking.'

McKay looked around them. 'We don't want to make a big deal of it. Like I say, most likely, you're right. But we should get the Examiners in to check over the scene. And we should talk to the widow as soon as she's in a suitable state.'

'That's her, sir.' The officer gestured towards an elderly woman standing further along the street being comforted by a couple of neighbours.

McKay nodded. 'Okay. I'll go and introduce myself. It doesn't look as if she's likely to abscond anywhere in the near future.'

As he moved away from the officer, he felt his mobile buzzing in his pocket. He moved back from the crowd before answering.

'Alec, it's Helena. Are you still up in Rosemarkie?'

'Aye. Just enjoying the scenery.' DCI Helena Grant was his immediate superior. She'd allowed him a couple of hours off to view the bungalow.

'How was the house?'

'Ach, you know. Bleak. Soulless. Shabby. Cramped.'

'You're taking it, then?'

'Obviously.'

'You're your own worst enemy, Alec, you know that?'

'I doubt it. I've made some bad ones in my time.'

'You deserve better than a place like that, though.'

'There's plenty would disagree with you on that,' he said. 'Anyway, what can I do for you?'

'We've just had an incident called in up there –'

'Aye,' McKay said. 'I think I'm standing next to it.'

'Some elderly gent fallen out his garden?'

'That's the one. Quite an achievement. To fall out of a garden, I mean.'

'Look, Alec, as you're already out there, can you take charge? Manage the scene, I mean. At least 'til the Examiners get there, and we get a better idea what's going on.'

McKay held the phone away from his ear for a moment and squinted at the screen, as if that might provide him with more information. 'Aye, well, I've already waded in with my size nines. I don't suppose the uniforms will object if I take it out of their hands. If you think it's necessary.' He frowned, wondering quite what had prompted Grant to make this call. She didn't generally do things without a good reason.

'I think it might be a wise precaution,' she said. 'In the circumstances.'

'Circumstances,' he repeated. He was gazing now at the elderly woman across the street, still surrounded by commiserating neighbours. 'What circumstances are those, exactly?'

'I don't suppose you've enquired about the name of the victim?'

'It wasn't high on my priority list,' McKay admitted. 'I was too busy bollocking the uniforms for not doing their job. I'd assumed the name of some poor old bugger in Rosemarkie wouldn't mean much to me.'

'Aye, well, always get your priorities right, Alec. But in this case, the name might just ring a bell.'

'Go on, then,' he said. But McKay was already ahead of her. The half thought that had been buzzing round his brain had suddenly settled, and he knew what she was about to say. And he finally recognised the elderly woman. Before Grant could respond, he said, 'Jesus. Jackie fucking Galloway.'

CHAPTER THREE

'Jackie fucking Galloway indeed,' Helena Grant said. 'You developing telepathy in your old age, Alec?'

'No. But, Christ, I just recognised Bridie Galloway standing across the street. The grieving widow.' He remembered the bungalow up on the high street now too. He'd been there once, years before, to drop off some of the stuff that Jackie Galloway had left behind at HQ. He'd not exactly been welcomed with open arms that day, but then, he hadn't really expected to be. Not, as Helena Grant would put it, in the circumstances. 'She's aged.'

'While you've remained younger than springtime?' Grant said. 'We've all aged, Alec. It was a long time ago. And, from what I hear, she's not had the easiest of times over the last few years.'

'If she stayed married to Jackie Galloway, I don't imagine she ever had the easiest of times,' McKay said. 'Man was an arsehole of the highest order.'

'I believe he spoke very highly of you too, Alec. But, aye, you're not far wrong.'

McKay was still watching Bridie Galloway across the street. She didn't exactly look the part of the grieving widow. Shocked, maybe, though that ashen pallor tended to go with the sunless territory up in this part of the world. But not greeting or wailing in the way he might have expected. But then, in this case, it probably wasn't what he'd have expected. Jackie Galloway would have been a handful even at the best of times. If he'd been suffering from Alzheimer's, then Christ alone knew what he'd have been like to live with. Maybe McKay's flippant remark to the young PC hadn't been so wide of the mark after all.

'Okay,' he said to Grant. 'I'll go and make my presence felt. Have the Examiners been called, do you know?'

'I believe Jock Henderson and his pals are winging their way to you even as we speak.'

'My lucky day. Just hope Jock doesn't forget his spectacles this time.' There was, for reasons neither could fully recall, a long-standing needle between McKay and the Senior Crime Scene Examiner. They treated their regular spats as jocular, but they never entirely felt that way to McKay.

'I'll leave you to it, Alec. Give my regards to Bridie.'

'Aye, I'm sure that'll make her day.'

McKay ended the call and stood for a moment in the weak sunshine, watching the scene in front of him. How long had it been since he'd seen Jackie Galloway? Twenty years or more. Chief Inspector John Galloway, in those days. Although not by the time McKay had last seen him, in that same bungalow up on the high street. By then, Galloway's police career was already behind him, and his once unignorable presence was already being discreetly erased from the collective memory. When it came to creating non-persons, the force could give the Soviet Politburo a run for its money.

Galloway had no one to blame but himself, of course. But that wasn't how he saw it. That had been the constant thread of Galloway's career. It was always some other bugger's fault. He'd got a long way on the basis of that mantra, and that had just made his eventual downfall even more spectacular. There'd been a moment, on that rainy evening when McKay had turned up on the doorstep with a tatty cardboard box full of Galloway's discarded junk, when Galloway had seemed almost like a tragic figure. It had been no more than a moment – lasting no longer than it took for Galloway to start spewing his usual invective at McKay's rain-soaked figure – but McKay had brought himself to feel some sympathy for the man. In the end, he'd dumped the box on the doorstep and told Galloway to go fuck himself.

He crossed back over the street and drew aside the young PC who was still unsuccessfully attempting to disperse the small crowd. 'You'll be delighted to know, son, that I've been asked to take charge here. There just the two of you?'

The young man nodded, clearly relieved to hand over responsibility to someone more senior. 'Roddy's up at the bungalow making sure no one tries to get in.'

McKay nodded. 'Good lad. The Examiners are on their way, so we'll all be able to sleep easy in our beds. You keep this lot at bay as well as you can, and I'll go chat to the merry widow.' He turned to the group of onlookers and held up his warrant card. 'Ladies and gentlemen. DI McKay. We fully appreciate your concern, but may I kindly request you return to your business? There's really nothing you can do here, and we need the space to carry out our work.'

Despite McKay's short stature, his authority was undeniable. The crowd, which had been blithely ignoring the pleas of the young constable, began almost immediately to move away, with only a few murmurings of discontent. McKay made his way over to where Bridie Galloway was standing. His initial assessment had been correct. She was pale but dry-eyed, he thought, as if she'd been shocked by the event but not necessarily distraught at the outcome.

'Mrs Galloway. DI McKay. I'm really very sorry –'

She peered at him. 'McKay? You used to work for Jackie, didn't you?'

McKay almost expected she'd spit in his eye. Instead, she gave an unexpected half smile as if his presence had confirmed something she'd been suspecting. McKay, not normally a man short of words, found himself at a loss. 'That's right,' he said, finally. 'I didn't expect you to remember me.' As far as he could recall, they'd met only once or twice at the force's Christmas shindigs.

'Aye, well. Jackie used to speak highly of you. Well, more highly than he spoke of most people, anyway.'

That was news to McKay. Galloway had never shown any obvious signs of approval when McKay had been part of his team. On the contrary, as the youngest member of the group, McKay had usually been selected as Galloway's primary whipping boy whenever anything went wrong.

'That's good to know,' McKay said. 'This must be an awful shock.'

She nodded. 'What's happened was a shock. I still don't really understand it. But – well, you know, Jackie wasn't a well man. Maybe it's a blessing, really.' She glanced at the two women beside her, as if seeking their approval for this sentiment. Both had backed away a few steps, McKay noticed. The police were loved the world over.

'Do you feel up to talking about it?' McKay said. 'Nothing formal at this stage. Just to give me an idea of what happened.'

'I'd rather not go back to the bungalow. Not just at the moment.'

He nodded. 'We've called out the Crime Scene Examiners, just to check the place over. We'll need to borrow your keys to give them access if that's not a problem?'

'The Examiners?' she said. 'Does that mean –?'

'It doesn't mean anything, Mrs Galloway. It's just routine. These days, any kind of unexpected – accident, well, we call them in just until we're sure of the circumstances.'

She looked unconvinced by his explanation. 'The back-door's open. I just came out looking –'

'Aye, of course. I wasn't thinking.' He gestured to the young PC. 'I'll let them know. Look, why don't we go and grab a tea at that restaurant place at the corner? Might do you good to have a sit down and a cuppa.'

It was too early in the year for the small restaurant to be busy, but there was a couple enjoying an early lunch by the window. They'd been greeted effusively by the manager who managed not to look too disappointed when McKay waved his warrant card and asked if he could bring a pot of tea to one of the tables outside.

'Not too cold?' McKay lowered himself on to one of the unoccupied picnic benches and gestured for Bridie Galloway to take a seat opposite. 'More private out here.' There was a breeze blowing off the sea, but it was mild in the sunshine.

'That's fine.' She seemed to have regained some of her composure in the short walk along the seafront. 'It's a grand place,' she said, looking back at the small restaurant. 'We could never afford to eat here.'

McKay shifted uncomfortably. 'Must have been a struggle for you both,' he said.

'Aye, well. Whose fault was that?'

McKay was unsure what answer she expected, and was relieved when a young waiter arrived with the pot of tea. They sat in silence as he distributed the cups, milk and sugar.

Finally, McKay said, 'I'm sorry about what happened to Jackie. Not just today but – well, everything.'

She shrugged. 'Most of that was the stupid bugger's own fault. He had nothing to complain about.'

Aye, but you did, McKay thought. *You were landed well and truly in the shite.* He was amazed that she could talk about her husband with such equanimity. But then he'd been amazed, at the time, that she'd stuck by him. He couldn't imagine that marriage to Jackie Galloway would have offered many other compensations. 'I hear he'd been unwell?'

'You could say that. Early onset Alzheimer's. Started only a few years after we moved up here.' She had the air of someone who wanted to talk, and McKay was content to let her. It was probably the first time in years she'd had an attentive audience. 'I didn't think much of it at first. It was the usual stuff. Being a bit forgetful. Standing in a room not knowing why he'd gone in there. You know.'

'Only too well,' McKay agreed. 'But it got worse?'

'He went downhill quickly.' She stopped, and for the first time since McKay had started speaking to her, she was showing some signs of emotion. 'I found him one morning searching for his uniform. Thought he was back on the beat. It just got worse after that. I mean, it came and went. There were good days – sometimes, days in a row – when he seemed fine, and you could fool yourself it was all miraculously going to be okay –'

'What did the doctors say?'

'Ach, they didn't pull any punches. It was a nightmare just getting him to hospital. He wasn't up to driving, and I'd never driven, so we ended up having to get the bus to the Raigmore every time. And there were times when he didn't know where he was or what we were doing. He once tried to arrest some wee lad who was being a bit gobby on the bus.'

'And you were his only carer?'

'We got some help from social services in the end. Came in a couple of times a day to help me feed him and get him into bed. But he was hard work. He'd go wandering off at home. I tried to keep the doors locked so he couldn't get out, but I'd find him wandering 'round the house. He got out into the street once, and a few times, he was out in the garden.'

'Is that what happened today?'

She didn't respond for a moment. 'I don't know. I don't know what happened today.'

'How do you mean?'

She took a mouthful of her tea. McKay's was growing cold in front of him. 'I used to have to keep an eye on him all the time. But the last couple of years, it's been different. He became more and more passive. The doctors reckoned that's the way it is sometimes. As if his brain was slowly shutting down. Like, you know, his batteries were running out.'

'So, he stopped wandering about?'

'It was gradual at first. He'd spend more time sitting in his chair in front of the TV. Then, I had to persuade him to get up when it was time for bed or, you know, if he wanted the lavvy. In the end, he stopped doing anything. He'd just sit there, staring at the screen. He wasn't really watching it. It was just the movement.'

'So, what happened today?'

'I don't know. I can't really believe it.'

'Talk me through it,' McKay said. 'If you're able to.'

She took a breath. 'I'd been shopping. Just over to the convenience store up the road. I get what I can there, these days, and just have the odd trip over to the Co-op at Fortrose. I was only out of the house for fifteen, twenty minutes or so.'

'How was he when you left?'

'Just the usual. I'd had the carer in earlier to help me get him dressed and give him breakfast. Then, I'd left him in front of the TV. He was the same as ever. Saying nothing. Just watching the screen.'

'What happened when you got back?'

'Something felt wrong as soon as I got into the house. It felt – empty, you know?'

McKay knew well enough. He'd felt it the night he'd returned home, after all that business along the shore here, to find Chrissie gone. He'd known the house was empty as soon as he opened the door.

'And it felt cold,' she went on.

'Cold?'

'The back-door was open.'

'You hadn't left it open?' He felt as if he were accusing her of negligence.

'No, of course not. It was always locked and bolted. I only ever went out there to hang out the washing, and I always checked and double-checked it was locked. I had the bolts fitted to make sure he couldn't wander out there.'

'So, what do you think happened today?'

She blinked. 'I don't know. I really don't know.'

'Do you think Jackie could have unlocked the back-door?'

'I'd have said not. I'd have said definitely not.'

'But he must have?'

'Well, aye. What else?'

'I don't know.' He paused. 'There was no sign of any other disturbance?'

'Disturbance? What, like a break-in?'

McKay shrugged. 'Anything like that. I don't know. I'm just considering the possibilities. What about the carers? Do they have keys? Is it possible they could have come back while you were out?'

'I suppose it's possible,' she said doubtfully. 'We've got one those key safe things on the front door with a spare key so they can get in if I'm not around for any reason. But I don't know why they'd have opened the back-door.'

'Could the key safe have been left open? Maybe someone else got in? Kids or something.' McKay felt as if he'd unintentionally begun to turn the conversation into an interrogation. *Aye, well done, son*, he told himself, *just the way to treat a grieving widow.* Even if she is grieving for Jackie fucking Galloway. 'Ach, I'm sorry,' he said. 'I didn't mean to subject you to the third degree. I'm just trying to work out how it could have happened.'

She shook her head. 'No, I want to know too,' she said. 'It was a shock finding him like that, even if –' She stopped, as if she'd been about to say something else, but then went on, 'Even if it's a blessing in some ways. But Jackie wouldn't have opened that door by himself. He couldn't have.'

McKay nodded. 'Well, let's not jump to conclusions. Stranger things have happened. Let's see what the Examiners have to say.'

'The thing is,' Bridie Galloway went on as if she hadn't heard him, 'I wasn't surprised. I wasn't really surprised that this happened. I should have known.'

'Known what?' McKay realised she was avoiding his eyes, staring past his shoulder at the open sea, the white scudding clouds.

'That he really was in danger,' she said. 'That the letters were serious.'

CHAPTER FOUR

Jock Henderson was leaning against the doorframe, smoking a cigarette. As McKay made his way up the path, Henderson blew out a cloud of smoke, not quite in McKay's face.

'They'll be the death of you, you know,' McKay said.

'Aye, like we've all got so much to live for.' Henderson dropped the cigarette on to the path, stubbed it out with his foot, then kicked it on to the garden. After a moment's thought, he jabbed the cigarette end with his toe to bury it in the earth. He was a tall, angular man with an uncontrolled mop of greying curly hair, and it was like watching a stork performing a mating dance.

'No white suit?' McKay asked.

'I've got Pete suited up checking out the rooms. I went straight down to do the body before the medics carted it away. And, yes, I wore protective clothing, even though the poor bugger had already been well and truly manhandled by those two jumped-up ambulance drivers.' He shrugged. 'Then, I was standing here enjoying the sun and a smoke. That all right with you, Alec?'

McKay ostentatiously pulled a packet of gum from his pocket. 'Your lungs, Jock.' McKay had been a forty a day man until a few years earlier. He wasn't generally evangelical about his new-found abstinence, but he was happy for any opportunity to wind up Jock Henderson. 'Gum?'

Equally pointedly, Henderson drew another cigarette from the packet in his top shirt pocket and went through the ritual of lighting it. 'Wouldn't have thought this one merited someone of your exalted rank,' he said. 'Too much time on your hands?'

'Have you been told the name of the deceased?'

Henderson shook his head. 'Not yet. No ID on the body.'

'Jackie Galloway.'

'Jesus. I didn't even recognise him. Is this how he ended up? Even that old bastard didn't deserve this.'

McKay nodded, wondering whether Henderson was referring to Galloway's death, the dementia, or maybe just the state and size of the bungalow. At least it was bigger than the place McKay had just agreed to rent. 'Not been easy for them. Was just talking to Bridie Galloway. Jackie's been away with the fairies the last few years.'

Henderson shrugged. 'He fucked up, that's the long and short of it. Well and truly.'

'She didn't, though,' McKay said. 'She just had to live with the consequences. In sickness and in health. 'Til death parts us. All that bollocks.'

'Ach, she fucked up as well,' Henderson pointed out. 'She chose to marry Jackie fucking Galloway. Probably thought she'd jumped on a gravy train.'

McKay chewed pensively on his gum for a few moments. 'So, what are your professional conclusions, then?' He placed a possibly satirical emphasis on the word "professional."

'Not much 'til Pete's finished with the rooms and the garden,' Henderson said. 'There was nothing suspicious about the body. Injuries looked consistent with falling twenty feet head first on to a concrete patio. Doc'll confirm, but I couldn't see anything to suggest the cause of death was anything other than the head injuries resulting from that. I took DNA samples from the two medics, so we can check if there's any sign of other DNA on his clothing, but I'm not hopeful of finding anything significant.' He shrugged. 'Doesn't mean he wasn't pushed, but there's not likely to be any evidence from the body. Any reason to suspect foul play? Other than the fact that at one time, the world and his wife would have been queuing up to push Galloway to his death?'

'Only the mystery of what persuades him to abandon the delights of daytime telly for the first time in months. And how he managed to get the back-door open.'

'People with dementia don't always behave consistently,' Henderson pointed out. 'Even when it's well advanced, they're sometimes capable of more than you think. In their more lucid moments.'

'You sound like you've some knowledge, Jock?'

'Aye, well. My dad, you know. He was far gone by the end, but there were odd times when he was almost his old self. It's a cruel fucking business.'

'It is that.'

'What about Bridie?' Henderson asked. He was looking mildly embarrassed, as if he'd unintentionally exposed more than he'd intended. 'You think she could be in the frame? Hell of a job looking after someone in that state.'

'The thought had occurred,' McKay said. 'She was away from the house for no more than fifteen or twenty minutes, so I don't suppose we'll be able to ascertain whether Jackie was dead before she got back. My instincts say no, but my instincts have been wrong before.'

'My guess is,' Henderson said, taking another draw on his cigarette, 'that even if she is the guilty party, no one's going to bust a gut to convict her. The poor woman's suffered enough, and Jackie Galloway was no great loss to the world. There won't be many back at HQ wanting to open that can of worms.'

McKay said nothing, but they both knew that Henderson had a point. 'Aye, well,' he said, finally, 'you tell your mate Pete to get his arse in gear. Some of us have things to do, you know.'

As if invoked by the mention of his name, a white-suited figure loomed into the doorway behind Henderson. 'Arse back in neutral,' he said. 'Job done.' This was Pete Carrick, a heavily-built, slightly lumbering Examiner who somehow had been landed with the unenviable role of Jock Henderson's sidekick. McKay wondered what sins the young man must have committed in a previous life. But he was an amiable and competent enough lad, all red hair and rosy cheeks.

'Anything interesting?' McKay asked.

'Difficult to say. Fair few different fingerprints in the sitting room and kitchen.'

'We'll need to exclude Galloway and Bridie,' McKay said. 'And get matches from the care workers. Beyond that, I can't imagine they had many regular visitors.'

'There's no sign of any struggle,' Carrick said.

'But then, I don't imagine Galloway would have offered much resistance,' McKay said. 'Poor old bugger would probably have done anything you told him. What about the bolts on the back-door? You check those for prints?'

'Obviously,' Carrick said, in a tone that he'd presumably learnt from Jock Henderson. 'There are a few partials. Look as if they're all the same.'

McKay glanced at Henderson. 'We'll have to get those checked against Bridie. She's presumably the only one who'd go in and out of that door normally.' He smiled at Carrick. 'Thanks for your efforts, son.'

'Suspect it's been a waste of time. We'll be lucky to find anything useful.'

'Time in this job's never wasted,' McKay said. 'Even by Examiners. Am I okay to go in there now?'

'Aye. Knock yourself out.'

McKay left Carrick and Henderson to stow away their equipment, and made his way through to the small sitting room. It was homelier than the place he'd agreed to rent – presumably because of Bridie's efforts – but probably no larger. There was an old-fashioned television, a couple of shabby-looking armchairs, a folded dining table that looked like it was never used, and a small sideboard. Nearly thirty years' service, and this was how Jackie Galloway had ended up.

McKay stepped over to the sideboard and pulled open the left-hand drawer. At the front of the drawer, as Bridie Galloway had said, there was a small stack of envelopes bound together with an elastic band. McKay dug out the pack of disposable protective gloves he always carried. There was probably little chance they could obtain any forensic evidence from the letters, but better not to risk missing any trick. He eased off the elastic band and looked at the top envelope. It was postmarked Inverness, dated about five weeks earlier. The address looked to McKay's inexpert eye as if it had been laser-printed. He slid out the letter. It was a single sheet of A4, folded to fit the small envelope, containing nothing but the printed words: "NOT FORGOTTEN. NOT FORGIVEN."

The other letters were identical, other than variations in the print and font. There was more than a dozen in total, dated roughly six months apart. Bridie had said she suspected there'd been earlier letters, but Galloway had destroyed them. It was only when he became incapable of looking after his own affairs that she'd seen and opened them as they arrived.

'I'd no idea what they meant,' she'd said. 'But they scared me.'

'You should have approached us,' McKay had said, though he knew fine well Bridie Galloway could never have brought herself to do that.

'Ach, what would you have done?' she'd said, and he'd had no honest answer.

McKay pulled an evidence bag from his pocket and slid the letters and envelopes carefully inside. There was no way of telling if they were linked to Galloway's death, even assuming his death was anything other than accidental. Galloway had made more enemies than most in his thirty years on the force, and some might well bear long-standing grudges. Whether that would have been enough to lead to murder – well, in Galloway's case, who could tell?

He looked at his watch. He'd left Bridie Galloway in the care of a neighbour who, even before McKay had left, had begun to subject her to an interrogation far tougher than his own efforts. He'd said he'd let her know when she could return to the bungalow, if that was what she wanted. However she might feel about Jackie's death, returning here might still be preferable to spending more time with the nosy neighbour.

It was already mid-afternoon, and he'd promised the letting agents he'd drop into their office on his way back into town. Then, he'd have to debrief Helena Grant on all this. Not to mention catching up on a stack of ongoing cases at various stages in the legal pipeline. He'd left his number two, Ginny Horton, dutifully working her way through a mound of paperwork. She was good at that sort of stuff, and seemed to enjoy it – a lot more than McKay did, at any rate – but he couldn't just abandon her to it.

Another late night, then.

But, then, he told himself, it wasn't as if he had anything much else to look forward to.

CHAPTER FIVE

Ginny Horton was watching the conversation with the air of a spectator observing an evenly matched game of tennis. Dialogue between McKay and Helena Grant tended to have that kind of adversarial quality. Finally, Horton said, 'Look, I'm sorry, but who exactly was Jackie Galloway?'

Grant leaned back in her chair and smiled, exchanging a look with McKay. 'Ah, the innocence of youth,' she said. 'Undisturbed by the troubled memories of the older generation.'

'Galloway,' McKay said, clearly choosing his words with care, 'was an utter shiteing bastard. A complete buggering arsehole. A —'

'We get the idea, Alec,' Grant said. 'I imagine he wasn't your greatest fan, either.'

'Funnily enough, that's where you're wrong,' McKay said. 'According to Bridie, he was a secret admirer.'

Grant raised an eyebrow. She was a short but nonetheless imposing woman, who, by now, had more or less learnt how to keep McKay in his place. 'Must have been a well-kept secret in the days when we were part of his team. Or maybe Bridie was flirting with you?'

'Jackie Galloway?' Ginny Horton prompted again.

'Like Alec says, he was the bastard's bastard, even in the days when all coppers were bastards. He was a DCI doing pretty much the job I'm doing now,' Grant said. 'Serious crime. He'd been with the force a long time. Not far off his thirty years. And he got results.'

'The question,' McKay added, 'was how he got them.'

'We're talking twenty years ago,' Grant went on. 'Things were different. But even then, Galloway was old school. His interrogation techniques were – well, let's say crude but effective. On the physical side.'

'That's one way of putting it.' McKay pulled out his customary strip of gum and began to chew. 'Ten, fifteen years before that, he'd have been getting away with it. But times were changing. There were complaints.'

'An increasing number of complaints,' Grant agreed. 'At first, he managed to ride it out. Usually by shifting the blame on to someone else.'

'Aye,' McKay said, with feeling. 'Including me, on one occasion. I was a young DC. Had just joined the team. Galloway was interviewing some drunken clown who'd gotten into a knife fight in a pub on Union Street. In the course of the interview, said drunken clown somehow ends up with two broken ribs. Galloway denies all knowledge and tries to pin the blame on me. You know, young lad, got a bit carried away. I hadn't even been in the sodding room. Only escaped a disciplinary because no bugger believed him, but they still couldn't prove he was responsible. Quietly dropped. There were a few like that.'

'Aye, but they were getting harder to ignore,' Grant said. 'There were too many rumours.'

'Some of us were sure he was on the take,' McKay said. 'That was how he got some of his results. Taking backhanders to protect one or two interested parties who then grassed up the competition.'

'I can see how he might have made a few enemies,' Horton commented.

'And very few friends by the end,' Grant said. 'He was a sexist bastard as well. I wasn't with his team long, but he made my life a bloody misery.'

'Happy days,' McKay said. 'And now look at you. Doing the same to me and Ginny.'

'Sod off, Alec.'

'So, what happened to Galloway?' Horton asked. 'It doesn't sound like he enjoyed a long and happy retirement.'

'Proverbial finally hit the fan,' McKay said. 'And you and I were both there to witness it, isn't that right, Helena, hen?'

'More or less.' Grant shifted uncomfortably in her seat, as if the memory was an unwelcome one.

'It was a drugs bust-up in the Ferry somewhere,' McKay said, referring to the area known formally as South Kessock. 'Some dealer operating out a council house. We were expecting trouble, so a bunch of us went up there. Safety in numbers, you know.'

Grant nodded. 'Aye, looking back, I reckon it was one of those tip-offs Galloway had got from his dodgy mates. Drugs supply was largely sewn up among a few suppliers in the city. This lot were interlopers. Kids, really, up from Edinburgh.'

'It went smoothly enough to start with,' McKay said. 'We turned up with the uniforms. Got the front door in. They didn't know what had hit them. All the gear was out there. Most of them were shit-scared and gave us no bother at all –'

'We were downstairs, getting them charged and out to the vans,' Grant went on. 'Galloway and a couple of his cronies went upstairs.' She stopped and looked at McKay.

McKay said, 'What happened after that – well, Galloway's version was that this wee ned was resisting arrest and pulled a knife from somewhere. There was a struggle, and the ned ended up with the knife in his stomach.'

'Christ.' Horton sat back in her chair. 'You said that was Galloway's version?'

'Aye, well. Obviously, there was an enquiry. Galloway was suspended. And some of the stories didn't quite match up. I don't know the full details, but at least one of Galloway's supposed cronies got the jitters that they might be dragged down with him. There was doubt about where the knife had actually come from, and whether the poor bugger had really been resisting arrest in the way Galloway suggested. Nobody was actually prepared to point the finger, but by then, other things were coming out of the woodwork about Galloway.'

'There was talk of a prosecution,' Grant said. 'But it never happened. In the end, Galloway was sacked for gross misconduct. Not just that incident, as I understand it, but a litany of things that were emerging. Lost his pension, everything.'

'But escaped prosecution?' Horton said.

'Aye, well, I suspect they didn't want the dirty linen washed too publicly,' McKay said. 'Galloway blustered about unfair dismissal and the like, but he knew he'd gotten off lightly.'

'Sounds a real charmer.'

'I suppose he suffered for it in the end,' McKay said.

'Though not as much as poor Bridie,' Grant pointed out, 'and none of it was her fault.'

'Which, after the history lesson, brings us back to the million-dollar question,' McKay said. 'Did he jump, or was he pushed? To coin a phrase.'

'You think Bridie could have done it?' Grant asked.

'Ach, it's possible, obviously. She had the motive, the means and the fucking opportunity. I had a look at that fence. It had been decent enough in its day, but it was rotting in various places, including the spot where Galloway fell through. It wouldn't have taken much – maybe just his weight, maybe that bit of an additional push.' He stopped. 'I shouldn't say it, but I'm with wee Jock Henderson on this one. If she did it, maybe good luck to her. No one but her's going to miss Jackie Galloway, and I don't see how we'd ever prove it either way.'

'I don't suppose forensics will be able to tell us anything,' Grant said.

'What could they tell us? No doubt Bridie's DNA will be on Galloway's clothes. Maybe her fingerprints were the ones on the back-door bolts. Unless they come up with evidence of some unknown third party in there, we're no further forward.'

'What about the letters?' Horton asked.

'What about them? Even if we get something from forensics on them – doubtful, if they've been sitting in Bridie's drawer all this time – all that tells us is that someone was sending Galloway vaguely threatening letters. Plenty of people had good reason to do that. Doesn't necessarily make them a killer.' McKay shrugged. 'And if they were, why wait 'til now? Galloway was probably not far from death's door, in any case.'

Grant nodded. 'Okay. So, we play it by the book. Get a formal witness statement from Bridie Galloway and anyone else relevant. The care workers who were there that morning, maybe. Anyone else?'

'No one seems to have seen him fall. It was Bridie who spotted the body. The garden belongs to a holiday let, which is currently unoccupied. Bridie went down there with a neighbour, and they called us in. We can interview the neighbour and the woman who runs the convenience store, just to confirm the time Bridie was in there. Maybe double-check with other neighbours whether anyone saw or heard anything. That seems to be about it.'

'Get someone on to that, and then, we'll wait to see if the forensics or the autopsy tell us anything we don't know. Not much else we can do.'

McKay had been sitting still for long enough. 'Fair enough, boss. Ginny and I have plenty on our plates as it is. Can't see this pushing its way up the priority list, unless something new emerges.'

'Thanks for the debrief, anyway.' Grant waited until McKay and Horton were both standing and then added, 'Actually, Alec, can you spare me a minute on something else?'

'Aye,' McKay growled, 'so long as it is just a minute. You seen how much crap's piled up on my desk?'

'And you'll welcome any excuse not to go back to it.' Grant waited until Horton had left the room, then said, 'Just wanted to check how you were, Alec.'

'Aye, well. I'm grand. Can I go now?'

'You get more like a naughty schoolboy with every passing day, you know that? What's the situation with Chrissie?' She knew that McKay would have told anyone else to bugger off and mind their own business, but the two of them had been through enough for him to recognise that, at some level at least, it was her business.

'She's staying up with her sister up near Strathpeffer,' McKay said. 'But that's not ideal for either of them. That's why I want to get out.'

'You don't have to do anything, Alec. She's the one who walked out on you.'

He shrugged. 'I've no great desire to be living in that place at the moment. Better if I bugger off and she goes back there. Might help her get her head straight.'

'And meanwhile, you're stuck in some pokey old dump up in the Black Isle.'

'Ach, it's got a sea view and everything.'

She shook her head. 'If I went in for cheap psychology, Alec, I'd say you were still trying to punish yourself.'

'It was cheap psychology got us into this mess in the first place,' McKay said. 'I'm just looking for a place I can afford to rent. I'm still paying the mortgage on the house, you know.' He stopped, as if thinking. 'Anyway, it'll only be short term.'

'Aye, I hope so, Alec. I hope so. I'm here if you want to talk, you know.'

'I'm not really the talking kind. Not that kind of talking, anyhow. You may have noticed that.' As if to prove the point, he was already on his feet, eager to leave the room. 'Now I'd best get back to the piles of crap.'

'Well. Like I say.'

'Aye, hen, and it's much appreciated. Thanks.'

He was already out of the door before she could offer any further response. She contemplated following him, but knew there was no point. He was just the typical middle-aged Scots male. If he felt like talking, he would, but the chances were, it would never happen. He'd bottle it all up and throw himself back into the job, and he and Chrissie would never sort it all out and get themselves back together.

As she sat there, staring ruefully at the closed door, Helena Grant wasn't entirely sure how she felt about that.

CHAPTER SIX

She looked up again at the clock on the mantelpiece. Not yet ten. There was no cause to worry at all.

But she always did, and she always had, although in the old days, she'd had a lot more cause. These days, the biggest risk was that Billy would have a coronary or stumble under a bus after one pint too many. As the years went by, both of those seemed increasingly likely.

The television was flickering away unwatched in the corner, a reality show featuring a bunch of supposed celebrities who meant nothing to her. Mostly they looked like children, though there were a couple of older faces she vaguely recognised. Someone from some sitcom decades ago. Another from a soap opera, though she couldn't remember which.

At ten, she'd switch over to the news, just as she always did, though these days the stories meant about as much to her as the unfamiliar celebrities. Usually Billy would be home by ten and they'd watch the news together, or at least they'd sit in the same room while she watched the TV and Billy snored noisily beside her. She'd wait until the news was finished, then wake him up and help him stumble his way, still half-asleep, into the bedroom.

These had been their evenings, pretty much, since Billy had retired all those years ago. It wasn't too bad, she thought, everything considered. Billy drank too much – everybody drank too much these days – but he'd never been a difficult or violent man. Not with her, at any rate. That must count for something. He was still decent company in the daytime. She'd be awake early, leaving him in bed to sleep off the night before. Sometimes they'd go and grab a bite to eat at the local café. Sometimes they'd even have a trip out, over to Beauly or Strathpeffer, or into Dingwall or even Inverness. Billy wasn't so keen on driving these days, but they both enjoyed these occasional excursions. All in all, it wasn't too bad a life, even if the evenings seemed to stretch out emptily.

When the clock reached ten, she switched over to the news. A story about a bombing in the Middle East. Politicians pontificating about something or other. A football team beating some other football team. It washed over her, and she hardly knew why she bothered with the nightly ritual of watching. It was just another activity to fill the evening.

Ten-twenty. Billy was usually back by now, though it depended who was there in the pub. If there was a group of them, they could blether away all night about the football or whatever it was they talked about, and Billy would lose track of the time and how much he was drinking. Those were the nights he came home well and truly stoshied. Not her favourite nights, though it was usually just a question of steering him towards the bedroom and letting him fall asleep in his clothes. It seemed likely that was what she had in store tonight.

When it reached ten thirty, they cut to the news "wherever you are." *Not much news where I am*, she thought as she always did, *except that Billy's even later than usual.* The news across Scotland didn't seem much more interesting. Another bill she couldn't be bothered with passing through Holyrood. Complaints about roadworks on various Highland routes.

Then, she peered more closely at the screen and turned up the volume. It was a location she recognised. The next village along the Isle, in fact. But that wasn't what had attracted her attention. It was the fact that she knew, not just the village, but the house that was in the shot.

'Police are not yet commenting on the cause of death, but neighbours have said that Mr Galloway had suffered for a number of years from Alzheimer's Disease ...'

She clicked off the sound. Jackie Galloway. It was years since they'd been in contact. Billy had tried to build some bridges in the early days, had approached Jackie to explain to him. But Jackie had made it quite clear he didn't want to talk, didn't want to meet, didn't want to have any communication. He blamed Billy for what had happened. But then, he blamed everyone for what had happened, everyone but himself. That had always been Jackie's way. She'd told Billy that. Told him again and again that none of it was his fault. But that hadn't stopped Billy feeling bad about it. Here they were, not exactly living in the lap of luxury but comfortable enough. And there was Jackie Galloway, stuck in that pokey little bungalow, living off his savings, struggling to make ends meet.

She suspected that was one reason why Billy had gone back to the drinking. Not that he'd ever really stopped, but he cut it back for a long time. Then, slowly, he'd begun knocking it back again. Partly it was just the boredom of retirement. He'd tried to find another job back in the force or with some local security company, but times were tight, and there was nothing available other than night-security stuff. In the end, he'd drifted back into the inertia of doing not much. The drink was an escape from that, no doubt. But she'd always felt there was something more.

She'd wait until the morning to break the news, even if he was in a state to take it in this evening. It was quarter to eleven now. Unusual for him to be as late as this. For the first time, with the news of Jackie Galloway's death fresh in her mind, she began to feel uneasy.

She made her way out into the hallway. She was tired but didn't want to head off to bed until Billy was safely home. She opened the front door and was met by the chill of the night air, a gust of the breeze from the sea. The drive and the street beyond were deserted. Her anxiety growing, she pulled her cardigan more tightly around her shoulders and stepped outside in her slippers. At the end of the driveway, she peered back down the street towards the centre of the village. There were a couple of young men lighting cigarettes under one of the orange street lights, but no sign of Billy. She could just about make out the lights of the bar.

She was tempted to walk down there, but she knew she'd look foolish if Billy was just sitting blethering with his mates. Unsure what to do, she turned back into the house.

She sat in her armchair, the television playing away unwatched, and waited until the clock turned eleven. Billy was never this late.

Finally, at a loss, she returned to the hallway and slipped on her coat and shoes. She checked she had her purse with the house keys inside and stepped out again into the night. The street was empty. She walked slowly down towards the bar, peering into every gateway and alley as if Billy might be hiding from her. She was feeling a cold grip of fear in her stomach now, though she couldn't really have said why. Yes, Billy was normally home by now, but that didn't mean he hadn't got talking and stayed behind for another pint. After all, what else could have happened to him?

When she reached the bar, she was relieved to see that the lights were still on. But when she pushed at the doors, they were locked. Then, she heard the sound of movement and voices inside. Perhaps they'd decided to have a lock-in. She was surprised at that. The Caley Bar had been closed for some months following all the trouble the previous year, but had recently been taken over by an enthusiastic young couple up from the south. The place had always been a bit of a dive, but he had ambitions for it – sprucing up the decor, selling food, aiming more at the tourist market than just locals. He'd happily tolerated Billy and his aged mates continuing to drink there, but wasn't likely to risk his licence by cutting them too much slack.

After a moment's hesitation, she pressed the bell. She heard bolts being slid back, and then, a puzzled face peered out at her. The young man. Callum something, she recalled. Callum Donnelly. She could already see that the bar was empty, except for a member of the bar staff wiping down the tables.

Donnelly blinked at her. 'Can I help you?'

He was nearly a foot taller than she was. She looked up at him. 'I'm sorry to bother you at this time of the night, Mr Donnelly. I'm Mrs Crawford. Billy Crawford's wife.'

He stared at her, clearly trying to compute what she was saying. 'Oh, right. Billy. Is something wrong?'

'I just wondered. Was Billy in tonight?' She wasn't even sure why she was asking. Where else would he have been?

'He was in earlier as usual, yes. I'm sorry. I don't really understand –'

'Do you know what time he left, Mr Donnelly? Roughly, I mean.'

'About half-nine or thereabouts, I think. That's what he usually does. I don't recall seeing him much after that.'

She felt as if she'd been struck a physical blow. Up until now, she'd been telling herself that Billy must be here, that he'd just stayed later than usual.

'Are you all right, Mrs Crawford?' Donnelly had stepped back and was gesturing for her to enter the bar. 'Do you want a sit down?'

She took a breath, telling herself to remain calm. 'It's just that – well, Billy's not come home yet, and I'm getting worried. It's like you say. He normally leaves around nine-thirty. He never stays much longer than that.'

'Perhaps he went to one of the other pubs,' Donnelly said. 'The Union or the Anderson.'

'He only ever comes here,' she said. 'This is where his friends come.'

'Perhaps he's gone back with one of them for some reason,' Donnelly said patiently. She could see he thought she was worrying unnecessarily. 'Does he have a mobile?'

She shook her head. 'He won't be doing with them. And he doesn't normally go anywhere.'

'I'm not sure what to suggest, Mrs Crawford. Perhaps you could call some of his friends?'

It was only a small village, and she had an idea who Billy's drinking companions were and roughly where most of them lived. She even knew one or two of their wives. But she couldn't envisage tracking down their names and numbers at this time of night. And she couldn't believe Billy would have done that. He never did. He just came here, had a few beers and the odd dram, and then came home.

In any case, she was becoming increasingly certain that, even if she did call Billy's mates, they would only confirm what, in her heart, she already knew.

That something had happened to Billy. Something bad.

CHAPTER SEVEN

Ginny Horton held up the bottle and stared into the green glass. 'Enough left for a small one each,' she said. 'Unless you want me to open another.'

Isla Bennett shook her head. 'Not for me. School day tomorrow. Just in the office, though. I'm getting sick of the London run.' Isla worked as a commercial lawyer with a practice in Inverness, but because she was qualified in English as well as Scottish law, she found herself shuttling to England on a frequent basis. That usually involved an early flight from Inverness Airport and, to allow for check-in, a crack-of-dawn departure from home.

'Makes me glad I've only got the commute into town,' Horton agreed. 'Not that that's not bad enough some mornings.' She poured them a half glass each and then eyed her own thoughtfully. 'I'm really tempted to open another one,' she said. 'But I know I'd only sit feeling sorry for myself. And I'd feel even sorrier for myself in the morning.'

'I shouldn't have told you,' Isla said. 'Sorry.'

'God, no. Of course you were right to tell me. I mean, I know you want to protect me and everything. But you can't do that by hiding stuff from me. Not stuff like this, anyway.'

'I know. It's just that — well, from what you've told me, that bastard has no right to start pestering you again. For any reason.'

'That won't be how he sees it. As far as he's concerned, he's the centre of the universe. He'll think I want to know what he's up to. He'll think I care.'

Isla nodded. 'And do you? At all, I mean.'

Unexpectedly, Horton hesitated before replying. 'No, of course not,' she said finally. 'But, well —'

'Blood thicker than water?' Isla took a small sip of her wine.

'Well, it's not even blood, is it? But Christ knows. It's certainly not because I've got any interest in him as a human being. If I never see him again, it'll be too soon. But maybe you're right. I can't escape the fact that he's part of my past.' She took another large mouthful of red wine. 'You see what I mean about being sorry for myself?'

'I do.' Isla stretched herself out on the sofa.

In Horton's eyes, both women looked distinctively English, especially up here. Horton herself looked almost a caricature of the English rose type – a rounded pretty face, slightly flushed cheeks and neatly bobbed dark hair. Isla, on the other hand, looked the horsey type – tall, fine cheekbones, well-scrubbed skin and long blonde hair. Both of these images contained a nugget of truth but were equally misleading. Horton sometimes wondered what their Highland neighbours thought of them, imagining they were dismissed as Sassenach degenerates. In fact, the welcome they'd received up here had been uniformly warm.

'Are you telling me you're not happy now?' Isla went on.

Horton threw a cushion at her partner, taking care to avoid the glass of wine. 'Stop fishing for compliments, Bennett. You know how happy I am. Just don't start taking any of it for granted.'

Isla laughed. The truth was that they were both more settled and content than they'd ever been. 'Anyway, what's all this "part of my past" stuff? Even as a police officer, you're not exactly about to pick up your pension.'

'Oh, you know. Childhood. A bloody miserable time, most of it. But still part of me.' She took a final mouthful of the wine and peered ruefully into the empty glass. 'Bugger it, I'm going to have one more. Glass, I mean, not bottle.' She pushed herself to her feet and went into the kitchen in search of the wine. It was a decent place they had here. Not large and not particularly luxurious, but comfortable and homely. When they got the woodstove going, as tonight, she didn't want to be anywhere else.

'You're getting attuned to the drinking culture up here,' Isla observed, as Horton returned with the opened bottle. 'When I was at the airport the other morning, it looked like everyone but me was topping up with alcohol. It wasn't even six o'clock. All these families going off on half-term holidays, knocking back the beer and the whisky.' She sounded amused rather than shocked.

'I'm not quite at that stage yet,' Horton said. 'Anyway, what exactly did David say?'

Despite her previous comments, Isla held out her glass for a refill. 'Well, he started by asking for you. But I reckon he knew what he was doing, phoning at that time. He knows you usually work late. I think he was expecting the voicemail. Was a bit taken aback when I answered.'

'I can imagine him squirming,' Horton said, with a note of satisfaction. Isla had been working at home finishing a report that afternoon.

'Anyway, I asked if he wanted to leave a message. There was a long dramatic pause, and then, he went into this spiel. Sounded to me like it was rehearsed, maybe even written down. That's another reason I think he was expecting the voicemail. Something to surprise you with when you got back.'

'You're even more cynical that I am, Isla Bennett.'

Isla shrugged. 'I'm not saying it wasn't sincere. But it was calculating as well. I suppose that's sort of impressive in the circumstances.'

'That's David, though.'

'He said he was desperate to talk to you. That he had something urgent to tell you. Something you needed to know.'

'Nothing else?' They'd already been through this several times since Horton had returned from work. She kept expecting some punchline. Something that David wanted from her. Money, quite probably.

'No, that was it. He just wanted to talk to you. Face to face, he said.'

'But he didn't leave a contact number?'

They'd already been through this as well. Isla looked quizzically at Horton. 'You're beginning to sound like you want to phone him back.'

'No, not at all. And he'd know better than to ask me to.' She stopped, thinking. 'But I know David. I know what he's like. He's always got some ulterior motive. He's always after something, even if it's not always easy to work out what.'

'So?'

'So, I'm curious about why he phoned. What he really wants.'

'Waiting for the other shoe to drop?'

'Something like that.'

'If so, he didn't give any clues.'

'He wouldn't.' Horton was staring at the woodstove, watching the play of the flames inside. She shivered. Partly, she thought, because the central heating had switched off for the night, the stove was dying down, and the weather outside was still chilly. Partly. 'That's the disturbing thing. He's up to something. I don't know what. But it's as if he's intruded here. Almost as if he's physically walked in the door.'

'He hasn't,' Isla pointed out. 'All he's done is make a phone call. And maybe he's not up to anything. Maybe he really does just want to talk.'

'Maybe.' Horton sounded unconvinced. She swallowed the last of her wine and placed the glass on the coffee table with a clunk. 'Okay, that's enough for tonight. I'm off to bed. Are you coming yet?'

Isla smiled. 'If you make it worth my while.'

Horton laughed and nodded. 'Oh, yes. I'll make it worth your while.'

CHAPTER EIGHT

The next morning, Horton felt relieved she'd not indulged further in the wine. She turned up at the office just before eight, as usual, to find McKay still wearing his battered anorak, feet up on the corner of her desk, ostentatiously chewing his ever-present gum.

'What time do you call this?' he said. 'We've got work to do.'

'Well, there's a first time for everything. You know you've still got your coat on?'

'We're heading out, Ginny. Up into the wild blue yonder. Well, the wild Black Isle, anyhow.'

'Something interesting?' When McKay was this excited, it was generally because there was a serious case in the offing. Something more stimulating that a bunch of neds beating each other up on an Inverness Saturday night.

His enthusiasm dimmed for a moment. 'Well, probably not. But I can always hope.' He was already on his feet, ushering her towards the door. 'You driving?'

'I usually do,' she said, following him out.

Once they were in the car and heading out of town, she said, 'Okay, so what's the story?'

'Body found up at Chanonry Point. Looks like it was washed up there this morning.'

'Recent?' She wasn't aware they'd had any reported mispers in the area over the last few weeks.

'That was what the officer who called it in thought. Didn't look as if it had been in the water long. Guess we'll find out more when we get there.'

'No one reported missing?'

'I checked the system just before you got there. Nothing showing up. But might not yet.'

He was silent for a few moments, staring out of the window. They were crossing the Kessock Bridge, the expanse of the Beauly Firth stretched out on their left. It was another half-decent day, plenty of blue sky visible between the scudding clouds.

They'd made this same journey up to the Black Isle at the start of their last big case. A case that had, if only indirectly, resulted in the crumbling of McKay's already fragile marriage. A case that was still dragging its way through the judicial process, leaving McKay seeming increasingly anxious, for reasons Horton didn't entirely understand.

'I'm assuming we're taking the Munlochy turning this time?' she said. She glanced across at McKay, wondering whether his thoughts were occupying the same territory as her own. But his face showed nothing, his eyes fixed on the road.

'Aye, that's the quickest,' he said. 'You know the way?'

'I know the way,' she confirmed. 'We've been dolphin spotting at Chanonry Point.'

'See any?'

'Quite a few. They were amazingly close to the shore.'

McKay was still staring morosely out of the window. His earlier excitement seemed to have dissipated. 'I've lived in these parts most of my life. Only seen them a couple of times.' He paused. 'Mind you, I've mostly not been looking.'

She turned the wheel to take the road towards Munlochy. 'We know anything more about this body, then?' she said.

'Fairly elderly looking, according to the uniform. Male. That's about all, as far I'm aware. The uniforms were leaving it all be until the Examiners get there.'

They passed through Munlochy and joined the coastal road through Avoch and along the edge of the firth to Fortrose. A few minutes later they reached the turn off down to Chanonry Point. There was a new housing estate on their right which seemed to have expanded further every time Horton came down this road. As they passed the entrance to the golf club, the road narrowed to a single track with passing places as it crossed the course itself.

In the summer, the road would be busy with tourists heading down to try to see the dolphins often visible from the Point. Even this early in the day and in the season, there would usually be a few vehicles coming and going.

At the end of the road, however, the uniforms had set up a roadblock with their own marked vehicle parked sideways across the road. As they approached, Horton pulled to a halt and peered out of the window, waving her warrant card. 'DS Horton and DI McKay,' she said.

The uniformed officer, a middle-aged man with ginger hair who looked vaguely familiar to Horton, crouched and peered into the car. 'Morning, Alec. Morning –?'

'Ginny,' she said. 'Ginny Horton.' She suspected all the uniforms knew who she was. It wasn't as if the place was overrun with female detective sergeants. But she always seemed to have to go through this ritual. 'I think we've met before.' In fairness, she thought, she had no idea herself where or when that might have been.

'Aye, maybe, ma'am. Good to meet you, anyway.' It was impossible to tell whether there was a satirical edge in his tone.

'This one look interesting, then, Andy?' McKay asked. 'I could do with an interesting one.'

'Who knows? Examiners have just got here.'

McKay raised an eyebrow. 'Quick for them. Not Jock Henderson, then, I take it.'

The officer grinned. 'No, the other guy. Carrick.'

'Well, let's be thankful for small mercies.'

They pulled into the car park. There was another marked car, an ambulance and the plain white Examiners' van parked in the spaces more usually occupied by sightseers. At the far end of the car park, there were a couple of large camper vans, both with German number plates.

McKay climbed out of the car and walked to the edge of the shingle beach, gazing out along the spit of land stretching out into the Moray Firth. To his left, there were a few houses, and set above the beach, the squat white-painted lighthouse that overlooked the Point and the bay. At high tide, the seas came up to the walls below the lighthouse, and it was necessary to take a footpath around to the end of the Point. For the moment, the tide was still low, and it was possible to walk along the rough beach. There was a uniformed officer standing twenty or so metres ahead of them to deter any pedestrians who might have bypassed the roadblock. Beyond that, a white-suited Examiner was crouched over an unidentifiable grey heap on the shingle.

McKay nodded to the uniformed officer as they passed. 'Morning, son. Grand way to start the day.'

Carrick looked up as they approached. His metal box of equipment was sitting on the ground beside him, and he had a digital camera in his hand.

'Morning, Pete,' McKay said. 'We okay to come closer?' His tone was noticeably less acerbic than when in Jock Henderson's company.

'Aye, close as you like,' Carrick said. 'Come and join in the fun. I've done all the important stuff.'

'Anything of interest?'

Carrick shrugged. 'Hard to say. White male. Mid to late sixties, I'd say. As far as I can judge, not been in the water long. Maybe twelve to twenty-four hours.'

'Any signs of foul play?' McKay leaned forward at peered at the body lying face down on the shingle. He could see grey hair, a sodden raincoat, a pair of black trousers and polished black shoes. Not a free swimmer, then.

'Nothing obvious,' Carrick said. 'There's some damage to the face and hands, but my guess is that was probably done by the impact against the shore. You'll need the Doc to confirm, though.'

McKay straightened and looked about them. Across the water, there was the imposing edifice of Fort George, built after the Battle of Culloden yet still operating as a working garrison, and some of the buildings in Ardersier. To their right, there were the coastal villages of Fortrose and Avoch. 'If he's not been in the water long, where might he have come from?'

'I'm no expert,' Carrick said, 'but I'd guess somewhere fairly close by. Drifted up the firth a bit, that's all. I don't think it would even have got over the water from the far side in that time, especially as the weather's been pretty calm. But, like I say, I'm no expert.'

'Sounds sensible enough to me, son. Wonder if anyone's missed him yet?' He turned back to the body. 'Any ID?'

'I've not checked yet. Was just about to turn him over and have a look at the other side.'

'I'll leave that task to you, son. I'm wearing my best shirt here.'

They watched as Carrick slowly eased the body over, then stepped back as he took more photographs and made brief notes in a pad. Finally, he finished and sat back. 'I'll check the pockets,' he said.

McKay had been walking slowly around the body and now stopped to peer at the corpse's grey features. He took another few steps back and crouched down on his haunches, staring at the prone body. Finally, he looked up at Carrick. 'Aye, you do that, son. But I don't need the ID now. I know precisely who the fuck this is.' He paused and pushed himself slowly to his feet. 'Ladies and gentlemen, may I introduce you to Mr Billy fucking Crawford.'

CHAPTER NINE

'Okay,' Horton said finally, 'I'll bite. Who's Billy Crawford?'
'Former DI Billy Crawford, to give him his full title,' McKay said. 'Former deputy and chief bag carrier to none other than equally former DCI Jackie fucking Galloway.'

Horton and Carrick were both staring at him. Carrick said, 'Galloway was the body over in Rosemarkie?'

'One and the same,' McKay said, beaming widely. 'One and the very same.' He appeared a changed man from the morose figure sitting beside Horton in the car earlier. 'Now isn't that an interesting coincidence?'

'You're certain it's him?' Horton said. She leaned over and examined the colourless, battered face.

'Oh, aye. Absolutely certain. I'd know that old bastard even if he had a stocking pulled over his head.' He paused. 'Which, at one time, wouldn't have surprised me.'

'Do you know where he lives?'

McKay gestured up the coast. 'Fortrose, somewhere, I believe. Couldn't bear to be too far from his old boss, even when it became crystal clear that his old boss wanted nothing whatsoever to do with him.'

'Do we know if he's been reported missing?'

'He wasn't on the system when I checked this morning,' McKay said. 'Maybe we should find out, eh?'

Horton extracted her mobile phone and dialled back to the office, wandering away down the beach in search of a stronger signal.

'If you're right,' Carrick said, 'that's a bloody odd coincidence.'

'I'm right, sonny, don't you worry about that. But, yes, bloody odd.'

'Did this guy have – well, medical problems like the other one?'

'Alzheimer's, you mean? Not that I'm aware of. Word on this one was that he had a bit of a thirst, if you get my drift.'

Carrick nodded. 'Well, that might explain how he came to be in the water. Wouldn't be the first drunk we've had to fish out.'

'True enough. Still, like you say, coincidence.' McKay looked up as Horton approached.

She nodded. 'Reported late last night. Had apparently been to the pub – the Caley Bar in Fortrose, would you believe? Didn't return home at the usual time. By eleven, wife got worried and went to look for him. He'd left the pub around nine-thirty. She tried phoning 'round various drinking buddies, but no sign of him. Eventually, around midnight, she called us, but no one got around to dealing with it properly 'til this morning.'

'Don't imagine there's anything that could have been done last night, anyway,' McKay said. 'He was probably already in the water by the time she reported him missing.' He frowned. 'Did you check where Crawford lived?'

Horton pulled out a notebook into which she had scrawled some details, and read out the address she'd been given.

'Interesting', McKay said. 'If Crawford had just been weaving his way back home, however pissed he might be, what would have taken him down to the sea?'

'People do stupid things when they're drunk,' Horton said. 'Or so I've been told.'

McKay peered at her with interest. 'You'll have to share some of your experiences some time, Ginny. Aye, you're right, but it's still a funny old route to take. Not something you'd do by accident, I'd have thought.'

'Maybe he walked back with someone?'

'But you wouldn't normally walk them home if it took you out of your way.'

'Unless it was a woman, maybe?'

'You think Crawford was playing away? It's possible, I suppose. Even at his age. Can't see many women drinking in the Caley, though, even though it's coming up in the world. Maybe he wanted to pay someone a visit.' McKay was looking thoughtful. 'All avenues to explore, anyway.' He peered back up the beach towards the car park. 'Who found the body?'

'Couple of German tourists, apparently,' Carrack said. 'Those two camper vans in the car park. They've been asked to stay put until you've spoken to them.'

'That would be the car park with the sign saying "no overnight parking,"' McKay said. 'We'd better get a statement from them, I suppose. Then we can go and break the bad news to Mrs Crawford, if nobody has already. What a job, eh?' He managed somehow to imbue the final question with an unexpected note of satisfaction.

Despite his disregard for the local parking regulations, the elderly German witness lived up to the national stereotype in the detail and precision of his account. He had described in perfect, virtually accentless English how he had taken an early morning walk down to the Point in the hope of seeing the dolphins. 'The low tide was early this morning,' he said. 'I understand that it is good to seek the dolphins an hour or so after the turning of the tide. It was a fine morning, so I went down to see.'

'You were alone?'

'Yes, my wife and our friends –' He gestured towards the second camper van. 'They were still asleep.' His tone implied that this constituted some moral failing. 'It was a fine morning. Six-forty. I know this because I had set my alarm for six-thirty. I spent ten minutes dressing.'

'When did you see the body?'

'I saw it when I reached the edge of the car park, above the beach. But, of course, I did not know what it was. It was just, you know, a grey heap. Something washed up by the sea, I thought. Which of course is what it was –' He trailed off, as if the reality of what he had found had only just struck him. 'I even thought it might be, well, a dolphin. But then I walked a few more metres and I realised.'

'You didn't touch or disturb the body at all?'

The man gave a visible shudder at the thought. 'No, of course not. I just went close enough to be sure what I was seeing. And also, to be sure that he was definitely dead.' The second sentence was added as an afterthought. McKay suspected that the man had gone no nearer to the body than he had needed to. Not that he blamed the man for that.

'We think he'd been dead for some hours,' McKay said. 'There was nothing you could have done.'

'I came back here to the van and woke my wife,' the man continued. 'And then our friends. Then, we dialled your 999. I think that is all I can tell you.'

The witness statement added little to their knowledge, other than to confirm that the body had been there first thing, presumably dumped on the shore as the tide receded.

He thanked the German and took contact details just in case any further questions should arise. They were heading further north, the man told him, wanting to explore the coast and maybe some of the islands.

'One word of advice,' McKay said, gesturing towards the signs at the entrance to the car park. 'Obey the parking restrictions. Some residents are less tolerant than we are.'

The German stared at him blankly. 'I'm sorry,' he said. 'My English is not so good.'

McKay nodded and turned away. 'If you say so, pal. If you say so.'

Horton was waiting by the car. Down on the beach, Carrick had finished his work and was packing up. The two paramedics were hoisting the body on to a stretcher.

'We'd better go and track down Mrs Crawford,' McKay said. 'My second grieving widow of the week.'

The Crawford's' house was a sizeable Edwardian detached villa, set a little way back from the main road in a leafy garden.

It was clear that Crawford had emerged from the South Kessock enquiry much more favourably than his boss. When the shite had hit the fan, it had become clear very quickly that Galloway had few real friends.

'Decent place,' Horton said, as they walked down the short driveway.

'The fruits of a life's honest toil,' McKay said. 'So they tell me.'

The door was answered almost immediately. Mrs Crawford was a slight, grey-haired woman who blinked up nervously at McKay. She took in Horton's presence behind McKay and her face dropped. 'You've come about Billy.' It wasn't a question.

'DI McKay and DS Horton. May we come in, Mrs Crawford?'

She led them through to a tidy living room. There was a general tartan theme to the carpets and decor. To McKay's eye, the place carried the ambiance of an upmarket Highland steakhouse.

McKay gestured her to take a seat on the well-stuffed leather sofa, then sat himself down on an armchair opposite. 'I'm afraid it's bad news, Mrs Crawford.'

Mrs Crawford looked around at Horton as if seeking a second opinion. 'What's happened to him?'

'I'm sorry —' When it came to it, there was never really any way to soften the blow. You couldn't afford to be ambiguous. McKay knew only too well that, given half a chance, people would cling on to any last shred of hope. 'I'm afraid he's dead, Mrs Crawford. He was found this morning.'

She was staring at McKay as if she hadn't understood what he'd said. There were no immediate tears, simply bewilderment. 'But how —?'

'We don't know exactly yet, Mrs Crawford. His body was found washed up this morning at Chanonry Point.' He didn't know whether she was ready for this detail yet, but he could see no way to keep it from her.

'Washed up?'

'We don't know how or why he entered the sea,' McKay said. 'It may be that he was taken ill or –'

'But why would he be anywhere near the sea?'

McKay glanced at Horton. 'We were hoping you might be able to give us some ideas about that, Mrs Crawford. We'll need to ascertain the cause of death and try to find out exactly what happened. But that can wait. I'm very sorry, Mrs Crawford. I appreciate this must be an awful shock for you.'

'Jackie Galloway,' she said unexpectedly.

'I'm sorry?'

She looked up at him. Her eyes were glazed, as if she were staring at some point in the distance. 'I saw on the news. Jackie Galloway. He's dead, too. That's right, isn't it?'

'Mr Galloway's body was found yesterday, yes. At his house in Rosemarkie.' He paused, unsure how to proceed. 'I believe your husband worked with Mr Galloway?'

She seemed about to answer, then she stopped and peered more closely at McKay. 'I know you, don't I? You used to work with Billy, too?'

'I did, Mrs Crawford. You're right. I should have said, but it was many years ago. I was a very junior officer. He was very well respected.'

'But why is this happening?' she said. 'Why now?'

'I understand your concerns, but this is most likely just a sad coincidence. As far as we can judge at present, Mr Galloway died from natural causes. An accident.'

She was gazing fixedly at McKay as if trying to imprint him in her memory. 'An accident like Billy's, you mean? Falling into the sea. But why was he anywhere near the sea? He'd just gone to the bar. It's a ten-minute walk back straight along the high street.'

'I'm sure there's a simple explanation,' McKay said. 'We'll be investigating the circumstances.' She was still staring at him, and it took McKay a moment to realise that the expression in her eyes was one of fear. 'We've no reason to suspect foul play.'

He hesitated. 'Unless you know of some reason why your husband might have been in danger?'

'He was a police officer. Like you. There are always people who want to hurt you.'

In his own case, McKay reflected, those people were probably mostly his own colleagues. But, of course, she was right. You made enemies in the job. The scrotes who decided to take their convictions personally, as if it was your fault they'd mugged some defenceless pensioner or committed an armed robbery. The toerags who thought their manhood would be questioned if they didn't swear revenge on you. Even the relatives sometimes – the wives or parents who blamed you for the fact they'd married or sired a malicious deadbeat. 'Your husband has been retired a long time, Mrs Crawford.'

'I know,' she said, her eyes still bright with fear, 'and that's why I'm asking you. Why Billy? Why now?'

CHAPTER TEN

They'd left Mrs Crawford in the care of a neighbour who had appeared promptly in response to a telephone call from the newly bereaved widow. McKay had the impression that, within the half hour, every female in the village over the age of sixty would have descended to pay her respects.

'She seemed genuinely scared,' Horton pointed out, as they walked back up the high street.

'Grief strikes people in strange ways,' McKay offered. 'Hard to see who would have bothered to take Billy Crawford out after all these years.' He paused. 'She's right, though. It's a weird coincidence. Two accidents. A day apart. Unexplained elements in both cases. Merits a bit more digging.'

Horton laughed. 'As if you were ever going to let it lie. You're desperate for a proper case to get your teeth into.'

'Nah, I'm just out for a quiet life,' McKay said. 'Let's go and pay a visit to the Caley Bar, shall we? For old times' sake.' He turned back to her, his face serious. 'If you can face it.'

The last time they'd been in the Caley had been at the tail end of the previous summer's major murder enquiry. 'Yeah,' she said. 'Back in the saddle and all that, you know.'

'I hear it's going up in the world,' McKay said. 'Mind you, it would have taken some sort of special genius to take it down market.'

From the outside, the Caledonian Bar looked much improved, with new paintwork and sparkling freshly cleaned windows. Once through the double doors, the changes were even more striking. The walls had been repainted a gleaming white, and the previously filthy floor had been stripped back and sanded. There were arty prints on the walls and vases of fresh flowers in the windows.

'Christ almighty,' McKay said. 'I think we've come into the wrong place.'

It had only just turned twelve, and the place was still empty. A tall young man with blond hair and Viking features was standing behind the bar. He looked up hopefully as they approached. 'Afternoon,' he said. 'How can I help you?' He had an accent, but it was barely discernible. Irish rather than Scottish, McKay thought.

McKay slid his warrant card across the bar. 'Not customers, I'm afraid. DI McKay and DS Horton. Mr –?'

'Donnelly. Callum Donnelly.' The young man was looking anxious.

'No need to worry, Mr Donnelly. We've not spotted anyone drinking underage or found you fiddling the till.' He gifted Donnelly on of his rare smiles. 'And frankly, you'd have to go a long way to surpass your predecessor in those departments. Denny Gorman wasn't exactly the model landlord.' He looked around. 'Nice job you've done with the place, eh, Ginny?'

Horton nodded. 'I'd barely have recognised it.'

Donnelly was looking relieved. 'We've only just begun, really. It's been a challenge, more than we expected.'

'Aye, I can believe that,' McKay said. 'I imagine Gorman would have left a few skeletons in the closets. And probably things less pleasant than that.'

'It's taken a bit of cleaning up,' Donnelly agreed. 'We're working on the kitchens now. Want to be able to do a proper range of food. Not sure we'll have that up and running for the start of the season, but we're giving it a go. Got to get the exterior sorted too.'

'Good luck to you,' McKay said. 'Nice to see some life coming back to the place.'

'How can I help you?'

'Billy Crawford,' McKay said. 'Was he in here last night?'

'He was,' Donnelly confirmed. 'He usually is. Then his wife came 'round later looking for him.' He stopped, staring at them. 'Oh, my God. Do you mean –?'

'I'm afraid so. His body was found this morning.'

'That poor woman. I'm afraid I didn't take her all that seriously. I thought he must have just gone on for a chat somewhere with his mates, and that she was being hysterical. I never imagined –'

'There were no signs of anything wrong with him earlier in the evening?'

'Not that I remember. Was he taken ill?'

'It's too early for us to be sure about the cause of death,' McKay said. 'His body was found washed up this morning at Chanonry Point.'

'My God. That's dreadful. How could that have happened?'

'That's what we're trying to find out,' McKay said patiently. 'You didn't see any evidence he was unwell?'

'I don't think so. He was pretty drunk by the end, though.' He paused, clearly wondering whether this raised any questions about his own responsibilities as the licensee. 'I mean, not incapable or anything. But he'd had a few. Four or five pints and a couple of chasers, I think.'

'Is that usual?' Horton asked. 'For Crawford, I mean.'

'If I'm honest, pretty much so. He usually came in about six-thirty. Didn't usually stay more than a couple of hours – usually away about eight or eight-thirty. But he often managed to knock back a fair amount in that time. The crowd he mixed with were all a bit like that, but some more than others.'

'Not the clientele you're aspiring to, I imagine?'

Donnelly shrugged. 'They're not so bad. It's hard to turn away business, especially outside the season. They're not trouble makers. They just sit there in the corner, gossiping away and getting quietly bladdered. The tourists are more likely to come in at lunchtime or early evening.'

'We'll need you to give us the names of Crawford's drinking companions, if you're able to. I imagine you may know them better than his wife.'

'I can do that,' Donnelly said. 'They're all regulars.'

'So what time did Crawford leave last night?' McKay asked.

'About nine, I think. I didn't notice exactly because we were fairly busy. But that's when he usually left, and I remember noticing he was gone a while after that.'

'Do you know if he left alone?'

'I couldn't say, to be honest. Most of them tend to peel off around that time, if not earlier, though there are a few who stay for the duration. If you want my honest impression, I'd say Crawford was less clubbable than the others. Most of them come in for a bit of company, have a couple of pints and then head off. I think Crawford came in for the booze, mainly, and possibly to get himself out of the house. He always seemed a bit detached from the others. He usually headed off on his own. I don't know whether last night was any different.'

'And this group,' Horton added, 'I assume they're all men?'

Donnelly laughed. 'Not much space for a woman among that lot. Why?'

McKay shrugged. 'Just trying to get a picture.'

Behind them, a young couple, presumably tourists, had just entered and were looking around the bar approvingly. 'First trade of the day,' Donnelly said. 'I'll see if I can tempt them with one of our deli-style sandwiches.'

'Jesus,' McKay said. 'Last time we were in here, you'd have been lucky to get a bag of stale crisps.'

They left Donnelly to his business, taking away with them the list he'd provided of Crawford's drinking companions. He'd come up with eight names in total, though not all had been present the previous evening. Donnelly had known where most lived, and McKay assumed they wouldn't have much difficulty tracking down the rest.

'What do you think?' Horton said, once they were back in the car. 'Worth taking further now?'

'Let's head back to town and have a chat with Helena. It's not like we've got capacity to spare. We need to decide whether there's anything in this one.' He paused, a small smile playing around his lips. 'Mind you, if the local media were to make anything of the unexplained deaths of two ex-coppers within a mile or so of each other, it might rise up the priority list a bit.'

'You're not thinking of tipping them off?'

'Ach, no, Ginny. What do you take me for?' He paused, still smiling. 'But, well, I might mention the possibility to Helena. Just in passing, you understand?'

CHAPTER ELEVEN

Ginny Horton spent the rest of the day working through paperwork, trying to get on top of the numerous cases she had on the go. It felt like a fruitless task – no sooner had she completed one form or dispatched another document than half a dozen more seemed to bounce into her inbox to take their place. But it was just as important, if not more so, than the other aspects of investigatory work.

She'd been happy to leave McKay in conference with Helena Grant. Despite his acerbic manner, McKay had the ability to wrap most people round his little finger, if he put his mind to it, and even Grant was no exception. If he wanted time and resources to devote to the two recent deaths, Horton was fairly sure he'd get it.

Sure enough, half an hour later, McKay reappeared, looking buoyant. 'Permission to carry on,' he confirmed. 'At least for the moment.'

'Helena thinks there's something worth investigating, then?'

'She agrees there's enough to warrant some further digging. And it's close to home. You know, police family stuff. Even if, in this case, we're talking about a couple of disgraced old uncles.'

'Crawford wasn't disgraced, was he?'

'Only just avoided it, the way I understand it. The word was that he was the one who shopped Galloway. I don't think he actually grassed him up as such. Reckoned he hadn't really seen what had happened in any detail. But, the way I heard it, his version of events cast enough doubt to pull the rug from under Galloway. Some said he'd done a deal to save his own skin. I don't know. He was disciplined, but he walked away on early retirement, kept his pension and all that.'

'Must have left Galloway well and truly pissed off.'

'No doubt about that. They were thick as particularly thick thieves, but haven't exchanged a word since, I heard. Not even an expletive.'

'Yet they were living within a mile or so of each other?'

'Aye, weird, isn't it? Assume it was accidental, but maybe the old attraction was too strong.' McKay returned to his desk, rebooted his PC and grimaced at the stack of new emails now filling his inbox. 'You got that list of Crawford's drinking pals?'

Horton pulled out her notebook. 'Here. Why?'

'I'll set someone on tracking them down. See if they can cast any light on Crawford's movements last night. Josh Carlisle got much on at the moment?'

'As much as everyone else, I'm guessing. But he's bogged down in the admin, like all of us. He'd probably welcome a trip out.' DC Carlisle was a young, enthusiastic member of the team, generally only too happy to do anything that would keep him in McKay's good books.

'His lucky day, then.' McKay was already back on his feet. 'Don't worry, I won't let him anywhere near your notebook. I'll photocopy the page.'

'You lose my notebook, Alec McKay, and I won't be responsible for my actions.'

***

The rest of the afternoon passed uneventfully. Sick of pounding at her keyboard, Horton left earlier than usual, heading out of the office just after five. The traffic on to the A9 was already heavy, tailing back into the city, and she was pleased when she finally reached the Aberdeen Road, heading for home.

Isla was unlikely to be home for another hour or so. Horton's plan was to stick on something for supper – probably one of the casseroles they made in batches to keep in the freezer – and then head out for an early evening run. She was a serious runner, but she was conscious that, at least by her own standards, she'd allowed the frequency of her runs to slip over the winter months. It was always harder to drag yourself out into a cold, frost-ridden morning or to force yourself back out into the darkness after work. But now the mornings and evenings were growing lighter, she was keen to get back into her former routine.

She parked in front of their neat little cottage, climbed out into the chill evening, and dug out her front door keys. It cheered her just to return to this place every day. It was only a small house on the edge of the village, but they'd spent time and money turning it into the home they wanted. The upper floors had a view of the firth, and in the summer, the garden at the rear formed a suntrap that retained the heat whenever they managed to get a few warm days in a row.

Above all, the place felt like a haven. It was somewhere that, at the end of each day, she could just put all the world – every crime, every investigation, every toerag they'd had to deal with – behind her. She knew Isla felt the same. They could lock the doors, draw the curtains, and it was just them.

She closed the front door behind her and bent to pick up the post. The usual junk. A clothes shopping catalogue addressed to Isla. A bank statement. A flyer for some new store in Inverness.

And an envelope, apparently hand-delivered, with her own name printed on the front. Virginia Horton. She couldn't remember the last time anyone had called her Virginia.

She took the envelope through into the kitchen and put the kettle on. She knew she was simply delaying. All her instincts were telling her to ignore the envelope, throw it away into the bin, unopened.

In the end, though, she knew she'd be unable to resist and she tore it open. Inside was a single sheet of paper, with a message handwritten in block capitals.

"Dear Virginia,

I don't know whether you got my message. I want to see you. There are things I need to tell you. I called this afternoon in the hope that you'd be here. I will try again.

Best,

David."

She stared at the words. The final sentence struck her with the force of a threat. "I will try again."

Too late, she did what she should have done in the first place. She screwed the letter and envelope into a tight ball and dropped them into the trash can beneath the sink.

She realised suddenly that she was shaking.

You're being ridiculous, she told herself. *You're a grown woman, a police officer. There is nothing he can do. Stop it.*

But then she rose, returned to the hallway, and double-locked the front door. She entered the living room and sat, curled in a corner of the sofa, still trembling, longing for the sound of Isla's returning car.

CHAPTER TWELVE

In the end, he took almost nothing. A few books. The portable CD player he knew Chrissie never used. A stack of his old CDs to play on it. A few other personal items – a framed photograph of his parents, a souvenir old-style bobby's helmet presented to him when he'd spoken at a conference years ago, a couple of ornaments that had belonged to his mother. He was able to get his clothes into a couple of suitcases. He hesitated, looking at the framed photograph of his and Chrissie's wedding day on top of the television. The two of them looking delighted and absurdly young. Full of hope. He picked it up for a moment and then replaced it.

There was no point in taking more. The bungalow was a furnished let, basic but with enough to meet McKay's limited needs. If there was anything else, he could pick it up from the supermarket in Inverness. He wanted to leave all this behind for Chrissie, as undisturbed as possible. At least pretend nothing had changed.

He'd sorted the details out with the agent the previous day, paying a month's deposit and a month's rent in advance. The young man still seemed slightly stunned that he'd managed to complete the deal so easily, and McKay hadn't even bothered to haggle about the rent. He just wanted it sorted. The place was vacant, and they'd been more than happy to hand over the keys immediately.

It took him only an hour or so to get packed, and it was still early evening by the time he reached the Kessock Bridge. The days were lengthening, but the first lights were coming on around the firth, and there was a low mist hanging over the water.

McKay wasn't sure if this felt like the end of something or the beginning. Time, he guessed, would tell.

Once he'd made the turn off the A9 into the Black Isle, he dialled the number on the hands-free. It rang briefly then a voice said, 'Ellie McBride.'

'Hi, Ellie. It's Alec. I don't suppose Chrissie's around.' He'd always got on well enough with Chrissie's younger sister.

There was a moment's hesitation. 'I think she's having a wee lie down just at the moment, Alec. I wouldn't want to disturb her.'

'Aye, no, quite right.' It was clear that Chrissie didn't want to speak to him. It was what he'd expected. 'Look, Ellie, I just wanted to let her know I've moved out now, like I said I would. Left everything as it was, so she can go back when she wants. Until we get this sorted out, you know.'

'Aye, Alec. I know.' She sounded kindly enough, though McKay guessed she'd mostly be relieved she wouldn't have to squeeze Chrissie into a house already barely large enough for herself, her husband and their three kids. 'What are you doing, though? Where are you staying, I mean?'

'I'm renting a place up over in the Black Isle. Rosemarkie. It'll do for the moment.' He paused. 'I've left details of the address and suchlike back at the house.'

'Look after yourself, won't you, Alec.'

'I'll do my best,' he said.

'Alec –' She stopped suddenly, as if she'd bitten back the words she'd been about to speak. 'I'll pass the message on,' she said, finally.

'Thanks, Ellie. And give my love to Chrissie.'

He ended the call before she could respond. Night was falling as he passed Munlochy Bay, and he could see a scattering of lights across the water. He still didn't know what had brought him up here, rather than just finding himself somewhere in Inverness. Partly, he wanted time to himself. Somewhere quiet where he could think. Partly, he wanted a complete change. A place where he wouldn't constantly be reminded of what he'd left behind.

There was something else as well, though, he thought. Something else he was seeking. Something to do with his daughter, Lizzie, who had somehow been lost to him even before her death. Something to do with the lost and the rootless. Wanting, perhaps, to engage with that.

He turned down into the small housing estate where the bungalow was located. It was at the end of a cul-de-sac, and there were no immediate neighbours – another reason he'd been attracted to the place. He pulled into the small parking space and turned off the engine. In the pale orange glow of the street lights, the bungalow looked as bleak and unwelcoming as ever.

Most of the houses back along the street would be occupied by couples and families, enjoying the warmth of an evening at home. It wouldn't take much to make this place homely, though it had sat unoccupied for some months. The owner was English, the agent had told McKay, and had inherited the property on the death of his grandmother, the previous occupant. He was waiting for the market to pick up before trying to sell it and had hoped to let it to holidaymakers, but the facilities were too old-fashioned, and the owner hadn't been prepared to invest in updating them. The agent had told McKay all this, with amusing candour, although only after he'd ensured that McKay's signature was firmly on the contract.

McKay hadn't cared much about all that, anyway. All it meant was that the property was being let at a price he could afford.

He sat for a few seconds longer, wondering how it had come to this. Then, he climbed out of the car and took out the front door key to what, for the moment at least, he was going to have to learn to call home.

***

When she finally heard the sound of the car pulling up outside, Ginny Horton hurried back into the hallway to unbolt the front door for Isla.

She wasn't sure whether it was some instinct or simply her mounting anxiety that made her pause and peer through the small window beside the front door. It had grown dark while she'd been sitting huddled on the sofa, and, other than in the kitchen, she hadn't so far turned on any lights in the house.

The car at the end of the drive was not Isla's familiar little Audi. It was something else, a model she didn't immediately recognise. It was parked across the entrance, catching the glow of the street light above. There was a figure in the front seat, but from there, she couldn't make out whether the driver was male or female.

She expected the occupant of the car to emerge and approach the house, but the figure remained motionless. She realised she was holding her breath.

Was it David?

There was no way of knowing. She had no idea what car he drove. She had no real idea even what he was doing these days.

She remained transfixed at the window, wondering what the hell to do. She could try to call Isla on her mobile, but she knew Isla turned her phone to silent when driving. She could call the police, but if this turned out to be just some random passer-by, paused to check directions or make a call, she'd just make herself a laughing stock. McKay would get more than his two-penn'orth out of that story.

In any case, she didn't want to move. She needed to keep watching. If the car door opened and David emerged, she told herself, she'd do something. But for the moment, she didn't want to look away, didn't want to risk the unknown. Didn't want to risk that David might approach the house without her even being aware of it.

She tried to calm her fears, telling herself she was being idiotic. Even if it was David, she wasn't the same person she'd been back then. She could look after herself. How old would David be these days, anyway? He couldn't threaten her physically. Just let him fucking try.

Somewhere behind her, back in the living room, she heard the buzz of her mobile, and momentarily, instinctively, she glanced away from the window. She hadn't even realised she'd left the phone in there. She hesitated, listening to the phone ring, wondering whether she should retrieve it. Maybe it was Isla to say she'd been delayed.

When she looked back out of the window, something had changed. The car door was open, and a figure was climbing out. A male, she thought, tall, thin, dressed in a dark suit. She still couldn't make out the face.

Then, there was the sound of a car horn, and the figure was turned into a silhouette by the glare of car headlights. Another impatient blast on the horn. The figure scrambled back into the car, as if in a hurry. Moments later, Horton heard the engine starting, and the car headed off down the road, wheels screeching from the acceleration.

Isla's Audi pulled into the driveway. Horton waited for her to emerge, as if expecting that, somehow, Isla might have been replaced by an impostor. It was only as Isla approached that Horton finally pulled back the bolts and threw open the door.

'Jesus,' Isla said. 'Stupid bloody tosser. Just stops in front of the drive without a second thought – What's wrong?'

'I –' Horton could barely speak. She led Isla into the kitchen and rummaged in the bin for the letter. Smoothing the crumpled paper on the table, she finally said, 'This.'

Isla took in the contents of the note and looked back at Horton. 'When did it arrive?'

'Today. It was there when I got back. Hand-delivered.'

'You mean he's here? I mean, up here somewhere.' She glanced towards the front door. 'Jesus, you think –?'

'I don't know. It might have been.'

'If it was him, he scarpered PDQ when I arrived.'

'Did you see his face?'

Isla shook her head. 'He was just a shape in the headlights. Then, he ducked back in the car and buggered off.'

'You didn't see the car reg?'

'I didn't take it in. I think it was a new one. This year, I mean. Maybe a hire car?'

'If he flew up here, he'd probably pick up one at the airport,' Horton agreed. 'I can't see him traipsing all the way up by car. Not his style.'

'We don't even know it was him,' Isla said.

'But we know he's around.' Horton was beginning to feel calmer now. 'Hang on.' She left Isla in the kitchen and went to find her phone in the living room.

She looked up as Isla followed her into the room. 'I had a call. Before he got out of the car. Just before you arrived.' She held up the phone, screen towards Isla. 'Number withheld.'

'Could have been anyone,' Isla said. 'Just a junk call probably.'

'Maybe he tried to call me before he left the car. See if I was in. Most of the lights were off, so he wouldn't have known if anyone was here.'

'Ginny, it could have been anyone. Why would he have called you? How would he even have your number?'

Horton sat down heavily on the sofa. 'I don't know. The whole thing's shaken me up. I'd been keeping watch on him out of the window. Then, the phone rang, and I was distracted. That was when he started to get out of the car –' She stopped, knowing she was sounding uncharacteristically hysterical.

Isla sat down and took Horton's hands in hers. 'Look, Ginny. Stop. Think about it. This isn't like you. The call was probably just coincidence. We don't know if it was David out there. Okay, so we know he's around. But maybe he's telling the truth, and he does just want to talk to you.'

'I don't want to talk to him.' Horton was conscious of sounding like a petulant child.

'I know that. We can make that clear to him, if we have to. But we don't know that he's got an agenda other than that.'

'So why is he approaching me like this? It all seems designed to unnerve me.'

Isla shrugged. 'Maybe he intends the opposite. Seems to me he might be nervous about approaching you. Calls when you're not likely to be here. Sticks a note through the letterbox when he knows you'll be at work. And, if it was him just now, sits in the car, unsure whether to ring the doorbell. Perhaps this is as much of an ordeal for him as it is for you.'

'If so, he really has changed.'

'People do, Ginny. Not always, I know. But sometimes. He's getting old. Maybe he's alone. That might be enough.'

'Maybe,' Horton said doubtfully.

'And you're a grown woman. Christ, you fight off hardened criminals with your bare hands. Why have you any reason to be scared of that fuck-up?'

There was a long silence. They were still holding hands, staring into each other's eyes. Finally, Horton said, 'He was a bastard. An utter evil bastard.'

'You've told me some of that –'

'I've not told you it all. Not the worst parts.'

'Okay,' Isla said. 'So, tell me.'

CHAPTER THIRTEEN

It took McKay even less time to unpack than it had to pack. He left the suitcase of clothes unopened in the bedroom, arranged the few trinkets he'd bought with him randomly around the sitting room, and sat down on the battered sofa to take stock.

The bungalow was less bleak than he'd remembered. Probably that had just reflected his mood the day he'd visited. It had seen better days, undoubtedly, and most of the furniture looked like it had been there for decades. But it was clean and comfortable enough. It wouldn't have taken much effort to make the place welcoming. But McKay knew even that much effort was likely to be beyond him.

He didn't even know whether Chrissie would take the cue to return home. She probably would, if only because she knew she was imposing on her sister. But whether she'd stay there any longer than she needed to – well, who knew?

Not McKay, certainly. He didn't even really know why she'd gone. He knew in general terms, of course. That was clear enough. All those years of circling each other, trying to offload their guilt at Lizzie's death, slipping further and further apart. And he supposed that last big case had acted as a catalyst, driven Chrissie to take the step she'd never quite managed before.

He'd finally brought himself to read the note she'd left on the night of her departure. He'd read it once, then thrown it away. It told him nothing he didn't already know. Nothing that helped him understand. Other than a few monosyllabic exchanges on practical issues, they'd barely spoken since. He had no reason to suppose things were likely to change now. All he could do was wait.

He'd known he'd be in no mood to prepare food tonight. He'd never been completely useless in the kitchen, but Chrissie had always insisted that was her role, and he'd not been inclined to argue. Maybe that was another part of the problem. On his way from the office, he'd stopped off to grab a supermarket sandwich, a bag of crisps and a six pack of beer, along with a pint of milk and a jar of instant coffee. They were sitting in the middle of the table, looking as enticing as everything else about this house.

It had only just gone seven. As far as he could recall, the pub in the village did food until eight. Maybe it was time to head out and get to know the locals. Find out what this place might have in store for him. *So much for being alone*, he thought. So much for giving himself time to think. He should have known by now that that was the last thing he ever wanted.

The small front bar of the pub was deserted, though he could hear some chatter from the back. There was no one behind the bar, but after a moment, a figure came trotting along the corridor. 'You okay there?' A young man, probably early twenties. Eager to please.

'You still doing food?'

'Sure. 'Til eight.' He reached behind the bar and slid a leather-bound menu across to McKay. 'Just yourself?'

'Just myself,' McKay confirmed. He skimmed quickly down the menu. Standard pub fare. He ordered a scampi and chips and a pint of the local Cromarty Brewery beer.

'You want to eat in here or go through the back?'

'Is it busy back there?'

The young man shrugged. 'Not so's you'd notice. Too early in the year for the tourists, and too early in the week for the locals. Just a few of the older lads, you know.'

McKay nodded. 'I'll go through there, then.'

He followed the young man through to the back of the building. The rear bar was laid out restaurant-style, and three middle-aged men were clustered round the bar. They fell momentarily silent as McKay entered. He took a seat at the far end of the room and nodded to them. 'Evening.'

One of the men nodded back. 'Evening.' They lost interest in him and resumed their chat. McKay sipped at his beer, watching them without curiosity. He'd spent too many years doing surveillance work to feel awkward eating alone, and the same experience had taught him how to make himself inconspicuous.

The food came quickly and was fine. McKay finished it off and knocked back his pint. Then, he made his way to the bar to get a refill.

While he was waiting for the beer to be poured, one of the men turned and regarded him curiously. 'You one of them newspaper types, then?'

McKay blinked, trying to translate this. 'Sorry?'

'You know, journalists. Or off the telly. You look familiar.'

'I think you've got the wrong man, pal. Nearest I ever get to the telly is falling asleep in front of it.'

'Oh.' The man sounded disappointed. 'You do look familiar, though. I thought you were maybe one of those – what do they call them? – investigative reporters.' There was something about the way he said "investigative," with an undertone of irony, that made McKay examine the man's face more carefully.

It took him a moment. Then, suddenly, McKay's imagination smoothed the man's wrinkles and redarkened his hair, and McKay saw him as he'd been twenty years before. Rob Graham. DI Rob Graham, in those days. Another one of Jackie Galloway's kitchen cabinet. Christ almighty, had they all settled in this neck of the woods?

'Like I say, you've got the wrong man. Can barely read a newspaper, let alone write for one.' McKay was already turning away. The last thing he wanted was to be recognised by Rob Graham. The one saving grace was that Graham had been the sort of senior officer who scarcely gave the time of day to his underlings. He probably wouldn't recognise McKay if he spat in his face.

Graham was looking unconvinced. 'Thing is, I thought you might be up here on account of these killings.'

McKay's hand tightened on the glass the barman had just handed him. 'Honest, pal, I don't know what you're talking about.' He took a large swallow of the beer. His only objective now was to get out of there as soon as he decently could.

'Police killings,' Graham said. He was clearly two or three pints to the worse. Not drunk, but far enough gone not to care what he was saying. There was something else in his tone, too, McKay thought. A note of anxiety. As if he wanted to talk about this to anyone he could. 'We were just discussing it,' Graham went on. He looked back at McKay. 'Bet the press would pay a pretty penny to anyone who could give them the inside track.' It was clear that, having somehow given himself the idea McKay was a journalist, he wasn't going to let it go easily.

'You've lost me,' McKay said. 'I just came in for a quiet pint and a bite to eat.'

'Leave him be, Rob,' one of the other men said. 'Poor wee bastard doesn't know what the hell you're on about.'

'What's he doing in here on his own, then?' Graham said, his drunkenness taking on an aggressive edge. 'Earwigging.'

'He's not earwigging, Rob. Poor bugger's just trying to drink his pint –'

Suddenly, McKay decided he'd had enough. It had been a crap day at the start of another crap week in what was rapidly turning into a crap year. He'd had to put up with this puffed-up bullying from Graham and his cronies twenty years before. He was buggered if he was going to put up with it now.

He turned to face Graham and put his pint down on the bar. 'Like your mate says, I'm just trying to drink my pint. If you reckon you've got information about criminal activity, you should be talking to the police, not trying to sell the story to imaginary fucking journalists.'

Graham laughed and looked around at his mates to share the joke. 'Police? You know who I am, sonny? Do you know who I fucking am?'

McKay allowed himself a smile. 'Aye, I know exactly who you are. Former Detective Inspector Robert fucking Graham.'

The amusement vanished from Graham's face as if someone had flicked a switch. 'How the hell –?' He peered again at McKay's face. 'Who the fuck are you, pal?'

'DI Alec McKay. At your service. Pal.' McKay's smile was unwavering.

'McKay. Christ, that little snot-rag. How the fuck you make DI?'

'Standards have slipped since your day, Rob. So, what's all this about killings?'

Graham looked back at his companions. 'I need a smoke. Let's go outside for minute, eh?'

'Anything you say.'

There was a small beer garden at the side of the pub. Graham sat himself at one of the tables and lit up a cigarette, waving the pack in McKay's direction. McKay shook his head. 'Given up.' As if to demonstrate, he slipped out a stick of gum and popped it into his mouth. 'Go on, then.'

'You know about Galloway and Crawford?'

'I know they're dead. Unfortunate accidents.'

'Aye, very unfortunate. You know they'd both been getting letters?'

McKay was stony faced. 'Letters?'

'Threatening letters. For years.'

'How'd you know they were getting threatening letters? I thought the three of you weren't bosom buddies anymore.'

'Jackie wouldn't talk to either of us,' Graham said. 'Reckoned we'd sold him down the river.'

'He wasn't far wrong, the way I heard it.'

'If we hadn't, he'd have taken us down the river with him.' There was no note of embarrassment or regret in Graham's voice. 'Billy and I got on well enough. We were never "bosom buddies," as you put it. Just people who ended up working together. Not close, but we rubbed along okay at work.'

'There was me thinking you were one tight little band of brothers.'

'Aye, well. Jackie had his own ways of promoting loyalty. But outside of work, not so much.'

'That why you were prepared to shaft him to save your own skins?'

For a moment, Graham looked angry, then he shrugged and smiled. 'Let's say, neither of us shed too many tears.'

'The letters?'

'I received them. Every six months or so. I checked with Billy, and he'd been getting them too.'

'What did these letters say?'

'Just "NOT FORGOTTEN. NOT FORGIVEN." Nothing else.'

'Did you keep the letters?'

'I threw most of them away. Thought it was just some gobshite with a grudge wanting to scare us. Wouldn't have been the first. When they kept coming, I held on to a few, just in case.'

'You didn't think to report this?'

'Not got many friends in the force. Wasn't going to make myself a laughing stock by reporting something like that. Not without good reason.'

'What about Galloway? How'd you know he was getting them?'

'I used to run into Bridie Galloway from time to time. Around the village. At first, we avoided each other. Then – well, after Jackie became ill, we'd stop and chat a little bit. I asked her about the letters, and she said they'd been getting them, too, though she only found out once Jackie was unable to deal with things like that.'

McKay nodded, as if this was news to him. 'So, all three of you.'

'Aye, same letters. Same frequency, roughly. I saw some of the ones that Billy got. They were identical.'

'When did you first start receiving them?'

'Maybe five years ago. Something like that. Then regularly after that.'

'Any idea who it might be?'

'Could be anyone. You know as well as I do, in our line of work, we get up a lot of people's noses.' He shifted on the wooden seat, and McKay had the sense that he might not be telling the whole truth.

'What about the wording? That mean anything?'

'Not that I can think of. Nothing specific.'

McKay decided there was no point in pushing it. 'But you think that the deaths of Galloway and Crawford might not be accidental?'

'Well, it's a bloody odd coincidence, isn't it? Let's put it this way. I'm watching my back.'

'And trying to sell the story to any passing hack?'

'Ach, that was the drink talking. But I'd feel better if someone was taking this seriously.'

McKay smiled. 'We're taking it seriously enough. But at the moment, we've no real reason to treat the deaths as anything other than accidental. Coincidences happen.'

'And the letters?'

'Aye, well, that's a consideration right enough.' McKay sat in silence for a few moments, reluctant to offer anything further. 'How come the three of you were all living up here?'

More shifting on the seat. 'How'd you mean?'

'Just wondered. Doesn't sound like any of you were bosom buddies. But you all ended up retiring up here.'

Graham looked away, making a play of lighting up another cigarette in the chill breeze. 'I was already up here,' he said. 'Lived here for years. As for the others, you'd have to ask them. Well, their widows.'

'You prepared to come in and give us a proper statement, Rob? Let us have a look at the letters? Mind you, we wouldn't pay you as much as the *Record* or the *Sun*.'

'Fuck off, McKay. Christ, I remember when you were the resident tea boy.'

'Long time ago, Rob. These days, we have business cards and everything.' He slid one of the cards across the table. 'Give me a call, Rob. We'll do this properly. If there's anything you need to be worried about, we'll sort it.'

'Aye, the tea boy's on the job. Fills me with fucking confidence.'

McKay pushed himself up from the table. 'You best get back to your friends, Rob. They'll be missing you.'

Graham looked up and regarded McKay thoughtfully. 'So, what is it you're doing up here, then, McKay? Eating alone in a bloody bar.'

'Must be this place, Rob. Coppers' bloody graveyard. Where we all come to die.' Before Graham could respond, he turned and walked out on to the main road. After a moment's thought, he turned left, taking the road down to the sea. *Some cold air*, he thought. *Some cold air to blow away the stench of the past.*

CHAPTER FOURTEEN

'So, tell me.'

'Tell you what?'

'Whatever you want. Whatever you can.' Isla paused. 'Whatever helps.'

They were back in the sitting room, an opened bottle of wine on the table between them. Ginny Horton had already knocked back one glass. 'I don't know that any of it helps,' she said. 'It feels like stirring up stuff I might rather let lie.'

'It's your decision. I'm not pretending to be a psychotherapist. Whatever feels best.'

Horton took a breath. 'Okay, I've told you some of this, haven't I?'

'You've told me that David was your stepfather. And that he treated you and your mother badly. Not much more than that.'

'Jesus. I thought I'd told you more than that.'

'Depends what you mean by told. I mean, I know you better than anyone else. I've worked out quite a bit.'

Horton nodded. She'd felt sometimes that there was some kind of telepathy between the two of them. There were things each understood about the other, without words having to be exchanged. She knew, for example – or at least she thought she knew – how much grief Isla had received from her own family simply because she was gay. She felt she knew what that had felt like, what the impact had been, even though the two women had never really discussed it. Maybe it was an illusion, but it was a comforting one.

'He wasn't even really my stepfather. Not legally, anyway. My mum never remarried. She stuck with the bastard for far too long, but at least she never married him.'

'What happened to your father?'

'He died.' She stopped and turned to Isla. Her eyes were damp. 'Before I was born. I never knew him at all.'

'Except that he's part of you.'

'Yeah. Except that.' She managed a smile. 'Which I suppose is everything.'

'So, tell me the story. Tell me what happened. How your mum came to be with David.'

There was a long silence. 'This is the bit I never tell anyone,' Horton said, finally. 'The bit I don't even want to tell you. Because it's so bloody corny.' She took another swallow of the wine. 'My dad – my real dad – was a police officer. Up in this neck of the woods.'

'You mean, that's why you're doing what you're doing? Why you dragged me all the way up to this godforsaken part of the world?'

Horton managed a laugh. 'As I recall it, you were the one who was desperate to get as far away from the home counties as possible.'

'Well, that's true enough. This suits me down to the ground. It's just I hadn't realised I had Dr Freud to thank for being here.'

'It was never conscious. I mean, I knew what my dad had been. What had happened to him. But that was just some vaguely interesting titbit from the past. Then, when I graduated, I didn't know what to do with my life. Spent a few years doing jobs I didn't enjoy –'

'You were a crap legal secretary,' Isla said. That was how they'd met. Isla had been a newly-qualified lawyer on some graduate scheme. Horton had been temping in secretarial roles.

'So that was why you encouraged me to apply for that police scheme,' Horton said. 'I always wondered.'

'That, and so I could have my wicked way with you without worrying about the office gossip,' Isla said. 'I'm very strategic.'

'I can see that. Anyway, I joined the police just because the opportunity was there. Never connected it with my dad. Didn't really think about it 'til we came up here, to be honest.'

'But that was why we came up here?'

'Not directly. When we started talking about getting out of London, getting somewhere that was right away, I thought about how my mum had always talked about the Highlands. That was what made me suggest it.'

'What happened to your dad?'

'Stupid accident, apparently. Hit by a car on his way back from the pub one Saturday night. Some drunk, probably, but then, he might have been drunk as well. There were no witnesses and a lot less CCTV in those days, and she reckoned they never identified the driver.'

'That's awful.'

'It's the way it is, sometimes. Today, he'd be caught on camera somewhere.'

'And David?'

'David was a copper, too. CID, apparently. I think he homed in on my mum as soon as she was – well, available. She was a decent looker in those days.'

'There was I thinking you were as English as they come, and you've got all this hidden Scottish ancestry.'

'Don't tell Alec, will you? It would blow his mind. He's got me well and truly pigeonholed.'

'So how come you ended up down south?'

'I don't know the full story myself,' Horton said. 'Not long after he and my mum got together, David decided to leave the force, and they headed for London. He'd got himself some junior management job with this private security firm. That's all I know, really. I was just a baby when we moved.'

'You ever tried to find out more about your dad? Force records and suchlike?'

Horton shook her head. 'I've never wanted to. I suspect Mum idealised him. You know, the golden days before everything went wrong. For all I know, he might have been as big a bastard as David. I don't want to know.'

Isla topped up their wine glasses. 'So, what about David? Tell me about him.'

'He was a bastard. That just about sums him up. He was controlling, manipulative, violent. Apart from that, he was a real charmer.'

'He was violent with you?'

'Sometimes. But most of it was directed at Mum. It was the usual story. Enough to keep her cowed, in her place. Not so much that the bruises would show. Mostly, anyway.'

'And this is the bastard who wants to get back in contact with you? I knew he'd treated you and your mum badly, but I hadn't realised –'

'It was the psychological stuff that was the worst,' Horton said. 'Looking back, I mean. At the time, I was terrified of his anger. He'd just go off on one, usually out of the blue and with no real cause. That was when he'd hit Mum. But between that, he used every trick in the book to put her down, make her feel stupid and small. He'd laugh at her with his mates. Would never let her get a job, but constantly criticised her because he was having to be the breadwinner. You know.'

'I know,' Isla agreed. 'What about you? Did he do the same to you?'

'Pretty much. The same kind of belittling. I think if I'd been older, it would have been worse. As it was, I was young enough that, after we finally got away from him, I was able to put it behind me and move on. As much as it's possible to do that, anyway.'

'How did you get away in the end?'

'We walked out. I had no idea at the time just how brave and smart Mum must have been. She'd got some savings from before my dad's death that she'd never allowed David to get near. She just upped and left. She'd had nowhere to go, but she had a couple of friends who let us stay while she sorted somewhere to live. It was a tough few years – not that I realised it at the time – but eventually, she got on an even keel, found herself a job. And it was okay.'

'What about David?'

'We basically hid from him for a year. He did everything he could to find out where we were living, but Mum's friends were loyal. They all hated the bastard as much as we did. She lived in day-to-day fear that he'd find her. He did, eventually, but by then, she was a different woman. He tried hard to frighten her, threatened to get violent. But she just picked up the phone and called the police. I can't even remember if anyone even came out, but he buggered off sharpish.'

'Just your usual bully, then?'

'I guess so.' She paused, thinking. 'I mean, you're right. You call his bluff, he backs down. Probably. But he's good at wrong-footing you. Making you feel small. Making you feel it's your fault. Like I say, psychological bullying.'

'That's why you're still afraid of him?'

'That's what it comes down to. I've not had many dealings with him since then. He turned up at Mum's funeral, even though no one had invited him and nobody wanted him there. He took the opportunity to pin me in a corner and harangue me about how badly he'd been treated. Someone had to virtually drag him away in the end. Then, he challenged her will. She'd left what she had to me, but he tried to claim the will wasn't valid.'

'Presumably didn't have a legal leg to stand on?'

'Not for a minute. But I don't think that was what it was about. It was about trying to put me in my place. Make me feel I'd got something I wasn't entitled to. Make me feel that even the inheritance was – I don't know, unclean, somehow.'

Isla took another sip of her wine. 'Did that work?'

'More than it should have done. I mean, it didn't make me want to hand it back, exactly. But it tainted things. Which is what he wanted.'

'And since then?'

'He turned up a few times. Always scared me more than it should have done. I keep telling myself I'm a grown woman, a fucking police officer, and he's the one who should be scared of me. But still. He turns me straight back into a child again. A five-year-old afraid he's going to hit me.'

'Do you think he would?'

'I really don't know. I think the answer's no. But I don't know what he's capable of.'

'He sounds to me like a small man who gets his kicks from scaring people he thinks are weaker than he is.' Isla laughed. 'Does he know you're a police officer?'

'It's a good point,' Horton said. 'I'm not sure he does. I don't know how long it has been since I last saw him. I'd joined the force down there by then, but I don't think I brought it up. I didn't say any more to him than I could avoid.' She was smiling now. 'It just occurred to me. As far as I know, David was still a DC when he left the force up here. Never made it to the dizzying heights of DS. Never passed his sergeants' exams. I outrank him.'

'Just tell him that, and you'll intimidate the life out of him.'

'I hope so.' Horton's smile had faded, almost immediately. 'But I don't like the thought of him out there. Maybe he's just a bully. Maybe he'd back off if I challenged him. But he scared me then. And he scares me now.'

CHAPTER FIFTEEN

I t was a fine, clear night, the sky full of stars, a low three-quarter moon scattering silver across the waters of the firth. The sort of night that didn't come around too often in these parts.

McKay hadn't been sure what had taken him down to the sea rather than along the more direct route to the bungalow. He didn't even know why the encounter with Rob Graham had left him so disturbed. He'd never much liked Graham. But he'd never liked any of Galloway's acolytes. Bastards who'd stitch you up in a moment, if it helped boost their conviction rate. Who'd beat a confession out of you, if they couldn't get it any other way. Who'd happily leave you for dead, if you got on the wrong side of them.

It was ironic to see Graham crapping himself about what might have happened to Galloway and Crawford, but McKay couldn't bring himself to feel amused. For a start, there was the possibility, however remote, that Graham's fears might be justified. That the two ex-coppers really had been murdered. That might mean that others, some of them less deserving than that bastard crew, might also be in danger.

Then again, McKay thought, if you were looking for justice, maybe Galloway and Crawford had faced that long ago. Galloway had ended his days a lost shadow of his former self, able to do nothing but gaze senselessly at a flickering TV screen. Crawford had been stuck in that far circle of hell where all you can do is deaden your days with alcohol in the company of blethering idiots. If anything, their deaths had released them from all that.

And where did that leave McKay? That, he supposed, was the real question that had brought him down here. What was there

81

left for him but solitary friendless suppers in near-empty pubs, listening to the likes of Rob Graham spouting endless bollocks? Then back home to a bleak, companionless shell of a house.

Ach, pull yourself together, man, he told himself. *This is temporary. Things will sort themselves out. You just have to get on with getting on. That's the way life works.*

The tide was high, the waters lapping at the top of the beach. To his left, he could see the spot where he and Ginny Horton had struggled with the young woman the previous summer. That was nagging at him, too. The case was still awaiting legal closure, but he knew that, whatever the formal outcome, his own doubts would remain unresolved. A police officer ought to be able to finish the case, close the file and move on, but that had never been McKay's way. It maybe made him a better detective, but a worse human being.

It was nearly ten. Time to be getting back, even if there was nothing much to get back for. He'd get an early start, throw himself back into work. Just get on with it. It was the only thing to do.

As he moved away from the railings, he heard a sound somewhere behind him, back up the narrow road towards the pub. Some sort of cry. He paused for a moment to peer up the street, but could see nothing aside from the empty roadway past the car park and the pub. Kids, probably, or some animal up by the burn. He turned to walk back along the shore, trudging slowly towards the rising moon.

***

He had fallen asleep more quickly and easily than he'd expected. The bed was comfortable, and the night was quieter than anything he'd known in Inverness. If he listened hard enough, he could hear the steady working of the sea against the shoreline. The soft rhythm had been enough to lull him gently out of consciousness.

He was woken by the buzzing of his mobile phone. It felt as if he'd been asleep for no more than minutes, but the lightening sky through the thin curtains told him the sun was already rising. He fumbled for the phone, glancing at the screen before answering. Helena Grant.

'This my early morning call?'

'Apparently,' Grant said. 'I like to make sure my team start the day right.'

'You driving 'round with the full Scottish, then? I'll have my eggs poached.'

'Your eggs are well and truly scrambled, Alec,' she said. 'We've another body.'

He sat up in bed, more awake. 'Even better than the full Scottish.'

'Ach, Alec. That's why I called you. I couldn't think of anyone else who'd be cheered at this time of day by the prospect of another corpse.'

'It's all I live for. What's the story?'

'That was the other reason I thought of you, Alec. It's another one up there for you. On your new doorstep.'

'Oh, for Christ's sake. I came here for the quiet life.'

'Like hell you did, Alec. You wouldn't have a clue what to do with a quiet life.'

'Okay, what's the story, then?'

'Body found this morning. Up in Fairy Glen.'

'It'll be the fucking fairies, then. A contract job.' McKay peered at his watch. 'How'd the hell anyone stumble across a body before six-thirty in the morning?'

'One of those young, fit types, out for an early morning run before work. You'll have heard about people like that.'

'Aye, mainly from young Ginny.'

'Body was in the woods, just off the car park. Face down in Rosemarkie Burn.'

'Lovely. Accident?'

'Who knows? Call came into Control about half an hour ago. They got a couple of uniforms up there to protect the scene, then

83

the call came through to me. After the last couple of days, I'd asked them to alert me to anything significant in that neck of the woods. Examiners are on their way. All we need now is a DI to take charge.'

'And your first thought was of me. Aw, hen, you're all heart.'

'Just get up there, Alec. See what you think.'

'I'll keep you posted.'

The house felt cold, and when he tried the shower, the water was icy. There was central heating, but it had been turned off while the house was standing empty, and McKay had forgotten to look at it the previous evening. Now, too late, he flicked the timer on and heard the boiler kick into action. A great start to the day.

He washed his face in the cold water, made himself a coffee and ate the previous day's sandwich as breakfast. This might be how things were going to be. A monastic lifestyle with supermarket catering.

The drive to the Fairy Glen car park took no more than a few minutes. The car park itself was deserted, apart from the inevitable German camper van and, at the far end, a marked patrol car. McKay parked beside it and climbed out to greet the two uniforms standing chatting by the entrance to the Glen. As McKay approached, one of them surreptitiously dropped his cigarette butt into the grass, screwing his heel on top of it.

'Hope you're not littering,' McKay growled. The two officers were both young, and though McKay didn't recognise them, he could see both were aware of his own reputation.

'Sorry, sir. I was just –'

'Aye, son. Just hammering another nail into your own coffin.' To emphasise the point, McKay extracted a pack of his trademark gum and popped a strip into his mouth. 'Where's our late departed friend?'

'Over there.' The other officer looked less cowed by McKay's presence. He pointed into the gloom of the woodland. The sun had not yet fully risen over the hills behind them, and it was difficult to make out the prone figure at the edge of the stream. 'I went over to check it really was what it looked like, and to make sure he really was dead. Yes, on both counts. Other than that, we've been careful to leave the scene untouched.'

'Male, then?'

'Yes, definitely.'

'What about the person who found him?'

'In the car. We assumed you'd want to talk to him.'

'You assumed right, son. Okay, I'll have a chat with him. Imagine he's keen to get away. Any word from the Examiners?'

As if McKay's words had summoned them, the Examiners' white van turned into the car park as he finished speaking. It pulled up beside McKay's car, and Jock Henderson climbed out.

'Thought you were avoiding me, Jock. Missed you at Chanonry Point yesterday.'

Henderson, his angular body looking as always as if it might topple over at any moment, peered at McKay as if not recognising him. 'Ach, Alec. They've not pensioned you off yet, then? I live in hope.'

'I know where too many bodies are buried. Speaking of which –' McKay gestured into the woodland. 'Looks like you'll be getting your white suit all dirty.'

'I'll leave some crap for you, Alec, don't you worry.'

'Story of my life, Jock.'

While Henderson donned his protective clothing, McKay opened the rear door of the police car and slid on to the back seat alongside a young ginger-haired man in a tracksuit. 'Morning, son. Dare say this has interrupted your routine.'

The young man blinked. 'It was a wee shock, right enough.'

'Aye, right enough. You okay now?'

The young man nodded. 'I'll survive.'

'Aye, well, that puts you one up on that bugger over there, anyhow,' McKay said bluntly. 'We'll not to keep you any longer than we need to. You're expected somewhere?'

'I'm due at work. In Inverness. I've left a message saying what's happened, and that I'll be a bit late.' The young man was talking too quickly, his brain and body still pumped with adrenaline.

McKay took out his notebook, unhurried, allowing the young man time to calm himself. 'You'll have given them something to talk about, anyhow. What's your line of work, son?'

'Graphic design. It's a small marketing agency. We do design, branding, all that stuff.'

'Very interesting,' McKay said in a tone that indicated his own interest in the matter was non-existent. 'And your name and address, son?'

'Redmond,' the young man said. 'Jamie Redmond.' He gave an address at the far end of the village, not far from where McKay was now living.

'Take your time and talk me through what happened. You were out for a run?'

'I go out two or three days a week before work, if I can, this time of year. It's harder in winter because it doesn't get light in time. But, now, it's just starting to be possible.'

'Rather you than me,' McKay said. 'Where'd you usually run?'

'It varies. If the tide's out, I might run along the beach. Other than that, mostly on the roads at this time of year.'

'But, this morning, you came up here?'

'I quite often run up here in the summer. It's harder if it's not fully light because the paths are rough, and I don't want to risk falling or twisting an ankle. But it was a beautiful morning and already quite light when I set off, so I thought I'd give it a shot. First of the year.'

'You spotted the body as you ran into the woodland?'

'No, on my way back. My original plan had been to run through Fairy Glen up to the main road, so I could come back that way. But when I got a little way in, I realised it was still too dark in the woods to run safely, so I decided to come back and try a different route. It was when I was running back towards the car park that I spotted the body.' He shook his head, as if trying to dislodge the memory. 'My eyes had adjusted to the dark in the woods. I just saw it out of the corner of my eye. It looked – wrong.'

'What did you do?'

'I just stopped at first and tried to work out if it was what I thought it was. I didn't really believe it, you know?'

'I know,' McKay said. 'Did you go closer?'

'In the end. Close enough to see. Then close enough to check that he was really –'

'I get the picture,' McKay said. 'You could tell it was a man?'

Redmond blinked as if he'd been caught out. 'Well, I thought so, but I don't know –'

'No, that's fine, son. I just want to be sure what you saw. Better to do it now while it's fresh in your mind. Memory can play tricks.' He paused. 'You didn't see anyone else around? On your run, I mean.'

'Not a soul. You occasionally run into dog walkers and the like, but not today.'

'Okay. Anything else you think you can tell us?'

'That was it, really. I had my mobile with me, so I dialled 999 and waited 'til your colleagues arrived, like they asked me to.'

McKay nodded. 'My Examiner colleague over there will want to take a DNA sample and your footprints, just for elimination purposes, but then, you'll be free to go. If we need anything else, we'll be in touch.'

McKay climbed out of the car and made his way back across the car park to the woodland where Henderson, now in his protective clothing, was still crouched over the body. An ambulance had arrived to remove the body once Henderson was finished.

As McKay approached, Henderson looked up from his work. 'Alec,' he said, 'something you need to know.'

'Oh, aye?' McKay took a step or two forward, careful not to risk disrupting the scene. 'What would that be?'

'Couple of things. First is that this looks to me like an unlawful killing. Subject to whatever the Doc might say, obviously.'

'Obviously.'

'It could have been an accident, especially if he was pissed. Might have tripped, banged his head, unconscious under water. Blah, blah. But it's difficult to see how that scenario would have panned out in practice. Looks to me like his head was held under the water. Deliberately drowned.'

'Doc should be able to confirm that, one way or the other,' McKay said. Something was beginning to make him feel uneasy. Something in Henderson's tone, and something in the back of his own head. 'And the second thing?'

'The second thing is that I know who our late friend here is.' Henderson paused. 'And so do you.'

The suspicion that had been growing in McKay's mind was beginning to take shape. 'Go on.'

'Another ex-colleague,' Henderson said. 'Took me a moment to place him, but then, I realised. Another blast from the past –'

'Rob Graham,' McKay interrupted. 'Rob fucking Graham.'

Henderson was staring at him, eyes wide inside his protective hood. 'How the hell did you –?'

'Because,' McKay said, 'apart from whichever bastard did this to him, I was probably the last person to see him alive.'

CHAPTER SIXTEEN

'Y ou know I've got to, Alec. I've no choice.'
'Aye, I know, but –'
'But nothing, Alec. Your position would be untenable.'
'I might agree with you, if I knew what that meant.'

Grant shook her head. 'You always were the original smart Alec. But you know I'm right.'

McKay was slumped back in his chair, looking as if all the life had been knocked out of him. 'That bastard Graham. Why get himself killed just then and just there?'

'I don't imagine he did it to inconvenience you, Alec.'

McKay pulled out a strip of gum and began to chew on it with a ferocity that made his feelings on the matter more than clear. 'Bastard, anyway. Always fucking was.'

'Are you looking to put yourself seriously in the frame for his death?'

'Oh, for Christ's sake –'

'Look, Alec. Ginny's already spoken to the landlord, who's reported that, in the course of his session in the pub last night, Graham got into a not particularly amicable-sounding conversation with some gentleman who was in there for a meal. Graham seemed to think that said gentleman – I use the term loosely, you understand – was a journalist of some kind. But then, it apparently turned out that this person was in fact a former police colleague of Graham's, who identified himself as a DI McKay. Am I getting the account right so far?'

'Aye, spot on,' McKay said morosely.

'Graham and this DI McKay then went out, supposedly because Graham wanted a smoke. But the landlord says that, while he was taking a crate of empties out, he saw the two of you standing outside, having a rather intense conversation. He and Graham's buddies assumed he'd return once he'd finished talking to you, but he never did, leaving them to finish their pints without him. Graham left half his pint unfinished, which apparently was most uncharacteristic.'

McKay shrugged. 'That all ties in with the statement I gave you, as well you know. I assumed he'd go back into the pub once we'd finished, as well. Don't know why he didn't.'

'He was still outside the pub when you left?'

'I got fed up with him. He just reminded me of everything that Galloway's regime had stood for. I left him and took a walk home along the seafront. Like I say, I just assumed he'd head back inside.'

'But you can see that, for the moment, if it turns out that Graham really was murdered, we've got to treat you as a potential suspect?'

'That's ridiculous. I left him my sodding business card, for Christ's sake. Anyway, why the hell would I want to kill Rob Graham?'

'You've just told me how much you disliked him.'

'Aye, but not enough to kill him. If I killed all the people I dislike, we'd halve the population of the fucking country.' He allowed himself a smile. 'I could kick off with a few members of fucking Holyrood.'

'Jesus, Alec, you really are incorrigible.'

'I've heard you use that one before. You don't fool me. You know fewer long words than you make out.' He stopped, his smile fading instantly. 'You don't seriously think I'm a fucking suspect?'

'No, Alec, I don't. But if you were anyone else, I'd at least be considering the possibility. You knew Graham. There was some needle between you. And you were the last person to see him alive –'

'Apart from the killer.'

'Apart from the killer. That's assuming he was actually killed, rather than just dipping his own head in Rosemarkie Burn. But we have to treat you as a possible suspect, at least until we've discounted you.'

'And how do you propose to do that?' McKay asked. 'You can't prove a negative. Like you say, I'd got at least the means and the opportunity, if not the motive. And you reckon I might have that.'

'And there lies our problem,' Grant said. 'That's why I've got to keep you at arm's length from any investigation and, if it comes to it, maybe even suspend you –'

'Suspend me?'

'For your own good, Alec. If there's any suggestion we've not done things by the book –'

'Aye, and everyone will assume that there's no smoke without fire, and what little career I have left will finally be flushed well and truly down the pan.'

'It won't be like that.'

'It's always like that.'

She sighed, knowing that, as always, he was at least partly right. 'Okay, Alec. You've got leave owing, right?' It was a stupid question. McKay always had leave owing. Probably another reason why he was living by himself in the back of beyond.

'Aye. Couple of weeks or so.'

Which probably meant at least three. 'Take it, then. You need a break, anyway. Give yourself chance to get your head straight. Maybe sort things out with Chrissie –'

'Is that any of your business, hen? With all due respect.'

'With all due respect, Alec, it is.' She leaned over the desk towards him. Normally by this point, he'd be prowling around her office, dipping his fingers into all manner of things that shouldn't concern him. It was a mark of his low spirits, she thought, that he couldn't even rouse himself from the chair. 'Look, we don't even know whether we've anything to investigate yet. We're still waiting on the Procurator's instructions on Galloway and Crawford's deaths. Until we get the post-mortem report on Graham, we don't know whether we've got an unlawful killing on our hands.'

'Even the Procurator's office can't write this off as a series of unfortunate accidents, surely?'

'If it had just been Galloway and Crawford, my bet is that they'd have decided exactly that. But if Graham was murdered – well, it puts a different complexion on things.'

'Aye, I'd say so. Three ex-coppers dead in a matter of days. All recipients of a long-running series of apparently threatening letters. Even the pen-pushers would have a struggle writing that off as Jungian fucking synchronicity.'

'But, as yet, we have no investigation. So, take yourself off home, Alec. Get yourself well away from here. If it turns out that Graham toppled into the burn while under the influence of an excess of beer and single malts, there's no harm done. If our suspicions are well founded, we have more of a problem. But we do it by the book, okay?'

'Ach. I suppose so. Can't pretend I'm happy, though.'

'No point in breaking the habit of a lifetime, Alec.' She paused and looked at him, her expression serious. 'This is about protecting your arse as much as anything else, Alec. You know that.'

'Aye, I know that. Doesn't make it any easier. I'll be climbing the walls at home.' He shook his head. 'If I can call it home.'

'Take the opportunity to sort things with Chrissie. You know you want to.'

'Maybe. But I don't know if I know how. Or if she wants to.' He allowed himself a smile. 'Christ, women, eh?'

'Aye, I know, pet. They're nearly as bad as men.' She tapped her pen on the desk in front of her. 'What do you reckon's going on here, Alec? With these deaths, I mean.'

'Christ knows. Back in the day, there'd have been plenty of people only too pleased to top those three. But now? Why would anyone still give a shit?'

'Someone gave enough of a shit to send them all periodic threatening letters,' Grant said. 'Assuming that's what they were.'

'Even so, why act now? It wouldn't have been long before Jackie Galloway popped his clogs anyway.'

'Maybe that was it,' she said. 'Maybe someone thought that would be too good for him.'

'If so, all they did was put him out of his misery. Or, more to the point, helped Bridie Galloway out of her misery. She'd still have been top of my list, but I don't see why or how she'd have killed Crawford or Graham.'

'Aye, well, maybe it's all just an unfortunate coincidence after all,' Grant said. 'Let's wait to hear what Graham's post-mortem tells us. And what the Procurator thinks.'

'Except I won't care, will I?' McKay said. 'Because I'll be sitting in my bungalow watching daytime TV, halfway to being Jackie fucking Galloway myself.'

'Alec, if you think I'm going to allow myself to be a staff member down for any longer than I can help, you've another think coming. We'll get you back before you get addicted to Jeremy Kyle.' She smiled. 'Now bugger off home, and let us get on with it, okay?'

CHAPTER SEVENTEEN

As she drove down the hill into Rosemarkie, Ginny Horton was almost tempted to turn off and pay McKay a surprise visit. But it was too soon, she told herself, and she had no idea how he'd react. He might be pleased to see her, but McKay could be a cantankerous old git, and he'd have taken his enforced exile badly, however temporary it might prove to be.

She was still feeling disturbed by her earlier conversation with Helena Grant. Horton had been surprised, returning to the office after a couple of off-site meetings, not only to find the office empty but also to see that McKay had left his desk tidier than he managed most evenings. Ten minutes later, Grant had popped her head around the door to advise that McKay had been, as she put it, encouraged to take his outstanding annual leave.

'You can't be serious,' Horton said. 'Nobody would really think Alec's a suspect.'

Grant was silent for slightly too long. 'No, of course not. It's just –'

'Just what?'

'I don't know. Alec never lets anyone get too close, does he? You never know what he's thinking.'

'I know he's not a murderer.' Horton was surprised at her own vehemence. Like most people, she'd had her run-ins with McKay. She was surprised now by how much loyalty she felt towards him.

'I don't think that. We've just got to do things by the book until we can eliminate him from the enquiry. But he makes everything so difficult for himself.'

Horton had been surprised by how emotional Grant had seemed. She'd always suspected there was something more between McKay and Grant than simply the fact that they were long-time colleagues or even long-time friends. After McKay's wife had walked out on him, Horton had wondered whether that something might blossom into a relationship. But the two had just seemed to keep stalking around each another, tense as barroom bruisers looking for a fight.

'So where are we up to with the investigation?' Horton asked, keen to move the conversation on.

'We've managed to expedite the post-mortem on Graham, so that should take place tomorrow. With any luck, that'll tell us whether there's evidence he was unlawfully killed. If so, then we obviously have to look more closely at the other two deaths. But even if not, I think the coincidence justifies our treating these as suspicious deaths. I've reported to the Procurator's office on that basis.'

'And in Alec's absence …?'

Grant sighed. 'I guess I'll have to take over as Senior Investigating Officer. It'll be you and me against the world, Ginny.'

Horton had a lot of respect for Helena Grant. She managed to operate very effectively in what was still a male-dominated profession without too obviously aping any of the worst traits of her senior colleagues. No mean feat, Horton suspected, and she was happy to treat Grant as a role model. Probably a more positive one than Alec McKay, for all his undoubted investigatory skills. 'I was scheduled to interview Graham's widow and to have a shot at tracking down his two mates from the pub, if you're happy with that?'

Grant had been more than happy with that, which was why Horton was now heading down the hill towards the shoreline in Rosemarkie. She passed the narrow road that led to McKay's rented bungalow, and instead took the seafront road. According to her satnav, the Grahams' house was just a few hundred yards along.

After the anxieties of the previous evening, Horton was cheered by the bright morning sunshine, the clear blue sea of Rosemarkie

Bay. She'd allowed herself to be spooked by David's unexpected appearance. In the light of day, her fears felt groundless, a child's lingering nightmares. If David should turn up, she could handle him.

She pulled up on the seafront and peered out of the car window to identify the Grahams' house. It was a far cry from the cramped bungalow where Jackie Galloway had eked out his final days. A solid-looking detached villa, elevated above the road, with views out over the bay. No doubt worth a bob or two.

The front door was opened almost as soon as Horton had pressed the bell. She had the impression that Shona Graham had been observing her progress up the steep drive.

'Mrs Graham?' Horton showed her warrant card. 'I was wondering if you were up to talking to me for a few minutes?'

Graham's widow was a handsome-looking woman, much younger than her husband had been. Horton guessed she was probably late forties, but doing her best to look even younger. Her hair was immaculately blonde, her face skilfully made-up. She clearly hadn't allowed the news of her husband's death to distract her from her usual routine.

'I'd assumed you'd want to. I know enough about how this sort of thing goes. Your two colleagues were here this morning.'

Horton nodded. The news had been broken to the widow by two trained uniformed officers. They'd offered her support, but reported that she'd seemed content to look after herself. Looking at her now, Horton could see no obvious signs of distress.

Shona Graham led her through into an impressively decorated sitting room. None of the decor was to Horton's taste – too much fine china and chintz – but she could see real money had been spent on it. Graham had done well for a DI.

'Can I get you a tea or a coffee?'

Horton shook her head. 'Thank you, but I won't keep you any longer than I need to. I'm sure you've a lot on your plate.'

Graham offered a smile that failed to reach her eyes. 'Less than you'd think,' she said. 'I can't progress the funeral arrangements until you release the body. I've just handed the rest over to the solicitors to look after.' She spoke as if completing a business transaction. 'How can I help you?' She gestured for Horton to take a seat.

'Mainly factual questions,' Horton said. 'Just so we can pin down what happened when.'

'You're treating Rob's death as suspicious?'

Horton felt as if she were being tested. 'We treat all unexplained deaths as suspicious. We don't yet know the circumstances of this one. We understand your husband was last seen in the bar last night. Can I ask what time he left the house?'

'You can ask, but I'm not sure I can give you an answer.'

Horton raised an eyebrow. 'No?'

'I don't want to give you the wrong impression,' Mrs Graham said, 'but Rob and I lived fairly separate lives. Not in a negative way, you understand. We'd come to an accommodation over the years, and he tended to do his thing and I tended to do mine. Last night, mine was a fairly boozy night out with the girls in Inverness.'

'So, you don't know what time your husband left the house?'

'I left around seven. He was still here then, watching TV.'

'Did he have any kind of routine? For going out, I mean.'

'Not really. We're retired, but we're not that stuck in the mud just yet. My guess is that, with me out of the way, Rob would have strolled down to the bar around nine, just to see who was in. There's a group of them collect there. Chances are, there's usually someone in to have a blether with.'

'Do you know who these people are?'

'Some of them. But you'd best ask the landlord. They're all regulars.'

Horton had already done just that and had obtained the names of the two men who'd been drinking with Graham the previous evening. 'What time did you get back last night?' Nobody had yet broached the question of why Shona Graham had failed to raise any alarm about her husband's absence.

Perhaps, Horton thought, this was another part of the couple's "accommodation."

'I didn't,' Graham said. 'That's why I didn't realise that Rob was missing. I drove into Inverness and stayed over with one of the girls. Thanks to you lot, you can't risk driving after a packet of wine gums these days, let alone what I'd drunk. And it's a nightmare trying to get a taxi to come out here late at night.'

They'd have to verify Mrs Graham's account, but Horton didn't have much doubt that she was telling the truth. 'So, you had no contact with him after you left yesterday evening?'

'I wasn't really expecting to.'

'What time did you arrive back this morning?'

'About eleven, I suppose. I didn't want to set off too early. Might have still been over the limit.'

That fitted with the notes Horton had seen. It had taken the two uniformed officers a little time to track down Rob Graham's address – there had been nothing in his pockets, other than a wallet containing some cash and a couple of bank cards. They'd initially visited the house just after ten, but had found it and the neighbouring houses empty. They'd returned a couple of hours later to break the news. 'You weren't surprised he wasn't here?'

She shrugged. 'Like I say, we didn't live in one another's pockets. I assumed he was out somewhere. He'd left the place tidy. But then, he was fairly domesticated.' She made her late husband sound like a pet dog. 'I didn't think anything of it until your people arrived.'

'I'm sorry to ask this,' Horton said, 'but is there anyone who might have wished harm to your husband?'

'You really do think he might have been murdered?' Mrs Graham's face gave nothing away.

'We can't discount any possibility, at present,' Horton said carefully.

'Well, he was a police officer.' She gave Horton another humourless smile. 'You make enemies, don't you? But that was all a long time ago. I can't think why anyone would want to harm him now.'

'You've received no threats? Threatening letters? Anything like that?' Horton knew from McKay that Graham had received the same mysterious letters as his two former colleagues, but she had no idea whether he'd shared this with his wife.

'No. We received the odd poison pen when Rob was still working. But nothing recently. Not that I'm aware of.'

'Your husband would have told you if he'd received anything?'

'Maybe. Maybe not. If he had received anything, I doubt whether it would have troubled him. You're barking up the wrong tree. I can't envisage anybody bothering to murder Rob.'

'Is there anyone else locally we should be talking to? Close friends. Other people locally who might have more idea about his movements last night.' The word "mistress" was hovering on Horton's lips, but she had no grounds even for raising the possibility.

Even so, she detected a momentary hesitation in Mrs Graham's response. 'I don't think so. Other than his drinking mates. And the landlord will know those better than I do.'

'I won't disturb you any longer for the moment, then, Mrs Graham.' Horton eased herself up from the plush sofa. 'We may need to talk to you again, if that's all right?'

'As much as you want to,' Mrs Graham said. 'Though I don't know how much I'll be able to say in return.'

'And you'll be okay here? On your own, I mean.' The question sounded absurd even to Horton.

'I think so, dear.' Shona Graham smiled. 'Don't you?'

CHAPTER EIGHTEEN

McKay managed to kill a couple of hours visiting the large Tesco in Inverness, stocking himself up with groceries for the empty week to come. Traipsing his way round the aisles with his trolley, he marvelled at his fellow humans' uncanny ability to block his path at every possible opportunity. It was as if, he thought, they had no sodding conception that other people even existed, let alone that they might want to complete their shopping sometime this fucking year.

He was at the point, just before he reached the checkout, of articulating this interior monologue out loud for the benefit of the two old biddies ambling along in front of him. *The halt and the fucking lame*, he thought. *Why are they even allowed out?*

He wasn't in the best of tempers. The thought of a week, maybe longer, stuck in that bloody bungalow with nothing to do, nowhere to go, no one to see, was already beginning to eat away at his sanity.

He took a breath and allowed the two elderly ladies to progress in front of him towards the checkouts. It was then that he spotted Chrissie.

She was heading towards the checkouts, too, her trolley even more laden than his own. His first instinct was to head off down one of the aisles, but he could see she'd already spotted him. 'Chrissie.'

'Alec.'

They stood for a moment in awkward silence, their trolleys parallel by the checkouts. 'Not like you to be out in daylight, Alec.'

'Aye, well. It's a long story.'

'Don't tell me they've finally found you out.'

'I'm just taking a few days' leave.'

She opened her mouth in mock astonishment. 'Christ, is this you turning over a new leaf, Alec? You barely managed a day off for your own daughter's funeral.'

He could see she regretted the words as soon as she'd spoken. She was right, though. She'd resented the way he'd thrown himself straight back into work after Lizzie's death. It had been his own way of coping. But he'd never really thought before about how it must have been for Chrissie, stuck all day in an empty house with only the memories in Lizzie's unaltered bedroom for company. 'Like I say, long story. You moved back into the house now?'

'Went back this morning.' Chrissie sounded reluctant to admit the fact, or perhaps just reluctant to let him know. 'Ellie was struggling to cope, so I thought I'd better.' She gestured towards his trolley. 'Looks like we're both in the same boat.'

'Mine's got a few more instant dinners,' McKay said.

'You're up in the Black Isle,' she said. 'Always thought of you as a city boy.'

'Just fancied a change. Breath of sea air rather than petrol fumes.'

'If you say so.' She looked back at the checkouts. 'I'd best be getting on.'

'Chrissie –'

'Alec?' She turned back, her face expressionless.

'We need to talk, Chrissie. Sometime. When you're ready.'

There was the faintest hint of a smile. 'Christ, Alec. You really have turned over a new leaf, haven't you?'

'When you're ready.'

'Okay, sometime. When I'm ready.'

He gazed at her for a moment, hoping to see something more in her eyes. 'I'll let you get on, then.'

'Aye, Alec,' she said. 'You do that.'

***

Ginny Horton spent the afternoon tracking down Rob Graham's two drinking buddies from the previous evening. As Shona Graham had suggested, the landlord had been able to supply her with names and approximate addresses. A couple of calls back to the office had given her the final details she needed.

Both lived in the village. The first, Rory Craig, was a retired farmer who'd sold up and was living in a well-appointed villa above the village with a view out across the bay. The other, Kenny Wallace, was a younger man who worked as an accountant in Inverness and lived in one of the seafront houses a few doors from Shona Graham. Horton wondered whether there might be any significance in that fact.

Craig was able to add little to what she already knew. She found him in his front garden mowing his lawn. He silenced the electric mower as she pushed open the gate. 'Can I help you, miss?' He sounded the kind of man who resented visitors accessing his property without permission.

She held out her warrant card. 'DS Horton,' she said. 'Mr Craig?'

He frowned, a worried expression flitting across his face. He was a squat man, with florid clean-shaven cheeks and a reddening nose that suggested a regular alcohol intake. 'What can I do for you?' To her slight surprise, the accent was English, noticeably upmarket.

'You know a Mr Robert Graham?'

'Rob? Yes, why?'

'I'm afraid I've some bad news. Mr Graham was found dead this morning.'

'Rob?' he said, again. 'I only saw him last night. What's happened to him?'

'That's what we're trying to ascertain, sir. Would it be possible to go inside?'

'Yes. Of course.' He led them through the half-open front door. 'Can I get you some tea? My wife's out at the moment, but –'

'That's fine, sir. Thank you. I won't keep you long, I hope. We're just trying to speak with those who saw Mr Graham yesterday evening.' She paused as Craig led them through to the living room. It was a blaze of tartans, the pattern on the sofa clashing violently with that in the carpet. A stag's head, apparently real, stared blankly down at her from over the fireplace. 'Mr Graham's body was found this morning just inside the entrance to Fairy Glen. We're trying to understand the circumstances of his death.'

Craig blinked, clearly struggling to absorb this information. 'Was he taken ill?'

'We don't know yet, sir. There'll be a post-mortem to help us determine the cause of death. Did he seem well when you last saw him?'

'As far as I'm aware. Just his usual self. Though, he'd perhaps had one or two too many.'

'Why do you say that?'

'Well, he accosted this poor chap having a meal. Seemed to think he was a journalist. But it turned out they knew each other. Well, sort of. Both in your line of work.' He frowned, and Horton could tell he was already thinking through the possible implications of what he'd just said.

'So we understand, sir.'

'Seemed a bit of needle between them. Not aggressive but a little tense. Rob went out for a smoke, and this chap went with him for a chat.'

'Did Mr Graham return to the bar?'

'No. We were a bit surprised. Seemed a bit rude, really.'

'And you saw no more of him?'

'Nothing. We left shortly afterwards, but there was no sign of him. We assumed he'd just headed off home. As I say, he'd seemed a little the worse for wear.' Craig hesitated. 'But then, he often was, if you know what I mean.'

'Do you think he might have been sufficiently drunk to be a danger to himself?'

'I wouldn't have thought so,' Craig said. 'He could hold his drink. He was a bit unsteady, but I've never really seen him really drunk.'

Horton suspected that Craig's definition of "really drunk" might be different from her own. 'Is there any reason he might have gone into Fairy Glen?'

'Not that I'm aware of. I suppose he might have just gone in there to take a – to relieve himself. I can't think of any other reason. His house is the other direction.'

'Was there anything else unusual about Mr Graham's behaviour last night?'

'Apart from accusing your colleague of being a journalist? No, I don't think so. Wife was away for the night, which always made him more chipper. Cat's away, and all that.'

'Is it possible he had other plans for last night? After he left the bar, I mean.'

Craig frowned. 'You think old Robbie might have had a bit on the side? Well, it's possible, I suppose. I never saw any sign of it, but then, I wouldn't necessarily. He was a pub buddy, mainly. Didn't know much about his private life.'

'We've no reason to think that, Mr Craig. But we have to explore every possibility.'

'Well, as I say, anything's possible. But I'm afraid I can't help you on that front.'

Horton supposed that, if Graham really had been murdered, then Craig was another potential suspect. But he and Kenny Wallace had both left the bar about half an hour after Graham had made his exit, and had walked back together along the high street. They'd each no doubt be able to vouch for the other, and as things stood, there was no good reason to question their account.

She said her farewells to Craig and drove back down to the waterfront to find Kenny Wallace's house. It was just gone five-thirty, and she half expected he'd still be at work, but she could at least leave a message for him to call her. Wallace's house was a few doors along from the Grahams', although that was hardly a major coincidence in a village as small as this. It was a recently built bungalow, with wooden decking to the front and sides and panoramic windows giving a view out across the bay. There was a newish Audi parked out front.

The door was answered by a harassed-looking woman, the sounds of shouting children rising behind her. She looked as if she'd made an effort to appear smart but events had somehow caught up with her. She blinked at Horton through a slightly over long blonde fringe, a disappointed expression on her face. 'Oh, Christ,' she said. 'I was hoping you were a mother.'

For a moment, Horton was bemused by this apparent comment on her maternal status. Then, the woman jerked a thumb behind her and added, 'One of their mothers, I mean. I was hoping you'd come early.'

'Mrs Wallace?' Horton held out her warrant card.

'Jesus, what now?'

'It's really your husband I needed to speak to.' The screams of children were growing louder inside the house. 'Is he available?'

'He's hiding somewhere, the bastard. I don't blame him, but he might at least have let me hide in there with him. You'd better come in while I track him down.'

As Horton followed Mrs Wallace into the house, the source of the noise became apparent. A host of small children were racing up and down the hallway, some carrying balloons and toys. Through the kitchen door at the far end, Horton could see a table laden with the remains of a birthday party tea – bowls of crisps, half-empty plates of sandwiches, an as-yet-untouched birthday cake. The party was reaching that manic point where the young guests were experiencing a sugar-rush with at least another half an hour to go before their parents arrived to collect them. No wonder Mrs Wallace had looked disappointed.

Mrs Wallace disappeared up the stairs and reappeared followed by a tall man who looked down bewilderedly at her. 'Can I help you?'

'Mr Wallace?' He was probably mid-forties but looked younger, his light-brown hair swept neatly back from a clean-shaven face. He was dressed in a dark blue business suit that looked out of place among the domestic chaos.

'That's me.' He reached the bottom of the stairs. 'Is there a problem?'

'Is there somewhere quiet we can speak?' The noise of the children was reaching the point where she found herself having to shout.

'You'd better come upstairs.'

She followed him back up the staircase, leaving Mrs Wallace to cope with the pandemonium by herself. Wallace led her into a room kitted out as an office. Silence fell as he closed the door behind them. 'Sorry about the bairns. Ellie's birthday. My daughter.'

'Many happy returns to her,' Horton said. 'How old?'

'Seven,' Wallace said, with a slight air of regret, as though the years were already slipping away from him.

'I'm sorry to trouble you, Mr Wallace. I believe you knew a Mr Robert Graham?'

'Rob? Yes, they're neighbours. Well, a few houses along.'

'You saw him last night?'

'In the pub, yes. For a while. What's the trouble?'

'He was found dead this morning. I'm sorry.'

'Well, no. I mean, I didn't know him all that well. Just someone to chat to, you know. But that's a shock. He seemed fine last night. Do you know how –?'

'We don't, for sure,' Horton said. 'That's why I'm making enquiries. His body was found just inside the entrance to Fairy Glen. By the burn.'

'Fairy Glen? What was he doing there?'

'That's what we're trying to find out. When did you last see him?'

Wallace ran through the same narrative she'd already heard from Craig. 'I don't think there's much more I can add,' he said. 'Except –' He stopped, as if considering what he was about to say.

'Except?'

'Well, it's probably nothing. But not long after Rob went outside with this police officer, I went to – well, you know, spend a penny. The side door of the pub was open. That was where Rob and the other guy had gone out. I didn't see any sign of them out there. I was still expecting that Rob would be coming back, so I assumed they'd probably just gone 'round to the garden for their chat. Anyway, as I was coming back, I heard this noise from outside.'

'What sort of noise?'

Wallace frowned. 'Like a shout or a scream, I suppose. I thought it came from the woods up towards the Glen. Assumed it was probably kids or maybe something like a fox screaking. They can make a racket, you know.'

'What time was this?'

'Don't know for sure. Maybe fifteen minutes after they'd gone out.'

'Anything else you remember?'

'I don't think so. Rory Craig and I left together. The night was as quiet as the grave then.' He realised what he'd said and added, 'Not the best choice of words.'

She handed him one of her business cards, as she had to Craig. 'If anything else occurs to you, give me a call. We may need to speak to you again, but I'll let you get back to the party now.'

Wallace showed no sign of moving. 'Bit of a shock this, to be honest. How's Shona taking it?'

Horton wasn't sure whether to be surprised that he knew Shona Graham's name. They were near neighbours, after all. But something in his tone made her wonder whether there might be more than that. Maybe another avenue to be explored.

'She seemed to be okay,' Horton responded. 'But, like you say, it must be a shock.'

'Aye, right enough.' After a long moment, he pushed himself to his feet and moved to open the door. 'I'll show you out. I think we're supposed to be doing the birthday candles.' He smiled.

'Then, I'm hoping we'll get rid of the little buggers.' The words were spoken as a joke, but it wasn't clear how much humour was in them.

Downstairs, the chaos seemed to be mounting as Mrs Wallace did her best to corral the youngsters back into the kitchen. Horton was only too happy to say her goodbyes and step out into the chill evening air.

It was still a decent evening. The setting sun behind her was casting long shadows out across the bay. Across the darkening blue waters, she could see the battlements of Fort George, the first lights beginning to come on. Her own house lay behind that, invisible from this angle.

A stiff breeze was blowing in from the water, and she shivered. Isla had been meeting a client in Stirling and was unlikely to be back much before nine, the best part of three hours away. Horton realised that, after the previous evening's events, she felt uncomfortable at the prospect of returning home alone. She'd managed, in the course of the day, to keep from thinking about David or what he might be up to. But now, as the evening shadows thickened around her, she could almost feel his presence. Almost as surely as if he was out there, staring back at her across the water.

Bugger him, she thought, as she unlocked the car. *I'm not a child any more. I've dealt with bigger bastards than him. There's no reason to be afraid.*

But she knew that she was. And she suspected that, deep in that part of her mind where she was still a small child, she always would be.

CHAPTER NINETEEN

Kelly Armstrong had noticed the changes when she'd passed by on the bus earlier that afternoon. On her return, curiosity getting the better of her, she'd hopped off the bus in Fortrose to have a closer look.

It was only her second day back and the first time she'd come through the village in daylight, so she hadn't noticed before. Now, she stood and looked in slight wonder at the transformation that had been effected.

It wasn't what she'd expected. She'd imagined that, after everything that had happened, the place would just be shut down and left abandoned. Maybe eventually turned into residential housing, like so many of the shop units out here. But instead, it looked as if somebody had bought the place and was trying to make a go of it. Well, good luck to them.

Still curious, she pushed open the door and stepped inside. The changes to the interior were even more impressive. What had previously been a dark and pokey bar, walls yellow with ancient tobacco stains and carpets sticky with spilled beer, had been stripped back to bare wood and whitewashed brickwork. The old bar had been renovated and now carried an array of polished handpumps and beer taps. The place wasn't busy at this time in the late afternoon, but a couple were sitting at the far end with beers and ornate-looking sandwiches, and a small group of middle-aged dog walkers were propping up the bar.

'You okay there?'

The man behind the bar had swept-back blond hair and angular features, and an easy-going manner which Kelly immediately found attractive. He was wearing a white T-shirt carrying the logo of a local craft brewery. Kelly remembered her own time working here and the grime and dust in the old cellar, and wondered how the man managed to look so smart. But probably the cellar, too, was a different place now.

'I'm fine,' Kelly said. 'Just amazed by how much this place had changed.'

'You knew it before?' the man said. He had the trace of an accent, but Kelly couldn't be sure whether it was a Scottish lilt or an Irish brogue. 'You don't look typical of the old clientele, if you don't mind me saying so.'

Kelly laughed. 'No, definitely not. I used to work here. Bar work.'

'Ah, that makes more sense,' the man said. 'Can I get you a drink?'

Kelly hesitated. 'Aye, why not? Just a Coke, though.' She reached into her handbag to dig out her purse.

The man held up his hand. 'No worries. On the house.' He smiled. 'You're just the kind of customer we're hoping to attract. Young, respectable – well, I assume you're respectable. Tell your friends.'

Kelly was warming to the man. 'How long have you been open?'

'Only a few weeks. Moved up at the end of last year. We'd have liked to have gotten it open before Christmas, but you can see how much work was involved. And the backstage areas were even worse than we'd thought.'

Kelly recalled her own visits to the dusty, spider-ridden cellar. 'You're from England?'

'Well, we lived down there for a long time. I'm Callum, by the way. Callum Donnelly.'

'Kelly Armstrong.'

'You live locally?'

'My parents stay in Cromarty,' Kelly said. 'I'm away at Uni at the moment in Stirling. Just back for the Easter vac.'

'Don't suppose you'd fancy coming back and doing a bit of bar work while you're here? We've got a couple of people working the odd evening, but we're looking for another person to help out in the afternoons and give some cover. Hoping that trade will start to pick up over the holidays.'

Kelly lowered herself on to one of the tall bar stools. 'I'm not sure,' she said, after a moment. 'I mean, thank you. But I had a slightly traumatic time here before.'

Callum Donnelly nodded. 'I've made a point of not enquiring too deeply into the background,' she said. 'But I know what happened to Denny Gorman. Were you involved in that? Not that it's any of my business.'

Kelly shivered involuntarily even at the mention of the previous landlord's name. 'Not directly. But I had a – run-in with Gorman before that. He didn't deserve what happened to him, but he was a creep.'

'I can see you might not want to be reminded. Sorry for asking.'

'But, actually, why not?' Kelly said. There was already too much stuff she was trying to avoid. Her now ex-boyfriend, Greg, for example. She managed successfully to avoid him during those last few weeks at Uni, but she'd been constantly expecting to run into him back up here. She didn't even know whether he'd actually come home for the vacation, but she still expected he'd be there around the next corner. It was going to take her a while to get over their split, but maybe one way was just to throw herself into new activities. 'What are you looking for, exactly?'

They agreed on a couple of hours in the afternoons to start with, enabling the Donnellys to focus on preparing the expanding food menu for the evenings.

'You'll find it a very different place, I promise,' Callum Donnelly said. 'Do you want to come and say hello to Maggie? She's out back.'

He led Kelly behind the bar into the rear part of the pub. A previously bleak-looking room which, as far as Kelly could recall, Gorman had used only for additional storage of his junk, had been transformed into a commercial kitchen. It was obviously still a work in progress, but a world away from anything that had been here previously. Maggie Donnelly, dressed in a chef's apron, was standing at one of the worktops, chopping carrots. She was an attractive woman, Kelly thought, with long dark hair which contrasted with the slightly startling crimson of her top.

'Maggie. You know we were looking for additional help over Easter?'

'You've found someone?' Her eyes swept over Kelly, and then back to Callum Donnelly. There was something in her expression Kelly couldn't interpret. Her hands continued chopping with practised inattention.

'Kelly Armstrong. She did bar work here before.'

'Under the old regime? Bit of a change from those days.'

'Just a bit,' Kelly agreed.

'Kelly's back from Uni. Happy to cover for us for a couple of hours in the afternoons and when we need her.'

Maggie Donnelly nodded. Her expression had softened but still seemed less than welcoming. 'Well, that's good,' she said finally.

'It'll be a great help,' Callum Donnelly said. He gestured towards the vegetables arrayed on the work surface. 'We want to start doing proper meals in the evening. Can't afford more trained kitchen staff yet, so Maggie and I will have to do the prepping. When can you start?'

'Soon as you like,' Kelly said. 'Tomorrow?'

'If you can, that would be perfect.' Callum Donnelly was beaming at them both as if they'd solved all his life's problems. His wife remained expressionless.

Kelly looked at her watch. 'I'd better be getting back,' she said. 'There's a bus due shortly.'

'See you tomorrow then.'

Kelly followed Callum Donnelly back out to the bar area. As they passed the open doorway leading down into the cellar, Kelly glanced involuntarily into the darkness.

'You probably know the layout of this place better than we do,' Donnelly said. 'The cellar's the one bit that hasn't changed too much. We've tidied it up, obviously. But we still need to tackle it properly.'

Kelly recalled the gloomy space beneath them, the shadows in the corners. The way that, even while he was alive, Denny Gorman had haunted the place like some malevolent spectre. She shivered slightly, wondering if she was doing right in coming back here. 'I think you should do that,' she said, trying to turn her words into a joke. 'Tackle it properly. Get rid of any trace of how it was.'

Donnelly laughed. 'You make it sound like the place is haunted.'

Kelly managed to smile back. 'Only for me,' she said. 'And only by memories.'

CHAPTER TWENTY

Still shaken by his unexpected encounter with Chrissie, McKay drove back up to the Black Isle in a pensive mood. The weather was holding fair, and as he'd crossed over the Kessock Bridge in the early evening, the waters of the firth were a deep blue under the empty opal sky. In other circumstances, it would have been a sight to lighten the heart, but McKay was feeling a long way from that.

He dragged the bags of shopping into the kitchen and began to unpack. Maybe now was the time for him to teach himself to cook properly, with time on his hands and the unenticing prospect of endless ready meals for one. He'd never been averse to the idea, but cooking had been Chrissie's territory, and she'd made it abundantly clear she didn't want him intruding. In those respects, their relationship had been all too traditional, and looking back, McKay couldn't really understand why. They'd drifted into the familiar Scottish stereotypes – the male breadwinner, the little woman left to look after the domestics. Neither of them had really wanted it, but neither of them had ever thought to question it.

He was contemplating these questions when the doorbell rang. His first instinct was to ignore it. Hardly anyone knew he was living here, so it was unlikely to be a welcome visitor. Most likely some young scrote supplementing his benefits by hawking sub-standard dishcloths. A quick flash of his warrant card was usually enough to send that type on their way.

But what if it was Chrissie at the door? She had his address. Maybe she'd thought over what he'd said and decided now was the time for a conversation after all. Stranger things had happened.

When the doorbell rang a second time, he hurried back through the hall and pulled open the front door.

'Alec? Sorry. You look like you were expecting someone else. Is this a bad time?'

'No. Christ, no. Who'd want to come and see me up here? Well, you, presumably.' He shook his head, conscious he was rambling. 'Ach, ignore my blethering. It's good to see you, Ginny. Come in.'

He led Horton through to the kitchen. 'Coffee? I'd offer you something stronger, but I assume you're driving.'

She nodded. 'I'll wait for that 'til I get home. I was up interviewing Rob Graham's drinking buddies, and it seemed rude not to call and say hello.'

'You're treating Graham's death as foul play, then?' McKay had his back to her, busying himself filling the kettle.

'Until we've a reason not to.' She paused. 'I shouldn't be discussing the case with you, really, Alec. Not in the circumstances.'

'Don't tell me you've got me pegged as a killer, too? I must be scarier than I thought.'

'Don't be daft, Alec. You know full well that Helena's done this for your own protection. We just need to do everything by the book.'

He finished spooning coffee into the mugs and turned to face her. 'Aye, I know. It's just a bit hard to take.'

'Don't think any of us are going to let you skive off for any longer than we can help, Alec McKay. You'll be back on board before you know it.'

'I hope so. I don't want to spend any longer than I have to in this place.'

She looked around her at the tiny functional kitchen. 'It's very – compact.'

'You hate it, don't you?'

'Well, it wouldn't suit me. But maybe it suits you, Alec.'

'Christ knows.'

'You're too good for this, you know, Alec. You don't have to punish yourself.'

'You reckon that's what I'm doing?'

'Looks suspiciously like it from where I'm sitting.'

He finished making the coffee and pushed one of the mugs across the small kitchen table towards her. 'Aye, well.'

'Have you been in contact with Chrissie? Maybe it's time to give it another go.'

'We've been in contact. She tells me she needs more time.'

'It's none of my business, but why did she walk out?'

He was tempted to agree that, no, it was none of her business, but he knew she meant well. 'She blames me for Lizzie's death. Just like I blame her for it.'

'You know that's bollocks, don't you, Alec? You don't really even know how or why Lizzie died. Whether it was just an accident or – well, something else. Either way, you can't hold yourselves responsible. She was an adult. She made her own decisions.'

'We brought her up,' McKay said. 'We created that adult.'

Horton shook her head. 'If she was depressed, that wasn't anything you created. You did your best. You did a decent job.'

'Doesn't stop either of us feeling guilty. Or trying to transfer that guilt to each other.'

'Jesus, Alec.'

Saying nothing, he rose and walked across to the kitchen window. 'Look,' he said. 'You can see the sea. It's not all bad.'

'You're changing the subject.'

'Of course I'm changing the fucking subject. What do you expect me to do?'

She picked up her coffee mug and rose to stand beside him, peering out through the glass. 'Okay. Where's the sea?'

'There.' He pointed between the row of houses. 'You might have to stand on tiptoe.' This was a joke. Horton was as tall as he was, if not slightly taller.

'Yes, I see it,' she said.

'This case of yours,' he said. 'Graham and Crawford and Galloway. You're not allowed to discuss it with me.'

'Well, nobody's actually said. But it seems sensible not to.'

'Aye, I can see that. Sensible. My middle name. But if I just talk at you, that's not a discussion, is it?'

'Alec –'

'That's just me shooting my mouth off. Feel free to ignore it, like you usually do.'

She took a long sip of her coffee and made no response.

'First thing. I'm sure Helena's on top of this, but still. You need to check out the other members of Galloway's team at that time. There were countless foot soldiers passed through, including me and Helena. I've never received letters like Galloway and his chums were sent, and I assume Helena would have mentioned it if she had. But it might be worth checking out former DSs Alastair Donald and Davey Robertson. Both retired now, as far as I know. Neither of them part of Galloway's real inner circle, but both would have liked to have been. Be interesting to know if either of them have been receiving the same letters.'

Horton was watching him. 'I'm just letting you talk at me.'

'Then, there are the people that Galloway's team put away. Particularly the ones where he might have used his – distinctive methods to get a result. Difficult to remember names after all these years, but I've had a shot at jotting down the ones I can recall.' He pulled a folded sheet of paper out of his pocket and tossed it on the table in front of her. 'That's a start.'

'You really are bored, aren't you, Alec? You need to get out more.'

'That's exactly what I want to do. Preferably back into the office. Anything I can do to push along the investigation –'

'Of course,' Horton said, 'if anyone really did think you were guilty, this might seem like an attempt to deflect attention. It's not a helpful look, Alec.'

'What else am I supposed to do, Ginny? I didn't kill Graham. Why the hell would I have done? Okay, I didn't much like the man, but if I killed everyone I don't like, I'd be the world's most prolific serial fucking killer.'

'I know, Alec. But Helena will be on top of all of this.' She paused. 'And think about it this way, Alec. If there's any challenge to Helena's integrity, however unjustified, she'll get taken off the case and replaced with someone more "independent." And that wouldn't help your position at all. I imagine there are a few people out there who wouldn't mind seeing you dragged down a peg or two.'

McKay nodded. 'Aye, you're right enough, Ginny. As always. Anyone ever told you no one loves a smart-arse?'

'Frequently. You, mainly. But be patient. Let us get on with it. We'll do it by the book, but we'll do it.' She picked up the sheet of paper from the table, and finally allowed him a smile. 'Mind you, since you've gone to the trouble, this might come in handy as well.'

CHAPTER TWENTY-ONE

'Christ. How much have you had?' He picked up the three-quarters empty bottle and held it in front of her.

She was sitting in her usual armchair, her eyes fixed on the television screen. 'Not enough, Ally. Not nearly enough.'

'For God's sake, woman, it's barely seven o'clock.'

'It's nearly eight. Where the hell have you been?' It was only the wine that gave her the courage to respond like this.

'Out. And?'

'Out where?'

'Is that any of your fucking business?' He slammed the bottle down on the table so hard, she thought the glass might shatter. 'I don't suppose you've cooked anything?'

'I had supper when I usually do,' she said. 'At six. You weren't here.'

She never knew what would drive him into one of his rages. She no longer cared what he said, although her physical fear of him hadn't diminished. The wine had deadened her emotions to that extent, at least. It was all unpredictable, anyway. Sometimes, an apparently innocuous word could send him into a fury. At other times, as now, he simply seemed uninterested in anything she might have to say.

'You'd better get me something, then,' he said and slumped down on the sofa opposite.

She was tempted to tell him to bugger off, but she hadn't the energy. She dragged herself to her feet and made her way through to the kitchen, making a point of taking her glass and the remaining wine with her. 'What do you want?'

'What did you have?'

119

'I just had a sandwich. Couldn't be bothered with anything more.'

'I want something hot.'

He sounded exactly like a spoilt child, she thought. A spoilt overgrown fucking child.

'There's a couple of frozen things. A curry and some Chinese thing. I could microwave one of those.'

'Fine. Whichever. Curry.' He put his feet up on the sofa and began flicking through the TV channels with the remote control. 'There's nothing but shite on TV.'

She suspected he might well have been drinking himself. He'd got himself a part-time job at the local garden centre, supposedly looking after security, but really, as far as she could see, just general dogsbodying. She couldn't understand why he wanted to do it. It wasn't as if they needed the money. They had a decent enough pension. But he was the sort of man who couldn't stand doing nothing. Whatever his actual job at the garden centre, she could imagine him bustling around, bossing the youngsters who worked there. He'd never risen above Sergeant in the force, but he'd behaved as if he was the Chief fucking Constable. That was the kind of man he was.

He finished at the garden centre at four, as far as she knew. So, he'd been somewhere for the last few hours. She couldn't bring herself to care where. Maybe he had another woman. If so, frankly, she was welcome to him. More likely he'd just stopped off and knocked back a few pints at the pub. He had no qualms about driving under the influence. He was one of those who thought it made him a better driver. And he was convinced that, if it came to it, his police background would be enough to protect him. *Well, good luck with that*, she thought.

She stuck the ready-meal curry in the microwave and set the timer. Then, she sat down at the kitchen table and poured herself the remainder of the wine. He was right, of course, at least about that. She was drinking too much. She was starting earlier in the day and not wanting to stop. But it wasn't as if she had much else to live for.

As if to prove the point, she heard Ally shouting from the sitting room, 'That curry ready yet? I'm fucking starving.'

That was far from literally true, she thought, judging from the way his fat stomach strained against his shirt. 'Two minutes,' she called.

'I'll have it in here.'

Like you've done with every meal for the last ten years, she added silently to herself. She waited until the microwave beeped and then, following the instructions to the letter as she always did, gave the food a stir and stuck it back in for another couple of minutes.

'How long does it take to microwave a fucking curry for Christ's sake?'

Two minutes, then lift lid and stir, she said to herself. *Then another two minutes. Then allow to stand for one minute.* Out loud, she said, 'It's coming.'

Finally, the microwave beeped again, and she took out the hot tray of food. She had a plate ready on a tray, and she carefully spooned the rice and pungent current out, adding a dab of the mango chutney Ally liked. There was a time when she'd have done that in the vain hope of trying to please him. Now, she did it only through habit.

'About fucking time,' he said, as she carefully carried the tray through into the living room. 'Any other wife would have had a meal waiting for me.'

Most other wives would have some idea what time their husbands were coming home, she retorted silently, as she placed the tray on his knee. Relieved to be finished, she returned to her armchair and left him to it.

The explosion came, as somehow she'd known it would, after only a few seconds. 'Jesus Christ, woman. This thing's fucking stone cold. Can't you even use a fucking microwave?'

She turned and then ducked back as the plate came flying in her direction, catching her glancingly on the cheek before shattering against the fireplace in a mess of rice and lurid curry sauce. She was expecting that Ally's fists would follow and turned her head away in anticipation. Instead, she heard him say, 'That's it. I'm going out again. Don't fucking wait up.'

Moments later, the front door slammed. She straightened and looked at the debris in front of her. The food had been fine. She knew that perfectly well. It was all part of the game Ally continually played in his head. Wrong-footing her. Doing what he wanted but always managing to make it her fault. Once, she'd have let it gnaw away at her. Now, she was numb to it.

The television was still playing silently, anonymous talking heads blethering about who knew what. She sat back, thinking about the next bottle of wine in the kitchen. And waited.

CHAPTER TWENTY-TWO

Ginny Horton had stayed chatting with McKay for as long as she could. McKay himself seemed ambivalent towards her presence. On the one hand, he was clearly enjoying the opportunity to chew the fat. They'd always got on well, and once past the sensitivities of McKay's enforced absence from work, they'd moved on to the usual inconsequentialities of office gossip and Scottish politics.

But she sensed there was a part of him that wanted to be alone. It was as if he'd chosen that pokey, soulless bungalow to cut himself off from civilised society, like some latter-day religious hermit. When she eventually announced she had to be going, he looked both disappointed and relieved.

Although Rosemarkie and Ardersier faced each other across the Moray Firth, only a mile or two apart as the crow flies, the journey home took her the best part of an hour, with a short hold-up for roadworks by the Kessock roundabout. She was happy enough with that. It meant she was likely to arrive home at roughly the same time as Isla. She was reluctant to admit it, but until she was sure David was no longer in the vicinity, she was keen to spend as little time alone there as possible.

As she turned out of the village towards their house, she was half expecting to see that same car parked outside their driveway. If it had been, she'd have kept on driving, turned back into the village and stayed well away until she'd managed to contact Isla. But the road was empty.

She pulled into the driveway and sat for a moment, the car doors still locked, overcome by a sudden panic. What if David was out there somewhere, waiting for her return? What if he'd left his car further up the road, so as not to alert her? The house itself was in darkness, and she could see nothing through the car windows.

She took a deep breath and pushed open the car door, the chill night air striking her face like a slap. There was a stiff breeze blowing in from the firth, and it felt as if a change in the weather was coming. Around her, she could hear the trees and bushes rustling like insistent voices in her ears. *It's you. It's your fault. You deserve this.*

She climbed out of the car and clicked shut the central locking, the flashing of the indicators throwing unexpected shadows around her. She fumbled for her house keys and took the half dozen steps towards the front door, thankful when the key slid smoothly into the lock.

She already had the door open when she sensed the movement behind her. She froze, unable to bring herself to look back, and heard the voice whispering, inches from her ear.

'Virginia.'

CHAPTER TWENTY-THREE

Ally Donald stumbled in the darkness, telling himself it was the gloom rather than the drink that had caused him to lose his footing. He'd only had – what? A couple of pints and chasers early on, then a few more pints and whiskies just now, after that bitch had driven him out of the house. Nothing he couldn't handle after all these years.

It was still quite early, only just gone nine. He was only out here because that bastard behind the bar had implied that maybe he'd had one too many already. Ally had thought of making an issue of it – well, he had created a bit of a stooshie until his mates had calmed him down – but it wasn't worth the hassle. It would be bloody embarrassing if the landlord called the police. Former Detective Sergeant in pub fracas. Even in his current state, he could see that wouldn't be smart.

So, in the end, he'd called it a night. After all, it wasn't as if he had to go home, necessarily. Not back to that bitch. Kirstie wouldn't mind if he called to see her. She'd just be watching TV, and she was always waiting for him whenever he called round. He'd sometimes wondered if it might be easier just to ditch the bitch and move in with Kirstie full time. But it wasn't that simple. The bitch had money, or at least the prospect of money, once her dad finally fell off the perch. And if he moved in with Kirstie, it would just be frying pan to fire. It worked because he could see her when he wanted to and then leave it all behind. It was a convenient arrangement for both of them, and neither wanted anything more.

He felt uneasy these days walking through Cromarty late in the evening. They'd lived here for ten years now, and though he'd never brought himself to admit it, there'd always been moments when the place gave him the creeps. It was full of little alleyways and vennels, deep in shadows. Any bugger might be hiding there, waiting to jump out.

Ally had never thought of himself as a nervous man. On the contrary, he'd usually been the first to go looking for a fight. But he wasn't getting any younger, and the last few years had knocked some of the stuffing out of him. Then, Rob Graham had called to let him know what had happened to Galloway and Crawford. Suddenly, all the years of those fucking letters hadn't seemed so funny after all. They'd none of them really taken it seriously. Not until now.

They'd had their worries, of course. They made plenty of enemies back in the day, on both sides of the law, and none of them had entirely trusted the others. Ally suspected that was one reason why they'd all found themselves living up in this neck of the woods, as if they were all surreptitiously keeping tabs on each other. But any anxieties on that score had faded as the years went by. Jackie Galloway, whom none of them trusted, had quietly gone gaga, and the rest of them had given themselves up to drink and boredom.

Then, Galloway and Crawford had died. Maybe accidents, maybe not. It was clear that Rob Graham thought not. When he'd called Ally, he'd sounded shit-scared. As if he'd known something Ally didn't.

Ally stopped, thinking he'd heard some sound behind him. The street was deserted, nothing moving in the pools of light below each street lamp. The wind from the sea was stronger, channelled up the alleyways from the shore. There was damp in the air, and he thought it would rain before morning.

He hurried on, peering into the shadows of each side road but seeing nothing but the occasional skittering of litter in the breeze. He was feeling more and more as if there was someone nearby, someone watching him. Someone following.

Cursing his own paranoia, he reached the corner of Kirstie's tiny cottage. To his relief, there were lights on inside. He realised now he'd actually been scared she might be out, though she rarely left the house in the evenings.

His anxiety draining away, he reached out to press the doorbell.

It was only then he felt the presence behind him, the warm breath on the back of his neck. The hand tightening slowly around his throat.

CHAPTER TWENTY-FOUR

Horton turned, her breath caught in her throat.

He was only a couple of metres away, his body silhouetted against the flickering lights on the main road. She had no doubt it was him.

'Just fuck off, David,' she said, struggling to keep her voice calm. 'Just leave me alone.'

'Virginia –'

'I don't want to talk to you, don't you understand? I don't want to see you.' Trying not to panic, she took a slow half step back, feeling for the edge of the door with her fingers. She couldn't read his expression in the darkness.

'Virginia.' There was no evident emotion in his voice. She knew that if she gave him the opportunity, he'd begin the familiar game playing. Toying with her feelings. Manipulating her into letting him back into her life.

'Just go away.'

He moved forward, but Horton had already stepped backwards into the hallway, slamming the door in his face. She could feel him pushing, trying to prevent the lock from engaging, but he was already too late. She slammed across the two bolts and stood back.

Shit, she thought. *Shit*.

Without turning on the house lights, she fumbled for her mobile, frantically searching for Isla's number. The call rang out for agonisingly long seconds but then cut to voicemail. Unless the flight had been delayed, Isla should have landed by now and be on her way back, but she disliked using the hands-free. Horton ended the call and dialled again, hoping that Isla would notice the repeated call and guess something was wrong. This time, she left a message, her voice trembling, asking Isla to call urgently as soon as she picked it up.

She moved to peer out of the window. There was no sign of David in the darkness. Perhaps he'd given up. Perhaps he was trying to find some other means of access.

Still leaving the house in darkness, she made her way through to the kitchen, wanting to reassure herself that the back-door was safely bolted. The bolts were firmly in place, the deadlock secured.

The house was relatively secure, but she didn't fool herself that David couldn't force his way in, if he really tried. The windows were mostly part of the original fabric of the house, the glass easily smashed. It was difficult to imagine David going that far. He generally preferred to inveigle his way into others' lives through more subtle means. But she knew he wasn't beyond violence, if he wanted to get his way.

There was no sign of him outside the kitchen window. She was returning to check the living room when she was startled by the phone buzzing in her pocket. She assumed it was Isla returning her call and answered without stopping to check the screen.

'Virginia.'

She forced herself to bite back the scream rising in her throat. Her first instinct was to respond, ask him how the hell he'd got hold of her number. But she knew it would be a mistake to engage. David had endless means of getting hold of any information he wanted. Maybe he'd tracked down one of her friends and used his persuasive wiles to extract the number. Maybe he'd used one of his dubious ex-police contacts. It didn't matter. He'd got it.

Tomorrow, she could change the number. But tonight, it felt like just another vulnerability, another hole through which he could crawl back into her life.

Still resisting the urge to turn on the lights, she felt her way into the living room. The curtains were open, and there, silhouetted against the twin doors to the patio, was a figure.

She knew the locks were strong enough, and unlike the majority of the downstairs windows, the patio doors were toughened glass. But if David failed to gain access there, he might start seeking other routes.

She jumped as the phone buzzed again. She pulled it out and stared at the screen. *Isla. Thank Christ.*

'Ginny, what's wrong? You sounded panicky.'

'It's David. Fucking David. He's outside. He was waiting for me. He's at the back of the house.'

'Jesus, Ginny. Call the fucking police. I'll get there as quickly as I can. I'm only five minutes away. I stopped after I turned off the main road to check your message. But call the police. Now.'

Horton ended the call and hesitated. Her normal instinct would have been to do anything rather than involve her police colleagues in this. But David was here, outside the house she shared with Isla, trying to gain entry, and there was now no getting away from that. When she looked up, the figure had vanished. Moments later, the front doorbell rang, shrill and insistent. She could see a face peering through the window by the door, trying to see into the house. The bell rang again, held down this time.

That decided her. She backed into the kitchen, feeling somehow safer there, and thumbed 999. 'Police, please. Urgent.'

'Police. How can I help you?'

Horton took a breath, trying to keep her voice calm. 'This is Detective Sergeant Horton. I've an intruder in my garden. Potentially threatening. I need help here urgently.' She gave the details to the call handler and heard the message being relayed to the dispatcher. 'There's a car fairly close by at the airport,' the handler said. 'They'll be there in a few minutes. Do you want to stay on the line until they arrive?'

'I'd better.' The doorbell was still ringing, unceasing now. The sound of someone who would not be ignored. 'You can hear that?' she asked the handler. 'He was waiting for me when I got back. I got into the house but he's still there.'

'Do you know his identity?'

'Yes. That's why I think he might be dangerous.'

Somewhere in the distance, behind the piercing sound of the bell, she could hear sirens. The doorbell stopped abruptly, and there were other sounds outside. A car door slamming, an engine starting. Horton remained motionless, listening for any clue as to what might be happening.

There was the sound of another car outside. The sirens were growing louder. Horton forced herself to walk back into the hallway and peer through the window beside the front door. Isla's Audi was parked by her own car in the driveway, and the trees beyond were pulsing with approaching blue lights.

She pulled back the bolts and opened the front door as Isla climbed out of the car. 'Has he gone?'

'I think so.'

The patrol car pulled up behind Isla's Audi, and two uniformed officers jumped out. Horton recognised one of them by sight, though she couldn't immediately recall his name. 'DS Horton?'

'That's me,' Horton said. 'And you're PC McCann.' She'd remembered the name as he'd drawn closer. *A decent lad*, she thought, *new to the force*. She'd had a couple of minor dealings with him, and had the impression he knew what he was about.

'Billy McCann,' he said. 'Well remembered. Where's this intruder, then?'

Isla turned and pointed down the drive. 'There was a car heading off just as I arrived. Doing a fair speed, so a pound to a penny, it was him.'

'We can put out a bulletin,' McCann said, regarding Isla with undisguised curiosity. 'Did you get sight of the car?'

Isla shook her head. 'It was too far away.'

McCann turned his attention to Horton. 'Any clues on the vehicle?'

Horton shook her head. 'No. There was a car parked out there the other night. I thought that was probably him too. I didn't get the make, but Isla thought it was a new car. We thought it was maybe a hire car from the airport. If it was David, he'd most likely have flown up here.'

'David?'

'My stepfather. That's who it is. He's left me messages. We think he was loitering 'round the house. Then, tonight, he tried to talk to me and follow me into the house.' As the adrenaline rush was dying away, Horton felt as if she could barely stand up, let alone answer McCann's questions.

'You think he's dangerous?'

'It's a long story. He was – abusive when I was younger. And he's been manipulative when I've met him since. I don't know whether he's dangerous now, but I wouldn't want to risk being alone with him.'

'You want us to try to pick him up?'

'I'm not sure there's any point. He'll just come up with some story. I've no proof that he intended to scare me –'

'Maybe he didn't.' This was the other uniformed officer, standing in the darkness behind McCann. Horton didn't know him. His voice sounded dismissive, as if she'd dragged them out here on a wild goose chase. Maybe she had. When David had been leaning insistently on the doorbell, when she'd seen his silhouette framed in the rear windows, dialling 999 had seemed the only option. Now, she was beginning to regret it. She could imagine how this would be relayed around the station tomorrow. Another woman who couldn't cut it in the job.

She looked past McCann at the second PC. He looked barely out of his teens, greasy hair and an acne-riven complexion. But with a cocky air McCann thankfully lacked. 'Maybe he didn't, son,' she said, thinking how McKay would deal with this one. 'But I couldn't be sure of that from what I know of his history.'

'No, I just –' The PC looked to McCann for support but realised none would be forthcoming. 'Aye, of course.'

'You think he's likely to come back?' McCann said.

'I don't think he's likely to come back tonight,' Horton said. 'I suspect he won't come back at all now.'

'Does he know you're –?'

'A police officer? I doubt it. We haven't been in contact for a long time.'

McCann nodded. 'Families, eh? Ach, tell me about it.' He gestured behind them. 'You're sure you don't want us to follow this up?'

She glanced at his colleague, still standing in the shadows outside. 'There's no point wasting your time.'

'We could put a bit of pressure on him. Make it clear he's not welcome.'

She allowed herself a smile. 'He knows full well he's not welcome. I've made that crystal clear.'

'Well, if he reappears, don't hesitate. It's what we're here for.' He glanced over at his colleague. 'Even if some of us might prefer to sit in the car with a fish supper.'

After the officers had gone, Horton watched as Isla slid the bolts on the front door, making sure the locks were fully engaged. She could see Isla was doing this deliberately, demonstratively, to reassure her that this place remained their refuge.

'I'm sorry,' Isla said, as she returned from the kitchen with an opened bottle of wine. 'I'm not sure if calling 999 was the best idea after all. That silly little bugger outside.'

Horton shrugged. 'There'll be a bit of gossip in the canteen tomorrow. Apart from anything else, I'm guessing your existence will be news to some people, though I've hardly kept it a secret. But they'll soon forget about it. And Christ knows what David would have done if they hadn't turned up.'

'You really think he would have done something?' Isla stopped pouring the wine and shook her head. 'Sorry. I'm sounding like that twelve-year-old they'd allowed to dress up as a policeman. I didn't mean it like that. I mean, do you think he'd have been physically violent?'

'Who knows? He's been violent enough in the past. But whatever he intended tonight, he scared the hell out of me.' She took a mouthful of wine and sat back on the sofa. 'The weird thing is that I almost feel better that it happened.'

'Better?'

'I don't know. It felt like it brought things to a head. It was worse when he was lurking out there somewhere, and I had no way of responding. Tonight, he showed his hand, and I made it bloody clear what my answer was.'

Isla nodded, her expression suggesting she wasn't entirely convinced by this assessment. 'Let's hope he takes no for an answer.'

'He will,' Horton said confidently. 'He's an arsehole, but he's not stupid. He won't risk another run-in with the police.' Her voice sounded calm, but her eyes were fixed on the still uncurtained patio windows. She rose, and with a finality that suggested she wanted to bring the conversation to an end, she pulled the curtains closed. 'Let's go and sort some food,' she said. 'I'm starving.'

CHAPTER TWENTY-FIVE

McKay stared balefully at the remains of his ready-meal lasagne. It had been okay, he supposed, though it would have been even better if he'd microwaved it until it was hot all the way through.

It was all a learning experience. A new house. A new lifestyle. A new bloody microwave, with half the power of the one he'd been used to at – His train of thought juddered to a halt, as he realised he'd stumbled unintentionally on the word "home." That was how he still thought of the place where he and Chrissie had lived. That had been home. But it wasn't anymore. Not for the moment, and maybe never again. This place was his home now. This bleak little bungalow where he owned nothing but a few basic household items.

He could already feel himself sliding, yet again, into melancholy. He pushed himself to his feet, grabbed his heavy waterproof from the back of the kitchen chair and, without hesitation, strode through the hall and stepped out into the cold night air. It was only when he was outside that he stopped to think about where he might be going and realised he had no idea.

The weather was beginning to change. The previously clear sky was heavy with clouds, and the air felt damp with the threat of rain. For want of any other destination, McKay turned down the narrow footpath to the seafront. The route was ill lit, illuminated only by the residual glow of the streetlights on the adjoining roads. McKay stumbled, cursing himself for not stopping to dig out the police torch he kept in his bag.

He was almost at the end of the path, the seafront road and the firth now visible before him, when he stopped and turned.

He'd suddenly had an uncomfortable sense that someone was watching him. There was no sign of anyone behind him, although there was plenty of shrubbery in which a covert observer could be hiding. But why the hell would anyone want to watch him?

Resisting the urge to look back again, he continued down to the road. The tide was high, and the beach along the front was reduced to a narrow strip. The wind was rising, and in the half light, the crashing waves were faintly phosphorescent. Across the firth, he could see the line of lights that marked Fort George and Ardersier. Ginny would be back over there by now, no doubt enjoying another evening of domestic bliss with her partner.

To his right, he could see Rob Graham's house, lights blazing, windows uncurtained. No longer Graham's house, of course, he added to himself. He wondered how Shona Graham was feeling tonight. Lost, alone? Or relieved to be rid of a burden of a husband?

The chill blast of the wind on his skin had woken him up but done little to improve his mood. Frustrated by his own misery, McKay trudged back up the hill. He needed some exercise and he needed a drink. It wouldn't be a great idea to return to the local bar. If nothing else, the small talk would be awkward. The only other option was the mile or so walk over to Fortrose, where he'd find a choice of places to drink.

Fifteen minutes of brisk walking found him on Fortrose High Street. He was already feeling in a more positive frame of mind, his face tingling from the chill of the rising wind. The rain had held off so far, though he could feel it was coming.

The smart move, he knew, would be to duck into the Anderson or the Union Bar, pubs where he could get himself a decent drink without risking any compromise of his own position. But, as he'd known from the moment he'd set off, he was already striding past those and heading towards the Caledonian Bar. In his head, he was rehearsing the conversation he'd have with Helena Grant if she ever found out. By the time he reached the door of the bar, he'd worked through a range of permutations but hadn't yet come up with one that didn't end with her giving him the mother of all bollockings.

He was less surprised by the new interior glamour of the bar this time, but was still disconcerted by the changes. It was like seeing a full-colour, high definition photograph superimposed on a sepia Victorian print.

Mid-evening, the bar was busy. There were a couple of families with children eating meals, a few younger couples, and over in the far corner, a group of more elderly men playing cards. Only the last group would have frequented the place in Denny Gorman's day, McKay thought.

He propped himself at the bar and surveyed the impressive array of beer pumps. Three cask ales, a couple of exotic looking lagers, an upmarket cider. Not to mention an impressive display of bottled stuff in the chill cabinets at the back of the bar.

As he was mulling over his choice of drink, the young barmaid turned from some task she'd been completing by the register. 'I know you,' she said, without any preamble. 'You're the policeman.'

So much for remaining incognito. 'Aye, that's me. The policeman. DI Alec McKay at your service.' He peered at the young face in front of him. 'Young Kerry, isn't it?'

'Kelly,' she corrected. 'Kelly Armstrong. But, yes. I didn't know you stayed 'round these parts.'

'Long story,' McKay said in a tone which confirmed he had no intention of sharing it. 'Mind you, I'm even more surprised to find you in here.'

She shrugged. 'Changed, hasn't it? And Denny Gorman's long gone.'

'No trace of him below stairs, even?'

'The lingering ghost of Denny Gorman? Jeez, I hope not.' She gave a mock shudder. 'I didn't want him anywhere near me even when he was alive.'

'Not many people did.' McKay gestured along the line of beer pumps. 'What would you recommend?'

'I'm not the one to ask,' she said. 'Callum always recommends the Cromarty Ales.'

'I'll try the stout then. I like things dark. Goes with the job. You still with that boyfriend of yours?'

She was pulling the pint and didn't look up at him. 'Aye, well. That's another long story.'

McKay took the hint. 'Still at Uni, though?'

'Just back up for the vac,' she said. 'Uni's great. Especially now I'm unencumbered, as it were.'

Unencumbered, McKay thought. That was how it felt if you were eighteen. Less so at his age. 'That's grand, anyway.'

She placed the pint in front of him and took his five-pound note. 'You're not here on business?'

McKay knew from his previous dealings with her that she was more astute than her young appearance might suggest. 'Purely social,' he said.

'Only, Callum said the police had been in asking about that poor man. The one who died.'

McKay nodded. 'Aye, that's right. But just routine, you know? Has to be done with any unexplained death.'

'Callum said the man's poor wife was in here looking for him the night he went missing,' Kelly went on. 'Do they know what happened to him yet?'

'It's not my case,' McKay said. 'Imagine they've an idea by now.'

Kelly gestured towards the cluster of elderly men in the corner. 'Those are his mates, apparently. You know, drinking buddies. Was chatting to one of them earlier. Nice old man. Remembered me being here in Denny Gorman's day. He was saying that your man –'

'Billy Crawford,' McKay prompted.

'Aye, that he'd been a bit jittery in the days before he disappeared. Not himself. Like he was worried about something.'

'That right?' McKay kept his voice neutral. As far as he'd been aware, this information hadn't emerged from any of the initial interviews they'd conducted following Crawford's death, though they'd spoken to several of Crawford's drinking partners. But that proved little. People were often cagey in what they revealed to the police. And, equally, people often exaggerated their recollections when chatting to their friends and acquaintances. This could be either, or nothing much at all.

'Is it right he was a policeman?' Kelly asked.

'Aye. Retired.' McKay gestured towards the group of elderly men. 'I should maybe go and pay my respects. I worked with him, years ago.'

Kelly nodded. At the far end of the bar, the father of one of the young families was waving his credit card, wanting to settle up. McKay left her to it and, cradling his pint, moved over to where Crawford's drinking buddies were sitting.

As he approached, the group, who'd been blethering away nineteen to the dozen, unexpectedly fell silent. McKay felt like the stranger who walks into the saloon in a low budget Western. 'I understand Billy Crawford was a mate of yours?' he asked, directing the question at no one in particular.

'Who's asking?' one of the men said.

McKay regarded the man who'd spoken. An overweight florid-faced man in a beige cardigan. Aye, one of Billy Crawford's drinking buddies, right enough. 'I'm an old friend myself.'

'That so?'

'Well, colleague,' McKay added. He brandished his warrant card to the assembled group. The silence, as he'd expected, grew even more profound. 'I worked with him when I first joined the force. Was sorry to hear the news.'

The man was still looking suspicious. 'This an official visit, then? Some of us have already spoken to you lot.'

McKay held up his pint, as if it were some token of his good intentions. 'Just popped in for a pint. Wanted to see how they'd done up the old place. It was the wee lassie behind the bar mentioned Billy's name to me. Just thought I'd come over to pay my respects.'

'You know any more yet about what happened to Billy?' The florid-faced man sounded keen to get any gossip that might be going.

'Not my case,' McKay said. 'Imagine there'll be an inquest to determine the cause of death, though.'

'Bit of a coincidence, him and Jackie Galloway,' the man said. 'And I hear there's been some new trouble over in Rosemarkie.' It sounded as if he already knew as much as McKay did.

McKay shrugged. 'Aye, sad times, right enough. You don't expect anything to happen just walking home from the pub.'

'That's if Billy did just walk home,' a second man said. For a second, the group fell silent again, as if the man had spoken out of turn.

'I'm just saying –'

'You're saying nothing,' the florid-faced man intervened. 'Let's not speak ill of the dead. Billy was a grand chap.'

'I'm not –' The other man finally recognised he was being silenced. 'Aye, he was that.'

McKay knew there was no point in pushing it. 'I'll leave you to it,' he said, raising his pint to them. 'Just wanted to pass on my condolences.'

He returned to sit at the bar, enjoying the continuing silence behind him. It took them a few seconds to begin chatting again. McKay finished his pint and ordered a second, along with a pack of upmarket crisps. 'Nice bunch,' he said to Kelly.

'Aye. Part of the old crowd. Not sure Callum really wants that kind of clientele, but they're harmless enough.'

McKay nodded, his eye still half on the group. The man who'd apparently said too much about Billy Crawford had had a packet of cigarettes on the table in front of him. McKay assumed that at some point he'd head for a quick drag outside the front doors. The only question was whether he'd go alone. McKay assumed there'd be more than one smoker among that group.

Sure enough, after a few minutes, the man picked up his cigarettes, said something to the group and made his way towards the doors. To McKay's relief, none of the others accompanied him. Maybe he was being cold-shouldered for shooting his mouth off.

Trying not to hurry, McKay finished his pint and the last few crisps, nodded to Kelly, picked up his coat, and headed towards the door himself.

Outside, the weather had turned colder, and a fine rain had started to fall. The streetlights and shopfronts along the high street were haloed with mist. The man was huddled in the doorway, drawing heavily on a cigarette.

'They'll be the death of you, you know?' McKay said, stepping past him.

'Aye. It's a race between this and the booze which'll get me first.'

'You seemed to want to say something about Billy Crawford in there?'

'None of my business,' the man said. 'But if you lot are looking into his death, you should know he didn't always go straight home.'

'That right?'

'Aye. He had a fancy woman. Widow. Meg Barnard. Nice little arrangement, I'm told.'

'How'd you know this?'

'Ach, everybody knows it. Well, everybody except Billy's widow. That's one reason Fat Bob in there doesn't like people talking about it. He's got a soft spot for Jeanie Crawford. He'll be in there, now she's free and single again. She'll be worth a bob or two as well.'

'You know where this Meg Barnard lives?'

'Aye.' He gave McKay a street name, just off the high street, down towards the sea. McKay's first suspicions had been correct, then. It might help explain how Crawford came to be in the water. 'Don't know the number. But it's a bungalow, down at the far end on the right. You'll find it.'

McKay nodded. 'Thanks. I'll pass on the information.'

'But you'll treat it discreetly, like? None of us wants to see Jeanie hurt.'

'Soul of discretion,' McKay said. 'You best get back to your mates. Or the cold'll get you even before the fags do.'

'Aye, bonny Scotland, eh?'

McKay stood for a moment after the man had gone, feeling the cold rain running down his neck. The smart thing to do was to relay this bit of intelligence back to Helena Grant in the morning. She'd want to know how he came by it, but he could give her an innocent enough answer to that. *Just chatting in the pub*, he'd say. *All blokes together. You know how it is.*

Aye, that was the smart thing to do. But Alec McKay had never had much of a reputation for doing the smart thing. Not when there was a chance to do something much dumber instead.

CHAPTER TWENTY-SIX

McKay looked at his watch. Still not eight-thirty. Not too late to be paying a social call. He pressed the bell. There were lights showing behind a couple of the curtained windows, but no other sign of movement or life. Maybe there was still time for him to salvage what might be left of his career, he thought. Then, he pressed the bell again. The rain was still falling, a fine mist that chilled McKay's skin.

After a moment, he heard sounds from beyond the door. It opened a few inches, held in place by a hefty-looking chain. 'Yes?'

In for a penny, McKay thought. He held out his warrant card. 'DI McKay. I'm looking for a Meg Barnard.'

There was silence. Then, the door closed and reopened, fully this time. The woman inside was short, blonde and buxom. McKay found it difficult to estimate her age. Younger than Jeanie Crawford, certainly, but probably not by much. 'This about Billy? I wondered how long it would take you.'

'Might have been better if you'd made contact with us yourself, Mrs Barnard.' He paused. 'It is Mrs?'

'Aye,' she said. 'The gay divorcee, that's me. You'd best come through.' She glanced at his sodden waterproof. 'And you'd better hang that out here.'

She led him through into a neat and, to McKay's eyes, feminine-looking sitting room. There was a preponderance of pink and frills, along with an array of cushions that seemed designed to deter visitors from taking any of the available seats. It was difficult to imagine Billy Crawford being comfortable in a room like this. But he imagined that Crawford hadn't come here for the decor.

McKay managed to accommodate himself among the soft furnishings. The television was on, the volume silenced. Meg Barnard took the seat opposite the television. There was a glass and a half-empty bottle of gin on the small coffee table beside her. Barnard's demeanour suggested she might have consumed much of the missing half that evening.

'I miss Billy,' she said, with no preamble. 'I didn't think I would, but I do. Poor wee bastard.'

McKay was still wondering how to steer round this conversation. 'Had you known him long?'

'Only twenty years,' she said. 'I used to work in the force. Admin.' She leaned forward. 'In fact, I remember you, Alec McKay. You were a cocky wee bastard.'

'Nothing changes,' McKay said. 'But that's a long time.'

'To be someone's mistress, you mean? Aye, I suppose. But it suited me. The one thing I learned from being married was that I'm not the marrying kind. I like my own company too much.'

'But you still wanted to see Billy Crawford.'

'Aye, well, that was just sex, wasn't it?'

McKay nodded. It was clear there was no need to go around the houses with this one. 'That was it? Sex?'

'Mainly. I mean, Billy could be a laugh. Decent company. But I wouldn't have wanted to live with him. I don't know how poor Jeanie managed.'

Poor Jeanie. 'You knew her?'

'Not really. I met her a couple of times in the old days. And I've seen her around the village. But it was just what Billy said about her.'

'What did he say?'

'Ach, that she was a fussing old hen.'

'You reckon she knew anything about your … arrangement with Billy?'

'Billy always reckoned not. I reckon women aren't usually that blind. Maybe it suited her as well.'

McKay raised an eyebrow. 'You think?'

'Got him out from under her feet.' She allowed him a smile. 'At least it wasn't golf.'

'Aye, there is that,' McKay conceded. 'Did you see him the night he went missing?'

She shook her head. 'He texted to say he might call in, but never turned up.'

'You weren't worried?'

'That wasn't the kind of relationship we had. If he turned up, he turned up. If he didn't, I'd spend the evening with my spiritual friend there.' She gestured towards the gin bottle. 'I might end up feeling a little horny. But there are ways of dealing with that.' She was still smiling.

McKay shifted awkwardly among the pile of cushions, feeling more uncomfortable than he'd have expected with Meg Barnard's directness. 'Was it usual for him to text you?'

'It varied. He'd usually have his tea with Jeanie, then head off to the pub early evening. If he felt like paying me a visit, he'd usually text me first. But sometimes, he'd text and then get caught up in some conversation and wouldn't make it over here before it was time to head back to Jeanie. He didn't like staying out too late. Knew she'd worry.'

'Very considerate.' None of this sounded much like McKay's idea of a relationship, or indeed of a marriage, but he was hardly in the best position to offer an opinion. 'What time did he text you?' As far as McKay could recall, no mobile phone had been found on Crawford's person. Most likely it was lying at the bottom of the firth somewhere.

'I can check.' She fumbled in a garish pink handbag by the side of her chair and pulled out a mobile phone. She scrolled back through the list of texts and passed it over to McKay.

McKay had been half expecting some romantic, or as least erotic, message but the text simply said: "Maybe see you later?" Perhaps Crawford had kept the wording of his exchanges with Meg Barnard neutral in case his wife should see them. But it seemed more likely that this was just the kind of man he was.

Barnard had texted back: "Aye. I'm around." *Touching*, McKay thought.

The texts were both timed at 7.03 p.m., presumably not long after Crawford had first arrived at the pub. Crawford had clearly been planning ahead. Callum Donnelley, the landlord at the Caledonian Bar, had said that Crawford usually left around eight or eight thirty. 'If he had come 'round, what sort of time would you have expected him?'

'Eight-ish, I guess,' Meg Barnard said. 'Much later than that and he wouldn't bother. He liked to get back to Jeanie not much after nine.'

'He didn't text you again?'

'That wasn't Billy's style. If he turned up, he turned up. If he didn't – well, I'd know he'd just stayed for another drink and then headed home. His loss, to be honest.'

McKay was silent for a moment. 'You reckon anyone else knew about your relationship with Billy?'

She laughed. 'I reckon the whole village knew but were too polite to say anything. Ach, you know how people are. Keep ourselves to ourselves. Not our place to judge.' She'd affected a high-pitched, prissy accent for the last two statements. 'All that crap. That's why I can't believe Jeanie didn't have an inkling.' She stopped, her voice suddenly serious. 'You really think someone might have wanted to kill Billy?'

'We just have to explore all the possibilities. The real question is how he got into the water.'

'We're close to the water's edge here,' she said. 'If you go a hundred yards or so past the end of the road, you can walk down to the firth. It's not far – another fifty yards or so. But I can't imagine what would have taken Billy down there. He wasn't exactly the sightseeing type.'

'Maybe went to relieve himself?'

She looked amused by the euphemism. 'He'd have been quicker just ringing the doorbell if he was that desperate.' She was watching him closely, as if trying to weigh up what else she ought to tell him. 'Look, I don't know if it's relevant,' she said, finally, 'but I don't reckon Billy was quite himself in those last few weeks.'

'How do you mean?'

'Well, you know Billy – you remember him, I mean. He wasn't a man lacking in self-confidence.'

That was one way of putting it, McKay thought. If McKay himself had been a cocky wee bugger in the old days, Crawford, like most of his senior associates, had been a full-blown egomaniac. 'Aye, so I recall.'

'That was Billy all over. Always thought he could do just as he liked.' She smiled, reading the expression on McKay's face. 'Just like he did with me, that's right. And we were all daft enough to let him get away with it. But the last few weeks, he wasn't like that.'

'In what way?'

'If it was anyone else, I'd have said he was scared. But I don't recall Billy being scared of anyone or anything.'

'We're all scared of something,' McKay observed. 'Maybe it just took Billy a bit longer than most of us to face it.' He paused, thinking. 'Could he have been ill? Something serious, I mean.' If there was anything like that, McKay thought, the post-mortem would reveal it.

'I wondered that,' she said. 'I guess it's possible. But it didn't feel like that. He wasn't just worried or preoccupied. He actually seemed nervous. As if he was constantly looking over his shoulder.'

'Literally?' McKay thought of the dark street outside, the shadows clustering at the far end, away from the street lights where the path led down to the firth.

'Maybe. He seemed rattled by noises. Even when we were in the middle of – well, you know – he'd stop as if he'd heard something downstairs. I could feel him tense.' She seemed to have abandoned any tendency to innuendo now, as if this was what she'd been wanting to say all along. 'He could tell I noticed. Tried to joke about it. Said it was just the old copper's instincts. But he never used to be like that.' She paused. 'I could see it when he left here. He'd started looking both ways, up and down the street. As if he thought there might be someone waiting for him.'

'How long had he been like this?'

'I'm not sure exactly. A few weeks.'

'You've no idea why?'

'Billy wouldn't even admit there was an issue. I tried to raise it once when it first started. You can imagine how he responded.'

'Aye, I can imagine.' Crawford hadn't been the type to show any kind of weakness, especially not to a woman. 'You didn't see anything that might have accounted for the way he was behaving? Anybody suspicious hanging around? Anything like that?'

'Nothing at all.' She allowed herself a laugh. 'I thought he was finally getting past it.'

He pushed himself to his feet. 'I'll leave you to it, Mrs Barnard. Thanks for your time. That's really been very helpful.'

She followed him to the door. 'You really think someone killed him?' It was the second time she'd asked the question. However blasé she might pretend to be, it was clear she was rattled.

'We've really no reason to think so, Mrs Barnard,' he said as he pulled on the heavy waterproof. It was true, as far as it went, at least until the post-mortem had been completed. 'But, like I say, we have to consider every possibility.' He paused as she opened the front door. 'Look, we'll be as discreet as we can in handling this. But I can't make any promises.'

'I understand. It may seem a bit late for this, but I really don't want Jeanie to be hurt.'

Aye, a bit bloody late for that, McKay thought. Out loud, he said, 'We'll do what we can. I imagine my colleagues may well want to talk with you further.' *Especially*, he added to himself, *when Helena Grant finds out what I've been up to.*

He stepped out into the chill night, watching his breath cloud the damp air. As Meg Barnard closed the door behind him, he found himself involuntarily echoing Crawford's behaviour and glancing down to the dark end of the street.

CHAPTER TWENTY-SEVEN

The rain had stopped for the moment, and McKay's first instinct was to head back to the bungalow. He'd done himself more than enough damage for one night.

Then, he took another look down towards the far end of the street. *Bugger*, he thought. That was his problem. He could never leave things be. Still muttering to himself, he trudged slowly down the final hundred metres to where the road ended. There was a fenced-off patch of ground to the left that looked as if it had been bought by a developer with the intention of building more housing. Now, it was overgrown and abandoned. Maybe the money had run out, McKay thought, or the market hadn't been there.

Ahead, beyond the end of the adopted road, the land fell away, grassland dotted with trees descending towards the firth. McKay took another few steps forward, feeling the wet undergrowth give beneath his feet. He moved to the right, peering into the dark until he found a clear line of sight to the sea. He could only just make it out, the water faintly translucent in the blackness, but it was no distance away – thirty or forty metres at the most.

He made his way further down the hillside, wondering how Crawford could have accidentally fallen into the water. Even if he really had been desperate for a piss, there was no reason to detour far from the road. It was possible that Crawford had entered the water elsewhere – there were other points in the village that gave access to the firth. But it was even harder to imagine what might have taken Crawford to any of those.

McKay was turning to head back up to the street when he heard the movement behind him. He froze, suddenly struck by an irrational sense that someone had been watching him all the time he'd been here. He'd been half-crouched, peering down at the water, but now, he straightened and stared back into the blackness. He could make out nothing but the slow sway of the trees against the buffeting sea wind.

Then, suddenly, he felt a weight against his back and the tight grip of gloved hands on his throat. He stumbled forward, flailing wildly against whoever was behind him, but could gain no purchase. The fingers on his throat tightened, the sharp edges of leather gloves biting into his flesh, forcing him down on to his knees.

His instincts working more quickly than his conscious mind, McKay rolled to his left, trying to pull his assailant on to the ground beside him, hoping that the impact would loosen the grip around his neck. He reached behind, straining for his attacker's face, his fingers searching for a point of vulnerability.

The grip slackened only momentarily as their two bodies struck the ground, but it was sufficient for McKay. Lying sideways on the wet earth, his feet found a grip, and he thrust himself backwards, driving his attacker's body hard against the trunk of an adjacent tree. He heard a brief gasp of surprise, and the hands on his throat loosened enough for McKay to pull free. He rolled forwards, twisting to see who was behind him.

He'd expected his assailant would be too winded to make an immediate move, but even before McKay could fully turn, the figure was up and running down towards the water. McKay lay, breathless, contemplating whether to give chase. But the figure was already out of sight, presumably heading back up towards the village, and McKay was in no state for running.

He dragged himself to his feet, looking down ruefully at his damp, mud-stained trousers. Jesus. What the hell was going on? Had someone been watching him all the time he was down here? Had they seen him visiting Meg Barnard's house? And why the fuck were they even interested in him?

Galloway, Crawford and Graham. A poisonous fucking trio back in the day. Watching each other's backs, but all too ready to stick a knife in them too. Lining their own pockets whenever they got half a chance, and not caring who they screwed over to do it.

Once upon a time, he could have named a dozen individuals who'd have been glad to see the back of all three of them. But that was a long time ago. Half those people would be dead, and the rest would be in their dotage. Why the hell would all this start up now?

He began the slow walk back into the centre of the village. The rain had started falling again, chilling the air and misting the orange street lights. McKay's body was bruised and aching, his clothes stained and damp. At that moment, even the bleak bungalow in Rosemarkie – the only place he could think of calling home – felt a million miles away.

And, of course, Helena Grant was going to be pissed as hell with him.

Well done, Alec, he thought. *Another great evening to write up in the fucking diary. Another fucking fine mess.*

CHAPTER TWENTY-EIGHT

'You know, Alec,' Helena Grant said, 'I think that's the first time you've ever begun a conversation with me by saying "you're not going to like this." Usually, you just try to brazen your way through whatever it is you've royally screwed up.'

'Aye, well,' McKay said from the other end of the phone line, 'it was a bit of an experiment. Thought I'd try a different approach.'

'Which means that, this time, even you know you've fucked up. It must be something really fucking serious.' She held the phone away from her and squinted at it, as if that might provide her some additional insight into McKay's unfathomable mind.

'Ach, well, it's not so bad,' he said. 'I just found myself getting a bit more – involved than I intended.'

'Go on, Alec. Tell me all about it,' she said wearily. The truth was, however much she might want McKay back in the fold, this conversation was the last thing she needed. She'd spent the first hour of the morning having an earnest heart-to-heart with poor Ginny Horton. Horton had been waiting outside Grant's office, looking more uncomfortable than Grant had ever seen her.

'Ginny?'

'I thought I'd better come and talk to you before anyone else did.'

Horton's confession, as it turned out, had been largely innocuous – essentially that she'd called out the uniforms the previous night for what sounded to Grant like entirely legitimate reasons.

'You did the right thing, Ginny. Obviously. You're not denied access to the emergency services just because you're a police officer yourself.'

Grant had nodded. 'Yes, I know. It's just – embarrassing. Especially as David had already buggered off by the time they arrived. I don't even know that he really meant me any harm.'

'It sounds as if, at the very least, he wanted to scare the hell out of you.'

'He succeeded pretty well on that front.'

She'd listened patiently while Horton had recounted her history with her stepfather. She'd encountered too many men like that – arrogant, manipulative, abusive. Plenty of them, truth be told, in the force. For a certain kind of copper, at least in the past, it had pretty much gone with the territory. She could only give thanks that the particular copper she'd chosen to marry had been a very different breed. But, of course, he'd been snatched from her far too early.

'You still think he might be a threat, though?'

'I honestly don't know,' Horton had said. 'Maybe there are things he really does want to tell me.'

'He could always write you a letter. He doesn't have to try to force his way through your front door.' Her guess was that, whatever he might want to share with Horton, the stepfather was playing the same games he'd always played. Making others dance to his tune. Men like that never really changed.

'Anyway, don't worry about it. No doubt there'll be a bit of gossip below stairs. But they'll always find something to gossip about. Give them twenty-four hours and they'll have moved on.'

Now, an hour or so later, Grant found herself having yet another heart-to-heart, this time with Alec McKay. Except, of course, that being Alec, it was far less straightforward.

She listened to his account of his visit to the Caledonian Bar in silence, already seeing where this was going. 'Please don't tell me you went 'round to see this Meg Barnard, Alec.'

There was a pause. 'Aye, well, I can see, with hindsight, it maybe wasn't the smartest of moves –'

'You can see that, can you, Alec? With hindsight? Just remind me again how long you've been a police officer?' She didn't really feel angry. Just very weary. But McKay often had that effect on her.

'Well, I know –'

'Look, Alec. Yesterday, I came within a hair's breadth of suspending you. For your own good. I tell you to take some leave and spend some time mending fences with Chrissie. Instead, you stick your nose back into the case and take it on yourself to interview a bloody witness. Potentially compromising anything she might have had to say.' She took a breath. 'You're not stupid, Alec. So, I can only assume you're doing this to drive me into an early grave.'

'It was only –'

'Don't even think of trying to justify this, Alec. Whatever I might or might not think, the truth is you're still potentially a bloody suspect in this case. I should do this by the book.'

There was an extended silence which told her that McKay knew he'd pushed it too far this time. Christ, he could be a numpty sometimes.

Finally, she said, 'I'm probably going to regret this, Alec. But I'll give you just one more chance. Stay at home. Mind your own bloody business. And, like I say, go and talk to Chrissie.'

'I ran into her,' McKay said, sounding relieved to change the subject. 'In the supermarket.'

'How was she?'

'Ach, you know. Civilised.' McKay made this sound like a disreputable quality. 'I said we should talk.'

'And what did she say?'

'She said, aye, when she was ready.'

'That sounds positive.'

'Maybe. She didn't exactly sound eager, though.'

'It'll take time, Alec. But you need to keep trying.'

'Aye, well. Maybe I'll give her a call. See how she responds.'

'You do that, Alec.'

There was another pause before he said, 'And thanks, hen.'

Before she could respond, he ended the call. Thanks for what, she wondered. For, once again, letting him off the hook? For encouraging him to talk to Chrissie? Either way, she knew it must have cost him to say it. Alec McKay wasn't a man to show his feelings, even at that rudimentary level.

Just as long as he really did keep his nose out this time. As it was, she'd have to arrange for someone else to go and talk to Meg Barnard. It didn't sound as if Barnard was likely to be a material witness, but she looked to be another piece in an increasingly complex jigsaw.

They'd had the expedited post-mortem and forensic results back for Jackie Galloway, but those had told them little. The cause of Galloway's death had been the trauma caused by the fall. There was no other evidence of foul play, but there'd been no reason to expect any. If Galloway had been pushed, it wouldn't have taken much force.

The forensics on the Galloways' house were equally inconclusive. There was a jumble of fingerprints and DNA traces, but Galloway had received care visits three times a day. According to Bridie Galloway, there'd been a handful of regular carers but a large rotating cast of stand-ins, with unfamiliar faces popping up several times in a week. They were in touch with the care agency, trying to identify all those who might have visited in recent months. But Grant wasn't confident much would result from those efforts.

The forensics on Crawford had told them nothing. The body had been tossed and turned in the firth for too long for any useful evidence to be left. There was some evidence of bruising that might have suggested a physical assault, but Jock Henderson had been reluctant to offer a view. The post-mortem report should be with them today. Maybe that would shed further light.

As for Graham, foul play looked more likely. It was difficult to see how he'd have ended up with his head face down in the burn otherwise, though Grant had come across stranger events in her career. They were still waiting on the forensics and post-mortem there.

She leaned back in her chair, gazing through the office window at the strip of grey sky visible above the Inverness skyline. There was something McKay hadn't told her, she thought, reflecting on her telephone conversation of a few minutes earlier. Not, in fairness, that she'd given him much chance to get a word in edgeways.

But, after all these years, she knew Alec McKay. There was something he hadn't said. And that worried her. If there was something he'd held back, it was either because of something he'd done or something he was planning to do. Either way, she thought, if Alec McKay was involved, the outcome was likely to be trouble.

CHAPTER TWENTY-NINE

McKay sat in silence, staring at the screen of his mobile as if it might tell him something more than the fact that his call to Helena Grant had lasted precisely four minutes and thirty-four seconds. That was the trouble with the modern world. You had every last scrap of useless information at your fingertips. But nothing that really mattered.

Why the fuck hadn't he told Grant about the previous night's attack? Was it because he'd been afraid she wouldn't believe him? That she might think he was concocting some story to demonstrate that he was another victim here, not the potential perpetrator? After all, in the cold light of morning, McKay could hardly believe it himself.

McKay had little doubt that the attacker had wanted to kill him. After the incident, he realised now, he'd been partly in shock. It was as if his emotions had shut down, preventing him from appreciating the impact of the assault. It was only as he lay down to sleep in that narrow, rented bed that he registered how lucky he'd been. If his instincts had been less acute, if he'd been a second slower in responding, those gloved hands would have tightened remorselessly around his throat. His body would have ended up tossed into the firth, just as Billy Crawford's had been.

This bleak thought had been confirmed the next morning when he'd looked in the bathroom mirror and seen the purple bruising on his neck, felt the skin tender to his touch. That had been no opportunistic mugging. It had been attempted murder.

Even so, none of that explained why he hadn't told Grant. If his life really was in danger, he ought to be shouting it from the bloody rooftops, not sitting here moping over a cup of coffee in this godforsaken bungalow, puzzling his own brain about why anyone might want him dead.

But it had never been his way to seek anyone's help. He was a proud bloody Dundonian male, too sodding stubborn to do anything just for his own good. Chrissie had always told him that was his trouble, or at least one of his troubles, and he hadn't honestly been able to deny she was right. It was why he'd never wanted to seek help in dealing with his daughter Lizzie's death or in holding his marriage together. Whatever the consequences, he'd rather struggle on, doing his own thing.

Now, someone out there, for whatever reason, wanted him dead. And he still couldn't bring himself to seek help. Without further antagonising Helena Grant, there was little he could do even to help himself.

All he could do was sit here, and wait and watch. And try to work out who the hell that someone might be.

***

That afternoon, they finally began to make some progress. Helena Grant had been trying to grab a spare five minutes in the company of one of the canteen's tuna sandwiches when her phone rang.

'Helena? Jacquie Green.'

Grant sat up straight in her chair. Dr Jacquie Green was the Senior Forensic Pathologist the local force mostly used for its post-mortems. 'Hi, Jacquie. What can I do for you?'

'More a question of what I've done for you,' Green said. 'Not that you'll necessarily want to thank me.'

'Go on.'

'I carried out the PM on Crawford this morning.'

'Something interesting?'

'You might say that. Not easy to be sure. The body had taken quite a battering in the water. But there were signs of bruising on the neck that suggest to me his death wasn't from natural causes. My view is that he was unconscious before he entered the water.'

Grant was silent for a moment. 'You're saying he was – what? Strangled?'

'That's exactly what I'm saying. The position of the bruising suggests he was grabbed from behind. Hands around the throat, I'd say.'

'That would be possible? To render him unconscious, I mean.'

'If you're strong and determined enough, definitely.'

'You're sure about this?'

Green laughed. 'You questioning my professional judgement, pal?'

Green was a tall, intense-looking woman with close-cropped dark hair. Most people, particularly her male colleagues, found her intimidating, but Grant had long ago discovered that she and Green were two of a kind. They got on well outside the workplace, especially when their conversation was lubricated with a decent bottle of shiraz or two. 'I wouldn't dare.'

'Very wise. I mean, there's always some element of doubt. In this case, more so because of the traumas that the body suffered in the water. But I'm pretty sure, yes. And not only that –'

Grant had already guessed that there was something else. 'Rob Graham?'

'Yup. In the circumstances, I thought I should get straight on to Graham. Exactly the same. And not much doubt there. Strangled. Unconscious. Then his head held in the water until he was dead. As clear as – well, as clear as Rosemarkie Burn.'

'Jesus. So, we definitely have a case?'

'I'd say you definitely have two cases.'

'Which means we probably have three.'

'Three?'

'Aye. Jackie Galloway.'

'Galloway? Died from the fall? You think that's connected?'

'Hell of a coincidence if not. Three ex-colleagues. All living in the same area. All dead within days of each other. And there are other connecting factors.'

'You want me to take another look at Galloway?'

'If you've time. But I imagine your original conclusions were right. If someone wanted to kill him, it wouldn't have taken more than a gentle push. Easy enough to make it look like an accident.'

'The killer might have managed that with Crawford, too, if the body had stayed in the water longer,' Green said. 'But it doesn't look as if any effort was made to make Graham's death look accidental. So, either the killer's getting more careless, or they're not bothered about concealing their intentions.'

'My guess would be the latter,' Helena Grant said. 'If you wanted to be discreet, you wouldn't commit three murders in as many days. This is someone who wants us to know what they're doing.'

'Fair point. So, the question is: have I made things better or worse?'

It was Grant's turn to laugh. 'Well, you've made them a lot clearer. At least we can confirm to the Procurator that we've got something worth investigating. Which means I can probably scrape up some half-decent resources to throw at it.' She paused, serious again. 'And this is police family business.'

'I'd heard that,' Green said. 'I'll get the reports to you by close of play. But I've told you the salient stuff.'

Grant ended the call and sat for a moment, thinking about what she'd just been saying. Police family business. That was true enough, whatever people might have thought about Galloway and his gang. This would be high profile. The top brass would be sticking their noses in. There'd be media interest. This would be national news.

That carried a lot of implications, for the force and for her as the Senior Investigating Officer.

One of which, she thought, was the question of just what she should do now about Alec McKay.

CHAPTER THIRTY

Ginny Horton had been trying to lose herself in work. She didn't want to think about what had happened the previous evening. She didn't want to think about what her uniformed colleagues might be saying about her. Above all, she didn't want to think about David. Where he might be or what he might be up to.

Luckily, throwing herself back into work wasn't difficult. With McKay absent, her workload was even heavier than usual. She had half a dozen or more cases on the go, some continuing investigations, others completed but with administration still to do. And then, there were the cases still to come to court, like last year's multiple murder. That was largely done and dusted from their perspective, but there would still be witness statements to give, briefings with the Advocate Deputy, all the usual paperwork associated with a major trial.

Horton still had an uneasy feeling about that case. It should have been cut and dried. The killer was dead, his daughter expected to plead guilty to his and another murder but with more than enough extenuating circumstances to limit her sentence. There wasn't much doubt how it was likely to go.

But there was something about the way McKay had talked about the case that left her uncomfortable. As if there was something that troubled him. Something he wasn't saying. As if he didn't believe the case was quite yet closed.

That was all a matter for another day. For the moment, she had more than enough to be getting on with. And that had been before Helena Grant had come in to break the news about the Crawford and Graham post-mortems. Grant had already been working the phones, pulling together all the resources she could, drafting in additional support from across the division. They'd had a planning meeting that morning, allocating officers to various tasks, and the Incident Room was taking shape downstairs. Grant was currently meeting with the Communications team to decide how to play the story for the media. They couldn't keep it under wraps for long now and, in any case, might well want to make an appeal for possible witnesses. But they all knew that the media would have a field day with a story like this.

For the present, they were supposedly making no assumptions about the linkages between the deaths, and Galloway's was still being characterised as "unexplained" rather than "suspicious." That was good practice – it was too easy to be seduced into drawing premature conclusions – but no one had much doubt this was a single investigation.

She was missing McKay, she realised, and more than she'd expected. She'd always seen him as a mentor, if not always a reliable one, and had come to see him as a friend. At times like this, she had grown to recognise the value not just of his experience and knowledge, but also of his chippy self-assurance and resilience.

Her last conversation with McKay, though just the previous evening, already felt like a lifetime ago. Still, she'd remembered McKay's advice to investigate more of Galloway's former colleagues and – without mentioning McKay's name – had shared that thought with Helena Grant. As she'd expected, Grant was already ahead of her and had drawn up a shortlist of those she thought worth approaching. Horton had been allocated to talk to some of these, including Alastair Donald and Davey Robertson.

She was on her way out of the office when she felt her mobile buzzing in her pocket.

'DS Horton? Sergeant Willock here.'

It took her a moment to place Willock. One of the small number of officers attached to the largely civilian Force Control Room. He was a heavily built man, who, from what she recalled, was one of the old school. She half expected he was ringing to take the piss, with a cluster of associates hanging out in the background.

Instead, he went on, 'You're part of this Crawford and Graham investigation, is that right?'

'That's right. But DI Grant's the SIO.' With anyone else, she'd be using forenames by now, but Willock wasn't one to encourage such niceties.

'I've been trying to contact DI Grant,' he said, with what sounded like a touch of impatience, 'but she's tied up at the moment. I was given your name.' His tone suggested this represented some kind of booby prize.

'How can I help you?'

'We've had another reported missing person. We thought it might be of interest.'

She'd returned to her desk and, with her free hand, was fumbling for a pen and notebook. 'Go on.'

'Call came in early this afternoon. A Mrs Donald.'

'Donald?'

'Aye. Ringing a bell, is it?'

'It might be.'

'Mrs Donald told us her husband had gone out last night and not returned. Interestingly, she apparently hadn't been too surprised or concerned about that. Far from the first time, was my impression. But then she had a call from his employer – local garden centre – enquiring why he'd not turned in to work.'

'And that was more unusual?'

'Seems so. Not one to miss a day's work, Mr Donald. That's how I remember him as well.'

Ah, she thought. *Willock had been saving that up.* 'This is Alastair Donald?'

She was gratified to hear a note of surprise in Willock's response. 'You're ahead of me, then?'

'Not on the missing person front,' she said. 'But Donald's on our list to speak to about the Crawford and Graham cases.'

'Aye, that'd be right,' Willock said. 'He was one of that unholy crew right enough. Wee bastard.'

Willock was beginning to sound almost human, Horton thought. It was clear that Jackie Galloway's team held a special place in his heart. 'You weren't a fan.'

'Well, to be honest, it takes a lot for me to feel any respect for you plain-clothes lot.' It wasn't entirely clear whether or not Willock was joking. 'But that bunch were worse than most. Arrogant wee gobshites, pardon my French. Thought they could do whatever they liked, or step on whoever they wanted.'

'And Donald was part of that?'

'I always thought he was a bit of a wannabe, to be honest. Not part of the inner circle. But that made him worse. Always trying to prove himself. You know the type.'

She knew the type well enough, and McKay had said much the same thing. 'What's your view on him supposedly going missing?' she asked.

'I'd be inclined to take it seriously. Donald was a tosspot, but he was always a stickler for discipline. Not the sort to miss work and not even phone in. Doesn't feel right to me. Shall I send the details over?'

'Yes. Send them to me. Donald was on my list to follow up anyway. I'll brief DI Grant.'

'Thanks. Only too delighted.'

Shit, she thought as she ended the call. Another one. Another retired officer. Another former member of Galloway's team. She logged into her email and saw that the information from Willock had already arrived.

It took her only a few seconds to read through the limited details in the note Willock had sent over. Donald's address was up in Cromarty. Yet another retired member of Galloway's gang living up in the Black Isle.

Grant's mobile was still going straight to voicemail, so she was presumably still locked in discussion with Comms. *At this rate, they might all find themselves overtaken by events,* Horton thought. She left Grant a brief message explaining what had happened and confirming that, in line with the original plan, she'd head up to Cromarty. The difference now was that it looked as if she'd be talking to Mrs Donald rather than her husband.

Well, she thought, *it ought to be an interesting conversation.*

CHAPTER THIRTY-ONE

McKay spent the afternoon pacing up and down the narrow spaces of the bungalow with the air of a cage-bound animal seeking an escape route. He could already feel himself growing stir-crazy. He cooked himself beans on toast for lunch, spent fifteen minutes watching the daytime news, and then started pacing again, pausing only occasionally to stare out of the kitchen window at the distant line of the sea.

After an hour or so of this, he threw on his coat and stepped out into the damp afternoon air. The weather had improved from the previous evening, but the sky was still heavy with clouds. The waters of the firth looked grey and forbidding, and a strong wind was driving the waves high up the narrow beach.

As he reached the main road, he turned his back to the sea and trudged up the hill to the high street. His plan, born mainly from the lack of any other ideas, was to visit the local convenience store, buy himself a few beers and one or two other items he needed. As a former heavy drinker, back in the days when it was almost a requirement of the job, he was acutely aware of the dangers of solitary drinking. But a few beers wouldn't do any harm, he told himself. He couldn't face the thought of a long solitary evening in complete sobriety. And he was gradually rendering most of the local bars out of bounds.

The shop was empty. McKay imagined it did most of its business during the tourist season. It was a well-stocked little place, aimed at holidaymakers in self-catering cottages and caravans who couldn't be bothered to traipse to the larger but more distant supermarkets. McKay threw some bread and a tub of butter into his basket, along with a pint of milk, and then selected some beers from the array of bottles on the shelves, most of them from the local breweries in Cromarty and Munlochy. He exchanged a few words with the bored-looking middle-aged man behind the counter then, laden with an embarrassingly clinking bag of bottles, stepped out into the daylight.

'Mr McKay?'

He looked up, surprised. 'Mrs Galloway.'

'Ach, call me Bridie.' Bridie Galloway looked a different woman from the person he'd spoken to a couple of days before. As if she'd dropped twenty years overnight. She was dressed in a neat, if slightly shabby, raincoat, but with a bright floral headscarf tied round her hair.

He smiled. 'You'd best call me Alec, then.'

'Aye, I think I can bring myself to do that.' She gestured towards the bag. 'What brings you back up here? Not just the quality of our local shops, surely.'

He blinked, slightly taken aback by her lightness of tone. A recently bereaved widow, her husband as yet unburied.

But then, the husband in question was Jackie Galloway. No wonder she was looking relaxed. 'Actually, I'm living up here these days. Temporarily, at least.'

She was astute enough not to follow that one up. 'Ach, well,' she said, 'there are worse places to live.' She paused. 'Look, I was just popping over to get some milk. Would you fancy coming back for a cup of tea? I could do with a bit of company.'

He hesitated. Every rational impulse was telling him he'd be a fool to accept. Helena Grant had already made it abundantly clear that it was approaching kicking-out time in the last chance saloon, and here he was, being invited back for tea by someone who was at least notionally a suspect in her own husband's killing. But the more prosaic truth was that she was simply an elderly widow looking for some companionship.

'Aye, why not? And I can save you the trouble.' He raised the bag. 'I've a spare bottle of milk in here.'

'If you're sure you can spare it.'

He'd only really bought the milk, along with the other few staples, because he hadn't wanted to be seen purchasing nothing but alcohol. 'I reckon so.'

He followed her across the street and waited while she unlocked the front door of the bungalow. Inside, he noticed she'd already rearranged some of the furniture. The sitting room looked brighter, though he couldn't immediately work out what she'd changed, other than to move what had been Jackie Galloway's favourite armchair away from the fireplace and the television.

McKay sat down and gazed around the room while she brewed the tea. There were no obvious signs that Jackie Galloway had ever lived here. There were no joint pictures of the Galloways, and nothing that would obviously have belonged to a man.

Bridie Galloway came bustling back through with the tea on a plastic tray, placing it on the table in front of him. She sat herself at the opposite end of the sofa and busied herself pouring the two teas.

'How are you managing?' McKay asked.

'Ach, you know. Keeping busy,' she said. 'It's a bit strange, having this place to myself. But I'm getting used to it.'

I bet you are, McKay thought. 'Have you seen much of other people?'

'The neighbours are very kind,' she said. 'There's been a lot to do. I had to let the carer agency know, and the local council. And I've had to start thinking about the funeral.'

'Have the police told you when you'll be able to go ahead with that?' McKay knew that Galloway's body was being held pending the decision on the investigation.

'I was hoping you might be able to tell me something about that,' she said pointedly.

McKay shifted awkwardly. 'I'm not working on the case, I'm afraid. I don't really have any inside track.'

She looked up at him in surprise. 'Oh, I'd assumed you were.' Maybe that was why she'd invited him back here for tea. McKay suspected that Bridie Galloway wasn't quite as guileless as her appearance might suggest.

'I'm afraid not,' he said. 'Not really sure why,' he added vaguely. 'Maybe they thought I was too close to it, having known your husband.'

'They called me this morning. Said the Procurator had requested the investigation should be extended. So, I don't know when it's likely to be.'

'I'm sure they'll keep you informed as much as they possibly can.'

'I'm sorry you're not involved in the investigation, Alec,' she said. 'Jackie rated you. And it would have been helpful to have someone who knew Jackie and his background.'

Don't you worry yourself, hen, McKay said to himself. *Plenty of people knew about Jackie Galloway and his background.* Out loud, he said, 'They'll have good people taking care of it, don't you worry.'

'Aye, I'm sure. There's three deaths now, aren't there? Three of Jackie's old team. That can't be coincidence.'

'It looks strange, right enough,' McKay said noncommittally. He could feel that Bridie Galloway was fishing for information. Fortunately, he had nothing he could have shared with her, even if he'd wanted to.

'I get scared, sometimes,' she said. 'Thinking about it. Thinking about those letters. Someone wanted Jackie dead.'

'It still might have just been an accident,' McKay pointed out. 'Coincidences happen.'

'You don't believe that, do you?' she said. 'Not really.'

'I don't know what I think about it.'

'Jackie made enemies. You all make enemies. It goes with the job.' She paused. 'And I know that Jackie – well, sometimes had his own way of doing things.'

That was one way of putting it, McKay thought. It was his turn to go fishing. 'How do you mean?'

'You know what I mean. He didn't always play by the rules. He did what it took to get a result. He used to boast about it to me sometimes. Said it made him a real copper.'

'Aye, well, it's a point of view. But I wouldn't know anything about any of that, Bridie. I was just a young rookie.'

'Aye, no doubt,' she said, sceptically. 'But if I were you – or your colleagues – I'd start looking at some of those last cases of Jackie's.'

'What makes you say that?'

'That last one,' she said. 'The drugs raid. That was the one that got all the attention because it all went pear-shaped. That was the one that ended Jackie's career.'

As well as ending some poor bugger's life, McKay thought. 'You think that's relevant?'

'I don't know,' she said. 'Maybe not that one. Jackie had already changed by then –'

'Changed?'

'He was a different man in that last year at work. He was coming up to retirement, anyway – that was why he was so angry about what happened – and I thought that was probably the reason.'

'How did he change?'

'It wasn't obvious. Well, it wouldn't have been to anyone who knew him less well than I did. But he became … I don't know … less brash, less cocky. Less sure of himself. Even slightly fearful, as if he was worried about something. Started taking a lot more care of security back home – this was when we were still living in Inverness.'

'You think this was something to do with an investigation?'

'That's the way it felt to me. As if something had happened that had rattled him. He wasn't someone who'd let that kind of thing show. But it was there, right enough.'

'But you don't have any idea what it might have been?'

'He never brought his work home. Not in that sense. He never talked about any of the investigations. Maybe occasionally, once they were concluded, he'd give me the gist. But not while they were going on. It was nothing he said. Just the way he behaved.'

McKay was inclined to take this seriously. Bridie Galloway struck him as an astute woman, and for all her sins, she'd known her husband better than anyone else had. 'And you think this was something to do with one of those last cases?'

'That was my impression. Whatever else he was, Jackie was no coward. He wasn't a nervous man, you know?'

'Aye, I know,' McKay agreed. That would have been the last word he'd have used to describe Jackie Galloway. The first one would probably have been an expletive. He sat drinking his tea, thinking. 'Have you told the police any of this, Bridie?'

'Not yet. It's only now that the dust's settled I've started thinking about it again. And it seems so – insubstantial. Do you think it's worth mentioning?'

'If Jackie's death was more than accidental – and I'm guessing that's still not entirely clear – they'll need all the leads they can get. Anything might help.'

'They?'

Aye, astute enough, McKay thought. He was already talking as if he was no longer part of all this. Maybe that was how he was feeling. As if, without realising, he'd already begun to put his career behind him. 'Like I say, Bridie, I'm not involved in the investigation. I can pass on what you've said, but it might have more impact coming from you. They'll be wanting to speak to you again, I'm sure.'

'Aye, they said that. Said they'd be in touch.'

'So, talk it through with them. Tell them what you felt. It may be nothing. But it may give them something to follow up.'

'Do you think I should be worried?'

'Worried?'

'If something happened to Jackie – and those others, Billy and Rob – someone out there's got a grudge. Should I be worried about my safety?'

In truth, McKay had no idea. None of this made much sense to him. But he could see little point in scaring an elderly widow. 'I can't see it, Bridie. The only victims so far – and that's if they even are victims – were retired police officers. If this is about revenge, they're the targets.'

She looked unconvinced. 'I've been locking up carefully,' she said. 'Stopped leaving the key in the key safe. I might see if I can afford to get the locks changed.'

McKay gazed back her, this frail elderly woman. The only thing she'd had to celebrate in the last couple of decades had been, maybe, the unexpected death of her husband. And even that had just left her with a different set of anxieties. 'Aye, Bridie,' he said. 'Better to be safe than sorry. And, while I'm up here, I'll do my best to keep an eye out for you.'

'Ach, you're a decent man, Alec McKay.'

It had been a long time, McKay thought, since anyone had said that about him.

CHAPTER THIRTY-TWO

'**W**eird,' DC Josh Carlisle said.

Horton glanced across at him. 'You must have been here before?' Carlisle had matured in the last couple of years – mainly as a result of working for Alec McKay, she assumed – but still looked fresh out of school. He had swept-back ginger hair, already threatening to recede, and the kind of rosy-pink cheeks normally provided only by a healthy hike through the hills or an unhealthy excess of alcohol. Neither, as far as Horton was aware, was high on Carlisle's list of vices.

'I suppose,' Carlisle said. 'As a child, maybe.' He made it sound as if this period was lost somewhere in the mists of time.

They were parked on the waterfront in Cromarty, looking out over the firth towards the industrial units at Nigg. A place where oil platforms and similar equipment were brought to be repaired or dismantled. The overall effect was mildly surreal – a peaceful maritime idyll mixed with the product of heavy industry. Horton always found the combination oddly satisfying, as if the two worlds were complementary.

The weather was continuing to improve, with shafts of sunlight periodically breaking through the cloud. Horton had parked up to return the call she'd just received from Helena Grant.

She thumbed Grant's number. 'Helena? Ginny. Just arrived in Cromarty.'

'Ally Donald? Doesn't sound promising in the circumstances.'

'No, we're losing ex-coppers a bit too frequently at the moment.'

'Tell me about it. I've just emerged from two hours with the Chief Super and the Head of Comms wanting to know what I'm doing about it. Everything I can, I told them, but oddly, they didn't seem satisfied with that. Last thing we need's another one.'

'Maybe this one's just a coincidence.'

'Aye, maybe. And maybe the Chief Super's really a sweetheart, but I'm not hopeful on either count. We're going to go live with the story this afternoon.'

'That'll set some hares running.'

'Right enough. But the word's already starting to leak out to the local media. They're not daft when it comes to putting two and two together. But given half a chance, they'll come out with an answer much bigger than four. Comms think it best we give them whatever hand we can with their arithmetic.'

'It's going to be a big story, however it's played.'

'No way 'round that. But we're going to keep it low-key for the moment. Keep Galloway's death out of the picture if we can – apart from the letters, we've still no evidence that wasn't an accident – and say we're pursuing various leads linked to Crawford and Graham's time in the force. What we don't want is for people to start thinking there's some sort of indiscriminate killer out there.'

'This one seems all too discriminating,' Horton agreed.

'We're also going to make an appeal for witnesses,' Grant went on. 'Crawford and Graham both went missing relatively early in the evening. Someone might have seen something, maybe without realising the significance of what they were seeing. It's a long shot, but we may hit lucky with a dog walker or a curtain twitcher. I thought you'd want the heads-up before the proverbial hits the fan.'

'Thanks,' Horton said. 'We'll let you know whether it looks like you've got another name to add to the list.'

The Donalds' bungalow was a neat-looking place on a small estate at the edge of the village. The sort of development that Horton could imagine being occupied by a mix of retired couples and younger families with parents who commuted into Inverness for work. Not exactly prosperous, but not short of a bob or two either.

Mrs Donald answered the doorbell as if she'd been standing awaiting their arrival. 'You'd best come in,' she said, when they'd introduced themselves. 'Would you like some tea?'

Horton would normally have declined the offer, but this time, with a brief glance at Carlisle, she accepted. She wanted time to get a sense of Mrs Donald, of the bungalow and, most of all, of what sort of marriage this had been. She'd been struck, on their arrival, by the apparent lightness of Mrs Donald's manner. Not quite the anxious wife. That was beginning to feel like a pattern in this enquiry.

'You reported your husband missing earlier this afternoon?' Horton began, once they were seated back in the sitting room.

While they'd been waiting, she'd looked carefully around the room. Nothing obviously untoward. The room was, to Horton's eyes, conspicuously tidy, nothing out of place. The only apparent blemish was an odd staining to the wallpaper by the fireplace. A good effort had been made to remove it, but the mark was still there and looked relatively fresh. It looked as if something had been spilled against it, but it was hard to see how that might have happened. There was, Horton thought, a faint smell of stale alcohol in the air.

Mrs Donald nodded nervously in response to Horton's question, her expression suggesting some fear of being wrong-footed. 'I wasn't sure anyone would take it seriously before then.'

'It always depends on the circumstances, Mrs Donald. I understand your husband hadn't returned home last night. Were you expecting him to be away?'

There was an unexpectedly long silence. 'He – sometimes stays away, yes. I wasn't entirely surprised.'

'He hadn't told you he was expecting to be away overnight?'

'No. Not as such. No.'

'Not as such,' Horton repeated. 'Look, Mrs Donald, I've no desire to be intrusive. But, in the circumstances, I do need to ask you. Where did you understand your husband to be last night?'

Another silence. 'He has a friend. I assumed he'd stayed with them.'

'And have you spoken to your husband's – friend?'

'I – No, that's not really possible.'

'Mrs Donald?'

'There's – well, another woman,' Mrs Donald said finally. 'Ally never made much secret of it. He never said it in so many words, but in every other way he used to rub my nose in it. As if it was my fault. As if I'd driven him to –' She stopped and took a mouthful of her tea. Her eyes, Horton noticed, were dry. There was plenty of emotion there, but little that looked like sorrow.

'You think that's where he spent last night?'

'That's what I thought. We'd had – words earlier. He stormed out. I imagined he was heading to the pub. When he didn't come back, I thought he'd spent the night – well, you know.'

'Did that sort of thing happen often?'

'Often enough. He's a difficult man. Difficult to please. If something made him unhappy –'

Horton could easily imagine. She'd spent the early part of her life under the influence of a man not unlike that. 'Was he often unhappy?'

'It didn't take much.'

Horton gave a pointed glance towards the fireplace. 'Can I ask –?'

'Aye. Well spotted. He lost his temper last night and threw his supper at me. I did my best to clean it up this morning.'

Because if you hadn't, Horton added silently to herself, the old bastard would complain about the mess. She remembered how her own mother had struggled with the same kinds of dilemma. 'Talk me through yesterday evening. What exactly happened?'

'Ally got in from work. That was about seven. He only works part time at the garden centre these days, so he'd have been finished long before that. I assumed he'd been to the pub.'

'Did he often do that?'

'Most days, unless some of them he went off to his fancy woman.'

'Was he drunk when he came in?'

'Not so's you'd notice,' Mrs Donald said. 'He knew how to hold his booze. Took a lot before you saw Ally drunk. He just became more and more aggressive.'

'He was aggressive last night?'

'No more than usual. He was complaining I hadn't got supper on the table, even though, as always, he'd given me no idea when to expect him. He complained I'd been drinking.'

'Had you?'

'A few glasses of wine. Not that it was any of his business.' Or yours, was the unspoken implication.

'Then what happened?'

'I got him some supper. One of those ready meal things. A curry. Cooked it for him and served it to him in here. He complained it was cold. Ended up throwing the plate at me.'

Horton had lived through many of the same kind of scenes. The man who could never be satisfied. Who always found fault with whatever was done for him. The man who could manipulate the women around him so they were always in the wrong. 'Did he hurt you?'

'Not this time. The plate missed me. He said he'd had enough and stormed out. I assumed he'd headed for the pub. That was his usual destination.'

'Where did he drink?'

Mrs Donald gave them the name of a pub down by the harbour. Horton knew it slightly. A respectable place where she and Isla had once or twice enjoyed a decent pub lunch. Not a place that would tolerate a punter too long if he started causing trouble. But no doubt Ally Donald had been a different person with his mates. 'You've not spoken to the pub?'

'I didn't bother. I thought that was where he'd gone, but I didn't much care. My only worry was that he might return three sheets to the wind and take it out on me.'

'Has that happened before?'

'Once or twice.'

'He's been violent with you?'

'Aye, you might say that.'

'You should have reported it, Mrs Donald. We'd have taken action.' Horton knew she was whistling into the wind, but it had to be said.

'Aye, well, you might,' Mrs Donald said pointedly. 'I'm not sure about some of your colleagues. Ally was one of the lads, you know. Don't tell me you lot wouldn't have covered for him.'

Horton knew better than to argue the point. Things might have improved in the force, but there were still plenty of unreconstructed bastards in there. 'But he didn't come back. And you heard nothing from him?'

'Can't say I was sorry. I waited up as long as I could. He liked me to be there waiting for him. In the end, it was obvious he wasn't coming, so I went to bed.'

'Did you expect him to come back this morning?'

'Maybe. That was his usual pattern. Turn up bold as brass. Shower. Change of clothes. Even get me to make him some breakfast. But when he didn't, I assumed he'd gone straight to work.'

'The garden centre?'

'Aye, reckons he's the head of security, but it sounds to me like he's just a dogsbody. He likes being the centre of attention.'

Horton had already called the garden centre. The manager there said that Donald hadn't turned up for work that morning and hadn't called in sick. He'd been surprised because Donald was normally what he called a "very reliable employee," who hadn't previously taken any unauthorised time off.

'You've heard nothing more since?'

'Not a word. I've tried his mobile, but it goes straight to voicemail.'

'Has anything like this ever happened before?'

'Not like this. I mean, Ally liked to keep me in the dark about what he was up to. Thought he was being clever. Pulling the wool over my eyes. Most of the time I knew but just didn't care. The work thing's different, though. Ally was a stickler for discipline. He complained all the time about the youngsters at the centre. How they'd throw sickies or suffer from Monday-itis. How they couldn't even be bothered to phone in if they were off. Ally wouldn't take a day off without very good reason.'

'You did right to call us, Mrs Donald. We'll need some information on your husband. His mobile number. A recent photograph, if you have one. A description of what he was wearing last night.' She paused. 'I'm sorry to have to ask you this, Mrs Donald. But do you know the name of the woman your husband was seeing?'

'Aye. Name and address. That was another area where Ally wasn't as smart as he thought. I've known fine well who she is for months now.'

Horton nodded, feeling slightly weary. She was tempted to wonder how people could live like this. But she remembered her own mother's endless compromises and concessions. How long it had actually taken her to do something. How she'd pretended, for years on end, that it was all tolerable. That it would improve. 'DC Carlisle will take down all the details,' Horton said. She sat for a moment in silence then added, 'One more question, Mrs Donald. Since your husband's retirement, do you know if he's received any – odd letters?'

'Letters?' Mrs Donald looked baffled. 'What sort of letters?'

'Letters than might be construed as threatening, for example.'

'Not that I'm aware of. But Ally wouldn't share that sort of thing with me. Is this relevant?'

'It might be.' Horton hesitated, then, deciding the news would be breaking in the next couple of hours in any case, she said, 'Are you aware that two of your husband's former colleagues, William Crawford and Robert Graham, both died in the last few days?'

'Somebody mentioned to me that Billy Crawford had been found dead. Drowned or something, they said.' Mrs Donald stopped. 'What does this have to do with Ally?'

'Very probably nothing,' Horton said. 'But it's looking as if Crawford and Graham were both unlawfully killed, and we think there's a possibility that their deaths might be connected.' The Head of Comms couldn't have put it more circuitously, she thought.

'They'd both been receiving threatening letters?'

'Letters that might be interpreted that way. We don't know if the letters have any connection with their deaths.' *And there's a faint possibility the Pope might not be Catholic*, Horton added silently to herself. 'You're not aware that your husband received anything like that?'

'You think Ally –?'

'We don't think anything yet,' Horton said firmly. 'But we have to look at all possibilities.'

'Ally never mentioned anything. But there were lots of things he didn't bother mentioning. I can have a look around, if you like. See if I can find anything.' She smiled. 'I know most of Ally's hiding places.'

I bet you do, Horton thought. 'If you come across anything that might be relevant, let us know.' She slid a business card across the table. 'We'll keep in contact, but if you need me, use those numbers.'

They spent a few more minutes collecting details about Ally Donald and then left Mrs Donald to her searching. As they walked back down to the car, Carlisle said, 'She didn't seem too troubled by her husband's disappearance.'

'That's one way of putting it,' Horton said. 'Can you blame her? If you ask me, her biggest fear is that the old bastard might decide to come back.'

CHAPTER THIRTY-THREE

They called in at the pub on their way back through the village. It was late afternoon, and the bar was deserted. They found the landlord behind the bar, busy polishing glasses. Horton waved her warrant card under his nose.

'This about underage drinkers?'

'Should it be?'

'Not that I'm aware. But that's usually what you lot pester me about.'

'Not this time. Do you know Ally Donald?'

'Ally? Aye, I know him. As a punter, anyway.'

'One of your regulars?'

'Helps keep me in business, you know.'

'Was he in here last night?'

'Aye, too right he was.'

'What sort of time?'

'Came in about seven, I guess. I threw him out just before nine.'

'Threw him out?'

'Well, in a manner of speaking.' The landlord continued ostentatiously polishing a pint glass, as if expecting that a genie might emerge from its innards. 'He'd had one too many. Well, several too many.'

'He was drunk?'

'Not incapable, you know. Donald can hold his drink usually. He ought to be able to, the practice he's had. But he was getting a bit belligerent.' He placed the glass back on the bar and appraised it for any remaining blemishes. Horton couldn't believe he treated each individual item of glassware with this level of care. 'He came

181

up to order another pint and a whisky. Lad behind the bar quite rightly asked him if he was sure that was a good idea. Donald got a bit pissed with him, asked if he was refusing to serve him. Lad said he thought perhaps Donald had already had enough. Donald offered to take him outside. You can imagine.'

'I can imagine,' Horton agreed.

'Part of the job. I'd been in the kitchen sorting out some stuff with the chef. Heard this ruckus out front so came to see what was going on. By that time, Donald's mates were already calming him down. I just gently suggested to him that maybe the lad had been right, and it was time to be making tracks. Donald may be a pisshead, but he's not a numpty. He took the hint.'

'You say this was around nine?'

'Aye, something like that. We stop serving food at nine, and we'd just got the last order out. That was why I'd gone into the kitchen.'

'Donald left alone?'

'As far as I know. I made sure he went out the door and kept an eye out that he didn't come back. His mates all stuck around.' He shrugged. 'I say mates, but it's just the four or five older regulars. I don't suppose they know each other beyond that.' The landlord put the pint glass back on the shelf and straightened up. 'What's this all about, anyway? Donald cause some trouble on his way home?'

'Donald never went home,' Horton said. 'He's been reported missing.'

The landlord's surprise looked genuine enough. 'Missing? Since last night?'

'Since he left here, as far as we're aware at the moment.' Horton decided to twist the knife slightly, on the off-chance it might provoke some further information from the landlord. 'You may have been the last person to see him.'

'Jeez. Well, Donald was a pain in the arse at times, but I wouldn't wish him any ill. You think he might have had an accident? The state he was in, I wouldn't be surprised.'

'We're not speculating yet,' Horton said. 'He may be perfectly safe and well somewhere. As far as you're aware, he was heading home once he left here?'

The hesitation was noticeable. 'I've no idea. I just assumed that.'

'You're not aware of anywhere else he might have gone?' It was worth checking, Horton thought, whether Donald's infidelity was common knowledge among his drinking associates.

'Look, it's none of my business. But in this game, you hear things.'

'What did you hear?'

'Everyone knew, really. Donald was never discreet about it. Boastful, even. He was having a thing with the woman who runs the gallery down by the waterfront. Lucky bugger, I'd say. She's no spring chicken, but she's still a looker –' He read the expression on Horton's face and stopped. 'He might have gone there.'

That answered one question, Horton thought. Donald's relationship, whatever its nature, was an open secret. 'We'll look into that. Thank you for your help.'

'Look, I hope you find him. He was one of you lot, wasn't he?'

'Once upon a time,' Horton agreed.

'Aye, he never let us forget,' the landlord said.

That, Horton thought as they turned to leave, *answered another question.* Ally Donald's past would have been no secret either.

They left the car in the small car park at the bottom of the hill and walked the last few metres along the waterside. The sky had largely cleared, and the Cromarty Firth was an unaccustomed deep blue, flecked by white wave caps. There was a stiff breeze blowing from the sea, and it felt as if spring might finally be starting to arrive. They cut up to the right, away from the sea, in search of the address Mrs Donald had given them.

Kirstie McLeod's house was in the middle of a narrow alleyway leading up from the sea to the main street behind. It was a two-storey, white-fronted cottage, with a front door on to the street.

To its left, half a dozen steps led down to a small courtyard with a shop front at the far end. A neatly painted sign read: 'Kirsty McLeod – Artist – Gallery'.

Glancing at Carlisle, Horton made her way down into the courtyard and peered into the shop window. It was filled with watercolours depicting what she took to be local landscapes. Competent enough to her untutored eye, but nothing special. She imagined they went down well with the summer tourists.

As they entered the shop, a woman looked up expectantly from behind the counter at the rear.

'We're looking for Kirsty McLeod,' Horton said.

The woman frowned. 'You've found her. How can I help?' She rose from behind the counter, a tall, statuesque woman with an undoubted presence. She had swept-back, silver-grey hair, and a face that Horton would have characterised as handsome rather than conventionally beautiful. Striking, though, she thought. She could see why the landlord had been smitten. Despite her name, McLeod's accent sounded more English than Horton's.

Horton showed her ID. 'You know an Alastair Donald?'

'I think you'd better come through.' McLeod led them back behind the counter into what was clearly her studio, and then through another door into a sitting room in the adjoining cottage. She gestured for them to take a seat on an overstuffed sofa draped in a flowered cover, and sat herself down in one of the other armchairs. 'What about Ally?'

'When did you last see him?'

'I'm not sure. A few days ago.'

'You didn't see him last night?'

McLeod looked from Horton to Carlisle and back again. 'What's this about?'

'Mr Donald has been reported missing,' Horton said. 'We're trying to trace his recent movements. We were advised you might be able to help us.'

'Were you, indeed? I wonder by whom.'

'Mr Donald was an acquaintance of yours?'

'You might say that.'

'What would you say?'

'Lover. Sexual partner. Maybe something more vernacular.'

'Friend?'

'If you say so.'

'Did you see him regularly?'

'Frequently but not regularly.'

Horton sighed. 'Can we cut to the chase, Ms McLeod? Our understanding is that you and Mr Donald are involved in a relationship. Is that correct?'

'That's correct.'

'And he visits you here?'

'Nowhere else.' McLeod shifted in her seat. 'Look, Ally and I have an arrangement. It suits us both. And frankly it's no one else's business.'

This was beginning to sound very like the way McKay had described Billy Crawford's relationship with Meg Barnard.

'Not even his wife's?' she asked.

'His problem. Not mine.'

'But Donald didn't come here last night?'

'No. Should he have done? I can let you organise my diary, if you like.'

'Our information is that he left his home around seven. From there, he went to the bar, and he was in there until around nine, when he left. He didn't return home, and he didn't turn up to work this morning. Nothing's been heard from him since he left the pub.'

There was silence for a moment as McLeod took this in. 'What makes you think he might have come here?'

'Would you have expected him to?' Horton said. 'In those circumstances.'

'Maybe. I'm not keen on him coming here if he's the worse for wear. If he's had a few drinks, Ally can be – difficult.'

'Violent?'

'Nothing I can't handle,' McLeod said. 'I've thrown him out physically before now. But I can do without that kind of grief.'

'So, you wouldn't necessarily have expected him to come here after a visit to the pub, even if he'd had an altercation with his wife?'

'Is that what happened last night? Well, that's not unusual. Sometimes, he'd come straight here when that's happened. If he chose the comfort of alcohol instead – well, Ally might have more sense than to treat me as second in line.'

'You've heard nothing from him in the last twenty-four hours?'

'I wouldn't expect to. We don't chat on the phone. If he turns up, he turns up. If I'm in, I'm in. If I'm not, he has to go without.'

'You said you last saw him a few days ago?'

McLeod thought for a moment. 'Thursday last week. He turned up late afternoon. I'd just shut up shop. He was on his way back from work. Stayed a couple of hours. Then, I assume he went home. Unless he went to the pub.'

'And you're sure you can't help us with Mr Donald's movements last night?'

'I had a quiet night in last night. The only thing that disturbed me was some fracas on the street out there.'

'Fracas?'

'Kids, I'm guessing. That would have been about nine-ish, as it happens. Something bumping against the front door. Sounded like someone fighting. I'm not a nervous woman, but I kept out of it. Last thing you want is some young ned with a knife.'

'Do you get much of that sort of thing?'

'What do you think? This is Cromarty not Sauchiehall Street. But we get the odd rumble after the pubs close. Usually drunks pissing in the alleyway. I waited until it quietened off then took a look outside. There was no sign of anything.'

'Thank you for your time, Ms McLeod.' Horton was already rising.

'So, what do you think's happened to the old bugger?' McLeod said. 'He's not just vanished in a puff of smoke.' She didn't sound unduly troubled by the prospect.

'We're not jumping to any conclusions,' Horton said. 'It may well be that Mr Donald is safe and sound somewhere.'

McLeod shrugged. 'As far as I know, there are only four points to Ally's compass. His wife, his job, the pub and me. Probably not in that order. But maybe he'll surprise me.'

'You don't sound too concerned by his disappearance, Ms McLeod.'

'Don't I? Well, maybe I'm more concerned than I sound. But I'm guessing not many people will be shedding tears if anything's happened to Ally Donald.'

Horton nodded. That, she thought, was beginning to look like yet another pattern in this case. Another possible victim. Another unmourned bastard.

CHAPTER THIRTY-FOUR

They were still only at the start of the tourist season, but the Caledonian Bar was doing well enough in its new guise. Most evenings now, alongside the usual regulars, there were clusters of couples and families here to try out the food. The kitchen was fully up to speed, with a decent menu of hot specials alongside the sandwiches and salads.

Kelly Armstrong could hardly believe this was the same place she'd worked in the previous summer. All memories of that time were behind her now – sadly, some of the good ones too. But she was well into a new year, a new start, and was generally feeling positive.

She was working most evenings now, as well as the afternoons, allowing Maggie and Callum to focus on getting the food out. It suited her well, keeping her busy and focused but allowing her plenty of time to get on with her Uni work in the mornings. The place was busy enough to keep her occupied, but not so much that she was rushed off her feet. She was mostly on her own behind the bar, but Maggie or Callum would help out if there was a rush.

She was serving one of their new range of cask ales when she realised the barrel needed changing. It was around seven, the busiest part of the evening, and for the moment, Maggie was working on the bar beside her. She glanced over. 'Give me a sec. I'll go down to change it.' So far, Maggie and Callum had insisted on doing the dirty work in the cellar, even though Kelly had learnt how to do it in her previous stint here. For her part, Kelly was happy to let them. The last thing she wanted was to be reminded of her previous experiences down there.

'Thanks, Maggie,' she said. Then, she stopped. The front door of the bar had opened, and three laughing young men had come in. One of them, she realised immediately, was her former boyfriend, Greg.

It shouldn't have been a surprise. The only surprise was that he hadn't been in here before. She knew that his favoured bar was the Anderson, just up the road, which served an even more imposing array of beers. But he was bound to try this place out, if only for a change of scene.

She couldn't face talking to him, not yet. She was the one who'd initiated their split. Even now, she couldn't quite have articulated why, but it had felt like the right decision. Something to do with growing up. Becoming her own person. In retrospect, she thought they'd made the wrong decision in choosing the same university. They'd assumed it would enable their relationship to survive and flourish, but once there, she'd felt almost the opposite. She wanted to do new things, be a new person, but felt Greg was an anchor from her past, dragging her back into the same person she'd always been.

She'd split up with him after Christmas. They'd been due to go to a party at one of his mates for Hogmanay, but she hadn't been able to face it. Instead, she'd spent the evening by herself, her parents out at some local shindig, listening to gloomy music through her headphones. Happy New Year.

In fairness, she knew that Greg would have had a worse one. Whatever her reasons, she'd treated him badly. As far as he was concerned, the news had come from nowhere and knocked him flat. He'd assumed she must have someone else, but that hadn't been the case. Whether that would have made him feel better or worse, she had no idea.

They hadn't spoken since. They'd managed to avoid each other back at Uni. They were doing different subjects, and there was no particular reason for their paths to cross. Back here, she'd half expected to run into him at some point, but so far, it hadn't happened.

Now, it had. But he still hadn't noticed her, and she turned to Maggie. 'You look busy. I can go and sort out the barrel. I know how to.'

'Well, if you're sure. It's still a bit of a mess down there.'

'It must be better than it used to be. I'll be as quick as I can.' She could see Greg and his mates moving towards the bar. Before he could spot her, she turned and disappeared through the door at the rear of the bar, heading for the cellar steps.

The cellar could hardly have been described as pristine, but, like the rest of the pub, it was changed from the old days. The previous forty-watt light bulbs had been replaced by bright halogen spots to ensure the business end of the room was fully illuminated. Denny Gorman's old junk had been cleared out, and the place had been repainted. The new range of cask and keg ales had necessitated a reordering of the barrels and pipes. Whereas before the room had felt narrow and cramped, now it seemed relatively spacious. *Farewell, ghost of Denny Gorman*, she thought. This place had been her last lingering phantom from the old regime, and with one visit, it had been exorcised. She wished she'd made herself come down here before.

It took her only a couple of minutes to change the barrel – even that task was so much easier with proper lighting and more space. She completed the job and then turned and stopped.

There was a figure standing in the cellar doorway, silhouetted in the light from the stairs. For just a moment, her mind was whisked back to the previous summer when Denny Gorman had stood in that same spot, refusing to let her pass. It was as if, despite everything, his spirit was still haunting the place.

'Kelly?'

Oh, Christ, she thought. *Not Denny Gorman. Worse than Denny Gorman.* 'Does Callum know you're down here, Greg?'

'Who the fuck's Callum? Your new boyfriend?' He sounded like a spoilt child, she thought.

'Callum's the owner,' she explained patiently. 'My employer. Get back upstairs before you land us both in the shite.'

'I'm already there.' He sounded angry, she thought. Angrier than she'd expected after all these weeks. 'Why don't I drag you in with me?'

She walked back across the room. Already the echoes of her last encounter with Denny Gorman felt too strong. 'Grow up, Greg.'

'I thought I had done. I thought we'd grown up together.'

She was only a couple of metres away from him now. 'We did. But now, we're finished. I'm sorry, Greg. I didn't mean to hurt you –'

'Well, you did a fucking brilliant job. I'd hate to see what you're capable of, if you really try.'

'Greg –'

'Why did you do it, Kelly? You humiliated me. You didn't care what I felt. You didn't care about anything.'

'Look, let me past, Greg. I've a job to do.'

'I don't care about your fucking job.'

She moved to push past him. As she did so, he grabbed her by the shoulders and thrust her back against the wall. Just as Denny Gorman had done.

But even Gorman, she thought, had seemed desperate rather than furious. 'Greg, stop it –'

'You okay, Kelly?' The voice came from the stairs behind Greg. Then, 'Hey, son, what the hell are you doing down here?'

Immediately, Greg released his grip. He turned to face Callum who was standing glowering at the bottom of the steps. 'I was just –'

'I don't care what you were doing,' Callum said. 'This place is off-limits, except to staff. Get the hell out of here.'

Greg didn't need to be asked twice. Head down, he scuttled back up the stairs as Callum called after him, 'And if you and your mates are still there when I get back up, I'm calling the police.'

He turned to face Kelly. 'What was all that about?'

'I don't know. He just –'

'Do you know him?'

It felt like the final betrayal, but she didn't know what else to say. 'Not really. We were at school together. He just appeared.'

'You sure you're okay? Do you want me to call the police?'

She took a breath. 'No, no. I don't suppose he meant any harm, really.'

Callum gave her a smile. 'I'm not so sure about that. I knew we shouldn't have let you go and change the barrel.'

'Changing the barrel wasn't the problem,' she said.

'No, I suppose not. Bloody wee toerag.' He was already making his way back up the stairs, muttering to himself.

She followed, a step or two behind. At the top of the stairs, she glanced back down into the stairwell, half expecting the ghost of Denny Gorman to be staring back up at her.

CHAPTER THIRTY-FIVE

Horton was almost home when the mobile buzzed on the car seat beside her. It was her personal phone rather than the office one, and she hadn't bothered to connect to the car's hands-free arrangement. She rarely received urgent calls on that phone, and Isla knew to call the work number if she wanted to speak while Horton was driving.

Keeping her eyes on the road, she fumbled for the phone and glanced at the screen. A number she didn't recognise. If it was anything important, they'd leave a message.

It was nearly seven-thirty. She'd stayed late at the office, partly because there was plenty to get done and partly so she wouldn't have to be home on her own. Isla had had a late meeting but expected to be home by seven. In a day or two, Horton knew she'd feel comfortable in the house again, but for the moment, after everything that had happened, she didn't want to be there alone.

It was already dark, and as she pulled into the driveway, Horton felt a slight frisson, knowing she'd have to navigate the short distance between her car and the front door. But Isla's car was already there, and she'd have heard Horton's car arriving.

There was a moment, as Horton fumbled with the key in the lock, when she half expected to hear that voice again whispering threateningly in her ear. She pulled open the door, stepped inside and, feeling as if she'd finally reached sanctuary, closed the door firmly behind her.

Isla was in the sitting room watching Channel 4 News. She'd already opened a bottle of wine and set it out on the low table with two glasses. 'I thought you might need it,' she said.

'Too bloody right,' Horton said. 'It's been quite the day.'

'Go and get changed,' Isla said. 'Dinner's cooking.'

'You've been busy.'

'It was a real effort, taking it out of the freezer and sticking it in the oven. I'm glad my efforts are appreciated.'

Horton made her way upstairs to change out of her office clothes into something more comfortable. That was part of their ritual – putting the day behind them. Tonight, those domestic rituals felt more important than ever.

She threw jacket and handbag on to the bed and began to dig out a suitable sweatshirt and pair of jeans. As she did so, she remembered the call she'd received in the car. She retrieved the phone from her bag and checked the screen. Whoever it was had left a voicemail message. There was also another more recent missed call, received while she'd been chatting to Isla, this time from a number she recognised.

She thumbed the return call button. 'Alec?'

'Hi, Ginny. Sorry to trouble you in the evening. Thought it might be better than office hours, in the circumstances.' McKay usually made a point of not disturbing his team outside work time unless it was absolutely necessary.

'I think I'm still allowed to talk to you, Alec.'

'You sure about that?'

'As long as we don't discuss the investigation.'

'Aye, well. About that –'

'Alec.'

'Not a discussion. I just want to tell you something.'

She sighed. 'Go on, then.'

'I ran into Bridie Galloway today.'

'"Ran into"?'

'Ach, it's a wee village. I can't avoid everyone. It was in the local store.'

'And?'

'She was talking about Jackie. Well, she would, wouldn't she? She thought we ought to be looking at the last few cases he was involved with. Before his retirement.'

'Well, obviously –'

'The thing is, she reckons his whole attitude changed around that time. He became less cocky. More anxious. Worried about his own safety. Not your typical Jackie Galloway at all.'

'This was before that last case that finished him off?'

'She says so. Sometime in that last year or so.'

'We're going back through those last cases anyway. But I don't see why someone would have waited twenty years to follow through.'

'Me neither. But I promised Bridie I'd pass on what she said. You might want to talk to her again. Get it from the horse's mouth. But don't tell Helena I sent you.'

'It's a deal. How are you doing, Alec?'

'Ach, you know.'

'I can imagine.'

'I saw the news tonight. Crawford's and Graham's deaths being treated as suspicious. I'm guessing that means I'm not off the hook yet?'

'Alec –'

'I'm not fishing. Just acknowledging I'm not likely to be readmitted to the fold in the immediate future.'

'We all want you back, Alec. As soon as possible, as far as I'm concerned.'

'Aye, I know. And it's much appreciated.'

'Have you heard anything from Chrissie?'

'Not a dickie bird. I'm not sure if the ball's in her court or mine.'

'If neither of you picks up the phone, nothing's going to happen.'

'I can't argue with that. Doesn't make it any easier, though.'

'Let me know if I can help.'

'Aye, lass, I will. Don't think I don't appreciate it. Beneath this curmudgeonly exterior lies – well, a deeply misanthropic interior. But you get my point.'

'I think so, Alec. Keep well.'

'Aye, and you.'

She ended the call and finished getting changed. She knew she was delaying checking the voicemail, increasingly certain what it would be. Isla would probably advise her simply to delete it. Then get the number blocked.

That was the sensible response. But she couldn't bring herself to do it. For one thing, if it was David, he'd find other ways to try to contact her. She could try to take legal action to stop him, but on what grounds? She felt threatened by him, but there was no evidence that he'd actually threatened her. All he wanted to do, he said, was talk.

In the end, just as Isla was calling up the stairs that dinner was ready, she played back the voicemail. It was exactly as she'd expected. 'Virginia. David. Look, I'm sorry about the misunderstanding last night.' Misunderstanding. 'I didn't mean to frighten you. But I really do need to talk to you. There are things I need to tell you. Important things. Urgent things.' There was a pause, and she could hear him down the phone. 'Look, Virginia. I've found out what it is you do now – funny old world, isn't it? – and I don't want to make more trouble for either of us. But I do need to talk to you. Whenever you like, wherever you like. If you're worried, we can meet somewhere public. Bring someone with you, if you want. Maybe that – friend of yours. Think about it. Call me back on this number. I'm staying up here as long as it takes.'

The message ended. 'As long as it takes.' Another sign-off that felt like a threat, however David had intended it.

'Ginny?'

She looked up. Isla was standing in the bedroom doorway.

'Something wrong?'

Horton held up the phone. 'David. A message.'

'Shit. Can't that bastard just leave you alone? You should have deleted it.'

'I need to bring this to a close. I can let it keep running on.'

'So, get a restraining order.'

'He wants to speak, he says. He has things to tell me.'

'He's playing with you.'

'I know.' She shook her head. 'He says he'll meet me anywhere I want. Somewhere public. He says I can bring you too.'

'If you did that, do you really think that would be an end of it?'

Horton shrugged. 'For the moment, probably. It wouldn't guarantee he'd leave me alone forever.'

'Well, it has to be your decision,' Isla said. 'If you want me along, I'm there. Come and eat, and then, we can think about it.'

CHAPTER THIRTY-SIX

McKay had spent the rest of the afternoon trying to maintain his sanity. After leaving Bridie Galloway, he took a long walk along the beach, traipsing around the bay towards Chanonry Point. It was a fine afternoon. He stood at the far end of the bay, looking back along the curve of the beach and the scattering of buildings in Rosemarkie, enjoying the chill wind off the water. He wasn't normally one to enjoy walking for its own sake, but this at least made him feel less imprisoned by the small bungalow and his own head.

When he reached Chanonry Point, he sat for a while on one of the wooden benches, watching the early tourists mill around him. There was no sign of the famed dolphins this afternoon, but, in any case, McKay preferred watching the dolphin seekers. They ranged from the serious enthusiasts, who'd sit there on their foldaway stools, expensive-looking cameras set up beside them, through to the casual tourists, shrieking to each other whenever they mistook some wave cap for a dolphin or seal.

The walk back felt longer and harder work, perhaps because there was only the bungalow to look forward to at the end of it. By the time he reached the outskirts of Rosemarkie, the sun was low over the hills, throwing shadows across the water. Another day drifting to its end. Another day of going nowhere, doing nothing.

Still lacking the will to cook for himself, he microwaved a frozen chilli con carne, and watched the news as he ate. The Scottish national news carried a short piece on the investigation into Crawford's and Graham's deaths. The regional news included a lengthier clip of the press conference featuring Helena Grant alongside the Chief Super.

Grant had acquitted herself well, as he'd known she would. She was good at that kind of thing, sounding authoritative and reassuring without actually giving away much of substance. The script had presumably been carefully prepared by the Comms team, focusing on possible linkages between the two deaths and the men's previous lives as police officers. The implication was that this might be some kind of revenge killing. Fortunately, it didn't seem to have occurred to any of the attendant reporters to ask how long the officers had been retired or why anyone might have chosen to exact revenge at this particular time.

He poured himself a beer and made the call to Ginny Horton. He could tell that Ginny, for all her politeness, was wondering why he was telling her how to do her job. Even without Bridie Galloway's prompting, they'd be looking carefully at the cases investigated by Galloway's team. If this was some kind of belated revenge killing, that was where its roots would lie.

Afterwards, unable to face any more television, he'd booted up his laptop and sat aimlessly exploring the internet. One of the few facilities the bungalow did have was half-decent Wi-Fi, presumably a legacy from the days when the owner had had aspirations to use it as a holiday let.

Grant had forbidden him from getting involved in the investigation, but she couldn't stop him searching the web. He found the website for one of the local papers and began to search for any reference to Galloway or members of his team.

The search was frustrating. The public archive of material went back only for the last decade, long after Galloway had retired. He could find nothing other than a couple of mentions of Rob Graham being on the winning side in some seniors' amateur football competition a couple of years before.

He tried other local journals, but found no more. It seemed easier to obtain copies of local newspapers from the nineteenth century than from the 1990s. Running out of ideas, he explored some social media sites to see whether any of the men had any presence there. He could find only a page for Shona Graham which looked as if it hadn't been updated for many months.

So much for all human life being exposed on the internet, he thought. It might be the case, if you were a teenager, but not so much if you were a sexagenarian retired ex-copper. For McKay himself, it was an alien universe. He'd never used any kind of social media and had no understanding of why anyone might want to.

Irritated by his lack of progress, he took a second beer out of the fridge. *Another slippery slope*, he thought, as he opened the bottle. But for the moment, he was feeling just like letting himself slide.

It was as he was walking back into the sitting room that an idea struck him. He couldn't fool himself that Helena Grant would approve, but he couldn't see it would do any harm. After all these years, he could rely on Craig to be discreet.

He scrolled through his phone's address book until he found Craig Fairlie's mobile number. It was seven-thirty. Craig was a stereotypical Scotsman in many ways and would have finished eating long ago. He'd probably be settling himself down to a beer and the telly.

He dialled the number, and after a moment, the call was answered. At first, all McKay could hear was an incomprehensible roar. He held the phone away from his ear, assuming here was some technical problem with the line. Then, he heard a voice say, 'Alec? That you?'

'Craig. Where the hell are you?'

'Where do you think I am? At the Caley.'

'They're playing tonight?'

'You know nothing? Celtic tonight. Just about to kick off.' Fairlie was shouting to make himself heard above the crowd.

'Not my thing, football. You know that.'

'Long time, no hear, Alec. What can I do for you?'

'It's maybe not really the time to try to explain. But I'm looking for a favour.'

'Ach, well, that figures. You never call, you never write –'

McKay and Fairlie went back to university days. They'd been good mates at the time. They didn't see much of each other now, but both had ended up living in Inverness, and they got on well enough when they met. Fairlie had become a journalist and found himself what he described as the least secure job on earth as a reporter on the local paper. They'd done each other a few favours over the years – Fairlie had dug out some bits of useful information for McKay, and McKay had occasionally given Fairlie early notice of some impending story in return. Nothing untoward – McKay was always scrupulous about that – but enough to keep Fairlie onside.

'How far back do your archives go?'

'Dunno exactly. Far enough. What are you looking for?'

'Stories from about twenty years ago. Would that be possible?'

'Aye, I should think so. Everything should be available either electronically or on microfiche, I imagine. We're gradually digitising everything, but it's a slow process.'

'Would I be able to have a look?'

'Aye, of course. It's theoretically open to the public anyway, but we tend not to advertise the fact.'

'Wouldn't mind picking your brains, too, if you can spare me a few minutes.'

'For you, Alec, anything. Cost you a pint or two, mind. How about tomorrow morning? I'll be in the office, barring any local catastrophes.' He paused, the crowd still loud behind him. 'Alec?'

'Aye?'

'You going to give me some gen on this latest story? These ex-coppers?'

'That's a very long story,' McKay said, imagining how Grant would react if she knew he was even making this phone call. 'I can't afford to step out of line.'

'That right? Things have changed, then.'

'Ach, I'll tell you what I can tomorrow. Thanks, Craig.'

'No bother.' Behind Fairlie's voice, the roar of the crowd was increasing. 'I'd better go. They're kicking off.'

'I'll leave you to your pain then.'

'Don't you start taking the piss, pal –' There was a pause, and then more crowd noise. 'Shit.'

'What is it?'

'We've only sodding conceded already, that's what.'

CHAPTER THIRTY-SEVEN

McKay wasn't sure whether he felt better or worse for having contacted Fairlie. Better, in that at least he was doing something. Worse, in that he really should be doing anything other than sticking his nose back into the investigation. Fairlie would be discreet, but it wouldn't take much for word to get back to Helena Grant.

Ach. He was what he was. He couldn't help himself. Grant knew that better than most. If he got himself suspended or even sacked, well, that was how it would be.

Still restless, he took another sip of the beer and picked up the phone again. *Okay, Alec*, he told himself, *if you're so fucking impulsive, just dial the number. Dial it.*

He hesitated a moment longer, then flicked through the phone's address book until he found the entry still labelled, poignantly enough, "HOME."

The landline rang out until it clicked to voicemail. McKay ended the call. He wouldn't have known what message to leave. She was out, then. Maybe back at her sister's. Maybe doing something more enjoyable. Perhaps, after all these years, Chrissie had decided the single life was for her and was making the most of it. Or, worse still, maybe she was already looking to bring her temporary single status to an end.

McKay was on his way into the kitchen to fetch another beer when he heard the mobile buzzing on the table behind him. He picked it up and looked at the screen. HOME.

'Chrissie?'

'That you, Alec?'

'Aye, who else?' He could feel himself slipping back into their old sparring ways. 'I just tried to call you.'

'Aye, I know, you numpty. That's why I'm calling you back.'

'I thought you were out.'

'Where would I would be going out to?' she said. 'I've just got a bit nervous about answering the phone at night.'

McKay felt a chill finger run down his spine. 'Nervous? Why nervous?'

'Since I've been back here, I've had a few odd calls,' she said.

'In what way odd? Threatening?'

'No. Not as such. Just silent.'

'That's those autodial things. Cold calling. You know. Just dial loads of numbers but they don't always connect –'

'This isn't like that, Alec. There's someone there. I can tell.'

'How often have you had these calls?'

'I don't know. A few times. It's always the evening. That's why when you phoned –'

'No, of course. There's not been one tonight, then?'

'Not so far.'

'Do you want me to report it? See if we can get the call traced?' The chances of tracking down the caller were minimal, he knew. 'Assume it's one of those "number withheld" calls?'

'Seems to be,' she said. 'I feel as if I'm making a fuss about nothing.'

'It probably is nothing,' he said, doing his best to sound reassuring. 'But it's making you nervous. We should do something about it.'

He was thinking about Chrissie rattling around in that empty house. If someone did want to harm him, it wouldn't be that difficult to get hold of his address, even though he dutifully followed all the usual security protocols associated with being a police officer. That someone, whoever it might be, maybe didn't even realise he wasn't still living there.

Or, he added silently to himself, might know fine well he wasn't there.

'I'll get someone to look into it,' he said. He had a decent security set-up back at the house – again, the need for it went with the territory – but like any domestic security, it had its vulnerabilities. If someone knew what they were doing, it wouldn't be difficult to penetrate.

'Well, if you really think it's necessary.' She sounded irritated rather than reassured. They'd only been on the phone for five minutes, and already he'd started to play his familiar "white knight" role, bounding in to save the poor wee vulnerable woman. All he'd really done was give her more cause for concern. 'Anyway, what can I do for you, Alec?' It was the voice he could imagine her deploying in her days as a medical receptionist.

'I just thought we ought to talk.'

'We're talking, Alec. Do you have anything much to say?'

'I –' It was no good, he thought. They were back into it. The same old routine. 'We need to talk properly, Chrissie. Sit down and really talk through what the problems are. Try and work it out.'

'Do you think there's any point, Alec?'

'I don't know. We need to give it a shot.'

'I don't think I'm ready for it, Alec. Look, I'm prepared to give it a go. There's too much between us to let it drift away without trying. But not yet. I need to get my head together. Need to think through properly what I need to say. Otherwise, we'll fall back into the same rut.'

'Maybe we need someone else to help. Some third party.'

'Aye, and that worked out so well last time, didn't it?'

'That wasn't –'

'I know. Rather unusual circumstances. And, yes, you might be right. But I think we maybe need to try to talk to each other first.'

'Whenever you want.'

'Give me a few days, Alec. Maybe not even that. Just time to think about it. I'll call you. Okay?'

There was nothing else he could say. 'Okay.'

She ended the call without saying goodbye. So where did that leave them? It felt like a step forward. Or maybe two steps forward and one back. Some sort of progress, anyway.

He ought to feel pleased. But, more than anything, he was feeling anxious. Thinking of her there in that otherwise empty house. Thinking of who might be on the end of those silent phone calls, and what it might be they wanted.

Thinking of the relentless grip that had tightened around his own neck just twenty-four hours before.

***

'You're sure about it?'

'Not remotely. But I don't know what else to do.'

'I've told you. Ignore him. If he carries on pestering you, get a restraining order.'

They'd finished eating and were back in the living room, the wine bottle half empty.

'I can't carry on like this,' Horton said. 'I need to find a way to bring it to an end.'

'He'll be back. You know that, don't you? You'll have given him what he wants. So, he'll just know he can still manipulate you. He might leave you alone for a while. But he'll be back.'

'Even so –' They'd been round this loop half a dozen times over the meal. Horton wanted to make contact with David in the way he'd suggested. Isla thought that, given that Ginny Horton was an intelligent woman, this was the world's stupidest idea.

'I'm not going to stop you, though, am I?' Isla said finally. 'You're going to go ahead and do it, whatever I say.'

'Look, tomorrow's Friday. What if we offer to meet him after work in one of the bars in the city centre? The place will be busy. There'll be no way he can do anything – inappropriate. If he starts playing up, we get him thrown out. How does that sound?'

'Idiotic,' Isla said. 'What he does then isn't the point. The point is that you'll have given him what he wants. He'll have won. Again.'

'It's not about winning and losing –'

'It is for him. That's the man he is.' Isla took a breath. 'But I can see you're not going to be happy 'til you've done it. And I can't say I blame you. If I were in your shoes, I'd probably do the same.'

'Tomorrow, then. About six?'

'Okay, I can be away by then. You come to the office, and we'll head over there together. I don't want any risk you'll have to deal with him on your own, even for a few minutes.'

'Fine by me. I've no desire to spend any time alone with him.'

Horton couldn't bring herself to call David back. Instead, she sent a text to the number saying she was prepared to meet him in the Black Isle Brewery Bar in Inverness. She'd be there at six p.m. with Isla. If David didn't turn up then, he'd have missed the only chance she was prepared to give him.

Two minutes after she'd texted, the phone began to ring. The same number.

'You're not going to answer it?' Isla said.

'Christ, no.' They both stared at the buzzing phone until it fell silent. 'Jesus, he knows how to scare the shit out of me, doesn't he?'

'Of course he does,' Isla said. 'That's the point.'

A moment later, the phone buzzed again. The sound of an incoming text. Horton picked up the phone, holding it between them so they could both read the screen.

"See you there," it said.

CHAPTER THIRTY-EIGHT

'You okay, Ginny?'
Horton blinked at the sunlight streaming in through the office window. 'Sorry. Was completely lost in this lot.' She waved her hand at the mass of files accumulated on her desk.

Helena Grant lowered herself on to the seat opposite Horton's desk, looking with slight trepidation at the unsteady tower of box files. 'You do realise you might literally get buried under paperwork?'

'It's a dangerous job, but someone's got to do it.' Horton had volunteered to work through Galloway and his team's final cases at that morning's planning session, without mentioning her conversation with Alec McKay. It was an obvious line of investigation in any case, though no one had seemed very keen to take it on. Probably, she reflected now, because it was among the most boring tasks imaginable.

The material was all archived, and when she'd first called the records unit, Horton had expected it would take some days to retrieve the files. But the unit head had seemed only too keen to oblige. 'We all want to see this one sorted,' she'd said. 'It'll probably take us a day or so to pull out all the records, but we can send them over to you as we go, so you can make a start.' Sure enough, later in the morning, the first couple of crates had been delivered to her office.

'Any luck so far?' Grant asked.

'Nothing obvious. It's like you'd expect. Most of the cases are routine stuff, especially twenty-odd years after the event. Stabbings and fights in the city centre on a Saturday night. Domestics. The individuals involved are all small-time. I can't see there's anyone or anything in here that might come back to bite Galloway or the others two decades later. Mind you, I've plenty more to go through. And I've been promised a couple of other crates to come.'

'Lucky you. Do you want me to find some more resource to help?'

'I'll see how it goes. But it might be better to stick with one person doing it. There might be links or patterns that tell us something.'

'Maybe,' Grant said. 'And, of course, it might be that none of this has anything to do with a specific investigation. Might have been more about what Galloway was up to behind the scenes.'

'But you'd expect some sign of it somewhere. If it was anything dodgy, I mean.'

'Galloway was always good at covering his tracks. And we don't know that it was necessarily dodgy. Maybe, for once, Galloway managed to make the wrong enemy for the right reasons.' She paused. 'Though, frankly, that doesn't sound like the Jackie Galloway I remember.'

Horton nodded. 'Even from these files, reading between the lines, I get the impression of a nasty piece of work. Some of the interviews just sound too neat, you know?'

'Aye, I know,' Grant said. 'He was pretty adept at getting the answer he wanted.'

'I had a look at that last case of his. The drugs bust that went wrong.'

'Must have made interesting reading, even after all this time.'

'Very interesting,' Horton said. 'There's nothing on the file about Galloway's disciplinary hearing. Assume that's all held confidentially somewhere?'

'It was handled by the Complaints Commissioner, so they'll have all the files. We may need to get access to them.'

'Seemed an odd one, even more than Alec said. Galloway's original statement reckoned he hadn't seen where the knife had come from or who'd stabbed the victim, but that he wasn't responsible.'

'That was Galloway all over,' Grant said. 'He was never responsible.'

'It was one of the others – Crawford, I think – who said that Galloway was grappling with the young man over the knife. He described it fairly neutrally – that the young man was stabbed in the course of the struggle. But the stories didn't tally.'

'Doesn't surprise me,' Grant said. 'Could have been either or both of them. Or Graham. All more than capable of shafting each other. You think the key to this might lie there somewhere?'

Horton shifted uneasily. 'In principle, I suppose it could. These were people trying to muscle into the city drug circuit. Alec reckoned that Galloway had been tipped off by one of his dubious friends. So, all that might have got up the wrong person's nose, especially with the way it turned out. But my impression from the file is that these guys were low-life chancers, not big players.'

'Or maybe,' Grant said thoughtfully, 'somebody used this as an opportunity to bring down Galloway. If so, it worked.'

'There's one other thing,' Horton said, after a pause.

'Go on.'

'I had a call from Alec last night.' She'd been considering not telling Grant this, but was feeling increasingly uncomfortable holding back the information, however trivial it might prove to be. She could almost see Grant stiffen in her seat at the mention of McKay's name.

'Oh, aye,' Grant said. 'And what did Alec want?'

'He ran into Bridie Galloway yesterday –'

'Ran into?' Grant's voice was icy.

'Just that, from what he said. It's a small village. He met her in the corner shop.'

'Very cosy,' Grant said. 'Was she complaining about the price of Tunnock's Wafers?'

'She was just encouraging us to look at these last cases.'

'Well, thanks for the tip, Bridie. Remind me to invite you in as a consultant.' Grant shook her head. 'Sorry, shouldn't take it out on you. Just finding Alec increasingly hard work on this. I'm putting my backside on the line for him as it is.'

'He knows that,' Horton said. 'But this is Alec's life.'

Grant sighed. 'Aye, I know. He must feel he's lost everything. First, his daughter. Then, Chrissie and his home. Now, it must feel like even his job's slipping away. But that's why he's got to behave himself. Anyway, what about Bridie Galloway? Was that all she said?'

'No. That's the point. She said that Jackie Galloway had changed, even before that last case. That he seemed anxious about something. Frightened, even.'

'Galloway never struck me as the type to be easily frightened.'

'That's the impression I've gained.'

'Maybe he'd got on the wrong side of someone. It's needle in a haystack territory, though, isn't it? But I suppose those case files are as good a place to start as anywhere.'

'I guess so,' Horton said dispiritedly. 'We seem to be running out of other leads. I don't suppose there's any word on Ally Donald?'

'Nothing so far. We've circulated his picture, and we've got door-to-doors going on in Cromarty, but we're running out of resources, so it's slow going, unless I can get some more bodies drafted in.'

'What about the other guy Alec mentioned? Another retired DS. Davey Robinson?'

'Robertson. Just got word back on him this morning, funnily enough. One of the titbits I'd come to share with you. Seems like he shuffled off this mortal coil just a few weeks back.'

'Can't have been that old, presumably?'

'Early sixties. Accidental death.'

'Accidental?'

'Aye. I'm trying to get more info on it. Another Black Isle resident, apparently.'

'That place is beginning to live up to its name. What happened to him?'

'Fall, apparently. He was a keen walker. Used to do the real hard stuff, Munros and the like, but this was just a leisurely stroll from Rosemarkie. You can walk up to the cliff top at Hillockhead. Main path goes inland, but there's another route along the cliffs. For some reason, he took that route and managed to slip and fall. At least, that's the assumption. His body was found washed up on the beach towards Rosemarkie.'

'Not treated as suspicious?'

'It was recorded as an accidental death. Reading between the lines, it looks like they suspected suicide. Robertson lived alone, but a couple of his neighbours reckoned he'd not been himself in the weeks before. Depressed. Anxious.'

'Any reason?'

'No one close enough to him to say. Suspect that's why the suicide angle wasn't pursued.'

'But it might not have been accidental?'

'Who knows? I've asked for the report on his death, just in case. But the last thing we need is to open up another front in this case, unless it's going to tell us something new.'

'Point taken,' Horton said. She realised that Grant was watching her. 'What is it?'

'When I asked if you were okay,' Grant said, 'I didn't just mean the case. I meant with – well, the other stuff you told me about.'

'David, you mean?' She pulled another file off the stack in front of her, wanting to move the discussion on. 'Yes, I think so.'

'He's not made any reappearance?'

Horton hesitated. She trusted Grant well enough to share her problems, as she had the previous day. But she also didn't want to bring any more of this into work than she had to. 'Not so far,' she said finally. 'I'm hoping that's the end of it.'

'Let's hope so,' Grant said. 'But if there's anything I can do, just ask.'

'Thanks. I'll be fine now. Honestly.'

Grant nodded, not looking entirely convinced. 'That's good, Ginny. I don't want to lose any more officers.'

CHAPTER THIRTY-NINE

'Alec. Good to see you again.' Craig Fairlie was a tall, well-built man, with a tight mop of curly blond hair. McKay had always suspected he worked out, but had never actually caught him doing it.

The newspaper offices were on a business park on the outskirts of town, a small oasis of tranquillity far removed from McKay's stereotypical idea of a busy newsroom. But he supposed that was how it was now. They ran a chain of regional papers on little more than a skeleton staff – locally, the team comprised a couple of all-purpose reporters, a network of freelancers and a core administration and IT team. The biggest group of staff, predictably enough, was the advertising sales team.

According to Fairlie, the old days of reporting real news were largely gone. 'It's mostly rewriting press releases these days,' he said. 'If a real story comes up, we'll cover it as best we can, and we do the local human-interest stuff. But it's not exactly Woodward and Bernstein. It's more putting enough in the paper so people will pick it up and see the adverts.'

Whenever they'd met over the last few years, Fairlie had complained that redundancy was on the horizon. 'Budgets get tighter and tighter. And it's the bloody hacks who're most disposable.'

'But without news, they're not a newspaper,' McKay had protested.

'You know the old saying,' Fairlie had responded bleakly. 'No news is a local free sheet. Wall to wall adverts and a few puffs for local traders. You don't need much else.'

Even so, he'd managed to hang on. 'It's not much of a life,' he said. 'But it's better than being a bloody PR. At least I'm rewriting the press releases, rather than drafting the crap in the first place.'

Today, Fairlie was in a more cheerful mood, maybe because he was still hoping to get some inside dirt on the investigation. *Well, good luck with that, old son*, McKay thought.

He led McKay to a small room at the rear of the building. It was a bare, functional space, the walls lined with grey filing cabinets. In the middle of the room was a small table just large enough to accommodate a microfiche reader and a computer terminal. 'Welcome to what we grandly call The Archive,' he said. 'Not exactly the British Library, or even the National Library of bloody Scotland, but more than a century of editions.'

He spent a few more minutes explaining the set-up to McKay and helped him log in as a visitor to the online system. 'That's about exhausted my expertise,' he said. 'But it you have any problems, speak to young Liam. He's the acned youth on the desk outside. Knows this place inside out. He reckons the stuff you're looking for should be available digitally, so you won't need to go fighting the microfiche. This was long before the current production system, so the editions are just digitised facsimiles of the original hard copies.'

'Can't wait,' McKay said morosely. He was already asking himself why he'd embarked on what was almost certainly a waste of time.

'Anything particular you're looking for?'

'Not really. I'd like to say that I'll know it when I see it, but I'm not even sure that's true.'

'Is this to do with those ex-coppers?'

'I'll let you think that, Craig. Will make life easier for both of us.'

Fairlie laughed. 'You've not changed, Alec. Only forthcoming when it suits you.'

'You wouldn't want it any other way. Think how bored you'd get if I told you everything.'

'I'll leave you to it, then. Give me a shout when you're done.'

Left by himself, McKay flicked idly through the electronic records, working out how to identify and examine a particular edition of the newspapers. He wasn't even sure where to begin. Galloway had resigned in mid-1997, and Crawford and Graham had retired a few months later. From what Bridie had said, Galloway's anxiety had sprung up some months before he left the force. To be safe, McKay probably needed to consider stories any time in, say, the preceding year and maybe even longer. That meant potentially going through some three hundred or more editions. And even then, there was no guarantee – and, in all honesty, maybe not even much likelihood – that he'd spot anything relevant. Still, what else did he have to do with his time?

Sighing, he brought up the first edition, which he selected arbitrarily from early June 1996, and began to skim through it. In practice, the process proved easier, though no less boring, than he'd envisaged. He soon realised there was little point in looking beyond the first few pages of each edition. After that, it was all human-interest features, television and sport. He developed a routine of working in detail through the first couple of pages, skimming through the next few and ignoring the rest. On that basis, he was able to get through it in only a couple of minutes. Just another ten hours or so to get through the rest, then.

After another hour, he was feeling even less encouraged. He'd found few stories that seemed even remotely relevant, and most of those were banal reports of the kinds of cases Galloway's team would have investigated. He'd found no references to Galloway himself or to any of his immediate colleagues. Quotes from the force were generally attributed either to a "police spokesman" or, occasionally, to senior officers. This was increasingly feeling like the wildest of wild goose chases.

'How's it going?' Fairlie had entered the room without McKay realising and was standing behind him, gazing blankly over McKay's shoulder at the computer screen – no doubt trying to divine the significance of that particular front page. *Well, that's easy, son*, McKay thought. *It has no fucking significance. Like every other page I've looked at.*

'It isn't really.'

'Ah. Maybe you'd be better picking the retentive brains of a seasoned newspaper man.'

'Aye,' McKay said. 'You recommend anyone?'

'Funny boy.' Fairlie rested his backside on the edge of the table next to McKay, as if settling in for the duration. 'Seriously, though, if you give me an idea of the sort of thing you're looking for, I might be able to point you in the right direction.'

Fuck it, McKay thought. He was getting nowhere as it was. 'Okay,' he said. 'But, Craig, if you even mention outside these four walls that you've spoken to me – well, I'll find ways to make the rest of your life even more miserable than it's been so far.'

'You forget I'm a Caley supporter. We're immune to misery.' Fairlie smiled. 'Look, Alec, I'm a journalist. A proper one, not like the unpaid interns they bring in these days. Aye, my instinct is always to look for a story, and I'm grateful for some of the morsels you've tossed in my direction. But it's in my interests to keep you sweet, not shaft you. If I can help you with this at all – well, I'm sure you'll do me a similar favour one day. Either that, or I'll get my rewards in heaven.'

'Ever optimistic,' McKay said. 'Spoken like a true Caley supporter.'

'Aye, well. It's what keeps us going. So, what's this about, Alec?'

'You mentioned the ex-coppers. You'll have your memories of Jackie Galloway, I'm guessing.'

'Everyone's got memories of Galloway. Not many fond ones, though. Still, poor bastard, from what I hear of his last days. I wouldn't wish that on anyone.' He paused, watching McKay intently. 'But if you're looking for dirt on Jackie Galloway, I'd have thought there was plenty in your own files.'

'Aye, maybe,' McKay said vaguely. 'We've got people going through all that. I'm just looking for a different perspective.'

Fairlie's face was expressionless. 'That right, Alec? You always were one for going your own way.'

Chances were, McKay thought, that Fairlie had already picked up some whispers on the grapevine. The only question was how much he knew. 'Every avenue and all that.'

'What sort of stuff are you looking for?'

'Galloway's last days in the force. Any evidence he might have got on the wrong side of the wrong people.'

'From what I remember of Galloway, that was his standard working method. Although word was he was very much on the right side of some of the wrong people, if you get my drift. You must know better than me. You were part of his team.'

'No comment,' McKay said. 'I was just the rookie tea boy. But I'm looking for something a bit outside the norm. Galloway was an arrogant bastard. There wasn't much that fazed him. But there are rumours that something did in those last few months. I've no recollection of it – to me he was just the big boss. I did what I was told.'

Fairlie leaned over and peered at the front-page McKay had brought up on the screen. 'We talking twenty-odd years ago?'

'Nineteen ninety-seven. You remember. Tony Blair. Charlie Kennedy. The devo referendum.'

'Oh, aye. Bliss in that dawn it was to be alive.' Fairlie closed his eyes as if hoping to commune with his younger self. 'I don't know, though,' he said, after a moment. 'As far as I can recall, Galloway was pretty much his usual self in those last months. Even when the shit hit the fan, we all assumed he'd emerge unsullied.' He shrugged. 'But it was always an act, wasn't it? If there were vulnerabilities, he wasn't going to reveal them to the likes of us.'

'Did you see much of him around that time?'

'I wasn't exactly close to him. He used to leak a few titbits to me when it suited him. And he tried to squeeze whatever intel he could out of me. We'd meet periodically for a pint. Or several pints in his case.' He paused, thinking. 'Like I say, he was an arrogant wee prick. Knew it all and more. Not a man unduly troubled by self-doubt. But I could imagine he might have thought his grip was slipping towards the end.'

'In what way?'

'Things were changing. He wasn't getting any younger. A lot of his old underworld contacts were dying off – or retiring on their ill-gotten gains to the Costa del Sol. There were new players coming on to the scene. Maybe he felt things were slipping away from him.' He closed his eyes again. 'There's something else nagging at me, though. Hang on a wee second.' He paused, his eyes still closed.

McKay watched him with some fascination. He'd seen this before. Fairlie didn't exactly have a photographic memory, but it was as if he was rummaging through some interior filing cabinet, flicking through the memories until he found the one he was seeking. It was one of the qualities that made Fairlie an effective – and from the authorities' point of view, occasionally an irksome – reporter. He not only knew where the bodies were buried, he sometimes recalled their locations years after everyone else had forgotten.

'There was a particular thing he kept badgering me about. Didn't make much sense at the time, and it still doesn't. Some guy killed in a hit and run. Here –' He leaned over McKay and tapped some words into the search field. Then, he scrolled down through the resulting file names until he highlighted one. 'That looks like it.'

The story was on the front page of an edition from late in 1997. It was a short piece about the death of a young man, Patrick O'Riordan, in a traffic accident the previous Saturday night in the centre of Inverness. O'Riordan had been crossing one of the backstreets late in the evening when he'd been struck by a passing vehicle. He'd been found some time later by a passer-by and rushed into Raigmore, but was dead on arrival. The story reported only that O'Riordan was an electrical fitter who'd moved to the area from Belfast some months before and had left a partner and small daughter. Police were still trying to trace the driver of the vehicle involved.

'What was Galloway's interest?' McKay said.

'You tell me. He kept asking me if I knew anything about this O'Riordan guy.'

'And did you?'

'Why would I? He was an electrical fitter.'

'So why would Galloway be asking you about him?'

'That's the question, isn't it? My sense was that he thought O'Riordan was connected.'

'Connected?'

'Underworld connections, I mean. That O'Riordan was associated with one of the big players.'

'And was he?' McKay was racking his own brains, but the name meant nothing to him.

'Not that I'm aware. And not that I could discover at the time. As far as I could see, O'Riordan was just what that story said. A poor wee bastard unlucky enough to be crossing the wrong street at the wrong time.'

'You think Galloway might have been the one driving the car?'

'Ach, that's always possible. Jackie Galloway didn't have too many scruples about driving after a pint or two. Or five. But if it had been an accident, he'd only have been worrying about covering his own arse. He wouldn't have had any interest in who the victim was.'

'Not unless he had a reason to,' McKay agreed. 'But you're sure that's what he was asking about? It was twenty years ago.'

Fairlie tapped his temple. 'Surprisingly resilient old beast, despite all the whisky it's had to deal with over the years.' He shrugged. 'Have to be reminded where I'm supposed to be tomorrow, but remember stuff from twenty years ago as if it was yesterday. It stuck with me because it was so unexpected, I suppose. We were chewing the fat about other stuff in the pub when he came out with it. I said I'd do a bit of digging, but I assumed it was just some passing whim rather than anything he was really concerned about. But then he phoned me back about it, wanted to know what I'd found. Called me three or four times in the end. That was definitely out of character.'

'But you'd found nothing?'

'Nothing at all. Made enquiries among all the usual suspects. Nobody knew anything about Patrick O'Riordan. Or if they did, they weren't saying.'

'You think they might have been concealing something?'

'Anything's possible. But if there's something there, you usually get an inkling. Often from the way they talk, or from what they don't say as much as what they do. But in this case, I thought that O'Riordan was just what he appeared to be.'

McKay nodded. 'Well, it's something to follow up, I suppose.'

'Not much, I know. But it's all I've got to offer. Had a few other dealings with him around the same time, but nothing out of the ordinary.'

McKay gestured towards the computer monitor. 'You reckon it's worth my while spending more time on this?'

'It's your time, old son. But I wouldn't. Anything interesting about Jackie Galloway and I'd have remembered it. You should have asked me in the first place.'

'Aye, so I should,' McKay said wearily. 'But, like I say, not a word about any of this.'

Fairlie held up his hand in mock outrage. 'Silent as the grave, pal. You know me.'

'Aye, only too well, Craig. Only too well.' He pushed himself to his feet, allowing Fairlie a faint smile. 'I'll leave you to it, then. And thanks for the info. Much appreciated.'

'It's not much, and it probably doesn't help you. But, aye, you owe me a pint some time.' Fairlie paused. 'Or, one of these days, maybe even an exclusive.'

CHAPTER FORTY

Ginny Horton was pulling off the Raigmore roundabout on to the A96 when McKay called. 'Alec?'

'You driving?'

'Yes. I've got the hands-free on, though, so carry on.' She slowed for the second roundabout at the retail park, watching the stream of Friday night traffic heading into Tesco.

'Got a little something for you, maybe.'

'Alec –'

'Don't worry. I'm not going to put you in a difficult position.'

'You've already done that. I had to tell Helena about your conversation with Bridie Galloway.'

'Aye, well, I assumed you would. How'd she take it?'

'Not best pleased, let's say. But she was interested by what Bridie Galloway had to say. We've sent someone to have another chat with her, see if we can find out any more. I've been going through the case files from that time. Haven't spotted anything so far, though.'

'That's why I'm calling. I've just been talking to an old journo pal of mine.'

'Turned gregarious in your old age, Alec?'

'You know me. Life and soul of the bloody party.'

'So, what did this pal have to say?'

'He knew Galloway in the old days. I was asking him what he remembered about Galloway's last few months in the force. Anything out of the ordinary.'

'And?'

'There was one odd little titbit. He said that, around that time, Galloway had got himself into a stooshie about some hit and run killing in Inverness.'

Horton's hands tightened on the steering wheel. 'Hit and run?'

'Some electrical fitter. Patrick O'Riordan. Northern Irish.'

Horton released the breath she hadn't even realised she'd been holding. Not her father, then. 'Why was Galloway interested?'

'Galloway seems to have got it into his head that O'Riordan had underworld connections. Kept badgering my pal to find out what they were.'

'And did he? Have connections, I mean'

'Didn't seem so. Just what he appeared to be – a poor wee bastard who'd got on the wrong side of a speeding lump of metal.'

'Why would Galloway have cared? You think he was the driver?'

'It's not beyond the bounds of possibility. But I wouldn't have expected him to care who the victim was. He'd have been more concerned about possible witnesses or CCTV.'

'He might have been worried if this guy O'Riordan really did have underworld connections.'

'Galloway wasn't the sort to run scared of the local villains. Even the biggest players up here were small fry in those days. Galloway had them where he wanted them. I can't see him getting jittery, unless there was something bigger at stake.'

'You think there might have been something your friend missed?'

'He's a good journalist, and he'd have known all the local players. But if this guy had wider connections, the local crowd might not even have known.'

'You said O'Riordan was Northern Irish,' Horton said. 'That would open up a few possible avenues.'

'Aye. Right enough. That would have been enough to give even old Jackie something to think about. It's one thing to get on the wrong side of some two-bit local dealer. It would have been another to get on the wrong side of the Provos or the Loyalists back in the day.'

'Wouldn't this have been around the time of the Good Friday Agreement?'

'Just before,' McKay said. 'This was around the time the IRA committed to a ceasefire. But there were still trigger-happy nutters around. So, aye, I suppose it's possible. Though Christ knows what anyone with those connections would have been doing in Inverness.'

'Sounds worth looking into, though. Given we're not exactly inundated with leads.'

'You've not managed to get me off the hook yet, then?'

'Our enquiries are continuing, Alec.'

'Aye, point taken, lass.'

'It's Helena's backside on the line.'

'Aye, I know that. I don't envy her that. This one's got the potential to screw us all over. Ex-coppers. A multiple killer.'

'And now, you're suggesting the paramilitaries might have been involved, too. That's sure to lower the heat.'

'You can always rely on me to make life easier.'

She finished the call as she reached the turn off to Ardersier. She'd stayed on at work until she could ensure her arrival home would coincide with Isla's. She didn't believe David would play anymore games, particularly now they'd set up the meeting for the next day. Even so, she was still reluctant to be in the house by herself.

It was already nearly dark as she approached the village, the sky clouding over again after the day's brief respite from the rain. Behind her, over the city, the setting sun reddened the western sky. Ahead, there was only a looming blackness that presaged more rain.

As she pulled into the driveway, she was surprised to see the house still in darkness. Her first thought was that Isla must have been delayed in the office, but Isla's car was already there. Perhaps she'd only just arrived back herself. The front door, Horton could now see, was ajar.

She climbed out into the darkness, involuntarily glancing behind her. The path and the road beyond were both deserted, the evening silent except for the rustle of leaves. The air felt damp, as if rain were imminent.

She stepped into the dark hallway, fumbling for the light switch. 'Isla?'

The interior of the house was as silent as the night outside. Horton blinked at the brightness of the hall light, pausing till her eyes had adjusted. 'Isla. I'm back.'

There was no response. Puzzled, Horton moved towards the kitchen. Then she stopped. There was a dark shape on the kitchen floor below the front window, half concealed in the shadow cast by the kitchen door. 'Isla?'

Horton stepped forward slowly, her eyes fixed on the doorway and whatever lay beyond. Reaching inside the kitchen door, she found the switch and turned on the lights. Then, she released a sharp breath that she only just prevented turning into a scream.

Isla was face down on the kitchen floor, head twisted away from Horton, her body motionless. Beneath her hair, a small trickle of blood was visible on the stone floor tiles.

For a moment, Horton stood frozen. Then, barely thinking coherently, she crouched beside the prone body, desperately feeling Isla's neck for a pulse. She realised that, probably for the first time in her life, she was praying.

It took her a few agonised seconds to find the pulse, her senses confused by the pounding of her own heart. But there it was, strong and steady. Isla was unconscious but not dead.

Horton twisted round, her relief allowing her the presence of mind to recognise that she had her back to the kitchen door. Someone had done this to Isla. Someone who could still be in the house.

She dug in her pocket for her mobile, thumbing 999 even as she was dragging it out. There was an interminable moment until the call handler answered, and then, Horton found herself babbling, 'I need an ambulance and the police. My partner's been attacked —'

The handler, with calm professionalism, talked her back into coherence until Horton was able to provide the details and the address. 'You think the attacker might still be there?'

'I don't know,' Horton said. 'The front door was open when I arrived.'

'We've made it a priority call,' the handler said. 'Stay on the line 'til they arrive. There's a car coming from the airport, so it should only be a few minutes. The ambulance won't be far behind.'

Mumbling thanks, Horton lowered herself to sit beside Isla's body, her eyes fixed on the kitchen door. Was it possible David had done this? Could he have turned up here, got into some kind of argument with Isla?

She reached for Isla's hand. As their fingers touched, Isla stirred and her eyelids flickered. 'Ginny,' she murmured.

'There's an ambulance on its way.' Isla's eyes had already closed again, as if she were drifting back into sleep.

She could already see the reflection of blue lights on the surrounding trees through the kitchen window. Moments later, she heard a car pulling up in the driveway outside. She said to the call handler, 'I think the police are here.'

'Do you need to let them in?'

'No, I left the front door open when I came in.'

She heard the call handler relaying the message to the dispatcher in contact with the officers. Almost immediately, the front door opened and the comfortingly familiar face of PC Billy McCann peered round the kitchen door.

It took McCann a moment to take in the situation. 'How is she?'

'Alive, anyway,' Horton said. 'Unconscious, but her pulse seems strong enough. She stirred a moment ago.'

'Ambulance should be only five minutes or so behind,' McCann said, crouching over Isla's body. 'Any idea what happened?'

'None at all. When I got here, the front door was ajar, and I found Isla like this.'

'You think whoever did this could still be in the house?' McCann glanced back to his companion.

'I don't know. I just came straight in here. I've not heard any movement.'

'We'll check it out. You think this is connected with what happened the other night?'

'You mean, did David do this? It's possible.' Horton was still clutching Isla's hand tightly, as if afraid she might literally slip away. 'If he lost his temper –'

McCann nodded. 'Aye. I know the type. I'm sorry about my mate the other night, by the way. Arsehole.'

'No worries.' Outside the window, there were further blue lights flickering through the trees. 'Looks like the ambulance,' she said.

The second officer was already at the front door, waiting to greet the two paramedics as they alighted from the vehicle. Horton reluctantly released Isla's hand and stood back to let them get on with it.

'We'll check out the house,' McCann said. 'If there's no sign of anybody, we'll get a bulletin out on the surrounding roads. Mind you, there won't be a lot of spare resource on a Friday night.' He gave her a smile. 'But you'd know that.'

The paramedics were going through their routine of tests. One of them, a tall, skinny young man with floppy ginger hair, looked up. 'I think she'll be fine. Unconscious, but she's stirred a couple of times while we've been moving her. Doesn't look too deep.'

'She did the same while I was waiting. I thought at first she was going to wake up.'

'The head wound looks worse than it is. Lot of blood but a fairly superficial gash. We'll take her in and get her checked out, though. Might be concussion. Do you want to come in with us?'

'I'll follow behind,' Horton said. 'If you're sure she's okay.'

'Sure as I can be,' the paramedic said. 'Obviously, until the docs have looked her over. We'll probably need to keep her in overnight.'

Horton nodded. 'I'll get some night things and a washbag sorted, then I'll follow you over.' It would be a relief, she thought, to busy herself with some prosaic tasks.

The kitchen door reopened, and McCann stuck his head in. 'I think you'd better have a look at this.'

Puzzled, she followed him out into the hallway. McCann was standing by the living room door. 'You'd best prepare yourself,' he said. 'It was a shock for us. You don't need to look, if you don't want to.'

'What is it?'

'A body.'

'A body?' She couldn't process this for a moment.

'It's a man. That's really all we can tell. I'm no expert, and we've tried not to disturb things any more than we could help, so we don't get the usual bollocking from you lot.' He gave her a smile, and she could see he was doing his best to play down what he was saying. 'But there are rough red marks on his neck. I'd say he'd been strangled.'

Horton's first thought was to wonder whether Isla could have been responsible. If she'd been attacked and fought back, maybe. But while Isla might conceivably have used a kitchen knife or a heavy object to defend herself, she was hardly likely to strangle an intruder.

She could see McCann had been following the same train of thought. 'Do you feel up to taking a look?'

'I imagine I've seen worse.'

'That's what we thought. But it's different when it's your own house, isn't it?'

He wasn't wrong there, Horton thought. 'Let's give it a go,' she said. 'If we can do it without contaminating the scene. I don't want a bollocking any more than you do.'

'We were careful,' McCann said. 'Went in there just long enough to check he really was dead. Artie's upstairs making sure there's no one else about. You should be able to see his face from the door.'

She followed McCann and peered round the door into the sitting room. McCann had turned on the lights when they'd first begun their search of the house so she had no difficulty in making out the body spread-eagled on the carpeted floor, its white face twisted towards her.

It still made no sense, but somehow, she was unsurprised by what she saw.

The dead man in their living room was, of course, David.

CHAPTER FORTY-ONE

Helena Grant had known the call would come. It was always an evening like tonight, at the end of a total shitehole of a day when all she wanted was a half a bottle of wine, a microwaved supper and an early night.

Today had been worse than most. She'd spent most of it either getting nowhere or briefing chief officers who wanted to know why she was getting nowhere. Then, there'd been another media conference where they'd still had nothing of substance to say, so she'd had to spend half the morning with the Head of Comms working out how they were going to say it. Then, a series of other meetings had dragged her away from where she should have been focusing her energies. All while she was still several officers down on her establishment, including the irritatingly indispensable Alec McKay.

She'd hoped for a few hours' break, but was far from surprised when her work phone buzzed almost as soon as she was back in the house. It was one of the sergeants from the Control Room. 'Another one for you, I'm afraid.'

She almost didn't need to ask. 'Another body?' Ally Donald's remains finally turning up somewhere, she assumed. Washed up at Munlochy Bay or dumped at Chanonry Point.

'Aye. Over in Ardersier.'

'Ardersier?' A quiet but insistent alarm bell was sounding in the back of her mind. 'Where?'

He read out the address, confirming her fears. 'One of your lassies, I believe?'

'One of my detective sergeants,' she corrected, her mouth dry. 'What do we know?'

'Male. Late middle-age. Your lass reckons it's her stepfather or some such, though we've not had a formal confirmation.'

Grant released her breath in relief, wondering whether the sergeant had been deliberately playing with her. Of course, she added silently to herself, this still didn't mean the news was necessarily positive. 'Do we know the cause of death?'

'Again, not confirmed. But the PC on site reckons it looks like strangulation.'

'Strangulation? How the hell could he get strangled?'

'That's your job, isn't it? Finding out, I mean.'

Smart-arse, Grant thought. *Sometime, when I've more time on my hands, you may find yourself regretting this conversation.* 'How's DS Horton?'

'Fine, as I understand it,' the sergeant said. 'But her … friend's being taken into Raigmore.' The mid-sentence pause was brief but undeniable. Another officer who still hadn't grasped what diversity meant. 'She was unconscious when your colleague arrived home. Some sort of head wound. They don't think it's serious, but they've taken her in to be checked out.'

'I'll get over there. Have the Examiners been called?'

'On their way.'

Grant sighed and ended the call. Another perfect Friday night, then. She knew it went with the job, and it wasn't as if she had anything much else planned. But, just once in a while, she'd have liked the chance to enjoy the place she'd moved to after Rory had died. Her plan had been to start a new life in this new house – not to forget Rory but to allow his memory to take its due place in her emerging future. Instead, she felt in stasis, lacking the time or the energy to take on anything new. Every day felt like yet another call-out to yet another incident.

The last thing she needed was another unconnected murder. She'd obviously need Horton to stand back from this one, which left her staffing even more depleted. All she could do was find out as much as she could, and then decide how to handle it.

Wearily, she slipped her shoes back on and reached for her coat. As she did so, the phone buzzed again. The same Control Room sergeant. 'You're not going to believe this.'

'Somehow, I think I am.'

'We've got another one for you.'

'It's my lucky night, isn't it? Go on.'

'Body found washed up by Munlochy Bay. PCs have just arrived. Looks like the body's been in the water a day or two, but they found some ID in the clothing –'

'Alastair Donald?'

There was a moment's silence. The undetectable sound, she thought, of thunder when it's been stolen. 'Aye, that's right.'

So, her prediction had been right, even down to the likely location. She'd known, even when Donald had first been reported missing, that it would come to this. Another ex-copper. Another member of Jackie Galloway's team. Another dead body. 'Okay,' she said, 'I'll get someone there as soon as I can.' *Though Christ knows how*, she thought. 'We're thin on resource at the moment –'

'Aye. Tell me about it.' There was no trace of sympathy in the sergeant's voice. 'I can't afford to leave our lads out there for too long.'

'You'll have to leave them there as long as it takes,' she said shortly. 'Give me the details, and I'll see what I can do.'

The truth was, she thought as she left the house moments later, there was no one she could send. All her officers were either tied up or unavailable, apart from the odd rookie she couldn't trust with either job. She was already conscious of the sensitivity of the Galloway enquiry, with the media sniffing at their heels. She wondered what the media would make of a body at the house of the detective sergeant working on the case. She could imagine them adding two and two and coming up with whatever the hell they wanted.

She couldn't see any real alternative but to visit the two scenes herself. Attending the Ardersier scene was the priority, as that was a live crime scene with the body in situ. Ally Donald's body, not to mention the PCs who were babysitting it, would just have to wait. She imagined the Examiners were under similar pressure.

It was only as she was turning the ignition key that she finally thought, bugger it. There was one solution staring her in the face, though she'd be taking a risk. But if anyone challenged her decision later, she'd ask them what better ideas they'd have come up with. She hesitated a moment longer then dialled the number.

The phone barely rang before it was answered. 'McKay.'

'You fancy getting back into harness, Alec?'

There was a momentary pause as he processed the question. 'You saying what I think you're saying?'

'I'm asking,' she said, patiently, 'if you want to get back on the job. If you'll pardon the expression.'

'If you're serious, I'll pardon you anything. Does this mean I'm off the hook?'

'You were never on the hook, as far as I was concerned, Alec. I was just trying to do you a favour. Nothing's changed, as far as that's concerned. You're still the last person to see Rob Graham alive, apart from whoever killed him. You were still seen talking to him outside the pub. You still don't have any kind of alibi – Shit, I'm being an idiot. I hadn't thought it through, Alec. I can't bring you back yet.'

'I haven't done anything, Helena. You know that.'

'Aye,' she said. 'I know that. But if I don't play this by the book, we'll both end up crucified.'

'So, why did you call me?'

'Ach, because I'm desperate, Alec. You heard about Ginny?'

'What about Ginny?'

She recounted what had happened at Horton's house that evening. 'Ginny's off to Raigmore with Isla. And I couldn't involve her in this anyway. I've no other senior officers available.' She realised, with something approaching shock, that she was on the brink of tears. It was as if all the pressures had crept up on her, overwhelming her without her realising. She couldn't remember the last time she'd felt so far from being able to cope.

She could tell that McKay could read at least some of this. 'What do you want me to do?'

'Alec, I can't –'

'Look, you need help, Helena. I can provide it. Simple as that.'

'It's not that simple, Alec.'

'If there's a problem, sling the blame in my direction. Tell them I went off piste. Against your orders. Mind you, I don't know if the powers-that-be would believe that of me.'

Suddenly, as unexpected as the previous moment's near-tears, she laughed. 'You bastard, Alec. You never change. I can't allow you to take that on. If it came to that, it really would be the end of your career.'

'At the moment, I'm feeling like it's ended anyway,' he said. 'I can't carry on like this, Helena. It'll be the end of me.' He hesitated again. 'Anyway, it's Ginny.'

'Okay,' she said, finally. 'But we might both end up falling on our swords over this.'

'Well,' McKay said, 'if we're going to do that, hen, let's at least do it in style.'

CHAPTER FORTY-TWO

'How are you doing?'

It was the quiet time, late afternoon, before the dog walkers and the families came for a drink and a bite to eat. A couple of elderly men were having a blether in the corner, painstakingly working their way through a single pint each, but otherwise, the place was empty. Kelly was behind the bar polishing glasses.

She hadn't heard Callum emerge from the kitchen. 'Oh. Fine. You know.' She gestured at the empty bar room. 'Not exactly rushed off my feet.'

'It'll fill up later.' He'd been prepping some food for the evening menu and was dressed in his chef's whites. They suited him, she thought. There were times – and increasingly, she was beginning to realise, these were times in the company of Callum Donnelly – when she thought she might go for an older man. Someone with a bit more maturity than the likes of Greg, anyway. It was a pity that Callum was spoken for.

'You've not seen any more of that wee bampot?'

'No.' Kelly imagined that Greg would be steering well clear of her now. 'I don't think he'll be back.'

'He better not be.' Callum had moved to stand beside her. He was holding one of the kitchen knives, twirling it casually between his fingers with practised ease. She knew its blade would be razor sharp. 'If he shows his face in here again, I might have to start applying my knife skills.' He flipped the knife into the air, allowed it to spin once, and deftly caught it by the handle.

'You wouldn't –' She stopped, realising he was laughing at her.

'Ach, of course not. But I'd kick his backside down the street.'

Kelly realised she'd allowed herself to move closer to him. Suddenly self-conscious, she took a step away and resumed her industrious polishing. 'I don't think he meant any harm.'

'It didn't look that way to me.' Callum leaned forward, and for a moment, she was convinced he was about to put an arm around her. Instead, he reached to adjust one of the beer pump clips. Kelly released her breath, aware she didn't know how she'd have reacted if Callum had touched her. She stepped away along the bar, making a pretence of checking the row of optics, conscious he was still watching her.

'You need someone to take care of you, Kelly,' he said, after a moment.

She didn't look back. She wanted to ask him whether he had anyone particular in mind, but couldn't bring herself to speak. Finally, she said, 'I'm fine. Really.' She forced herself to face Callum.

As she had expected, he was watching her, his hands still juggling idly with the knife. She wanted him to say something more, but after a second, he shrugged and smiled. 'I'd better get back to the kitchen. That veg won't prep itself.' He waved the blade in the air in the manner of a costume-drama swordsman.

Kelly smiled back, feeling as if she'd lost the power of speech. She could hear movements from the kitchen, then the sound of Maggie Donnelly's voice calling for Callum. Maybe, Kelly thought, Callum had heard those noises a moment before she had and knew his wife had returned from her trip to the cash-and-carry. Maybe that was why he'd said nothing more.

The bar doors opened and the first of the evening crowd came in – a middle-aged couple with their dog. Kelly took a final glance towards the kitchen door and then moved to serve the couple, trying to stop herself from thinking about what, if anything, might have just nearly happened.

***

'I see the walking cadaver's already arrived, then?'

McCann blinked as McKay's figure loomed over him. With all other rooms currently being treated as potential crime scenes, McCann had been sitting on the stairs writing up his notes while he waited for CID to arrive. Now that CID had done so, in the intimidating form of DI Alec McKay, McCann wished he'd been standing to attention instead. 'Sir?' McCann knew McKay by reputation, but had never had any dealings with him. It seemed best to keep things on a formal footing until he received some guidance otherwise.

'Yon Jock Henderson. Examiner.'

'Oh. Right. He arrived about ten minutes ago.'

'Punctual by Jock's standards.'

McCann had risen to his feet. 'PC Billy McCann.' He held out a hand for shaking, but McKay ignored it.

'Pleased to meet you, son. So, what's the story?'

McCann glanced at his notebook, wondering whether he should retrieve it to support his account.

'Just the headlines for the moment, son. You can save the details for when we've all got time to blether.' McKay leaned against the wall and gestured for McCann to sit down again. 'Mind you, if we're waiting 'til old Jock's finished his perusals, we've probably got all the time in the world. Best make yourself comfortable.'

McCann hesitantly lowered himself back on to the stairs and quickly summarised what had happened after his arrival at the house.

'Ginny seemed okay?' McKay asked.

'I think so. I mean, she was obviously concerned about the condition of –' McCann hesitated, clearly wondering what terminology would be acceptable to McKay.

'Her partner. Aye, well, obviously. How did she react to the sight of chummie in the living room there? The body, I mean. Not Jock.'

'Seemed to take it in her stride. Is it right it was her stepfather?'

'Aye, something like that,' McKay said vaguely.

'She didn't know he was here, though? Tonight, I mean.'

'She hadn't seen him for years,' McKay said. 'Then, he turned up out of the blue a few days ago.'

'He'd been harassing her,' McCann said. 'She called us out the other night because he was prowling round the house.'

'So I understand,' McKay said.

'When I first saw the body, I thought –'

'Aye, son. I think we all did. But you reckon he was strangled?'

'That's what it looked like. I'm no expert, though.'

'We'll see what old Jock thinks. Not that he's much of an expert either.' McKay tapped his fingers on the wall. 'You don't strangle someone in self-defence, though, do you?'

'I wouldn't have thought so,' McCann agreed.

'So, who the hell killed him?' McKay sounded as if he was asking himself rather than McCann, so the young man offered no response. 'Tell me again what Ginny said to you about what she saw when she got back.'

'There wasn't much. She said she'd been expecting her partner to be back first, so she was surprised the lights weren't on. Then, she found the front door ajar. She came in, went into the kitchen first, and found her partner on the floor there.' He pointed to the spot where Isla had been lying. 'Then, she called us. That was about it.'

'She hadn't gone into the living room?'

'No. She stayed in the kitchen 'til we arrived. We were the ones who stumbled across the body when we went to check the rest of the house. Looks like the patio doors have been forced, so that's presumably how he got in.'

'You've checked out the gardens and the surrounding area?'

'As soon as we could, yes. The two of us did a scout round. No sign of anything, but difficult to be sure in the dark.'

'Your mate's gone now?'

McCann nodded. 'We had a couple more call-outs. Routine stuff, but we thought there was no point in both of us sitting here. I said I'd stay as long as needed then get him to pick me up.'

McKay nodded, his expression suggesting that while he'd been talking, his brain had been pursuing other avenues of thought. 'Okay, son. That's very helpful. You can get off when you like. I'll finish up with old Jock in there and get this place sealed off. I'm assuming Ginny's over at Raigmore?'

'Yes. She left a set of keys over there. I said I'd leave them for her at HQ.'

'Thanks, son. I'll look after all that then. And now, I'll go and chivvy old Jock along. He's probably fallen asleep in there.'

***

McKay watched Jock Henderson as he hunched over the body, clad in his rustling white protective suit. *At times like this*, he thought, *you could almost believe the old bugger knew what he was doing.*

'Nearly done, Jock? That body's cluttering up the place.'

'Aye, well,' Henderson said, without looking up, 'some of us do a proper job, you know, Alec?'

'Aye, so I hear. But somehow, I always get landed with you, Jock. How's it looking?'

'Not much to see, to be honest. At least I've not had to wade through pools of blood on this one.'

'Must be a disappointment. Cause of death?'

'Asphyxiation, I'd say. Strangled.' He looked up and regarded McKay over the top of his face mask. 'We seem to be having rather a lot of those lately.'

McKay nodded, thinking back to the hands that had gripped his own throat in that dark corner of Fortrose. The way Rob Graham had been killed. It was hard to conceive of any connection between that and the body lying in front of him. But then, he knew almost nothing about this man. 'Must be in fashion,' he said. 'Any ID on him?'

Henderson held up an evidence bag containing a brown leather wallet. 'Aye. Various cards, driving licence and so on.

Name of David Kirkland. Address in Surrey somewhere. I wrote down all the salient details before I bagged it up.'

McKay frowned. David Kirkland. The name rang a distant bell, though he couldn't imagine how or why it should. Maybe Horton had mentioned it to him some time. It didn't feel like that, though. It felt like something from further in the past.

'Anything else?'

'Not obviously. I've dusted for prints, especially 'round where the door was forced open. But there doesn't seem to be much. We'll get the clothing checked over for DNA traces. You never know.' He pushed himself to his feet. 'I'll take a few photos, and then, we're done in here. You want me to check the kitchen and the rest of the house?'

'Probably worth checking whatever we can,' McKay said. 'As I understand it, nobody's disturbed the place, except for the two uniforms when they checked it out.'

'What's the story, then, Alec? Word on the street is that this is Ginny Horton's place. And that it was Ginny's other half attacked in the kitchen.'

'You frequent some dubious streets, Jock. But, aye, this is Ginny's. My understanding is that yon corpse is Ginny's stepdad. We're assuming some kind of intruder. Maybe interrupted a burglary.'

'What kind of burglar strangles someone?' Henderson asked.

It was a reasonable question, and McKay could offer no answer. 'One who's good with his hands? Christ knows, Jock. But we've had stranger cases.'

'If you say so, Alec.' Henderson was prowling round the room, taking an array of shots with his digital camera. 'Your job to worry about that side of it, I'm glad to say. I'll leave that in your incapable hands.'

'Aye, you do that, Jock. Are we okay to call up the ambulance to take away our pal here?'

'Whenever you like,' Henderson said. 'Though I don't think he's in any hurry.'

CHAPTER FORTY-THREE

*P*erfect, Helena Grant thought.

As she'd headed up the A9, the rain had begun to fall again, buffeted by a rising wind from the sea. The Black Isle often seemed to have its own weather, and she wasn't surprised that the rain grew heavier as she passed through Munlochy and took the turn off to the bay. She was a skilled driver, but in the dark and rain, she found herself struggling to navigate the twists and turns of the single-track road.

She'd been down here once before when there'd been a spate of burglaries and damage to holiday cottages in the area, and she recalled that the road deteriorated further as it approached the shore. It was nothing that her small four-by-four couldn't cope with, even in bad weather, but it required all her concentration.

It was another few minutes before she spotted the cluster of lights through the trees. The rain was lashing almost horizontally from the sea as she drew in behind the patrol car, its blue light still throbbing in the darkness.

Ahead of her, there was a small cluster of holiday cottages. An idyllic spot in the summer, she thought, with views out over the waters. Cold and exposed on a night like this. Outside the nearest cottage, she could make out two figures obviously seeking whatever shelter they could find on a small roofed veranda. One of them was already moving to greet her.

'DCI Grant,' she said.

'PC Tommy Burns,' he said, reaching out a hand to shake.

She recognised the man slightly. He was a red-faced figure, approaching middle-age and slightly overweight. 'I hear you've found something.'

Burns led her under the shelter of the veranda. 'Aye, well, not us, really. Couple renting the next place along. Must have fair ruined their holiday.' Burns gestured towards the figure beside him. 'My partner in crime, Andy Gordon.' Gordon was a younger man, eyes blinking under a mop of blond hair. He looked anxious, Grant thought, though she couldn't tell whether he was more intimidated by her or the nearby presence of a dead body. 'Where's the body?'

Burns waved his hand into the darkness. 'Down there. We didn't want to move it 'til the Examiners got here. Looks like he's been in the water a while, poor bugger.'

'You found some ID?'

'Aye. He's wearing a suit, completely sodden, but we thought we'd better give the pockets a quick check. There was a wallet. Cards, driving licence all that. Someone called Alastair Donald.'

She nodded. 'Aye. Reported missing in Cromarty a day or two back.'

'Surprised he washed up here then, rather than in the Cromarty Firth.'

It was a fair point. She was no expert, but the entrance to the Cromarty Firth was relatively sheltered. She'd have expected a body entering the water in Cromarty to be washed back into the firth rather than around the Isle into the Moray Firth to the south. 'I suppose it depends on the tides,' she said.

'Or where the body actually went into the water.'

Burns was clearly no numpty. 'Aye,' she said. 'That too.'

She could see another set of car headlights approaching along the track, the glare smeared by the steadily falling rain. The Examiner, she hoped.

'Who are the people who found the body?'

'Couple renting the cottage next door,' Burns said. 'English.' He gave the word an emphasis which wasn't exactly disparaging, but implied that only the idiot Sassenachs would take a holiday in this part of the world at this time of the year. 'Nice enough, though,' he added. 'They'd been over to Fortrose to get some shopping. Came back to go for a short walk before the rain set in and found the body washed up down there. Bit of a shock, I imagine.'

'Did you take a statement?'

'Aye. There wasn't much more they could tell us. I think they just fled back inside and called us.'

The approaching vehicle had drawn up behind Grant's. One of the Examiners' white vans, with the lumbering figure of Pete Carrick climbing out. She imagined that Jock Henderson would have ensured he drew the longer straw of dealing with the body in Ginny Horton's house rather than braving this one.

'Evening.' Carrick looked characteristically untroubled by the prospect of examining a corpse in the pouring rain. 'Where's our customer?' His face was invisible inside a hefty waterproof.

Burns led Carrick and Grant down towards the shoreline, holding his flashlight steady so they could find their way across the uneven ground. 'Over here.'

The tide had receded since the body had been washed up, and the shapeless black mound was several metres back from the water. Carrick nodded, as if responding to some unspoken question.

'I'll leave you to it,' Grant said to Carrick. 'I'll go and have a quick chat with the couple who found the body.'

As Burns had indicated, there was little more the two holidaymakers, a Mr and Mrs Renshaw, were able to tell her. They both still looked slightly in shock. 'I still can't believe it,' Mr Renshaw said for the third or fourth time. 'I mean, it's not what you expect, is it? We were halfway down towards the sea when we saw it –' He stopped, as if the memory had startled him.

'We didn't know what it was at first,' Mrs Renshaw said. 'I thought it was some sort of animal. A large dog or a pony. Something like that.'

'We got a bit closer,' Renshaw said. 'And then it was obvious. I still can't believe it.'

'Do you know who it is?' Mrs Renshaw asked.

'We think so,' Grant said. 'Someone reported missing in Cromarty recently.'

'The poor thing,' Mrs Renshaw said. 'It must be so cold out there.' She made it sound as if Ally Donald had been for an ill-advised swim.

'Have you seen any other objects washed up? In the last day or two, I mean.' There was no reason to think that Donald might have been carrying anything that wasn't on the body, but it was worth checking.

'Not that we've noticed,' Mr Renshaw said. 'We go for a stroll along the shore every day, so we'd probably have spotted anything.'

'Do you come here regularly?'

'We've been booking this place for a few years now,' Renshaw said. 'We like the peace and quiet.'

'And the views,' Mrs Renshaw said. 'We love the views.'

'We usually come up a couple of times a year. We'll be back again in the summer.'

Grant nodded. 'You've given a statement to the PC, I believe. We'll leave you in peace now. We'll get everything sorted outside, so you'll see some comings and goings, but don't worry. Did the PC take contact details for you?'

Mrs Renshaw nodded. 'Will you need anything more from us?' she asked, anxiously.

'I don't imagine so,' Grant said. 'But sometimes, there are things we need to double-check at a later stage. We won't trouble you unless we need to.'

Neither of the Renshaws looked reassured by this statement.

'I mean,' Renshaw said, as Grant rose to leave, 'it's not what you expect, is it?'

***

Outside, the rain was still coming down, the chill wind roaring up the firth. Carrick's protective tent was flapping and clattering away in the wind, as if it might leave the ground at any moment.

He emerged a few minutes later, pausing as he removed his face mask to check the tent moorings. Then, resembling an ungainly phantom in his white suit, he hurried over to join them. 'Done about all I can,' he said. 'Not much chance of finding anything useful on him. Been in the water too long. Although –' He paused, as if thinking. 'When did you say he went missing?'

'Couple of days ago. Why?'

'Difficult to be sure, especially in these conditions. But I wouldn't have thought he'd been in the water that long. Overnight, maybe. You'll need to get the doc's view.'

'What do you reckon on cause of death?'

'Again, hard to be certain. There are some odd-looking cuts and lesions on the body. I'm not the expert, but I'd say made before death rather than in the water. It almost looks –'

'What?'

'I'm probably going over the top. But I'd say he'd been subjected to some pain.'

'Pain?'

'Pain.' Carrick seemed hesitant to proceed. 'Lesions. Some cuts. Maybe burns.' He took a breath. 'Almost as if he'd been – well, tortured.'

'Tortured?'

'Ach, well, I'm probably being ridiculous. Doc'll laugh at me. And tortured is maybe too strong. But, like I say, pain.'

'Christ. The poor bugger. Not many people seem to have had a good word to say for Ally Donald, but no one deserves that.'

'Donald,' Carrick said. 'Is this another ex-copper, then?'

'Aye. Another member of Jackie Galloway's happy band.'

'Before my time,' Carrick said. 'We seem to have a pattern though.'

'Aye,' Grant said. 'We do. And if you're right about this one, it seems to be escalating.'

CHAPTER FORTY-FOUR

McKay hated hospitals. Others might have called his dislike irrational, but McKay thought it was reasonable enough. Hospitals were full of sick people. If you were in there, it was either because you were sick or because you knew someone who was. Or because you'd broken your toe and knew you'd be spending the next eight hours twiddling your thumbs in A&E with only piss-poor vending machine coffee for comfort.

Nobody wanted to be here. Not even, as far as McKay could tell, most of the staff. They were a decent bunch on the whole, he knew, but too many of them looked overstretched, exhausted, pale and dead-eyed in the face of another endless shift. He'd already had a brief argument with a security officer who'd told him he couldn't come in outside visiting hours and who'd initially seemed unimpressed even by McKay's warrant card. It was only when McKay began to make admittedly empty noises about the consequences of hindering a police enquiry that the man had grudgingly allowed him to pass.

It had taken him a further fifteen minutes to track down the ward where Isla was being treated. She'd been moved since her arrival, presumably because the staff were juggling beds, but nobody seemed to know where she'd been moved to. Eventually, he'd found a helpful auxiliary nurse who'd been able to extract the information and point him in the right direction.

Now, he was kicking his heels outside a locked ward, where everyone was clearly too busy to respond to the bell or pay any attention to a grumpy DI tapping vainly at the window.

Finally, a couple of porters arrived pushing a pale-looking elderly woman on a trolley. 'Waiting to get in, pal?'

'Aye,' McKay growled, wondering whether it looked like he was standing in the corridor for his own entertainment. 'No one answering the buzzer.'

'They like to make you wait,' the porter said. 'Makes them feel important.' He pressed his security pass against the locking mechanism, and the doors gently swung open. 'After you,' he said. 'We're in no hurry, are we, May?' He winked at the woman on the trolley who offered a half smile in return.

'Thanks,' McKay said.

A stern-looking nurse was already striding towards them. 'Can I help you?' she said, in a tone that suggested the answer was unlikely to be in the affirmative.

McKay waved his warrant card. 'I'm looking for Isla Bennett,' he said. 'Brought in earlier.'

'Ms Bennett's asleep, I'm afraid.'

'Aye, I imagine so,' McKay said. 'Is her partner still here? I'm assuming you don't throw everyone out after visiting hours?'

'Yes, she's still sitting with Ms Bennett. For the moment,' she added pointedly.

'And would you be able to point me in their direction?'

She finally conceded and gestured towards the far end of the ward. 'Last bay on the right,' she said. 'Please do try not to disturb the other patients.'

'I'll put the song and dance act on hold,' McKay said.

Horton was sitting by Isla's bed, looking half-asleep herself. 'Alec?'

'Aye. The bad penny. Looks like I'm back on the job. For tonight, at any rate.' He pulled up a chair and sat down beside Horton. 'How's she doing?'

'Not so bad. She woke for a while, but they've given her sedation for the night. They're keeping her in 'til they've got all the test results back, but they think she's okay.'

'And how are you?'

'I'm fine. A bit shocked about David. But mainly just because it happened in our house. It doesn't make any sense.'

'Did Isla say anything when she woke?'

'Not really. She was still very woozy. I don't think she saw anything. Like me, she hadn't been into the living room. Went straight into the kitchen to make a coffee. She can't remember much after that, but it looks like she was struck from behind with some heavy object. Fairly vicious blow, from what the doctor said, but luckily, Isla's got a thick head.' She gave a laugh only just the right side of forced. 'Could easily have been much nastier.'

'Small mercies,' McKay said. 'So, she knew nothing about –'

'David? I don't think so. She was spared that, anyway. Not that either of us is likely to be entering a prolonged period of mourning, if that doesn't sound too brutal.'

'From what you've said, it doesn't sound like he'll be much missed. At least he won't be around to harass you again. Do you think that was why he was there again last night?'

'I don't know. Even that makes no real sense,' Horton said. 'After all the hassle, I'd finally agreed to meet with him. On neutral territory, with Isla present, so he couldn't play any of his games. He'd agreed to that, so why would he change his mind?'

'Maybe neutral territory wasn't really what he wanted. Maybe he just agreed to the meeting to keep you stringing along.'

'Could be,' Horton said. 'But that doesn't explain who killed him. Or why they decided to do it in our house.'

'Do you know of anyone who'd want to kill him?'

'I imagine there were dozens of people. Some more serious than others. But, no, it's years since I've seen him properly. I don't know who he might be mixing with now. Or what he might be involved in.' She shrugged. 'I just wish he hadn't brought whatever it is to my house.'

'Aye, well, from what you say, that was the sort of man he was. His ID has an address in Surrey. Does that sound right?'

'Probably. He was living somewhere near Guildford the last I knew. That was a few years ago.'

'We'll have to liaise with the local force down there,' McKay said. 'I'm guessing that whatever's behind this is something that's followed him up, for whatever reason.'

'I'd assume so,' Horton said. 'I don't know that he had any business up here, other than with me. Mind you, he was the sort of man who had his fingers in a lot of pies. As far as I know, he'd never been back up to these parts since –' She stopped suddenly.

McKay frowned. 'Since?'

Horton shook her head. 'I was going to rabbit on, and then, I remembered that you don't know about any of this, do you?'

'From your tone, I'm guessing not.'

'I've never told you about my background, have I? Well, not much.'

'A fine English rose. The flower of the home counties. As English as – I don't know – double-dealing and exploitation. Something like that?'

'Except I'm not, really.'

'Not what?'

'Not English.'

'So, what are you, then?'

'If you weren't already sitting down, I'd tell you to sit down. The shock might be too much. The fact is, Alec, I'm as Scottish as you are. Well, nearly.'

For a moment, McKay found himself in the unaccustomed position of not knowing what to say. 'Well, that explains a lot,' he said finally.

'Does it?'

'Aye, I always knew you were far too capable to be English.' He shook his head. 'But, okay, take me through this slowly. How come you're Scottish? I've never heard anyone who sounds more fucking English. And, believe me, I've heard some gobshites over the years.'

'You say the nicest things. I spent virtually all my childhood in the depths of Surrey. But I was born up here.'

'So, what were you doing down there, then? Operating undercover? Missionary work?'

'My mother moved south when I was small. With David.' She recounted the story she'd previously told Isla.

McKay was having some difficulty processing all this. 'Your dad was a copper?'

'Apparently.'

'Killed in a hit and run.'

'Yes. He was a PC.'

'When would this have been?'

'Twenty odd years ago. I was just a baby.'

'What was his name?'

'Peter Horton. Mum kept his name. She and David never married.'

'Doesn't ring any bells,' McKay said. 'I'd have thought it would. Officer being killed's a big deal, whatever the circumstances.' He paused, thinking. 'David Kirkland does, though, now I think about it.'

'David?'

'Aye. When Jock Henderson told me the name on the ID, it set something buzzing in my mind. But I couldn't remember what it was. He was another one of us, wasn't he?'

'That's what he told me. Left the force when we moved south.'

McKay leaned back on his chair and regarded Horton for a second. 'You're really full of surprises, aren't you, Ginny? Why'd you never share any of this before?'

She shifted uneasily on her seat. 'It didn't seem relevant. Mum never wanted to talk about the time before we moved down south.'

'Yet, you've ended up back up here in the family business?'

'That's what Isla said. Paging Dr Freud.'

'Ach, well. None of us can escape our backgrounds, however much we might try.'

'That's a bit philosophical for you, Alec.'

'I'm in a philosophical mood, Ginny. That's what a few days of enforced inaction does to you.' He was silent for a moment, his fingers drumming softly on the metal frame of Isla's bed. 'David Kirkland, though,' he said finally.

'What about him?'

'He was a bit of an odd bugger.' McKay hesitated. 'Sorry, Ginny, I'm being insensitive –'

'Feel free,' she said. 'I've said much worse about him. But how do you mean?'

'I was just a young copper, so I only saw things from the margins. But there was a lot of gossip about Kirkland. He was nominally attached to Galloway's team. Major investigations. He was a DS, but he seemed to occupy his own position, do pretty much what he wanted. He was one of the few people I never saw Galloway bully. Galloway just steered clear of him.'

'What are you saying?'

'I don't know what I'm saying. None of us knew much about Kirkland's background. He was supposedly a local –'

'He always told me he was from Inverness,' Horton said. 'And I suppose you could just about detect an accent. But he'd probably have passed for English to most people.'

'Story was that he'd spent some years down south before he joined us up here. Worked for the Met. Nothing was ever said explicitly, but my impression was that he was on some sort of secondment arrangement rather than a straightforward transfer. Nobody seemed to know quite what his role was.'

'People like that are usually spooks or Special Branch,' Horton observed.

'Or just self-important arseholes,' McKay said. 'But, aye, that was the gossip, right enough.'

'He never gave a hint of anything like that.'

'Well, he wouldn't, I suppose. Depending on what he'd been involved in.'

'Why would he have been up here?'

'That's the question,' McKay said. 'Not exactly terrorist central up here. Ach, maybe it's all bollocks. Maybe he just wanted people to think he was more than he was.'

'Well, that would be David,' Horton agreed. 'I never saw him as a fantasist, but he didn't suffer from any lack of self-importance.'

'Intriguing, though,' McKay said. 'Another question is why he chose to leave the force after he got together with your mother. Why head back south?'

'He always reckoned it was because he'd had enough. Wanted a change. He certainly didn't go off to re-join Special Branch or MI5. He was working in some management role for a security firm. Did okay. Set himself up in something similar in the end. Agency security stuff. Made a penny or two out of it, though that was after Mum had left him.'

'And he ends up dead on the floor of your living room,' McKay said. 'I don't envy the poor bugger who gets landed with digging into all this.'

'You don't think it'll be you, then? Leading the investigation, I mean. When you said you were back on the job –'

'I'm just helping Helena out of a hole tonight. She's running on empty. But I'm not out of the woods yet on the Rob Graham thing. She's going to have to tread carefully. Anyway, this one we can throw back to our friends in the south. Like I say, we've no strong reason to believe the killing was connected with anything up here.'

'Good luck with that,' she said. 'I'm sure they'll be only too keen to take on a major investigation into a murder six-hundred miles away. Especially if there might be spook involvement.'

'Everyone likes a challenge.'

She laughed. 'Jesus, we need you back, Alec. You to keep me going.'

He looked at her for a moment, trying to gauge whether she was mocking him. 'If this is how I get treated because I've been away for a few days, I might plan to be away a lot more.'

'Ach, awa' and boil yer heid, McKay,' Horton said in a bad Scottish accent.

'By George,' McKay said, pushing himself to his feet, 'I think she's got it. Welcome home, girl.'

CHAPTER FORTY-FIVE

Outside, the rain was falling harder than ever, and McKay scurried to his car, head bent low against the freezing wind. He threw himself into the driving seat and dragged out his phone, thumbing for Helena Grant's number.

She answered almost immediately. 'Grant.'

The weather at her end sounded even worse than it was in Raigmore, her words muffled by the roar of the wind. 'Jesus, Helena, where are you?'

'Still up at poxing Munlochy Bay,' she said. 'Waiting for the ambulance to come and collect Ally Donald's body. Thought I might as well send the uniforms on their way so they can go and deal with drunks on Union Street or whatever's next on their list.'

'It is Donald, then?'

'We're pretty certain. He's been in the water a bit, but the ID checks out. Looks like we might have some worrying developments, though. Carrick reckons this one might be more than just murder. Reckons some pain's been inflicted on the body. Some form of torture.'

'Christ. Where the hell's this going, then?'

'You tell me. How's your evening been? And, more importantly, how are Ginny and Isla?'

'Ginny seems fine, and it looks like Isla will be, too, assuming the tests don't reveal anything unexpected. And my evening's been – enlightening. Has Ginny ever told you anything about her background?'

'Not really. From somewhere down south, isn't she?'

'As it turns out, no.' He repeated what Horton had told him.

'She's really Scottish? You're going to have to start treating her with some respect, Alec.'

'Aye, right. And when have I ever treated my fellow Scots with any kind of respect?'

'True enough. So, this stepdad, or whatever he was, was David Kirkland?'

'Ring any bells with you?'

'Vaguely. The one everybody reckoned must be Special Branch or some such. I assumed he'd been sucked back into the mysterious world of spookdom.'

'Turns out he was being an abusive stepdad to our DS Horton,' McKay said. 'Who knew? Maybe he was just a fantasist prick after all. Though, given someone had a reason to kill him tonight, maybe not.'

'I suppose he was a member of Galloway's team as well,' Grant offered. 'Notionally, anyway. Maybe this is part of the same deal.'

'He was barely part of Galloway's team. They stuck him there for the headcount, but I don't recall him having any operational contact with Galloway. Or much other kind of contact, for that matter.'

'If our killer's reaching those parts of Galloway's team, you and I can't be too much further down the list, Alec.'

McKay thought back to the hands tightening around his throat a couple of nights earlier. He needed to tell Grant about that, but the moment didn't seem right. Apart from anything else, if she was stuck out by herself in the wilds of Munlochy Bay, it wouldn't help to give her another reason to worry. 'Aye, that thought had occurred to me. I guess we need to take a bit of care.'

'Trust me, Alec, I'm taking as much as I can at the moment.'

'What about Ginny's father?' McKay asked, looking to change the subject. 'Her real father, I mean. This Peter Horton. That name mean anything to you?'

'Nothing.'

'Yet, he was supposedly killed in service. You've think that would have snagged in the mind.'

'I'd have thought so,' Grant said. 'I don't remember anything like that. You're sure he was based up here?'

'That was Ginny's understanding. I suppose, after all these years, she might have got the details wrong or misremembered what her mother said.'

'That's not usually Ginny's style. Worth looking into?'

McKay was silent for a moment. 'I don't know,' he said. 'I mean, I'd say it was Ginny's business. I can't see how or why it would have anything to do with what we're investigating.'

'But?'

'It's just that something's telling me that it might.'

'The old copper's intuition?'

'Aye, and I'm getting to be a very old copper. But you know how it is with these things. You just pull on threads in the hope one of them might lead you somewhere.'

'I'll look into it myself,' Grant said. 'Don't want to risk setting any hares running where Ginny's concerned.'

'Thanks for humouring me, hen. Speaking of which, am I off the job again now?'

'Let's play it by ear, shall we, Alec? I'm trying to look after both our interests. It's the weekend now, so you don't need to come in 'til Monday. Who knows how many corpses we'll have by then?'

'That's what I love about you,' McKay said. 'Your unbridled sense of optimism.'

'Aye,' Grant said. 'It's part of my Scottish character. You'd better break that news to poor Ginny.'

***

Grant finished the call with McKay and sat staring into the windblown night. She'd found a garden chair and made herself as comfortable as she could in the shelter of the unoccupied holiday cottage. Carrick had wrapped the body in a substantial body bag and then, with the help of the two PCs, carried it up out of the rain. So here she was, all alone in the pitch-black night, with nothing but a corpse for company. *And people say policing isn't glamorous*, she thought.

She wondered whether she should have left the two PCs to babysit the body. But they'd both got a full list of call-outs, whereas she was planning to do nothing more than head back for a whisky and a long hot bath. Carrick had offered to wait with her, but she couldn't see much point in both of them being cold and wet, and as the senior officer present, she felt an obligation to see this through.

She'd been told the ambulance would be there as soon as possible, but that had been nearly forty-five minutes ago. In the adjoining cottage, she could see the flickering of a television screen. She wondered about asking the Renshaws whether she could shelter inside, but felt reluctant to impose on them any further.

She wasn't by nature a nervous person, and she'd faced more than a few hairy moments in her police career. Even so, the conversation with McKay had left her uneasy. It was difficult to imagine why anyone should bear a grudge about her or McKay's involvement as junior officers in Galloway's team twenty years before, but whoever was behind this was playing by no normal rules. It felt as if that team, for whatever reason, was being picked off one by one.

The only reassurance was that, unlike Galloway, Crawford and Graham, she and McKay had never received any threatening letters. But she didn't know whether Ally Donald or Davey Robertson had received letters either, and both of them had ended up dead. Now Donald's body had been found, they'd at least have an opportunity to check through his possessions.

She'd turned off her flashlight to save the battery. The darkness closed in within a few metres, and it was impossible to make out anything other than the bulk of the trees along the shoreline.

There was no reason to think anyone was out there. No one could have known Donald's body would be washed up here tonight. No one could have known she'd end up sitting here by herself. Even if someone really was out to get her, she was arguably safer here than in her own home.

She forced her mind to focus on the case. Five deaths now, at least three of which they knew to be unlawful killings. Galloway's and Robertson's were still, in effect, open verdicts, but Galloway's at least was an unlikely coincidence. As for Robertson's death a few weeks earlier – well, who knew? The case notes had told her little. Robertson had lived alone, separated from his wife who was living in Inverness. He seemed to have no close friends, but neighbours had thought he seemed anxious and distracted in the weeks before his death. They'd have to do some more digging there, talk to the widow. But without some evidence to link it to the other deaths, it was likely to be a dead end.

Finally, she saw a glimpse of blue light hazed by the rain and the trees. She hadn't realised until that moment how tense she'd been feeling. She stepped over to the edge of the decking, holding her flashlight ready for the ambulance's arrival. The throb of the blue light was growing closer. She assumed they'd turned on the lights to alert her to their arrival.

The ambulance headlights appeared on the road along the shore. She turned on the flashlight and waved it to attract their attention. As she did so, she glanced down. The land to the right of the cottage was largely grassed over. At this time of the year, it was soddened with rain, patches of mud visible among the grass.

She held the flashlight steady and directed it back towards the ground, wanting to confirm what she thought she'd seen a second before.

She was oblivious now to the sound of ambulance pulling up, the shouts of the paramedics as they climbed out.

Her eyes were fixed on the ground.

On the trail of clear, apparently new footprints leading from the edge of the veranda away into the darkness.

CHAPTER FORTY-SIX

They usually served food until around eight-thirty, the pub staying open until eleven. Kelly had finally passed her driving test on the second time of trying and had received an aged handed-down car from her parents as a late Christmas present. It meant she could work the evening shift at the Caledonian Bar, without worrying how to get home. Callum generally let her go a little before closing time, unless they were unusually busy.

Tonight had been relatively quiet for a Friday, maybe because the weather had closed in. Around eight-fifteen, Callum had poked his head out of the kitchen and said, 'No sign of anyone else looking to eat?'

She was feeling uneasy about their earlier exchange, even though nothing had really happened. Nothing more than her own post-adolescent imaginings, a momentary schoolgirl crush. He was a decent-looking man, Callum, but he was hardly her type, even if Maggie hadn't been in the picture. Kelly might be looking for someone with more maturity than Greg, but not that much more. She forced herself to turn and smile. 'Doesn't look like it.' There was a family finishing eating, but the other occupants of the bar were regulars more interested in the beer than the food.

'Think you can hold the fort for an hour or so?'

'Don't see why not. Doesn't look like there's going to be a sudden rush.'

'Hope it doesn't stay like this,' Callum said. 'We were building trade nicely, but now it's stalled a bit.'

'It's still early in the year,' she said. 'And rubbish weather. You wait 'til the season starts. They'll be queuing outside.'

'I hope you're right. I'm just popping out for a bit, if you're sure you can cope. Maggie's having a lie down. One of her migraines.'

She thought she detected a slight disapproving emphasis on the last word, as if he were dismissing it as a bad habit that Maggie indulged in.

'I'll be fine,' she said.

'I'll be back by ten,' he said. 'Then you can get off early, if you like.'

She'd coped perfectly happily. Callum reappeared just after nine-thirty, looking wet and dishevelled. 'Cats and dogs out there. Miserable night.'

'Have you been far?' she said.

'Just to see one of the suppliers. Guy who sells us meat and game. Gets some grand stuff at a good price. Never like to enquire too closely where it comes from.' He laughed. 'But he reckons it's legit. He's in with the local farmers.'

Kelly thought was talking a little too quickly, sounding nervous. Maybe he was hiding something, she thought. Maybe he was having an affair. She'd assumed, when she started working here, that Callum and Maggie had the perfect marriage. They always seemed to get on well enough in her presence. But lately, she'd seen the odd crack in that façade. Maybe things weren't quite as smooth as they appeared on the surface.

Or maybe, she added to herself, *that's just your own wishful thinking.*

'Hope you didn't get too wet.'

'My own fault,' he said. 'Took a jacket without a hood. Got soaked just getting from the car.'

He joined her behind the bar, though none of the remaining regulars showed much sign of needing another round in the foreseeable future. It was at times like this, despite the refurbished decor, that the place felt most like it had in Denny Gorman's day. She glanced towards the passageway to the cellars, hoping that none of the barrels would need replacing tonight.

'I meant what I said earlier, you know,' Callum said.

'What was that?'

'About you needing someone to look after you.'

She turned away, conscious she wanted to avoid his eye. 'Did you have anyone in mind?' She'd finally brought herself to say the words and was aware that they sounded on the verge of flirtatious.

'Not really. But you deserve someone decent. Someone with a bit about him. Not like that young toerag the other day.'

'Ach, well. He's well and truly out of the picture. I guess I'd rather find someone –'

'Someone what?'

He was standing closer behind her than she'd realised. She turned, flustered. He wasn't exactly crowding her, but he'd never stood this close before. 'I don't know,' she said, scarcely conscious of what she was saying. 'Someone a bit more sensible. A bit more mature.'

'Is that right?'

'I –' She stopped, seeing that Maggie had entered the bar behind him. 'Oh, hi, Maggie. How are you feeling now?'

Callum had already turned to face his wife so Kelly was unable to read his expression. 'Oh, you've risen. How's the head?'

Maggie was regarding them both curiously. 'Not so bad,' she said. 'I can usually shake them off as long as I can get some rest. Thanks for looking after the place.'

'No problem,' Kelly said. 'It's been pretty quiet.'

'I was telling Kelly she should get off early,' Callum said. 'It's pouring down out there.'

'Don't suppose you could get me a coffee, Callum,' Maggie said. 'I need something to get my brain into gear again.'

'Aye, of course.'

Maggie watched as he disappeared into the kitchen, then turned to Kelly. 'Was that him up to his old tricks again?'

'I don't know what –'

'Don't worry, Kelly. I'm not blaming you. I know you're not leading him on. If you were, you wouldn't be still working here. You're a decent kid. I just know what he's like.'

Kelly could think of nothing to say. She was feeling – well, her age, she supposed. Smart as she might be, she knew she was little more than a kid. More than vulnerable to being exploited by someone better versed in the ways of the world. Her first feeling was embarrassment, but her second was anger, though she couldn't have said whether it was directed at Callum or at Maggie. 'He hasn't tried anything on,' she said finally. 'Really.'

'He will,' Maggie said. 'I can see the way his mind's working. Except it's not his mind that's mainly in charge. And when he does, don't be fooled. Tell him to bugger off, and then, tell me.'

'I –'

'Don't trust him, Kelly. If you're not careful, he'll tell you night is day, and you'll end up believing him. Now, get off home for the night, and we'll see you tomorrow.'

Kelly nodded, conscious she was on the verge of tears. She turned, grabbed her coat, and made her way out into the night.

CHAPTER FORTY-SEVEN

*T*his isn't me, Helena Grant thought. *I don't get nervous. I don't get scared. Not like this. Not after all these years.*

She was clutching the steering wheel tightly, head forward, staring out into the rain. She must be almost back up to the main road by now, but an anxious part of her was still expecting that the car would stick, wheels spinning vainly in the sodden ground. The last thing she wanted was to be stranded out here tonight.

She saw the glow of a street light up ahead and realised she was at the junction. Relieved, she paused to turn left on to the main road back towards home.

It was only then she admitted to herself that she didn't want to do it. That she was afraid to go home. That if someone really had been watching her tonight, that person almost certainly knew where she lived.

She turned right instead, heading further down the Black Isle towards Fortrose. She reached over, flicked through her phone's address book and dialled the number.

'Alec?'

'Helena? You okay?'

'Aye, I'm fine. Well, fine-ish.'

'Thought you'd have had enough of my blethering for one night.'

'Actually, I was wondering if you were still up to receiving visitors at your palatial new residence.'

'Tonight? Aye, well, I'll have to tell all the other guests at my Friday night soirée to clear out, but I don't suppose Nicola and Alex will be too offended. Don't know about Ruth and Kezia, though. They look settled in for the night. Where are you exactly?'

'Not far,' she said. 'Just past Munlochy.'

'My door's always open to you, hen. You know that.'

'See you in ten minutes then,' she said, when he'd told her how to find the place.

'The kettle will be singing on the hob for you,' McKay said, then added for the avoidance of doubt, 'Metaphorically speaking, that is.'

The rain had slowed by the time she reached McKay's bungalow, though there was still a fine drizzle misting the street lights. McKay had heard the car and was standing in the doorway.

'You must be freezing,' he said, bustling her in. 'You definitely drew the short straw tonight.'

She followed him through into the living room. 'You weren't kidding about the shabby and soulless bit, were you?' she said.

'Ach, I'm warming to the place.'

She looked around. 'With a bit of effort, you could make it quite cosy. But you're not going to put the effort in, are you?'

'I doubt it. What can I get you? Coffee? Tea? Something stronger?'

She hesitated. 'I'm driving. But to be honest after the night I've had, I think I need some fortification.'

'We can organise you a taxi back. Your car'll be safe here. And tomorrow's Saturday.'

'Which doesn't mean I won't be in at work.'

'Your choice,' he said. 'I can offer you a decent whisky. One of the few things I made sure to bring with me from home.'

'Home?'

'Ach, you know.'

'You've talked me into it,' she said. 'Whisky and a taxi.'

He returned from the kitchen with two unmatching glasses and an unopened bottle of Dalmore. 'So, what's been bad about tonight? Apart from having to deal with a washed-up corpse in the pouring rain.' She was slumped on the cheap vinyl sofa. He seated himself on the armchair opposite.

She told him what had happened while she was waiting by Munlochy Bay. McKay was silent for a moment. 'I should have told you,' he said finally.

'Told me what?'

'What happened to me in Fortrose the other night.' He placed the two glasses on the table and poured them a decent measure each.

'Which was?'

'That I was attacked. Out of the blue. After I left Meg Barnard's house.'

'Oh, Jesus, Alec. Why the hell didn't you tell me?'

'You seemed pissed enough with me already. I didn't need your sympathy as well.'

She allowed him a laugh. 'You do realise this is technically withholding evidence? Like you're not deep enough in the shite already.'

'That's always been my motto. If you're up to your oxters, keep digging. But, aye, you're right. I should have said something.' He took a mouthful of the Scotch. 'Sorry.'

'Worth it just to hear you say that word,' she said.

'Don't you think I'll be making a habit of it.'

She took a deep swallow of the whisky, with the air of someone forcing down an unwelcome medicine. 'What the hell's going on here, Alec? Jackie Galloway's team apparently being picked off one-by-one. You and me may be on the list, even though we were the most junior members of Galloway's crew. Who the hell would bear that sort of a grudge after all this time?'

'Plenty of people capable of bearing a long-term grudge,' McKay observed. 'The real question is why they've waited so long.' He stared into his glass as if seeking inspiration. 'I'm still interested in this Peter Horton.'

'Ginny's father?'

McKay swirled the whisky for a second, then took another mouthful. 'Aye. It's like a piece of the jigsaw that doesn't fit.' He paused. 'I made a phone call earlier.'

She eased herself back on the sofa, resting her feet gently on the edge of the coffee table. 'Is this something else I'm not going to like?'

'Nah, I was very discreet.'

'Go on, then.'

'Spoke to Craig Fairlie.'

'The journo. Oh, aye, very discreet, Alec.'

'Ach, he's an old pal.'

'Aye, they all are, if they think you'll give them some inside intel.'

'I just asked if he recalled any coppers being killed around that time. Craig's Mr Memory. If anyone would remember, he would.'

'And?'

'Not a scoobie. Nothing at all. He remembered a couple of officers who'd died in service, but they were both victims of the great Scottish coronary.'

'So why did Ginny believe it?'

'Because that's what she's been told, I'm guessing. She'd have been told this as a child. Her mother wouldn't have imagined she'd end up as a police officer back up here. Yes, there was always the possibility that she might start digging into her natural father's background, but maybe that wasn't foremost in her mother's thoughts at the time.'

'But why lie at all?'

'People lie for all kinds of reasons, don't they? We don't know who Ginny's father really was or what happened to him. Maybe her mother just wanted a positive story.'

Grant considered for a moment. 'In which case, all this might have no significance after all. Just a nice story to tell the wee one.'

'Except that David Kirkland was a copper.'

'Maybe that was what gave her the idea. And made it plausible.'

'And Kirkland's now dead. Apparently killed in the same way as the rest of Galloway's crew. And he'd been trying to talk to Ginny.'

'We don't know that he was really trying to talk to her,' Grant pointed out. 'It looked to me that he was trying to harass her. If he wanted to talk, there's always the phone.'

'Depends what he had to say,' McKay said. 'Some things are better said face to face.' Both their glasses were empty. McKay leaned forward and refilled them.

'Alec McKay, expert in interpersonal communications. What sort of things?'

'I don't know,' McKay said. 'Maybe something like everything you've been told about your background is a lie?' He paused, thinking. 'Or that the man you thought was your father didn't exist?'

'You're making an awful lot of leaps there, Alec.'

'I'm just thinking aloud. Never a pretty sight.'

Grant emptied her glass. 'I'll do some digging into it tomorrow. But surely Ginny's mother wouldn't have just made him up?'

'Who knows? If she had some reason to be embarrassed by the real identity of the father, maybe she thought it better to create some idealised figure instead.'

'If you're even half right about any of this, it'll be devastating to Ginny.'

McKay refilled their glasses for the third time. 'We seem to be getting through this Scotch.'

'Spirits evaporate,' Grant said. 'Scientific fact.'

'Aye, no doubt. You're right, though. It'll be a shock to Ginny if there's anything in this. But she's a tough little thing.'

'I hope so.' Grant leaned her head back on the sofa, looking as if she might fall asleep at any moment. 'I still don't see how this has anything to do with Galloway and his gang, though.'

'Me neither,' McKay acknowledged. 'A lot may depend on what it was that Kirkland wanted to tell Ginny.'

'We'd better start doing some digging into Kirkland as well.'

'Good luck with that. If the rumours were true, I imagine Kirkland's tracks will have been well and truly covered.'

'If the rumours were true,' Grant said, 'how come he ended up working as a glorified security guard down south?'

'Maybe he'd been compromised in some way. Time for him to get out. Who knows?'

'We don't, certainly,' Grant said, yawning. 'Christ, I'm tired.'

'You want me to phone for that taxi?'

Her eyes were still closed. 'I suppose.' She paused. 'If you want me to go.'

There was an extended silence. Finally, McKay said, 'I don't think it would be right for you to stay.'

'We're both single, Alec.'

'I'm not. Maybe I will be. Maybe I won't. But I'm not now.' He was silent for another moment. 'And you're my boss.'

Grant laughed. 'Jesus. How the hell did that happen? Alec McKay being the cautious sensible one. But, aye, you're right, Alec. It was the whisky talking.'

'I'll phone the cab, then.' As he climbed to his feet, he leaned over and poured her another measure. 'While you're waiting, you can let the Scotch have a few last words.'

'Christ,' she said. 'I'm going to regret this in the morning.'

It wasn't clear, McKay thought as he dialled the number of the taxi firm, whether she was referring only to the whisky.

CHAPTER FORTY-EIGHT

She was standing in the small car park at the rear of the bar, fumbling clumsily for her car keys, when he appeared. The rain had lessened to a fine mist, and it was almost as if he materialised from the darkness. She stood, frozen, car keys clutched too tightly in her hand.

'Kelly. I'm sorry –'

She took a breath. 'You'd better go back inside, Callum. I don't think it's a good idea for you to talk to me like this.'

'What did she say to you?'

Kelly was still feeling shaken by her conversation with Maggie Donnelly. It was only a couple of weeks until she went back to university. She could just jack all this in and focus on her studies. It would mean she had a bit less money for next term, but that would hardly be life-changing. She didn't need this hassle. 'You know what she said, Callum.'

He took a further step or two towards her. 'I know the kind of thing she'll have said, aye. You know it's all nonsense, don't you?'

'I don't know, and I don't care.' She was still feeling too much like a gauche teenager, but was determined not to show it. 'I don't want to get involved.'

'There's nothing to get involved with,' Donnelly said. He held up his hands. 'Have I done anything, Kelly? Have I tried it on with you?'

'Well, no –' She could already feel her initial certainty crumbling.

'That's not me, Kelly. It's not the man I am.'

'It's none of my business –'

'That's Maggie. She's a bonny woman. But she gets – well, jealous. She imagines things.'

Kelly was thinking back to that moment behind the bar. Something had happened then, but she couldn't have said what it was, or whether Callum had been responsible. Maybe she'd been imagining things too. 'Like I say, Callum, it's none of my business. Look, I need to get home –'

'Aye, I'm sorry. I shouldn't keep you. I just didn't want you to go away with the wrong impression. I'm sorry for what Maggie said. She gets things – out of proportion sometimes.'

Kelly couldn't read the expression on his face. When he'd appeared unexpectedly out of the darkness, her first thought had been of the previous landlord, Denny Gorman, lurking in the shadows of the cellars. Gorman had been a sleazy piece of work, and she couldn't see Callum Donnelly in the same light. But she didn't know what to think.

'It's none of my business,' she repeated. 'I'm just here to work behind the bar.'

'Things are difficult between me and Maggie at the moment,' Donnelly went on, as if he hadn't heard her. 'That's all it is.'

'Look, I really do need to be getting back.'

'Aye, of course. You're getting wet.' He said this with a note of surprise, as if he'd been unaware of the persistent drizzle gradually soaking both of them. 'You'll come back, though? Tomorrow, I mean.' His tone was that of a small child being left at nursery for the first time.

A few moments before, she really had been on the point of giving it up, driving off and not bothering to come back. 'Okay,' she said, finally. 'I'll be back tomorrow. But Callum –'

'What?'

'I really want nothing to do with this. If there are – problems between you and Maggie, that's your business. I'm not part of it, and I don't want to be. If Maggie starts to think –'

'Aye,' he said. 'Understood.'

She climbed into the car and turned on the engine, then reversed carefully out of the narrow parking space. Donnelly stood to one side, head dipped against the steadily falling rain.

As she pulled on to the high street, she glanced in the rear-view mirror. He was still there, head bowed, watching her drive away.

***

Ginny Horton had hoped they'd allow her to stay overnight with Isla, but the charge nurse had made it clear this was not hospital policy. 'I just want to make sure she's all right,' Horton had argued.

'Of course you do, dear,' the nurse had agreed. 'As do we all. And the best way to do that is for her to get as much rest as possible.'

McKay had returned the house keys. There was no reason why she couldn't simply go back and get herself a decent night's sleep.

Except that the idea still unnerved her.

She was being ridiculous, of course. Her only cause for anxiety had been David's behaviour, and that was something she need never worry about again. It was hardly pleasant that his body had been discovered in their home, and there still remained the unanswered question of who was responsible for his death. But unless David's death had been merely coincidental, it was difficult to imagine why the killer would have any interest in her or Isla. She didn't know what business David had been involved in. But he'd always sailed close to the wind, and she imagined the reasons for his death had nothing to do with his visit up here. Maybe his killers just preferred to avoid soiling their own doorstep.

In the late evening, the journey home took her little more than half an hour. When she turned on the hallway light, everything looked normal, as if the evening's events had never taken place. She moved quickly through the ground floor, turning on the lights in each room.

She suspected that McKay had done some tidying of his own once Jock Henderson had completed his work. There was nothing obviously out of place, no sign of where Isla had been lying on the kitchen floor, or of where David's body had been spread-eagled in the sitting room. She checked that all the downstairs doors and windows were locked, closing each set of curtains as if she were physically excluding the outside world.

She went through the same routine with the upper rooms, although there was no sign they had been disturbed. When she found herself compulsively wanting to double-check the rooms she had already visited, she decided it was time for bed.

In the end, she slept better than she'd expected. She lay awake for a while, listening to the rain against the skylight, and eventually, the soft white noise was enough to lull her into unconsciousness.

She woke once in the night, aware of the absence in the bed beside her. Half-awake, it took her a moment to recall the events of the previous evening, the fact that Isla was still sleeping in Raigmore Hospital. Lying awake, she was struck by a sudden unease.

Her first thought was that something might have happened to Isla. But the ward had her contact details, and she'd missed no calls to her mobile. Her second, equally irrational thought was that someone was in the house. She lay still and listened, but could hear nothing. The rain had ceased while she was sleeping, and the night was silent.

She climbed out of bed and, slipping on her dressing gown, she walked over to the window. Finally, she recognised the source of her unease, the probable reason why she had woken.

The security light at the rear of the house had been triggered and the back garden was flooded with light. The glare was bright enough to illuminate the square of the bedroom window through the curtains.

She lifted back the curtain and peered out into the night. As far as she could see, the garden was deserted, the wet leaves of the trees glistening in the white glow. Most likely, the light had been triggered by some animal. It had happened before from time to time.

She was about to close the curtains when she caught a movement at the edge of her vision. She pressed her face against the glass. For a second, she thought she glimpsed a human figure, dark against the green backdrop. Then, it was gone, if it had ever been there. A second later, the light was extinguished, and the garden plunged back into darkness.

Her rational mind told her it was nothing more than an illusion, a shape created by the night and the movement of the leaves. She stepped across the room and silently opened the bedroom door, listening intently for any sign of movement. But there was nothing.

She couldn't bring herself to go downstairs, even at the price of leaving her fears unchecked. In the end, she closed the bedroom door and pulled over a high-backed chair to wedge under the handle. It was primitive, but it would delay any intruder long enough for her to dial 999.

And, she told herself, *there is no intruder.*

She forced herself to return to bed. This time, sleep really did prove elusive, and she lay awake, her ears alert for any sound, falling into a fitful slumber only as the first glow of dawn showed through the curtains.

CHAPTER FORTY-NINE

Helena Grant's regrets the following morning were as she'd predicted. Mostly, she regretted the excess of whisky which had left her with a mild but nagging headache and a general sense of not being up to speed with the world. Partly, she regretted what she'd said to McKay. The words had been out of her mouth before she realised what she was saying. She still wasn't sure what had motivated her – a genuine desire, the whisky, or just her nervousness about coming back home alone. Whichever it was, the words had been said, and there was no way to take them back.

And there was part of her, she realised, that was regretful about Alec McKay's response. He'd been right, of course. He wasn't single, and in a soberer mood, Grant would never have wanted to risk hurting Chrissie. And she was his boss. She was already sailing close enough to the wind in her dealings with McKay. The last thing she needed was anything that might compromise her further.

Even so, it had taken all her courage to return home alone the previous night. She'd been tempted to reveal to McKay how nervous she was feeling, but she'd been afraid he'd invite her to stay merely out of sympathy. She'd asked the taxi driver, a young local man whom she knew from previous trips, to wait until she was safely inside the house. Then, she'd locked all the doors firmly behind her and checked all the rooms, before finally retiring to bed.

Now, as she sat drinking her coffee and gazing out over the firth, she decided her biggest regret was simply that she'd allowed herself to become so spooked the night before. In the light of a fine morning, her fears felt absurd. The rain had passed, and the sky was clear, reflected in the choppy waters below.

The footprints last night proved nothing. She'd assumed they were new, because otherwise the rain would have washed them away. But maybe they were less recent than she'd assumed. Perhaps they'd been left by one of the Renshaws or some passing walker earlier in the day. In hindsight, it seemed ridiculous to imagine that anyone might have taken the trouble to follow her down there, whatever their motivation. Alone, in the dark, with only a corpse for company, she'd allowed herself to get the jitters.

It was Saturday, but she was planning to head into the office in any case. With this investigation expanding by the day – not to mention the impending investigation into the death of David Kirkland – time off was a luxury she couldn't afford.

She organised a taxi to retrieve her car. There was no sign of life in McKay's bungalow, and after a moment's hesitation, she decided not to disturb him. There'd be time enough to face him later.

The traffic was light back into town. From the Kessock Bridge, it looked as if the world had been washed clean by the previous night's rain, the waters of the firth sparkling in the morning sunshine. The car park at HQ was almost empty, and inside, most of the offices were deserted for the weekend. The Major Incident Room for the investigation was a different matter. Despite the constraints on overtime payments, several of the team had made a point of coming in. It tended to be this way with any major investigation, and this had made a bigger impact than most.

Grant took a walk around the team, checking what was going on, what progress was being made. She made a point of reminding them not to push things too far, to make sure they got some rest over the weekend. Commitment was fine, but exhaustion wouldn't help anyone.

She returned to her own office and logged on to her computer, ready to face the stream of emails that would already have accumulated. Even putting aside the current investigation, she had a mountain of administration to catch up with.

She was barely seated at her desk before her mobile rang.

'Helena. Jacquie Green.'

Grant shouldn't have been surprised. Green was famous among her colleagues for her dedication and long hours. The mystery was how she managed to balance this with bringing up three very young children. But then, Grant thought, that wasn't a question that would even have occurred to her if Green had been male. 'Jacquie. Hard at work on a Saturday morning?'

'I'm guessing you might be, too,' Green said. 'There's a lot going on.'

'Aye, too much.'

'I came in partly because I heard about what happened at Ginny Horton's house. I understand this body we've got is her stepfather?'

'Well, almost,' Grant said. 'He never married Ginny's mother, so there's no legal relationship. Not much of any kind of relationship, in fact.' She never minded speaking openly with Jacquie Green.

'I thought you'd want me to look at him ASAP,' Green said, 'in the circumstances.'

'Appreciate that, Jacquie. At the moment, anything that makes our lives easier is welcome.'

'I'm not sure I'm going to make your life easier,' Green said. 'Wish I could.'

'I had a feeling you were about to say that.'

'I've not have chance to do more than take a preliminary look so far. But a couple of things,' Green said. 'First, the cause of death was asphyxiation. Strangulation. Pretty much identical to Graham and very similar to Crawford.'

'So, it looks as if this is part of the same pattern,' Grant acknowledged. 'It turns out that Kirkland's an ex-copper too. And was once attached to Galloway's team. This just gets bigger and bigger.' She paused. 'You said a couple of things?'

Alex Walters

'Well, maybe more than a couple. Next thing is that Kirkland wasn't killed where he was found. The body was moved after death.'

Grant was silent for a moment. 'You're saying someone went to the trouble of dumping his dead body in Ginny Horton's house?'

'That's the size of it.'

'But why the hell would anyone do that? And, before you say it, yes, I know it's my job to find that out.'

'The final thing is that, although asphyxiation was undoubtedly the cause of death, there were a number of other lesions and injuries to the body. All of which occurred before death.' Green paused, as if taking a breath. 'I'd say he suffered before he was killed. There are also lesions on his wrists and ankles that suggest he'd been tied up.'

'Jesus.' Grant was thinking back to what Pete Carrick had said the previous night about Ally Donald's body. 'Have you had chance to look at the other customer we brought in last night?'

'You're keeping us busy over here, aren't you? But, yes, I have. That was going to be my last point.'

'Same cause of death? Same type of injuries?'

'You have been told that nobody likes a smart-arse?'

'More times than I care to remember.'

'You're spot on. Pretty much identical.'

'Pete Carrick used the word "torture."'

There was another silence. Finally, Green said, 'I don't think that's an unreasonable description.'

'Christ, what are we dealing with here?'

'A lunatic,' Green said. 'With a grudge.'

'Hell of a grudge after twenty-odd years.'

'Aye, I'd say so.'

Grant ended the call and stared at her computer screen as if it might offer her some answers. All she ever seemed to get were more questions and an increasingly heavy workload. And she still had to decide what to do about McKay.

274

That thought brought her back to the mysterious Peter Horton. She really needed to check the records, see if anyone of that name had ever been employed as an officer here. But the HR offices would be closed until Monday, and she wouldn't be able to gain access to the old Northern Constabulary files without their help. After a moment's thought, she picked up the phone and dialled a number.

'Control Room.'

'DCI Grant here. Don't suppose Charlie Willock's on duty today, by any chance?'

'Sergeant Willock?' the operator said pointedly. Willock was old school and allowed only more senior officers to use his forename. 'Aye, he's in today. Did you want to speak to him?'

It took a moment to transfer the call. 'Willock.'

'Charlie, it's Helena Grant.'

She knew that Willock really wanted to call her "ma'am," but was smart enough to recognise it wouldn't be welcome. His compromise was usually to avoid calling her anything at all. 'What can I do for you?'

'Just want to pick your brains.'

'Pick away, if you can find them.'

Willock was one of the oldest serving officers in the region, less than a year away from retirement, with a reputation for an encyclopaedic knowledge of the force and its employees. 'Does the name Peter Horton ring any bells with you?'

'Horton? As in your DS Horton?'

'Same spelling, yes.' Grant said. 'With the force maybe twenty years ago.'

'Officer or staff?'

'Officer, as far as I know. Based in Inverness.'

'No. Rings no bells at all. Pretty sure we've never had an officer of that name. Not in my time.' He made it sound as if this period encompassed most of recorded history.

'Staff member, then?'

'It's possible, I suppose. I couldn't claim to know everyone who's ever worked here. But I don't think I've ever come across anyone of that name. Where did you get it from?'

'Just came up in conversation. Somebody reckoned he'd died in service.'

'Ach, no, that's nonsense.'

'No, that's what I thought. I wondered whether they'd got their wires crossed somehow.'

'Completely crossed, I'd say.'

'Aye, well. Thanks for the input, Charlie. You've confirmed what I thought.'

Whoever Peter Horton might have been, then, he'd never been an officer up here. The question was how much more of the story, if any, was actually true. Had Peter Horton existed? If he had, who had he been? And had he really died in a hit and run collision?

She dialled McKay's number. 'Alec? Helena. Recovered from the whisky yet?'

McKay sounded as if he'd only just woken up, but he often sounded like that, even in the middle of the day. 'Aye, just about. How are you? I see you got your car.'

'Aye. Thought it best not to disturb you.'

'I wasn't thinking straight last night. I shouldn't have let you go home alone.'

'Aye, well, let's not go there, eh? We'd both had a dram or two too many.'

'Long as you made it back safely.'

'I've just been talking to Charlie Willock,' she said.

'Lucky you. That man can bore for Scotland.'

'But he knows the Force. I was picking his brains about Peter Horton.'

'And?'

'He's pretty sure that Horton was never an officer here. Couldn't swear there wasn't someone of that name employed in a staff role, but he's no recollection of it. And the hit and run story sounds like complete bollocks.'

There was silence at the other end of the line. Then, McKay said, 'Shit. I've just had a thought.'

'First time for everything, Alec. Go on.'

'You know I said I'd spoken to Craig Fairlie? I asked him what he remembered about Jackie Galloway as well.'

'Oh, aye. This was you being discreet, wasn't it, Alec. And?'

'Well, maybe nothing. But it was when you mentioned the hit and run. With all last night's excitement, I'd forgotten about it.'

'Go on.'

'Fairlie reckoned that in Galloway's last few months in the force he got himself unduly worked up about the death of one Patrick O'Riordan. Hit and run death in the centre of Inverness.'

'At about the time we're talking about.'

'Exactly. It's another interesting coincidence.'

'Why would Galloway be interested?'

'Fairlie reckoned that Galloway was worried O'Riordan might be connected.'

'Connected?'

'Organised crime connections. Not local ones – that wouldn't trouble Galloway. But something bigger.'

'But why should that trouble Galloway, unless he'd been responsible for O'Riordan's death?'

'Good question.'

'Was there any evidence that O'Riordan was connected?'

'Well, presumably Galloway had nothing more than suspicions. Fairlie reckoned he found nothing. And Fairlie usually has the nose and sources to dig out anything if there's anything to be dug. So, I'd say not. Except that there's also the interesting fact that O'Riordan was Northern Irish.'

'Ah.'

'Again, may mean nothing. Lots of people are Northern Irish. Some of them are electrical fitters.' McKay was silent for a moment, and Grant could almost hear him thinking. 'One other thing,' he said. 'It just occurred to me. Fairlie said O'Riordan had a young daughter.'

'And lots of people have young daughters.'

'Aye. But not many get themselves killed in hit and run incidents.'

'Fair point.'

'Ach, it's probably all nonsense. But strikes me as enough to justify some digging.'

'Even if there's something to be found, are we likely to be any more successful than Galloway and Fairlie were twenty years ago? It's a long time ago.'

'Sometimes, you just strike lucky.'

'That's the best you can offer, is it? That we might strike lucky.'

'You never know,' McKay said. 'Like you say, there's a first time for everything.'

CHAPTER FIFTY

In the end, Ginny Horton slept longer than she'd intended. She'd fallen asleep only as dawn was showing through the curtains, and she'd slept fitfully even after that. But she'd been physically and emotionally exhausted – it had been a long week even before the previous night's events – and she'd finally fallen into a deeper sleep, waking only when her mobile buzzed loudly on the bedside table.

She thumbed the call button without even bothering to check the number. 'Horton.'

'Ginny. It's Isla. Just letting you know I'm back in the land of the living.'

'Oh, God. Sorry. I meant to call first thing. But I couldn't sleep and then I overslept –' In a mix of guilt and relief, she hardly knew what she was saying.

'No worries. I thought you'd be worn out. You must have had a hell of an evening.'

'How are you feeling?'

'A bit sore-headed. But otherwise okay. Consultant's just been round. He reckons everything's fine. No concussion. No serious damage. So, I'm free to go, whenever you can pick me up.'

'In that case, I'm on my way. Well, I'll need time to dress.'

'I think we'd all be grateful for that.' Isla hesitated. 'What's the story, Ginny? What happened last night? No one here seems very keen to enlighten me.'

'I'll tell you when I get there,' Horton said.

'I've got no memory of anything. Just walking in the house, going in the kitchen and then – nothing. Were we burgled?'

'It's a long story,' Horton said. 'But, no. Nothing's damaged or missing.' *Nothing physical at least*, she added to herself. 'I'll get straight over there, and then, I can tell you all about it.'

She showered and dressed hurriedly, then jogged down the stairs two at a time, eager to get going. More than anything, she just wanted to put all this behind them.

Outside, the weather was glorious. There were buds breaking through on the bushes around the house, and spring was finally arriving. All of that felt like a harbinger of better things to come.

It was as she was locking the front door that Horton sensed the presence behind her. She couldn't have said what alerted her – a scent, a sound, the movement of a shadow across her vision – but she suddenly knew she wasn't alone. She moved to turn, already raising her hands, jutting keys clutched in her fist, preparing to defend herself.

But she was too late. Before she could move, the gloved hands closed around her neck and began to tighten.

CHAPTER FIFTY-ONE

Kelly had almost decided not to turn in to work. She was still disturbed by the previous night's events – the conversation with Maggie, the even odder exchange with Callum in the car park. Now she didn't know what to think.

Whatever the truth, it was their business. Kelly had no desire to get involved, not even to find herself the confidante of one or other of them. So, her first thought had been just to walk out after all. She was only a casual bar worker, and she'd be gone anyway in a couple of weeks.

But then she asked herself why she should do that. Why should she forego a job she enjoyed and the extra money it gave her, just because the Donnellys made her feel awkward? She wasn't a quitter. She'd walked out from this place the previous year, but that had been unavoidable. She didn't want to make it a habit. That way, she'd begin to believe it showed some flaw in her own character.

So, in the end, she turned up, punctual as ever. At least until the tourist season was properly underway, the place still tended to be relatively quiet at this time of day. For the moment, there were just three regulars sitting having a blether around the log fire at the far end of the bar. Maggie Donnelly was standing behind the bar, watching them.

'Wasn't sure whether you'd be back,' she said as Kelly approached. It was impossible to read either her tone or her expression.

'I don't walk out on anything, unless I've a good reason to,' Kelly said.

'Maybe you've a good reason to.' Maggie Donnelly was silent for a moment. 'He spoke to you again last night, didn't he? Outside.'

'I –'

'I know. You told him not to. You told him to go away.'

'I did.' Kelly was damned if she was going to apologise. Callum had approached her. She'd done her best to tell him not to. There was nothing else she could have done.

'What did he tell you? That I get things out of proportion? That I'm jealous and paranoid about his behaviour?'

'Something like that.' Kelly could see no reason to deny it. It wasn't her job to protect Callum Donnelly. 'He said he hadn't done anything. Which he hasn't.'

'Yet.'

'Look, I've done nothing except try to do my job here. I'm not responsible for anything that Callum might or might not have done, here or anywhere else. For the record, he's not behaved inappropriately with me. If he's done things before – well, that's none of my business.' It was probably the longest speech she'd made to Maggie Donnelly. 'But if you don't want me working here – well, fine. I'll go.'

Maggie Donnelly was watching her intently. 'I think, in the circumstances, that might be best. Not because you've done anything wrong. But because of Callum. Because of what he's capable of. When is it you go back to university?'

Kelly was momentarily thrown by the non-sequitur. 'A couple of weeks. Why?'

'If I pay you two weeks' wages, does that sound fair?'

'You don't need to –'

'None of this is your fault. If anything, it's my fault. I thought Callum was – well, I thought he might have changed. But he hasn't. He's still the same. He still can't be trusted. So, it's better if you go. For your own sake. I'll get the wages sorted and send you a cheque. We've got your address, haven't we?'

'Yes, but –'

'That'll be for the best. I'm sorry about this, Kelly. Like I say, not your fault. But you're better off out of this.'

'Well, I won't argue. The money's always welcome. Thanks again.' She hesitated, looking past Maggie Donnelly towards the door into the kitchen. 'Should I say goodbye to Callum? I feel a bit bad just leaving.'

'I don't think that would be a good idea.' She gave what was presumably intended to be a smile, but there was no obvious warmth in it.

'Well, I'm sorry,' Kelly said. 'I hope it all works out for you both.'

'I've been with him a long time, Kelly. I know what he's like. What he does. What he's capable of. He needs keeping under control. I don't think there's anyone but me can do it.'

There was an intensity to Maggie Donnelly's tone that suggested she was talking about something outside Kelly's youthful experience. Something more than harmless flirting or even philandering. Something more serious. But none of this was her business.

'Well,' she said, finally. 'Say goodbye to him for me. I'm sorry it's ended like this.'

'Aye, Kelly,' Maggie Donnelly said. 'So am I.'

Kelly remained motionless for a few moments, expecting the other woman to say something more. But she remained silent, her eyes fixed on Kelly's face, as if waiting for her to leave.

'Goodbye, then,' Kelly said awkwardly. 'I'll see you around.'

She pushed her way out through the bar room doors. The sun was still shining, but the air felt colder, chill against her skin, as if the spring had decided to delay its return after all.

CHAPTER FIFTY-TWO

Isla Bennett checked her watch for the tenth time in as many minutes. It was nearly two hours since she'd spoken to Ginny. She'd assumed Ginny would leave home more or less immediately and would have been here long ago. Even allowing for the traffic, it shouldn't have taken her more than half an hour to make the journey from Ardersier into the hospital.

Maybe she was having trouble parking. Maybe there was some road closure or accident that had disrupted Ginny's journey in. But, in that case, Isla was surprised that Ginny hadn't phoned.

She'd tried calling a couple of times, feeling foolish at her own anxieties. The phone had cut to voicemail. That, in itself, was unusual. Ginny made a point of answering, if she could. She generally turned the phone off only if she was caught up in some police business that made interruption impossible.

Perhaps that was the answer. Perhaps Ginny had been called in unexpectedly to deal with some work commitment. Isla knew how much pressure Ginny and her colleagues were facing at the moment.

But that made even less sense. If Ginny had been called in to work, she'd certainly have phoned to let Isla know what was happening.

So, where the hell was she?

Isla forced herself to sit quietly until two hours had passed. She'd already had to repel one of the nurses who, no doubt with the best of intentions, had repeatedly enquired whether her friend had been delayed. Well, obviously she has, she wanted to respond. Instead, she'd just smiled and nodded and said she was sure Ginny would be along shortly.

At the two-hour point, she tried Ginny's mobile again. As before, it cut straight to voicemail. She'd already tried the landline at home, but both of them tended to ignore that, because the only calls they received were junk ones. As she expected, it rang then, like the mobile, cut to voicemail.

Unsure what to do next, she flicked through the address book on her phone, wondering if there was anyone else she could call. Maybe one of Ginny's work colleagues who might at least be able to say whether she'd been called back in.

The only relevant number in her list was Alec McKay's. McKay had given it to her the previous year when Ginny had been in hospital overnight after all that stuff up in Rosemarkie. 'If you need anything,' he'd said to Isla, 'just call me. Anytime. I'll do whatever I can.'

At the time, Isla had been unable to imagine any reason why she might need or want to call McKay. She had nothing against the man. From Ginny's accounts, he was a decent boss, his growling bark far worse than his bite, and a likeable enough individual once you got beyond his surface surliness. But Ginny had never shown any great inclination to mix with her colleagues outside work, other than the odd Christmas meal or swift drink at the end of the day, and Isla had been more than happy to go along with that.

The phone barely rang before she heard the distinctive voice at the other end of the line. 'McKay.'

'Alec. I'm really sorry to bother you. It's Isla Bennett here.'

There was a momentary silence, and she knew he was trying to work out who she was. Finally, he said, 'Ginny's Isla?'

'Yes, Ginny's Isla.' It was a reasonable enough description, she thought.

'Sorry. Bit slow today,' he said. 'Late night last night, with one thing and another. How's the head?'

'I seem to have survived,' Isla said. 'All okay, according to the docs.'

'Glad to hear it. Nasty business. Have they released you from the quackery, then?'

'Yes. But, well, that's why I'm calling.'

'What is it?'

'I'm waiting at Raigmore. Ginny was supposed to be picking me up. We spoke a couple of hours ago, and I thought she was coming straight over, but she's not turned up yet.' She felt like a small child complaining her mother was late collecting her from school.

McKay's response, though, was more serious than she'd expected. 'She told you she was coming straight in?'

'That's what she said. My impression was that she was just going to throw some clothes on and get over here.'

'This was two hours ago?'

'A bit more.'

'You've tried her mobile?'

'Yes, of course. Just goes straight to voicemail.'

'That's not like Ginny,' he said, echoing her own thoughts. 'She almost always takes calls. She's not left any messages, anything like that?'

'No. I've been checking my voicemail and texts in case I'd missed something.'

There was a longer, more ominous silence. 'Have you been told what happened last night?'

'Ginny said she'd fill me in when she got here. All I know if that some bugger hit me over the head.'

'This is something I should be saying to you face-to-face,' McKay said. 'But we found a body in your sitting room. Well, Ginny did.'

It was Isla's turn to be silent, as she struggled to formulate a response. In the end, all she could manage was, 'I don't understand.'

'Ginny found you unconscious in the sitting room. The front door had been left ajar. She called the police and ambulance and stayed with you till they arrived. Then, when the uniforms checked the rest of the house, they found a body in your sitting room.'

'A body?'

'David Kirkland.'

'David – Ginny's stepfather?'

'It appears he'd been murdered. Strangled.'

'My God. Poor Ginny.'

'My impression was that she wasn't exactly mourning his passing. But, aye, it must have been a shock.'

'But who –?'

'We haven't a clue who or why.' He paused. 'I suppose that's why I'm beginning to share your anxiety about Ginny. Whatever the reasons for Kirkland's death, I'd assumed it was something personal to him. It hadn't occurred to me there might be any threat to Ginny. But I don't want to take any chances.'

'You really think she might be in danger?'

'I can't see any good reason why she should be,' McKay said. 'It's much more likely that Kirkland's killing was linked to his own activities or background. Nothing that would involve Ginny. But – well, we don't know anything for sure. I'll head over to your house and see if I can find out what's happened to her. Can I get you on this number?'

'Yes,' she said. 'I'll call you if she turns up in the meantime.'

'Aye, thanks. And I'll call you when I get to the house.'

'I'm sorry to put you to all this trouble. I'm sure it's nothing. I'm just being paranoid.'

'Aye, well,' McKay said, 'let's hope so.'

***

The traffic on the A9 and A92 was light, even for a Saturday afternoon. McKay had seen nothing that might account for Horton's delay in reaching the hospital.

Even before he'd stopped at the end of the driveway, he'd registered that there were still two cars parked outside the house. He climbed out of his own car and walked slowly down the driveway. The fine weather was holding its own, only the faintest of breezes coming in from the firth. Somewhere beyond the house, McKay could hear the brush of the tide on the shore, the raucous cawing of a gull.

He stopped and peered in through the passenger window of Horton's car, then tried the door. The car had been left unlocked. McKay dipped his head into the interior and examined the front and rear seats, but neither offered any clue to Horton's whereabouts.

He slammed the door shut, then walked over to the front door of the house. He jammed his finger on the doorbell, and held it down.

There was no response. McKay pushed gently at the door. It was, as he'd expected, firmly locked, apparently with the full mortice lock engaged.

McKay looked around him. The front garden was laid mainly to lawn, with no obvious places of concealment. He made his way around the side of the house into the smaller rear garden. Again, it was largely lawn, with some trees and shrubbery along the boundaries. Other than a couple of gulls picking aimlessly at the grass, there was no sign of life.

There were no lights showing in the house. He approached the rear door and tried the handle. It was firmly locked. The two patio doors were similarly secured. He pressed his face to the glass and peered into the sitting room. Everything looked undisturbed, untouched since he'd tidied it the previous evening following the removal of Kirkland's body.

It seemed unlikely that Horton was still in the house, but there was no way to be sure without gaining entry. He walked back to the front of the house, thumbing through his phone's address book.

'Helena?'

'Alec. You sound like you're outside?'

'Aye. Outside Ginny's house, to be precise. I think we might have a situation.' It took him only a minute to update her.

'You really think she might be missing?'

'Something's happened to her. She told Isla she was leaving straight away. She's not the sort to just disappear. And her car's still here. Unlocked.'

'I'll get over there. Shall I stop off at the hospital and pick up Isla?'

'You'd better. She'll be climbing the walls. And she can give us access to the house. I'll let her know.'

His phone call back to Isla was even shorter. He tried to offer some reassurance, but they both knew there was little he could say. 'We'll get you over here,' he said. 'Then, we can see how things stand.'

He ended the call and walked to the end of the drive. The house stood some distance from the two neighbouring properties. They could check whether anyone had seen Horton leaving the house, but it seemed unlikely there'd be any witnesses. McKay was returning to the house when his mobile rang. An unfamiliar number.

'McKay.'

The voice on the line was young, nervous, stumbling over its words. 'Mr McKay. Can you spare me a minute? It's Kelly Armstrong. You know, from the Caley Bar.'

His first thought was to wonder how she had his mobile number, but then he remembered. She and her boyfriend had found the first body in that bizarre murder investigation the previous year. He'd given them his mobile number in case they had anything to add to their statements. He hadn't intended it as carte blanche to call him whenever they felt like it.

'Look, Kelly,' he said, 'it's really not the best time –'

'No, I'm sorry. I shouldn't have bothered you. It's just a stupid thing anyway.'

He decided to take pity on her. There was nothing he could do here in any case until Grant and Isla Bennett arrived. There was no sense in troubling the neighbours until they'd had a look inside the house. 'Ach, no, Kelly. I can spare you a minute. What's the trouble?'

'Well, it's just this.' She sounded embarrassed now that he was taking her seriously. 'I'm probably making a fuss about nothing. But after all that stuff last year –'

'Go on.'

'It's about the bar,' she said. 'Well, about the Donnellys. The couple who've taken it over.'

'They've done a decent job, that couple. What's the problem?'

She told him what Maggie and Callum Donnelly had said to her, recounting her final exchange with Maggie.

'With respect, Kelly, it doesn't sound a lot. A bit of a marital tiff, that's all. I understand they're quite common in some marriages.' *Aye, too right*, he added to himself.

'I know. I understand that.' She sounded deflated, as if she'd expected that McKay might accord her more respect. 'It wasn't that, exactly. It was something about the way she talked about him and his – well, his behaviour. It was as if she was talking about something more than just, you know, playing around. As if she was trying to warn me of something. I kept thinking about it afterwards, and it just felt odd.'

'In what way?' Kelly Armstrong was no fool, McKay reflected. She'd been more than right about that sleazebag Denny Gorman. If she felt there might be something wrong about Callum Donnelly, it was at least worth listening to, even if now wasn't the ideal moment.

'It was the tone, I think. She didn't exactly sound jealous or anything like that. It was more that she was concerned about me. About my safety. I don't know – as if he might be some kind of threat.'

'Maybe she just thought you might be vulnerable. Emotionally, I mean.'

'I know. That's what I assumed at first. But it felt more than that. I can't really explain. Just, well, you know –' She stopped, as if unsure where she was taking this.

'Intuition? Aye, I know. The copper's best friend and worst enemy.' He paused, struck by a sudden thought. 'I'm not saying you're wrong. You're smart enough. There's not a lot I can do, though. Donnelly didn't actually do anything, did he?'

'Nothing, no. I felt a bit uncomfortable, but that might have been my fault as much as his. I'm just wasting your time, aren't I?'

'We'd always rather people talk to us, Kelly. Better safe than sorry. Look, I'll try to find an excuse to talk to the Donnellys. See if I share any of your concerns. There's not a lot more I can do –'

'No, I understand that.' She sounded as if she didn't believe him.

'I will do it, Kelly. Trust me. I'm not fobbing you off. I can't promise it'll go anywhere, but I will talk to them.'

'Thanks. I know I'm being stupid but –'

'Like I say, better safe than sorry.'

It was no more than instinct built on instinct, he thought as he ended the call. Or, to put it another way, nothing based on bugger all. Even so, he dialled the number that had been established for the Major Incident Room, hoping someone would be there on a Saturday morning. In the middle of an investigation, the odds were on his side.

Sure enough, the phone was answered almost immediately. 'MIR. Carlisle speaking.'

'Josh. Alec McKay here.'

'Guv?' He could almost hear Carlisle jumping to attention. Josh Carlisle was a bright, serious hard worker, always keen to please his superiors. In normal times, McKay found it almost impossible not to take the piss out of him. It had taken him months to stop Carlisle calling him "sir."

'Wonder if you could do me a small favour, Josh? I want to get some intel on a guy called Callum Donnelly. Can you get on to the PNC team and find out what they've got.'

'Anything in particular?'

'Any past convictions. Cautions. Anything, really. There may be nothing, but I'd like to know.' McKay gave Donnelly's current address at the Caledonian Bar. 'That's all I've got. From his accent, I think he's Irish or Northern Irish – probably Northern, when I think about it. Don't know if that's right, and if so, how long he's been over here.'

'The Caledonian Bar?' Carlisle said. 'Isn't that –?'

'Aye, the very same. Just coincidence, though. Unless there's a curse on that bloody place.'

It was clear that Carlisle wanted to ask more, but McKay was in no mood to share. 'Just see what you can find, Josh. It's probably a waste of time, but give it a go.'

'If you say so, guv.'

'Aye, Josh. It's the privilege of high office to bugger your underlings about. Humour me, eh?'

'I'll get back as soon as I can.'

'Much appreciated, Josh.'

Moments later, Helena Grant's car pulled into the end of the drive. McKay stepped forward to help Isla Bennett out of the passenger seat. He'd always found her a mildly intimidating figure, but today, she looked slight and pale, as if diminished by everything that had happened. Her head was bandaged, but there was no other sign of any injuries.

'How are you feeling?' McKay said.

'Physically fine,' she said. 'Emotionally shot to hell. What's happened to Ginny?'

'I wish I knew. Her car's there, unlocked. The front door of the house is double-locked, as far as I can tell.'

Isla fumbled in her handbag for a set of keys. 'Let's see if there's any clues inside.'

It took her a moment to unlock the front door. Grant sat in the kitchen with Isla while McKay checked the rest of the house.

'No sign of her,' he said. 'The bed's unmade. Looks like the shower's been recently used.'

'What about her coat? Handbag?' Grant said.

Isla rose and peered into the hallway. 'She usually wears her waterproof at this time of the year. It's normally hanging up in the hall.' She paused. 'It's not there.' She turned. 'I don't know about her handbag. She usually leaves it in the bedroom at night. It's got keys and bank cards and suchlike in it.'

'I didn't see it up there,' McKay said. 'I had a good look round for anything like that.'

Grant took a breath. 'So, it looks like she left the house, locked up behind her, unlocked the car, but then, for some reason, didn't drive off.' It was a statement of the obvious, but it felt more shocking to hear it said out loud.

'So, where the hell is she?' Isla said.

'Is there anywhere she could have gone?' Grant asked. 'Neighbours? Some kind of emergency she might have got caught up in?'

'I can't see it. We're friendly enough with the neighbours when we see them, but we don't know them well. There are only a couple immediately adjacent to us. Even if there'd been some sort of emergency, she'd have found the time to call or text. She knew I was waiting.'

'Things happen, though,' McKay said. 'There's probably some simple explanation that we haven't thought of.' He exchanged a glance with Grant. 'Look, Isla, you make yourself a cup of tea or something, if you feel up to it. Helena and I will check with the neighbours. We'll be right back.' He was reluctant to leave her, but wanted to speak to Grant alone.

Outside, he said to Grant, 'What do you think?'

'I think we've a problem. Whatever the circumstances, I can't see that Ginny would have gone off voluntarily without letting Isla know what was happening.'

'Me neither. I'll go and check with the neighbours, see if anyone saw anything.'

'Okay. I'll get an alert out in the area. I can always stand it down if you find Ginny sitting patiently next door with an ailing neighbour and a dead phone.'

McKay returned a few minutes later, stone-faced. 'Nothing,' he said. 'Both neighbours were in. Couples, about the same age as Ginny. Neither had seen any sign of her this morning. One of them heard a car pulling away at a silly speed earlier. Thought it was kids messing about. They get them up here joyriding on the back roads sometimes. Though not usually on a Saturday morning.'

'You're thinking what I'm thinking?'

'That someone's snatched Ginny. It's beginning to look that way, isn't it? But why the hell would they want to do that?'

'For the same reason they killed David Kirkland?' Grant said. 'And maybe the same reason they've been picking off Galloway's cronies?' She paused, thinking. 'Doc Green reckons that Kirkland wasn't killed here.'

'How'd you mean?'

'He was killed elsewhere then his body was brought here. And before he was killed –' She stopped, as if unable to say the words. 'There were various lesions on the body. It looks as if he'd suffered some pain. The same was true of Ally Donald's body, apparently.'

'Jesus.' McKay was staring at her. 'So, if Ginny –'

'Exactly.'

'Christ. We need to find her. But why Ginny? I mean, we can connect all the others with Galloway, one way or another. But Ginny's nothing to do with any of that.'

'God knows. I don't care at the moment. I just want to find her before any harm comes to her. I've put an alert out, for what that's worth. I've set someone trying to scour the cameras on the main roads, in case they spot anything. And I've asked for a couple of the team to come up and speak to the rest of the neighbours. I'll get an Examiner over to check over Ginny's car and the area around it as a crime scene. But none of that feels very promising without more of a clue where we should be looking or what we're looking for.'

'Why the hell Ginny, though?' McKay had hardly heard her. 'There must be –' He stopped, conscious of his mobile buzzing in his pocket. 'Hang on,' he said, thumbing the call button. 'McKay? Oh, Josh.' He'd almost forgotten his previous conversation with

Josh Carlisle. Now it felt like little more than displacement activity, something to fill the time and allay his anxieties until Grant had arrived. 'Okay. Right. That is interesting. Look, it's not a priority now, but we'll need to do some more digging there when we get the chance. You've asked them to send the details over? Good lad. And thanks.'

Grant was staring at him quizzically.

'Josh Carlisle. It's probably nothing. I was just filling the time 'til you and Isla got here, really.' He told her about his conversation with Kelly Armstrong, his request for Carlisle to dig out anything he could find on Callum Donnelly.

'And?'

'Donnelly's Northern Irish. From Derry. And he's got a record.'

'What sort of record?'

'Mainly petty stuff from years ago. Looks like he was mixing with the Provos at the tail end of the troubles. Just a kid, really. Involved in a couple of instances of what seemed to be sectarian violence, as well as a few bits of petty theft, drugs. That kind of stuff. Six months inside in his late teens.'

'When are we talking?'

'Twenty years,' he said. 'Donnelly's in his late thirties now. The most interesting thing is that Josh reckoned there was a Special Branch flag on the file. We may get a call from our buddies down south.'

'Twenty years,' Grant said. 'Jackie Galloway's heyday. The time when David Kirkland was plying his mysterious trade up here. The time when Ginny's father was supposedly killed in some hit and run incident.'

'And when one Patrick O'Riordan, electrical fitter from Belfast, really was killed in a hit and run,' McKay said. 'Be interesting to see how the various dates align.'

He could see that Grant's mind was running through the possibilities. 'Okay,' she said. 'So, we're pulling out some interesting jigsaw pieces. But how do they fit together?'

'Christ knows,' McKay said. 'But it feels to me like it might be worth talking to Donnelly.'

Grant gestured towards the house. 'Do you think –?'

'That this has anything to do with Ginny's disappearance? I haven't a clue. But it feels like another piece of the jigsaw.'

'Are you saying you want to go and talk to Donnelly now?'

McKay shook his head, though the gesture was one of despair rather than denial. 'Christ, I've no idea what to do, Helena. But I want to be doing something. There's nothing useful I can do here. It's better for the Examiners to look over the car and the house, rather than me conducting more clumsy searches with my size nines. I could go and speak to more of the neighbours, but do you really think they'll have anything useful to tell us? I'd just be going through the motions, and time's running out.'

'You really think that bearding Callum Donnelly in his lair might be more useful?'

'Ach, I've no idea. But I'm not sure it could be less useful.'

'Okay. Look, you go and do it. If there are any developments here, I'll call you.'

'Thanks, Helena. I'm probably just being a total numpty, but, you know –'

'Aye, Alec,' she said. 'I know.'

CHAPTER FIFTY-THREE

McKay was crossing the Kessock Bridge when Helena Grant called. He assumed there'd been some development, and she was summoning him back. 'Helena? Any news?'

'Nothing here. But one or two things that might be relevant to you.'

'Go on.'

'First thing is, I had a call from the officer I've got working with the camera team. They've been looking at footage over Kessock Bridge at the appropriate times this morning.'

'I'll give them a wave. And?'

'Vehicle behaving erratically. Speeding and then cutting up other vehicles, as if in a hurry.'

'Sounds like just another day on the Kessock Bridge.'

'Aye. Except that when we checked this vehicle had false plates.'

'That right?'

'Plates relate to a blue Ford Focus registered in Stirling. This was a silver four-by-four Kia. We're trying to check the cameras further up the A9, but no luck yet.' She paused. 'Then, there's the second thing.'

'I'm all ears.'

'I'm getting worse than you, Alec. Can't stop digging. I was standing here, trying to offer some support to Isla, but both of us just wanted to be able to do something. So, I made a call to an old mate in Edinburgh who specialises in counter terrorism. As luck would have it, he was in the office and was able to do a bit more searching on their systems into Callum Donnelly. Like Josh said, most of his record is trivial stuff.

But the old Special Branch flagging was interesting. My friend was being very circumspect but he reckoned Donnelly was once a – I think the phrase is "person of interest" to Special Branch. Small fry but looking to ingratiate himself with the Provisionals. There was some suggestion he might have been involved in the Manchester bombing, though he wasn't one of the main suspects –'

'That was a murky old business anyway, from what I recall,' McKay said.

'Aye, so I believe. It looks as if after the Belfast Agreement Special Branch's interest in Donnelly lessened. There's nothing recent on there. Nothing to suggest he was ever any more than a peripheral figure, even if he wanted to be more. He was only a kid, really. Late teens.'

McKay pulled over into the outside lane to take the right turn on to the Black Isle. 'So, what does any of this have to do with Galloway, let alone Ginny?'

'Christ knows. But there's a third thing.'

'Go on.'

'I asked my mate about David Kirkland. Asked him bluntly whether he was Special Branch.'

'And?'

'I didn't expect a straight answer, and I didn't get one. But he didn't leave me in much doubt that the answer would have been yes.'

'So, what was his role? Why was he up here?'

'The word used was "nursemaid."'

'"Nursemaid"?'

'Witness protection.'

'That would explain why he had bugger all to do with Jackie Galloway. Presumably just attached to Specialist Crime for want of anywhere better to put him. So, who was he protecting?'

'That's what I've been wondering. And the name that keeps popping back into my head is Patrick O'Riordan.'

McKay slowed as he headed through Munlochy, then pulled out on to the main road to Cromarty. 'Any real reason for that?'

'Bugger all,' she said. 'Your mate Fairlie found no connection.'

'Craig's the best,' McKay said. 'But only in a local context. And, to be fair to him, if it was that kind of connection, he might have decided not to probe too deeply. But we don't have much, beyond the fact that he came from Belfast.'

'And the way he died. But, aye, I know. It's just the usual copper's hunch.'

'I'm not saying you're wrong, mind,' McKay went on. 'And if you're right, the next obvious question is who killed O'Riordan. And why.'

'We've a hell of a lot of questions,' Grant said. 'And bugger all in the way of answers. And meanwhile, Ginny's out there, somewhere, facing Christ knows what.'

'Tell me about it. What I'm doing feels like a wild goose chase, but I don't know what else to do.'

'There's not much. I've got a team doing door to doors of the neighbours, but not hopeful they'll tell us much. We've got an alert out on that vehicle. The Examiners are on their way to check out the house and Ginny's car. Beyond that, I'm running out of ideas.'

'Let's hope this produces something. Text me the vehicle details. They might ditch the registration plates when they get up here, but it's something to look out for.'

As he pulled up outside, the Caledonian Bar looked peaceful enough. Inside, the bar was quieter than the last time McKay had been in here, with just a couple of old boys in the far corner. A bored-looking young man was standing behind the bar, playing a game on his mobile.

'I'm looking for Callum Donnelly,' McKay said.

'Aye, aren't we all?' the young man said. 'Let me know if you find him.'

McKay drew out his warrant card. 'Don't get smart, son. I'm on a short fuse today. Do you know where he is?'

The young man looked unfazed by McKay's credentials. 'That's what I'm saying. They called me in at the last minute, because that wee lass had let them down. Then, I get in to find a note asking me to open up and take charge. No sign of either of the bloody Donnellys. And no food prepared, so I've had to send people away if they're looking to eat. Then, I get all the abuse for not being able to provide food –' He stopped, clearly sensing McKay's impatience.

'Can I check through the back?' McKay asked, moving towards the rear door.

'Knock yourself out.' The young man had already returned to his game, oblivious to McKay and what he might be doing.

The kitchen was deserted, with no sign of any food preparation. McKay made his way upstairs and peered into the two bedrooms. Both were tidy enough, with no evidence of any hurried departure. He hurried downstairs and checked the cellar. Again, there was no sign of anything disturbed or out of place.

He returned to the ground floor and found the exit into the rear yard. In Gorman's time, this had been another gloomy space cluttered with junk. The Donnellys had cleared the rubbish and opened up the rear entrance to create a car park. At the far end, in the corner by the wall, there was a small outbuilding.

It was locked, but both the door and the lock itself were old and rusting, the doorframe warped by damp. McKay wasn't a large man, but he leaned his full weight against the door, pulling the lock away from the frame. Almost immediately, it gave, and the door opened.

The space within was less tidy than the other rooms McKay had explored. There was a workbench scattered with nails and screws, shelves lined with paint pots, and below those a neatly stacked pile of logs, presumably for the woodstove in the bar. There were a couple of drawers beneath the worktop. McKay pulled them both open and peered inside.

One contained nothing more than a selection of battered-looking tools – a screwdriver, a hammer, a hacksaw. None of them looked recently used.

The second drawer contained a pile of newspapers, the upper ones at least looking relatively new. They were editions of various local papers, and at first, McKay assumed they'd been kept as protection while decorating. He pulled out the copy on top and flicked quickly through the pages.

On the inside first page, there was a report of Jackie Galloway's death, a short innocuous piece which characterised the death as an apparent accident. McKay lifted out the second newspaper. A different journal, this time with Galloway's death reported in a small column on the front page. McKay pulled out a handful more and skimmed quickly through them. Each newspaper included a story about one of the recent deaths – Galloway, Crawford and Graham as well as the supposedly accidental death of Davey Robertson some weeks before. The overall effect was chilling – a morbid equivalent of a proud parent collecting newspaper accounts of their offspring's achievements.

Towards the bottom of the pile, the newspapers were older, dating back a couple of years. McKay turned the pages trying to identify any relevant story.

It took him a few moments to spot it. He'd been expecting another report of a death in the news pages, but there was nothing there. He turned a few more pages, skimming through the usual array of human interest stories that bulk out any local newspaper. Towards the centre of the paper, there was a pull-out special, a guide to careers aimed at school-leaving teenagers. There were pieces on options for university, technical training, apprenticeships and a range of possible workplaces. Almost lost among them was a short interview on the experience of being a woman detective in today's police force. An interview with Detective Sergeant Ginny Horton.

CHAPTER FIFTY-FOUR

McKay pulled out another newspaper from a month or two earlier. Now he had a better idea what he was looking for, it took him only a few seconds to find it, this time in the sports section. A short report of a local marathon, with photographs of the winning runners. In second place, Ginny. A third newspaper carried a similar report about a half marathon Ginny had run over in Nairn.

Other than the pile of newspapers, the drawer was empty. The remainder of the room was equally unenlightening. If he'd been hoping for some clue as to the Donnellys' current location, it looked as if he'd be disappointed.

He dialled Helena Grant's number.

'I was just about to call you,' she said. 'Anything?'

'Not a wild goose chase, anyway,' he said. 'I've no idea what's going on here, but it looks as if Donnelly's our man. Just wish I knew where the hell he was now.'

'We might have a lead,' she said. 'That's why I was calling. I've just had a call relayed from the Control Centre. They had a complaint phoned in from some irate cyclist who reckons he was nearly knocked off the road by a speed demon in a four-by-four.'

'Our four-by-four?'

'Looks like it. Being an irate cyclist, he made sure to take the number.'

'Where was this?'

'North side of the Black Isle. Up near Culbokie. Ten minutes ago, or so. Best thing is they seemed to be turning into a private road, so we may have them.'

'Do they know they were spotted?'

'Cyclist reckons they didn't even notice he was there. Can't be sure, though, obviously.'

'Did this guy see who was inside the car?'

'Not clearly. Had the impression there was more than one person. Said they seemed distracted.'

'I bet they bloody did. Do we know the exact location?'

'Pretty much. I'll email you the map link. You can get that on your phone?'

'Aye, no bother.'

'I'm setting up roadblocks on the roads out of the Black Isle,' Grant said. 'I'll get back up there as soon as I can.'

'I'm on my way.'

The email arrived just as McKay was getting back into the car, and he spent an agonising few seconds trying to match the image to his knowledge of the Isle. Then, oblivious of other traffic, he U-turned and put his foot down hard as he headed back towards Avoch and took the right-hand turn up into the hills.

It was a single-track road over the top of the peninsula, initially through scatterings of relatively new bungalows and then out into more open country. The traffic was light, but the road was winding and narrow, and his frustration grew with every stab at his brakes.

At the summit, he took the left turn towards Killen. Once through the tiny village, another turn took him on to the road heading north towards Culbokie. Minutes later, he emerged on to the main road along the north of the Isle. He slowed, his eyes fixed on the roadside for the expected private road.

He almost overshot it. The entrance was obscured by overgrown shrubbery which had covered the two crumbling gateposts. At the last moment, he hit his brakes and pulled into the roadside.

He climbed out of the car and peered through the gateway. A rough wooden farm track led down from the road, twisting off to the left a hundred metres or so below. Beyond the trees, the waters of the Cromarty Firth were blue under the clear sky, the summit of Ben Wyvis seeming almost close enough to touch.

Clutching his police baton – the only weapon he'd had available in the car – he walked slowly down the track. Beyond the bend, the path stretched only a short distance further, ending at a battered-looking static caravan. A silver four-by-four was parked to its left.

McKay moved back into the woodland. There was no sign of life. The only sound was the shuffle of leaves in the breeze off the sea.

He worked his way around the edge of the trees, eyes fixed on the caravan, until he was close enough to see into one of the small windows. He could make out nothing in the dim interior.

He moved further round to the rear then stepped up as close as he could. Inside, he could now make out a figure standing, its back to the caravan door, and one other seated figure. Beyond that, the scene was lost in shadow.

It was then he heard the scream.

It was like nothing he'd ever heard before – a howl of anguish from the depths of pain. There was no way to tell whether the voice was male or female, old or young. It was like a wailing from the heart of hell.

All caution gone, McKay flung himself at the caravan door. It was outward opening, and for a moment, he expected it to be locked. But the handle gave, and the door opened.

McKay's brain struggled to process what he was seeing. Callum Donnelly was lying supine on the ground, stripped to the waist, his hands and feet bound with plastic ties, blood pulsing from a glaring crimson gash in his stomach. As McKay entered, Donnelly screamed again, even more blood-curdling than the first in the close confines of the caravan.

Maggie Donnelly was standing over him with a butcher's knife in her hand. She seemed not to have registered McKay's appearance, and was preparing to lower the blade once more to her husband's naked chest.

McKay had no time to take in anything else. He kicked out at Maggie Donnelly's arm, his foot striking her wrist, sending the knife across the small room. As if she'd only now seen him, she turned. She looked inhuman, her features twisted in a savage scowl, her eyes blank.

McKay moved towards her, but she had already retrieved the blade, slashing it blindly in the air. She was unrecognisable from the woman McKay had met days before, spittle running from her mouth, scatterings of darkening blood on her blouse.

She lunged at McKay, the blade arcing perilously close to his face. He took a step back, trying to judge his moment. Then, as she approached a second time, he swung the baton and struck her hard across the side of the head. She reeled back, losing her footing, stumbling across her husband's bleeding body.

McKay had heard all the clichés about the strength and resilience of the insane, but had never believed them. Maggie Donnelly, though, was rising again, even as he fumbled for the handcuffs in his pocket. He turned, trying to raise the baton for a second blow. But she was already too close, the blade inches from his chest.

He fell backwards, trying to find purchase for another strike. Then, he became aware of movement to his left.

Ginny Horton had been bundled behind the door, feet and hands bound like Callum Donnelly's. She had managed to half roll, half throw herself across the floor, colliding with Maggie Donnelly's legs from behind. Donnelly fell forward, the knife slipping from her grasp, its momentum carrying it past McKay's face.

Immediately, McKay was on top of her, dragging her hands behind her back and snapping on the handcuffs with a practised movement. She struggled fiercely beneath him, but he pressed his weight hard on her back, trying to keep her immobile.

Outside, he could hear the wail of police sirens growing closer.

'About fucking time,' he said breathlessly to no one in particular. 'The fucking cavalry.'

CHAPTER FIFTY-FIVE

'One question,' Helena Grant said, 'is how much we tell Ginny?'

'We can't withhold anything we know,' McKay said. 'So, another question is, how much do we *know*?' He placed a delicate emphasis on the last word.

'We don't know much,' Grant agreed. 'That's the trouble with dealing with the spooks and semi-spooks. It's all nose-tapping and winks.'

'Aye, they're a bunch of winkers, right enough.' They were in Grant's office, and McKay was staring morosely out of her window at the Inverness skyline. Grant could tell he wasn't quite back to his usual self because he still hadn't started wandering round the room peering into her papers and possessions.

'What we can infer from the little they're prepared to say,' Grant went on, 'is that Patrick O'Riordan was an informant. He was passing on intel about the Provos to the security services. He got found out and had to be shipped out of the Province PDQ, ending up on our doorstep.'

'Nursemaided by David Kirkland.' McKay nodded. 'Was O'Riordan his real name?'

'I'd guess not. He comes over here, leaves his wife and young daughter behind. Gets set up in a new life, new identity.' Grant spoke as if to herself, wanting to get this straight in her own head.

'How the hell do you do that?' McKay asked. 'Just leave your wife and daughter behind like that?'

'Maybe the plan was for them to join him later. Although the fact that he almost immediately got his new partner pregnant over here suggests it wasn't his priority.'

'Aye. And he didn't just leave them behind,' McKay went on, as if he hadn't heard. 'He actually left them in danger. What if O'Riordan's pissed-off ex-colleagues decided to vent their anger on his wife or daughter?' McKay sounded personally affronted by O'Riordan's behaviour twenty or more years before. It was possibly not the time to delve too deeply into the psychology of that, Grant reflected.

'I don't know,' she said. 'Maybe there's honour among terrorists. Maybe O'Riordan was just a bastard.'

'Aye, well. I suppose there is that faint possibility. Then, he gets himself killed anyway. Coincidence?'

'I'm guessing not,' Grant said. 'I'm guessing someone wanted him discreetly taken out. And that someone gave Jackie Galloway an incentive to have it done. More things we'll never know for sure.'

'But why Galloway? And why the hell would he agree to it?' McKay shook his head.

'I suspect that discreet removal services were part of Galloway's offering. One way of keeping the right people sweet and justifying the backhanders he was getting. Easier for Galloway to make sure the job was done properly, and that any investigation would run into the sand.'

'Must have been a bloody idiot to take on this one, though.'

'He wouldn't have known, would he? He'd have just been given the target by one of his local contacts. He'd assume that O'Riordan was just some toerag who'd got too far up the wrong noses.'

'It has a kind of brilliance,' McKay conceded. 'The Provos getting a copper to do their dirty work. Even if it comes out, the security services aren't going to want to wash that dirty linen in public. Then, after the event, Galloway starts to suspect the truth or part of the truth and is crapping himself about exactly whose toes he's trodden on.'

'I suspect he never knew for sure. He probably found out O'Riordan was connected with the Provos, but didn't know which side was breathing down his neck.'

'Ach, it'd take a heart of stone not to laugh,' McKay said. 'So, when they all start getting threatening letters a few years later, they assume it's the boys in balaclavas finally come to collect.'

'Whereas we now know it was O'Riordan's estranged daughter. The poor wee lass he left back in Ireland. Now all grown up, married to Callum Donnelly, and with the mother of all grudges. Or, more accurately, father.' She paused. 'You have to wonder about the psychology, don't you? She doesn't blame O'Riordan for deserting them. But she wants to wreak her revenge on the people responsible for his death.'

'She probably persuaded herself that, if he hadn't been killed, O'Riordan would have eventually brought them over here. People can talk themselves into any old bollocks. But how the hell would she have found out about Galloway?'

'Aye, that's an interesting question, isn't it?' Grant was silent for a moment. 'But I imagine whoever was responsible for ordering O'Riordan's killing wouldn't have been too averse to letting the word get around.'

'Aye, I suppose not. Doesn't explain why she waited so long, though.' McKay sat back in his chair, looking thoughtful. 'She's been living over here a long time.'

'I wonder if all she wanted to do at first was scare them?' Grant said. 'Give them a taste of what it was like for her, stuck back in Ireland, always looking over your shoulder. Then, gradually, the anger and resentment grew, until we ended up with this.'

'You know what I reckon?'

'I never know what you reckon, Alec. Tell me.'

'I don't think this was just about revenge. Or not just revenge for her father's death, anyway.' He paused and extracted a strip of gum from his pocket. 'I think it was about men.'

'Isn't it always?'

'Look,' McKay said. 'Maggie Donnelly. She's off her head. We can agree on that?'

'I'm not sure that's the technically acceptable terminology. But, aye.'

'Whoever wants to come up with a better name for it can face her armed with a knife in a static fucking caravan,' McKay said. 'You didn't see the expression on her face.'

'I'm not disagreeing, Alec. Go on.'

'We don't know how long she's been that way. Or what finally tipped her over from just sending letters into doing all this. But I'm wondering whether Callum Donnelly's philandering might have been a factor.'

Grant shrugged. 'Aye, your young woman was bang on about that.'

'Kelly Armstrong? She's an astute wee thing.' McKay looked wistful for a moment, and Grant knew he was thinking of his own lost daughter.

She and McKay had interviewed Callum Donnelly as soon as he was well enough to be seen. The stomach wound had been serious, the paramedics who'd picked him up reckoning it would be touch and go. When they finally saw him, after he'd spent a week in intensive care, he was white faced and still shell-shocked. They were still unsure if they were interviewing him as a potential accomplice or as a victim. Another question, Grant reflected, that they might never answer satisfactorily.

'Tell us what you can,' Grant had said. They'd been ordered by the medics not to press Donnelly too hard for the moment.

He shook his head. 'She's always been – I don't know – unbalanced. She'd just go into blazing furies for no reason at all. She could become obsessive about the smallest things. But I never imagined –'

'We think,' Grant said, 'that she was involved in some other deaths locally. Do you know anything about that?'

Donnelly's momentary hesitation had suggested to them that he might know more than he was saying. 'No. I can't imagine –'

There'd be time to push him on that later. 'Do you know why your wife wanted to harm you, Mr Donnelly?'

'I –' He stopped. 'I don't know exactly. We'd been having some blazing rows.'

'About what?'

Another hesitation. 'What brought it to a head this time was the young girl we'd had working in the bar.'

'Kelly Armstrong?'

Donnelly looked surprised. 'Aye, Kelly. Maggie thought I was trying to, you know –'

'And were you?'

'Maybe. I don't know. It wouldn't have been the first time.' He shrugged. 'I'm not proud of it.'

Aye, like hell you aren't, Grant had thought. 'You think that was it? That was what made her attack you.'

'I don't know. I don't understand any of it. She's assaulted me before, when she thought I was – well, you know. But nothing like this. She attacked me at home. That morning. Out of the blue. Hit me over the head with something. When I recovered, she'd already got those plastic ties on me and was dragging me into the back of the car. I couldn't believe she was strong enough to do it.' He blinked. 'We bought that bit of land when we took over this place. Where the caravan is, I mean. The plan was to build a house there, when we'd got enough money together, so we wouldn't have to live over the bar. I hadn't been there for weeks, but Maggie used to go over there to work on the garden. That's what she said, anyway. She bundled me out of the car and dragged me into the caravan. That's when I saw that other woman –'

'Detective Sergeant Horton,' Grant said.

'Detective – Dear God. I didn't know who she was.'

They hadn't pushed the interview any further. Donnelly had been in no state to respond, and they didn't want to risk invalidating any evidence that might emerge from his testimony.

'You think that was it?' Grant said sceptically. 'That's what pushed her over the edge?'

'Ach, no. Not in itself. But I was thinking, all of them – Galloway, Crawford, Graham, Donald, the whole bloody lot of them – were bastards, one way or another. In every case, their widows will be better off without them. You know, the way Sutcliffe believed he was doing the Lord's work. Maybe she was the same.'

'Ridding the world of chauvinist bastards? I've heard of worse motives. And a proxy revenge on the father who abandoned her? You might have a point, Alec. Or you might just be telling me something about where your own head is at the moment.' She paused. 'She attacked you too.'

'Aye, well, there is that.'

'And, to come back to my first question, how much do we tell Ginny?'

'About having a sister? Or a half-sister, I suppose.'

'A half-sister who wanted her dead because she'd usurped her position. Christ, I've heard of sibling rivalry –'

'That'll all need to come out at the trial, won't it? Not much we can do about it.'

Grant nodded. 'Of course. But there's something else.'

'Something more than being nearly murdered by the sister you didn't even know you had?'

'I'm sharing this with you because I don't see why I should be the only bugger having to decide what to do about it.'

'The benefits of seniority. Go on.'

'When the Examiners were reviewing the crime scene after David Kirkland's death, they took samples of DNA from Kirkland, Ginny and Isla for exclusion purposes.'

McKay looked up, his expression suggesting he knew where this was going.

'I had a call from the lab today. They wanted to check the identities of the individuals involved because they were worried there'd been some cross-contamination of the samples.'

'Ah.'

'There were similarities between Kirkland and Ginny's DNA.'

'Shit. You mean that bastard might have been her real father?'

Grant shrugged. 'It sounds as if her natural father was a bastard either way. But at least Ginny could have some illusions about O'Riordan, or whoever he was. I don't think she has many about Kirkland.'

'It's not relevant to the case,' McKay said. 'We don't know for certain. And the prosecution is going to be a nightmare in any case. We don't even know if Maggie Donnelly will be fit to plead. She's virtually catatonic at the moment. I'd say, let it lie.'

'That's the way I was thinking. I'm just not keen on secrets.' She paused. 'Speaking of trials, not long now 'til the Hamilton trial starts, is it?'

McKay shifted awkwardly in his seat, with the air of a schoolboy worried about being caught out in a lie. 'Few weeks. Why?'

'Just thinking it'll be another nasty one.' This had been their major investigation of the previous year. Elizabeth Hamilton had been responsible for the death of her father, himself a suspected serial killer, and of Denny Gorman, the former owner of the Caledonian Bar.

'She's expected to plead guilty to the murders. Assume they'll argue diminished responsibility. It'll be one for the experts to fight over. That's all.' His tone sounded less confident than his words.

'I hope you're right,' she said. 'And that nothing else comes out of the woodwork.' Her eyes were fixed on his, as if she were challenging him to say more.

'Aye, I hope so, too.' McKay pushed himself to his feet, clearly wanting to end the conversation. 'By the way, I'm meeting Chrissie tomorrow night.'

She looked up in surprise. 'That right?'

'Neutral ground. Dinner in some fancy place in the city. Try to clear the air. See if we can find a way to make a new start. All that.'

'Aye, well, that's good,' she said. Her face was expressionless. 'Good luck with it. You hopeful?'

McKay looked back at her as if unsure what she was really asking. Finally, he said, 'I just keep buggering on, you know. But, aye, pet, I'm hopeful. I'm always fucking hopeful. In the end, it's about all we've got, isn't it?'

The End

ACKNOWLEDGEMENTS

Thanks, as ever, to all those who helped make *Death Parts Us* happen.

Much of the book was written while finally trying to plan and organise a permanent move to the Black Isle. This has proved as challenging as major life-changes always do (don't be surprised if an unreliable house-buyer appears as a victim in my next book…). But I'd like to express my thanks and appreciation to all those on the Black Isle and in the surrounding area who've shown us typical hospitality and friendship while we've been trying to make this happen. And I hope they'll forgive me for yet again turning their beautiful landscape into a hot-bed of fictional serial killing.

As always, I want also to thank all those wonderful people at Bloodhound Books for their professionalism and enthusiasm—Sarah, Sumaira and Lesley in particular for their various input and support. And of course, to Betsy and Fred for simply being the best publishers around.

Finally, thanks to Helen for her input on the earlier drafts (including helping me to resolve at least one major plan conundrum), for the moral support, for the wine, and for everything else.

Lightning Source UK Ltd.
Milton Keynes UK
UKOW04f2136211217
314874UK00001B/122/P